BOUND BY OATH AND DEEDS. . . .

They are the Renunciates, the Free Amazons, warriors, healers, teachers, some even gifted with the powers of *laran*, but no matter their skills, no matter the backgrounds from which they originally came, all become equals when they take the Renunciates' oath and enter the Guild house.

These are their stories, adventures that could only happen on a world like Darkover, tales which take us from a fateful meeting with a woman who is only half human but whose predicament is one that crosses all racial boundaries . . . to the trial of a young Renunciate accused of murder and cursed by the gift of *laran* . . . to the perilous encounter between three women seemingly helplessly caught in a war to the death between their clans. . . .

RENUNCIATES OF DARKOVER

A Reader's Guide to DARKOVER

THE FOUNDING:

A "lost ship" of Terran origin, in the pre-empire colonizing days, lands on a planet with a dim red star, later to be called Darkover.

DARKOVER LANDFALL

THE AGES OF CHAOS:

1,000 years after the original landfall settlement, society has returned to the feudal level. The Darkovans, their Terran technology renounced or forgotten, have turned instead to free-wheeling, out-of-control matrix technology, psi powers and terrible psi weapons. The populace lives under the domination of the Towers and a tyrannical breeding program to staff the Towers with unnaturally powerful, inbred gifts of *laran*.

STORMQUEEN!

HAWKMISTRESS!

THE HUNDRED KINGDOMS:

An age of war and strife retaining many of the decimating and disastrous effects of the Ages of Chaos. The lands which are later to become the Seven Domains are divided by continuous border conflicts into a multitude of small, belligerent kingdoms, named for convenience "The Hundred Kingdoms." The close of this era is heralded by the adoption of the Compact, instituted by Varzil the Good. A landmark and turning point in the history of Darkover, the Compact bans all distance weapons, making it a matter of honor that one who seeks to kill must himself face equal risk of death.

TWO TO CONQUER

THE HEIRS OF HAMMERFELL

THE RENUNCIATES:

During the Ages of Chaos and the time of the Hundred Kingdoms, there were two orders of women who set themselves apart from the patriarchal nature of Darkovan feudal society: the priestesses of Avarra, and the warriors of the Sisterhood of the Sword. Eventually these two independent groups merged to form the powerful and legally chartered Order of Renunciates or Free Amazons, a guild of women bound only by oath as a sisterhood of mutual responsibility. Their primary allegiance is to each other rather than to family, clan, caste or any man save a temporary employer. Alone among Darkovan women, they are exempt from the usual legal restrictions and protections. Their reason for existence is to provide the women of Darkover an alternative to their socially restrictive lives.

THE SHATTERED CHAIN

THENDARA HOUSE

CITY OF SORCERY

AGAINST THE TERRANS
—THE FIRST AGE (Recontact):

After the Hastur Wars, the Hundred Kingdoms are consolidated into the Seven Domains, and ruled by a hereditary aristocracy of seven families, called the Comyn, allegedly descended from the legendary Hastur, Lord of Light. It is during this era that the Terran Empire, really a form of confederacy, rediscovers Darkover, which they know as the fourth planet of the Cottman star system. It is not apparent that Darkover is a lost colony of the Empire, until linguistic and sociological studies reveal that Darkovans are of Terran extraction—a concept not easily or readily acknowledged by Darkovans and their Comyn overlords.

> THE SPELL SWORD
> THE FORBIDDEN TOWER

AGAINST THE TERRANS
—THE SECOND AGE (After the Comyn):

With the initial shock of recontact beginning to wear off, and the Terran spaceport a permanent establishment on the outskirts of the city of Thendara, the younger and less traditional elements of Darkovan society begin the first real exchange of knowledge with the Terrans—learning Terran science and technology and teaching Darkovan matrix technology in turn. Eventually Regis Hastur, the young Comyn lord most active in these exchanges, becomes Regent in a provisional government allied to the Terrans. Darkover is once again reunited with its founding Empire.

> THE HERITAGE OF HASTUR
> SHARRA'S EXILE

THE DARKOVER ANTHOLOGIES:

These volumes of stories written by Marion Zimmer Bradley herself, and various members of the society called The Friends of Darkover, strive to "fill in the blanks" of Darkovan history, and elaborate on the eras, tales and characters which have captured their imagination.

> DOMAINS OF DARKOVER
> FOUR MOONS OF DARKOVER
> FREE AMAZONS OF DARKOVER
> THE KEEPER'S PRICE
> THE OTHER SIDE OF THE MIRROR
> RED SUN OF DARKOVER
> RENUNCIATES OF DARKOVER
> SWORD OF CHAOS

Marion Zimmer Bradley

Renunciates Of Darkover

DAW BOOKS, INC.
DONALD A. WOLLHEIM, FOUNDER
375 Hudson Street, New York, NY 10014

ELIZABETH R. WOLLHEIM
SHEILA E. GILBERT
PUBLISHERS

First Printing, March 1991

1 2 3 4 5 6 7 8 9

DAW TRADEMARK REGISTERED

U.S. PAT. OFF AND FOREIGN COUNTRIES

—MARCA REGISTRADA,

HECHO EN U.S.A.

PRINTED IN THE U.S.A.

Contents

Introduction

AMAZON FRAGMENT

Every one of these anthologies at once takes on its own special character, created by the stories I get to choose from, and this year it has assumed a form I never expected. Story after story came in, and, with very few exceptions, they all dealt with a theme I had never thought of: Renunciates with *laran*.

As I say, this was an idea that had never occurred to me. When first I created the idea of the Renunciates, I had structured it as either-or; basically there were three paths for women. An ordinary woman on Darkover would follow one of these paths: to marry and have children; to go into a Tower, if she had *laran;* or, if she had no calling to either of these, she could become a Renunciate.

Why is this so much of a surprise to me?

Probably because the way I had structured Darkover, I thought of the two as mutually exclusive. Every game has its rules; one does not play chess by the rules of checkers; but today people are impatient of rules. In the SCA women insist on fighting and being knighted, quite disregarding the fact that in the Middle Ages being re-created, there *were* no female knights! As a historian, I cringe. I hasten to add that as an ex-tomboy, I can sympathize with a little girl's wish to play knight, and in a purely imaginary world, that would be fine; but not in the Middle Ages.

And there's another thing; when I was a young girl, my experience with girls was that, by and large, they were all only too happy to be restricted; most of the ones I knew in school were entirely happy with their lot . . . they contentedly read soupy romantic novels

(when I was reading science fiction), and I swear that
most of the girls I knew in school had no interests but
fashionable clothes, makeup, and—always—*boys*. I
was—or would have been—happy to have nice clothes;
but makeup didn't interest me, and my mother's most
uncomplimentary adjective for a girl—obscenity
aside—was "boy crazy." As a result, although I liked
men well enough, I have always disliked the adolescent
male of the species. The ones I met in high school
were only interested in football, except for a few na-
scent science fiction fans. Since football (and cars)
bored me (and still does—blasphemous as that may
seem), I never developed any interest in the adolescent
male of the species. I learned to think well of teenage
boys when I was teaching, though; the girls did little
but compare jewelry and talk about boys. (At least
some of the boys had some interest in learning the
music or English I was trying to teach them.) I lost
count of the girls (and female teachers) who took me
aside and told me that I really should try to conform
more, learn to dance, pretend to like sports and dance
music—in short, catch myself a boy and start conform-
ing. The fact that I really didn't *scared* them. A girl,
I thought then, was someone who *existed* to find a boy
friend. I very seldom met an "exception" until I was
grown up.

If this sounds bitter, it's only because I am.

It was only when I got into the science fiction world
that I met men—or boys—who honestly didn't care if
I was female.

As you can see from this, I am not a whole lot of
aid and comfort to people who are anxious to make
me into some kind of symbol of the perfect feminist.
I am fond of telling doctrinaire feminists that science
fiction is the one place where I have never found the
slightest hint of discrimination; attempts to enlist me
in the holy cause of abused women writers (my editors
are women) don't get very far. I am not—to put it
mildly—very popular with feminists, which is fine with
me. (Where were all these feminist types when I
needed them?)

But today's women want to have it all; and perhaps that's why, when I announced this anthology, story after story came in, showing Free Amazons who had, in addition to everything else, *laran*.

I still don't think it's very realistic. One thing I find totally unrealistic is the notion of a Keeper who becomes a Free Amazon; the life of a Keeper is so demanding that a woman who could not accept the discipline associated with it wouldn't be accepted for one. And if she didn't like the life, she'd find it out in the long and difficult training.

But, short of that, I have decided that this flood of Free Amazons with *laran* must mean something profound to the imaginary inhabitants of Darkover; and thus I present a selection of stories about Renunciates of Darkover with *laran*. How do you feel about this? Do you agree with the writers?

In any case I hope you enjoy these stories as I did. One of my fans recently told me that in writing about Free Amazons I had alienated some of the early readers. I'd hate to think so. Hey, it's all just a game. We're all having fun here.

Strife

by Chel Avery

I didn't know at first if "Chel" was the name of a man or woman; it is short for Michel, "which I rarely use because everyone wants to change to Michelle or to Michael. I fight enough other battles."

My writers have a fascinating array of unusual jobs; Chel is a "Conflict Response Specialist" for the Friends Conflict Resolution Programs, a Quaker organization. I must admit that a story called "Strife" seems just right for this. She says she's done a lot of nonfiction writing, but this is her first fiction sale.

One by one, Shaya n'ha Margali cautiously released her sisters from the five-way link, trying to ease them through a gentle coming apart. But the psychic separation was painful, and she winced as each one dropped out of rapport. In a transition that seemed sudden and harsh, she found herself mentally disconnected, sitting in a circle with four other women bent around a glowing blue stone and a young herding dog. She bent her head down to rest on her knees.

"Look, Minka is standing on that paw as if it had never been hurt," Caitha gloated, greedily scooping a handful of snowberries from a fruit bowl. "We did a great job."

"Shaya is disappointed again," said the more observant Mellina, reaching to take Shaya's hand. "What is it, love? The rest of us are so happy with what you've taught us to do together. Why can't you enjoy it, too?"

"The rest of you have no standards for comparison. The rest of you don't know what a real matrix circle feels like," Shaya snapped. Then she sighed. "I'm sorry. I'm tired and hungry, and, yes, I'm disappointed. But I shouldn't take it out on you. Caitha, pass me some of those berries, please."

Caitha pushed the bowl toward her. Dorelle brought a plate of nuts and bread to Shaya's side and sat down close beside her, and 'Lista scooted over, so the four women sat huddled around Shaya, embracing her with their love. Mellina squeezed her hand. "Talk to us, Shaya. Help us understand what's wrong."

Shaya waited until the tears that threatened to slip down her cheeks were under control. "My foster father, Damon Ridenow, told me that once someone has been part of a telepathic circle, no other kind of intimacy is ever enough. If you lose it, you will either find a way to re-create it, or you will grieve over it for the rest of your life. And if you haven't experienced it, there's no way to understand it."

"But haven't we experienced it?" 'Lista asked. What were we just doing? And you're right about the intimacy, it's like . . ."

"Like having your skin off," Dorelle offered.

Shaya laughed sadly. "Those are the exact words people always use. But there's more to it than that. It's not just being inside each other's minds, it's not just knowing each other's every thought. When it's right, there's such a precious sense of closeness, of trust, of love. . . ." She stumbled on her words and paused for an awkward moment. "That sounds all wrong. I mean, I do love you all, and I'd trust you with my life. You know that. But something's missing."

She went on. "Growing up in the Forbidden Tower was like being held all day, every day, in the arms of a dozen people who loved me. Even when we had arguments, even when I was naughty and was being punished, I could still feel all that caring wrapped around me. I thought I could make that happen again with all of you."

Dorelle spoke in a voice so low the others had to hold their breath to hear her. But at the psi level, her thoughts were urgent. "Living with you four is the best thing that ever happened to me. It is better than I could ever have dreamed was possible.''

Shaya hugged her tight. "Oh, please, don't ever think this little Guild House in the hills isn't exactly the place I would choose to be in the whole world. And I am as happy as could be . . . in the *normal* scheme of things. What I'm talking about is something more than normal. I'm talking about magic.''

Caitha stretched and yawned. "What we really need is a good night's sleep, plus half a day. Do you realize how late it is? I think Shaya's problem is just that she's tired, and so are the rest of us. Good night, dears.'' And with a quick kiss on four cheeks, she left the room.

Curled in the comfort of Mellina's arms, Shaya worried. "It must be my fault. I'm no Keeper, just a junior technician. If my *breda*, Cleindori, were with us, instead of closeted in Arillin Tower, maybe. . . .''

"Don't blame yourself,'' Mellina squeezed her. If it's someone's fault, blame the rest of us. Except for you, we're all total commoners. Our *laran* may not be powerful enough.''

"Don't let those Comyn myths fool you. At Mariposa, we had more than a few commoners working in our circle. That's why I was so sure we could do it here.''

The dream was so vivid. When she lived in Thendara Guild House, she had noticed the disproportionate numbers of Renunciates with *laran*. It made sense. Women from the common classes gifted with psychic abilities were flukes. They had none of the acceptance and training available to the nobility. Misfits in their own world, they frequently sought the refuge of the Sisterhoood, a community which at least allowed them to be themselves.

Shaya also noticed the crucial need for emotional, and sometimes physical healing among new members, many escaping to the Guild House from desperate situations. With the urgency of her vision, she had persuaded the Guild-mothers to let her take a hand-picked group of Renunciates and found a small Guild House away from the city where a circle of telepaths could develop their skills, then offer training to wild telepaths in the Sisterhood who had not learned to control their *laran*. They would also provide a center of retreat and healing for initiates whose emotional scars were too deep to endure the rigorous training required of new members.

Mellina was following her thoughts. "And it's working. We're succeeding wonderfully. We *are* learning to heal."

"You're right, of course. I'm sorry to gripe. We are succeeding in everything I asked the Guild-mothers to let us do. I just hadn't realized how much more I wanted—I wanted that deep belongingness that I gave up when I left Mariposa."

"You do belong. We all do, love."

"Yes, but it's flat somehow. I can't describe what's missing, but if you knew what it was, you would say the community we feel now is like a spring snowfall in the plains compared to a Hellers blizzard."

"Well, maybe when we've gotten more used to being with each other, when we get to know each other more. . . ."

"I don't think so. I chose this group so carefully, not just because we all have *laran*, but because we are all so well suited to each other. I care for each of you, and I made certain each of you could care for all the rest. No Tower circle since the Ages of Chaos was ever so carefully selected for compatibility."

She took a mental roll call. In the matrix link, she experienced each of them as a weather image. Caitha was a spring breeze, strong, exuberant, and sometimes unpredictable. 'Lista was a sunny sky, warm, open, peaceful. Dorelle was a summer snowfall, caressing everything she touched so gently that she seemed to dissolve on contact.

"And me?" Mellina was still following her thoughts.

Shaya imaged for her a rare night sky she had seen in her childhood, clear, but without a single moon in sight. The stars glimmered brilliantly against a back-drop of darkness and mystery.

"You flatterer," Mellina kissed her. "If I weren't so tired. . . . Oh, but I *am* tired. Let's sleep. Tomorrow everything may seem different.

Shaya recalled those last words in the midst of the turmoil that erupted the next day. She was carrying hot water for the laundry when she heard a knock at the door. She assumed it was the tanner with some hides Caitha had spoken for in the market. "Mellina, can you get that? My hands are full."

A few minutes later, when she was up to her elbows in suds, Mellina came back to the room. "Shaya, I think you should come out. We have an interesting problem."

In the receiving room, an elderly woman, dressed in a delicately embroidered gown with fur trim, sat before the fire. Her back was held perfectly erect, yet she seemed at ease on the crude wooden stool. She stood as Shaya entered the room. "You will be Shaya n'ha Margali. It is my honor to meet you, *mestra*. I am Magwyn Delleray."

The woman was polite, even friendly in her address, but Shaya was unused to such confident directness in women outside the Guild. "How is it you know my name, *domna*?

"It was my son, Regald Delleray, who leased you this lodge. He was reluctant, at first, to do business with only women, but I persuaded him that Renunciates have a reputation for honesty and fair dealing, and that you would make good tenants."

Shaya thought the relationship with Regald Delleray did no credit to the mother. He had tried to overcharge them. But no woman should be judged by her male kin. Lady Magwyn seemed to be cut of a different cloth.

"Then we are in your debt, *domna*. How may we be of service to you?"

"It is not I who need your help, but my grandson, Dennor. May we sit while I speak? It is a situation that will need some explaining, and I am afraid if I stay on my feet, you will find it too easy to send me back out the way I came, before I've had a chance to persuade you to join my cause.''

Shaya smiled. She liked the woman's frankness. ''I promise you, my lady, neither you nor any woman will be sent from this room without a full hearing. But, please, do sit down. Your story must be a long one because I can think of no way that we can have anything to do with a young boy.''

''He is not so young a boy, nearly eleven years. And while he's always been a handful, recently he's been especially hard to control. I believe he is showing early symptoms of threshold sickness. His mother had *laran*, and I believe that gift, or curse, may be descending on Dennor.''

''Then it is not us you should be speaking to, but a *leronis* from a Tower.''

''Of course, that's obvious,'' Magwyn said impatiently. ''But Regald will have no part of it. He has no *laran* himself, and he treats his son's unruliness as bad behavior, nothing more. His solution is to beat the child, and to punish him with extra work. He distrusts the Towers, and he will not allow a *leronis* within the house.''

''Oh, the poor child,'' Mellina interjected. Shaya had forgotten Mellina was listening, and she spoke quickly to prevent her sympathies from running away with her and involving the Renunciates inappropriately. ''Yes, it is a sad matter, but I fail to see how we can be of help.''

''The child could be in danger,'' said Magwyn. ''He needs protection and instruction. I want to remove him from his father's care. I will say he has gone on a hunting trip with his cousins, but I will bring him to you, and you will help him.''

Shaya spluttered. ''*Domna* . . . I'm sorry. We can't, I don't see how. . . . First of all, we do not allow boys over the age of five in our Guild Houses. And even if we did, what makes you think we could be of any help whatever?''

Mellina was staring at her questioningly. Shaya
wished she would stop. Magwyn spoke, "First of all,
you can do whatever you like. I have heard your oath
of the Order of Renunciates, and it does not prohibit
what I ask. You speak of custom, no more. As for what
you can do, well, I am not Tower-trained myself, but
I am enough of a telepath to recognize *laran*. I have
observed you women in the market, and every one of
you has *donas*. Now, don't try to fool me into thinking
that you are all here to earn your way as midwives in
this little village that has hardly one birth for each time
Kyrrdis waxes full. I have seen you start no craft or
industry, nor are you offering your services as guides
or mercenaries. This house is a *laran* circle. That I
know."

Shaya put her face in her hands. Images of curses
and threats against the Forbidden Tower crowded her
mind. All it would take in this provincial, superstition-
ridden town was a few rumors, and they would be run
out like diseased chervine.

Magwyn spoke more softly. "Don't be afraid. I will
not tell stories, and I think most people in these parts
lack the imagination to guess what I did. It was only
a guess—until you confirmed it by your reaction."

Magwyn took Shaya's hand in one of hers, and Mellina's in the other. "Now, I promise you, no matter
what you decide, I will speak no ill of you. But I also
promise you that if you do help me, you will have a
strong ally in me, and I will come forward on your
behalf if you ever need help. I will go now. Tomorrow,
Dennor and I will be at the market, near the horse
traders' stalls where he can spend hours and not notice
the time passing. If you will help me, show up there,
and I will send him away with you."

She stood. "Thank you for listening to my request.
You have much to discuss. I can find my own way
out."

Shaya controlled a sigh of relief as Magwyn's back
receded through the doorway. Then she glanced at
Mellina's pained face. There was going to be a problem.

"It's out of the question, love," she said firmly. "I know this woman's story breaks your soft heart, but it's impossible."

But Mellina, usually so gentle, could turn into a catwoman with unweaned young when her instincts to protect were aroused. "Of course it's possible. We need to discuss this with all of us together."

By dinnertime, Mellina had spoken to everyone, and Shaya found herself outnumbered. "Why not?" asked 'Lista. "It's not as if we were too busy doing other things. Let's give it a try."

"So what if it's against custom to have a boy of his age in a Guild House," said Caitha. "I think we can handle it. It will give me someone *enthusiastic*"—she glowered playfully at the other four—"to practice swordplay with."

Dorelle, as Shaya could have predicted, was anguished over the story of Regald's roughness with his son. "After all, an eleven-year-old is still a child, really. Half the problem with men in the Domains is they're forced to be men and soldiers before they're old enough. We could make a real difference in the boy's life."

Shaya groaned. "Aren't you women paying attention? The boy's father beats him because he is 'hard to handle.' In other words, he's undisciplined and unruly. He will ruin everything. He has already. Do you realize this is the first time we've quarreled?"

But it was a lost battle. The next day, three Amazons strode toward the horse stalls in the market, Shaya hoping to establish some authority and discipline from the start, Caitha impatient to see the lad's sword arm, and Dorelle eager to caress the poor waif and shelter him from the roughness of the other two.

It had not occurred to them that Dennor would not want to come. Magwyn had to pull him aside and speak sternly with him. The exchange was out of earshot, but from the sight of the two, and from the psychic reverberations, it was obvious that there were complaints and curses from Dennor matched by stern warnings from Magwyn.

The old woman could be formidible, as Shaya already knew, and whatever power she wielded, it was effective in the end. But the Dennor who joined them was sullen. "Send me off with a bunch of *dames*, and not even pretty ones. Well, you'd better just know," he brushed off Dorelle's tentative arm across his shoulder, "no old witch is going to make a sandal wearer out of me."

Dorelle was obviously bewildered. Shaya thought grimly to herself that at least, at this rate, it wouldn't take long to convince the others to end this foolish venture and send the boy back. Caitha was undaunted, though, and actually managed to stop the boy's grumbling when she said, "We'll find out what kind of sandal wearer you are. As soon as we get back to the house, we'll have a swordplay lesson and see if you can live up to all this male pride that means so much to you."

Thankfully, Caitha wore him out with her lesson, or things might have been worse. By dinnertime, Dennor had managed to terrorize Minka into cowering behind the horse shed whenever she saw him. He had broken a mug by accident, and another deliberately in a fit of temper when Mellina admonished him to be more careful. And he had complained so much and made so much noise that everyone but Caitha had a headache. "Is this what you *ladies* eat for dinner?" he snorted when they gathered at the table. "I'm a man. I need meat. I need ale. I'll *die* on this stuff."

Shaya, her temper long since lost, grabbed Dennor by the shoulder and shook him. "Listen, you spoiled *cralmac's* brat, when the snows lie thick on Nevarsin and folk are housebound for months, they would be thrilled with the fresh vegetables and milk on this table. When there is red tide at Temora and the fish are not good to eat. . . ." She choked.

Caitha stepped in calmly. "If you don't like our food, Dennor, you don't have to eat it. In the meantime, please be quiet and let the rest of us enjoy our supper." Dennor shut up and ate.

After supper was cleared away and Dennor sent off to his room, they almost decided not to gather a matrix circle that night. Shaya was in a vile mood, Caitha was exhausted, and the others were troubled and unhappy. The irritation they had all felt toward Dennor, now that he was out of sight, threatened to erupt at each other. Shaya decided, however, that they should practice. "We need the discipline. We can't always expect ideal conditions." So they went into rapport and rehearsed some simple psi exercises, concluding by setting a soothing spell on poor Minka's frazzled nerves. Surprisingly, it all went more smoothly than they had expected, although afterward they were too drained for conversation. Stumbling off to bed, 'Lista muttered, "At this rate, Minka is going to be the healthiest dog in all the Domains."

Shaya was jerked awake, several hours later, by anguished screaming that went on and on and did not stop. When she stumbled, barefoot and disheveled, into Dennor's room where the shrieks originated, 'Lista and Caitha were already there. Dennor crouched on his bed, perspiration streaming down his shaking body. "Stay away from me," he shouted. "I said, stay *away!*" Then he put his arms over his head and wailed. "The walls, the walls are dancing, they're moving in to crush me."

"Good Goddess, what's the matter?" said 'Lista. "He won't let us touch him."

"It's threshold sickness," Shaya answered. "You're lucky if you don't know what it is. Go fetch a pitcher of water, and a mug—I see he's broken the one in here. And Caitha, check the herb closet. There should be a small bottle of *kirian*. It smells like . . . no, don't smell it. Just bring me all the small bottles."

Then she sat on the edge of the bed and spoke firmly. "Dennor, pay attention to me. I know what's happening to you. I've had it myself. It feels terrible, but if we treat it right, you'll get over it. Now, it seems like you're mad, but you're not. Do you hear me?'' She wasn't sure she was getting through. ''You're not mad.''

When Mellina stumbled into the room a few minutes later, Shaya was able to get Dennor onto his feet, walking about the room with the two women on either side.

It was a long night. Dawn was coming when a weary Shaya sat beside an even more exhausted Dennor as he drifted off to sleep, still disoriented, but calm. ''My father punishes me when I get like this. He says I'm being weak and hysterical, I'll turn out a sandal wearer.''

Shaya wanted to say that there were worse things to be, but instead she said, ''No, you have *laran,* and there's nothing weak about it. You're body's just getting used to it, and you have to be very strong to bear it well. Tomorrow, I'm going to begin teaching you to control it. If you go to sleep now, I'll tell you about *Dom* Esteban of Alton who was captain of the Guard and the finest swordsman of his day. But the greatest battle he ever fought, to rescue his own daughter from the catmen, he fought with *laran* from his bed.

The next day, Dennor looked wan and pathetic. Mellina and Dorelle would have cosseted him if he would have let them, but he acted rude and surly, taking every opportunity to scoff at the ways of these ''women''—the word loaded with distaste—who didn't know their place in the world.

Shaya called him to her in the afternoon. ''I know you don't want to be here, Dennor, but I realize now that Magwyn was right to bring you to us. What happened to you last night could kill you if you aren't treated properly, and your father clearly has no understanding or respect for threshold sickness. We are going to get you through it safely, and I am going to teach you enough about using your *laran* that you won't hurt yourself or someone else with it. You should be sent to a Tower, but that can't be helped.''

''Me go to a Tower? They're the scourge of the Do-

mains. They turn healthy young men and women
into. . . ."

Shaya interrupted. "I see you're quoting your father. Well, I have my own quarrels with the Towers,
for other reasons. That's not the point. The point is
that someone, and I guess it's going to be me, has to
teach you to be master of your *laran,* or it will be
master of you. Do you understand?"

It was the right argument. Dennor nodded.

"All right. Now, we should postpone your training
until all the threshold sickness is passed, but I'm afraid
we don't have that leisure. See this stone? I want you
to look into it. You won't like it, but I'm sure you're
strong enough to handle the feeling it gives you."

She coaxed him through his first lesson with shame-
less appeals to the boy's idea of manliness. Her first
rapport with him hit her like a jolt. The experience of
Dennor in her mind was like being on the edge of a
tornado, recklessly tossing with outraged emotions and
raging, unfocused will.

That night there were no complaints about supper.
Dennor tossed down the vegetable stew and nut bread
as if it were the best meal he'd ever had. So did Shaya.

There were more attacks of threshold sickness in the
two tendays that followed. Usually, they followed bouts
of particularly bad temper and unruly behavior on
Dennor's part, but they were growing milder and less
frequent. Shaya was no happier than before about his
presence among them, but she accepted his protection
and training as a grim responsibility, and she had to
admit that the boy showed real talent for matrix work.
Caitha gave him a sword lesson every morning and
thoroughly enjoyed the exercise, if not Dennor's condescending attitude about a woman practicing combat.
His scorn may have covered his shame that he repeat-
edly failed to best her in mock battle.

They settled into a strained routine. Dennor took
his morning and afternoon lessons, went to his room
after dinner, and then the women gathered their matrix
circle in secrecy. Dennor adapted to the unwanted tu-

telage, but his attitude remained irritable and rebellious, often jarring the nerves of Renunciates. Dorelle
and Mellina, who subscribed to a belief in gentleness
toward children, showed the strain by taking it out on
their Guild-sisters. For Shaya, frustration and hurt cul-
minated the day Mellina, who never criticized, angrily
charged her with "overbearing bossiness."

In the matrix circle that night, they succeeded in
focusing their minds together at a deeper level than
ever before. They persuaded a runt chervine calf to
take nourishment from its mother, almost certainly
preventing its abandonment and death. Yet Shaya enjoyed no exultation. Her awareness of the others was
disturbed, as if, beyond the hills, she could hear the
faint roar of an approaching tornado.

The next day, 'Lista scolded Dennor for running
carelessly through the vegetable garden and breaking
several nearly-ripe melons. Angered by the repri-
mand, Dennor turned on her and shouted, "Leave me
alone, you sorceress! I could have you all driven
away." His voice went high with fury. "It's bad
enough you're unnatural women, not tolerated by decent folk. But I know you're witches, too. You do sorcery circles. I see you in my mind at night, all hunched
around a gleaming starstone, doing evil, unlawful
things. When I tell, you'll be lucky if you aren't burned
to death."

'Lista came to Shaya in tears, truly frightened. "The
villagers out here are conservative and superstitious.
What if he does say those things?" Shaya calmed her.
"I'll have a word with him and convince him it's
something he dreamed in his threshold sickness. But
we should be careful. We won't gather again until he's
left us and, please Avarra, that will be soon.

Shaya was not surprised to be woken that night by
a piercing scream from Dennor's room. It was after
such difficult days that his threshold sickness most often erupted. As she slipped from her bed and pulled
on a robe, she listened for more screams, or the hys-

terical sobbing that sometimes followed. Instead, there
was silence, then a thin, panicked voice calling her
name, "Shaya, Shaya, wake up!"

She caught him stumbling toward her in the hallway.
"Easy, *chiyu,* it's all right. Come, I'll take you back
to your bed."

"No!" He struggled free from her arms. "It's my
grandmother. Something terrible happened. She's hurt.
She's dying. We have to go to her. We have to go
quickly." His eyes were dilated, and he shook Shaya's
arm in frenzy.

Shaya tried to pull herself out of sleepy grogginess.
"It's just a dream, Dennor. Another bad dream. Try
to calm yourself."

"No, it's *not* a dream. You have to believe me. I felt
it happen. I saw her in my mind with my *laran,* the
way I saw you and the others in the matrix circle."

Shaya started. She had to take him seriously, even
if she did not want to betray the truth of his other
vision. She spoke sharply. "Even so, you must calm
yourself. Self-control is the first principle of everything I've been teaching you. If what you say is so,
you must be in charge of yourself to help your grandmother. Now, master your thoughts. I want you to
show me what you saw."

Standing in the dark hallway, she took Dennor's
hands in her own and linked her mind into rapport
with his. As always, the storminess of his thoughts and
feelings buffeted her. Fighting seasickness, she stilled
them both. Then she relived with Dennor the dream
or memory of Lady Magwyn Delleray falling helplessly backward, a sharp, striking pain on the side of
her head, a thrusting out with her mind, groping, calling for help from the one nearest her, her only grandchild, then slipping away into unconsciousness . . . or
death.

"No," insisted Dennor, following Shaya's thoughts.
"She's not dead, or I would know it. But we have to
go to her quickly."

'Lista's calm voice at Shaya's elbow said, "I'll get
the horses." Shaking herself free of the rapport, Shaya

saw her Guild-sisters gathered around. Their grasp of
the situation followed her own understanding.

"Dress quickly," Shaya instructed Dennor. "You
will need shoes and a warm cloak. Hurry, everyone."
There was no question that any of them would wait
behind.

In what seemed like ages, but was only moments
later, six horses trotted quickly down a narrow road
that led to the bottom of the hill. Fortunately, Liriel
was full, and two of the others moons nearly so. Dennor called back from the lead, "We must turn off at
the little trail just beyond the bridge. Since my mother
died, my grandmother has lived by herself in a cottage
on my father's estate. She has only one waiting woman
in residence, and Iniya is deaf."

They swung themselves off the horses at the door of
the cottage, Caitha running forward to knock and
shout, "*Domna* Magwyn. Lady. Iniya. Someone,
please answer." Dennor was only a few steps behind,
and he spent no time in knocking. Dragging a long,
wooden key from a hollow in a tree, he made short
work of opening the door, just as a serving woman in
a disheveled nightdress stumbled into the entryway
waving a poker. As she recognized Dennor, the poor,
stupefied woman dropped her weapon and stared at the
Renunciates. "Iniya," Dennor shouted, "where's
Grandmother?"

A soft moan answered them, and they followed it
into the next room. At the foot of a stairway, Magwyn
lay, half her face wet with blood, Iniya gave a little
shriek and rushed to the side of her mistress. Shaya
stooped beside her and drew her back. "*Mestra*, let
my sister 'Lista examine her. She is a midwife and
healer." It was a lie, but easier to explain than that
'Lista was the group's best monitor. Iniya was sent to
steep some reviving herbs in boiling water, leaving
'Lista free to explore Magwyn's injury.

She reported in the practical, passionless tone of the
discipline she had studied. "Lady Magwyn has had a
bad fall, but her spine is not hurt, and there is no

internal injury except a few bruises. The serious matter is that she has struck her head, and there is bleeding inside her skull. If it does not stop soon, and I do not think it will of its own accord, her brain will be injured permanently. She is likely to die in two or three hours.''

Dennor began to sob. "She cannot die. She is the only one who ever loved me. I don't remember my mother. I can't lose her, too.''

Dorelle put her arms around him, and for once he did not resist. "*Chiyu,* a time comes for each of us. Your grandmother has had many good years, and now she is going easily, without pain. You will always have her love in your memory.''

Dennor wrested free and faced Shaya. "You can help her. I know you can. Use your sorcery—or is it just for party tricks?'' The words and tone of a challenge masked an anguished plea.

"It is so much more than we've ever attempted,'' Shaya spoke doubtfully. "I don't know whether even a skilled Tower circle could save her.''

"What do we have to lose?'' asked 'Lista.

"Nothing that I can tell. We'll try,'' she put her hand on Dennor's shoulder, "but truly, it is a matter of Avarra's will and Avarra's mercy.'' She looked at the stricken, bloody face that had been so proud and yet so honest. "I want her to live, too, you must understand, Dennor. But wanting and trying are not always enough.''

They carried Lady Magwyn to her bed and made Iniya understand that there were to be no interruptions. "That means you, too,'' Caitha pushed Dennor toward the door. "We will send to you as soon as we've done all we can.''

Dennor balked. "I want to help you. I want to be in the circle.'' Caitha raised her eyebrows and looked to Shaya.

"That wouldn't work, I'm afraid,'' Shaya said gently. "The five of us have practiced together, and we know how to join our *laran.* You don't have enough training, and you would disrupt us.''

"But you said I was very good with the starstone. Please, let me help. Can't you use all the strength you can get? I'm strong. I'll do whatever you say."

"Dennor," Shaya was stern, "even if you were a regular part of our circle, we would have you stay away at this time. Your emotional bond with your grandmother could interfere with our work. And if she dies while you are in rapport, it could be too much for you to bear."

"No, no, I must." Dennor was nearly in tears. "If she dies without my helping to try to save her, I will always think it was my fault for not making you let me help. If I'm part of the circle, and we fail, then I will know that Avarra willed it."

There was some truth in what he said. Shaya recognized it and felt the others acknowledge it. And they could use his strength. Yet rapport with this child was stormy. Would he interfere with the delicate work ahead?

Mellina pulled her aside. "Please, Shaya, ask yourself if you are saying no to him because you do not like to work with him. If that's the reason, please think again."

Shaya sighed. "I'm afraid you're right. We'll do the best we can, all six of us."

Shaya brought Dennor into the circle last. She wanted the strength of their familiar five-way union before touching the tornado that was Dennor. First the sunniness of 'Lista, then the snowiness of Dorelle, the breeze of Caitha, and the starlight and mystery of Mellina—all woven together, solid, strong, resilient. Gently, gently, she reached for Dennor and gathered him in. . . .

The blast knocked them loose from one another. Dorelle literally fell down, gasping. The others looked as if they had been slapped.

"What happened?" asked Dennor, confused. "Did I do something wrong?"

"It's not what you did," Shaya explained, touched by the consternation in the boy's voice. "You just have

a different nature than we're used to. All right, everyone,'' she scanned the group closely. ''We'll try this
one more time before we give up. This time, I'll bring
Dennor in first. I'm more used to him. That may make
it easier for the rest of you.''

Again, she gazed into her matrix, then reached out
for Dennor. He was trying to contain his psychic energy. She appreciated the gesture but knew that any
withdrawal would limit the strength he could bring to
the task, that she must work with all six of them as
they truly were, trusting the rapport, or not work at
all. She linked minds with him, opening herself as she
never had before to the turbulence of his presence. She
tried somehow to *absorb* his chaos into herself. She
wondered, momentarily and for the first time, what
kind of sky or weather she herself might seem to be.
Leaving this irrelevancy behind, she added the other
four, one by one. The link was unfamiliar, like a rough
sea, but it held. 'Lista monitored the circle and indicated that they could proceed.

Following 'Lista's deep sense of Magwyn's injury,
Shaya slowly sank consciousness, the consciousness of
all of them, into the damaged vessel of the injured
brain. Slowly, so delicately that a random thought
could have blown them off course, they located the
damage, found the weak place that had been suscep-
tible to injury and the tissues that ached under the
pressure of escaping blood, and they went to work.

Who went to work? When Shaya tried to remember
later what had happened, it seemed that there was only
substance and motion. The substance was cell bodies,
cell walls, the cohesion between tissues, and gathering
fluids. The motion was that of wind and snow, stars
and sunlight, and a wildness that mixed them all together in a glorious and purposeful confusion.

It was rough to handle, demanding the hardest effort
Shaya had ever made as center of the circle. Dennor's
turbulence threatened, again and again, to break loose,
to shred the cohesion weaving them together, just as
the pumping blood in Magwyn's brain threatened to
tear apart the new cell walls so carefully knitted by

the power and direction of joined minds. Against this
disruption they rallied and gathered, extending awareness ever more deeply into one another until Shaya felt
she herself was all of the things she loved about the
others, that she herself was sunlight and stars and
spring breeze and snowfall, that she herself was also
a tornado. For Dennor joined in the struggle for unity,
pitching his strength into holding the center within all
their grasps. He no more wanted to tear apart their
rapport than the pulsing blood *wanted* to destroy Magwyn's brain.

It may have lasted a few moments, or it may have
lasted all night. Of all the elements and passions that
wove and worked together, time was not one. But finally it was over, and Magwyn lay peacefully sleeping, her breathing regular and deep. When Shaya
lovingly broke the circle, releasing them from the most
personal intimacy that can be imagined, there were
tears running down her face.

For a long time, no one spoke or felt any need to.

Then someone, touching someone's hand, yes,
Shaya's hand, said, "That was what you were telling
us about, wasn't it? That's what a "real" matrix circle
feels like."

Shaya nodded, then laughed softly. "I know why it
took us so long. I picked this group so carefully. We
all tried so hard to be loving with each other. We were
too compatible. What we needed was *strife*.

Dennor just grinned.

Amazon Fragment

by Marion Zimmer Bradley

One of the pleasures and privileges of editing these anthologies is getting my obscure out-takes (this one from the first draft of THENDARA HOUSE) into print. When this appeared in a Darkover fanzine, some readers wrote to me that two women with their hands chained together couldn't undress; well, this is, after all, fantasy and I'm using poetic license. Anyhow, I like this, and it stars two characters my readers seem to like: Camilla n'ha Kyria and Rafaella, who both appear in THE SHATTERED CHAIN (DAW 1976).

In printing my own stories in this anthology I am using the well-known principle of "Thou shalt not muzzle the ox that treads out the grain" or "Rank Hath its Privileges."

As for biographical information—if you don't know who I am, what are you doing here anyhow? If that sounds ungracious, put it down to my general bad-temperedness . . . I started this whole Darkover thing.

News here is that I'm just out of the Rehabilitation Hospital after my latest stroke, and I am a pretty lucky individual; brain scans show a lot of my brain is turned to granola—but I can still read and write and walk and talk. (And edit.)

Years afterward, neither Camilla nor Rafaella could ever remember exactly what had triggered their original quarrel. Somewhere there must have been some initial remark, some small individual episode, which set off a series of silly, pointless squabbles, of rude remarks and covert insults, of endless bickering; but neither of them could ever trace it back and find the spark which had set all this tinder ablaze.

But it seemed to Rafaella, this winter, that Camilla had for no known reason taken a bitter dislike to her, and went out of her way to pick quarrels over everything. She remembered one bitter dispute over a barn-broom which they were both using in the stable one day, as a result of which Camilla had—accidentally, she insisted—shoved her into the manure pile. And another, in the kitchen, where she had stumbled and scattered a pile of trash which Camilla had laboriously swept up, and because Camilla had loudly accused her of doing it on purpose, she did not, (as normally, she insisted, she would have been glad to do) help the other woman sweep it up again.

But Camilla—it seemed to Rafaella—was forever making remarks about women who flaunted their lovers, and when Rafaella, one night in the music room, had laughingly admitted to one or two of the younger women that she had reason to believe she might be pregnant, Camilla had muttered ''Harlot!'' and gotten up to leave the room. Rafaella had flared, ''None of *your* lovers would ever give you so much,'' and Camilla had slapped her face.

That episode had gotten them both called up in House meeting before the Guild-mothers, who, without listening to the remarks they had exchanged— Mother Lauria said sharply that she had heard all the insults young women could put on one another and was not interested—admonished them to try and live at peace. Afterward the Guild-mothers, aware of their hostility, tried to assign them separate tasks; Camilla was working in the city, and Rafaella living in the house and working in the Guild House garden, so that they really did not come in contact very often. Not nearly often enough to quarrel as often as they did. It soon seemed that they could not be in the same room without quarreling, and they made a point of seating themselves at opposite ends of the room in dining room and House meeting.

The final episode was triggered one night when they happened to be at the same time in the third-floor bath, and (by accident, Rafaella always insisted) Rafaella ran without looking into Camilla, knocking her off balance and splashing her with dirty water. Camilla turned on her furiously.

"Now see what you have done, you fat bitch!" Her thick nightgown was clinging wetly to her knees, sopping.

"Bitch yourself," Rafaella retorted, angry because for once it had really been an accident and she had actually opened her mouth to apologize, to hand Camilla the towel in her own hand, when Camilla turned on her.

Camilla did not answer. She picked up a basin at hand, and doused the gallon or so of cold, soapy bathwater over Rafaella's head.

Shocked, spluttering, furious, frantically pushing ice-cold, soapy hair out of her face, blinded, Rafaella picked up a pitcher and flung it at her.

"I'll break your head, you *emmasca* cat-hag!"

The pitcher, which was made of stoneware and heavy, struck Camilla on the shoulder, knocking her almost to the floor. She stumbled and went down; a woman behind her caught her and helped her to her feet. Camilla whirled; her clothes were spread out on a stool, and she caught up her dagger from her belt.

"You filthy whore, how dare you!" She rushed at Rafaella, and Rafaella gripped at the knife in her boots, in sheer reflex—self-defense, she justified herself later. And then they were fighting in deadly earnest, slipping on the wet stone floor of the bath, Camilla hampered by her long nightgown. It took four women to drag them apart, and both were bleeding from long, painful cuts; Kindra, roused from sleep to deal with the matter, looked grave.

"You two have been keeping the house in an uproar for half a season," she accused. "This cannot go on. While it was only harsh words, we held our peace, but this—" she looked, shocked, at the slash along Rafaella's bare arm, the two cuts on Camilla's face, "this is serious, this is oath-breaking. You are sworn, like all of us, to live at peace, as kin and sisters."

Camilla hung her head. In the slashed, dripping nightgown, she looked ludicrous. Rafaella saw Kindra's eyes on hers and wanted to cry.

Kindra said quietly, "Daughters, I ask you now to kiss one another, beg each other's pardon, and swear to live at peace as sisters should. Will you not obey me, and we need carry this no further."

Rafaella looked at Camilla with cold, fastidious distaste—as if, Camilla said later, I was something with a hundred legs that you had found in your porridge. "I'd rather kiss a *cralmac!*"

"Rafaella, my child, this is not worthy of you," Kindra said.

Camilla said, in shaking rage, "Let her keep away from me, and I will promise to keep my hands off her dirty throat. I will promise no more!"

Kindra stared from one to the other of them, angry and appalled. "We cannot have this here! You know that!"

"Then send me away," Camilla flared, "where I need not listen night and day to her taunting! There are other Guild Houses in the Domains!"

Rafaella's eyes rested on Camilla; she felt her lip curl as she said, "Perhaps that would settle it best. I am trying to stay as far away from her as I can, but it seems the House is not big enough for us both. If she chooses to leave here, that would solve everyone's problem."

Kindra shook her head. "You are my oath-daughters, both of you; that would be no solution. Children," she pleaded, "will you not, for my sake, sit down together and talk this through?" She held out a hand to each of them; Camilla lowered her eyes and pretended not to see, and Kindra said in despair, "Will you leave me no choice but to bring this before the judges?"

"Oh, Kindra," Rafaella said, and her eyes filled

with tears, "I have tried, truly I have, but I can't live with her! One of us must go, even if—" she heard her voice catch in a sob, "even if it must be me!"

Would Kindra actually send her away? She thought, wretchedly, *Does she care more for that* emmasca *than for me?* A year ago she would have flung herself into Kindra's arms and cried, promising to do everything Kindra asked. She moved toward Kindra, on the verge of breaking down, longing for Kindra to take her into her arms, but Kindra frowned and drew back. She said, and her voice was hard, "It is not to me, Rafaella, but to Camilla, that you must make your apology."

"To *her?*" Rafaella was cold and incredulous. "Never!" She wanted to cry out, *Kindra, don't you love me anymore at all?* But she swallowed the words back, knowing she had no right to speak them.

Kindra took Camilla's long fingers in hers. She said "Kima, my child, you are the elder, and you have been one of us longer. She is a child. Will you yield? I should not ask it. Yet I do."

Camilla's voice was husky; but her eyes were tearless and her face like stone. "It is unfair for you to ask it, Kindra. You know I would do anything for you save this, but I have done nothing to merit her persecution—"

"Nothing?" Rafaella cried, "You—"

"*Rafi!*" Kindra's voice was not loud; but it cut Rafaella off in mid-syllable.

Camilla went on, steadily, "If she will apologize, I will accept her apology, and carry this no further, but I will not crawl to her and beg forgiveness for allowing her to ill-use me!"

Kindra sighed. She said, "You have left me no choice," and summoned the women who had disarmed them. "Keep them in separate rooms while I send for the judges."

Left alone, frightened as the night crawled on, Rafaella heard the words of her oath echoing in her mind. *And if I prove false to my oath, I shall submit myself to the Guild-mothers for such discipline as they see fit, and if I fail, let them slay me like an animal and consign my body unburied to corruption and my soul to the mercy of the Goddess. . . .*

Oath-breaking. She had once heard her father say that the most vicious crime was to turn drawn steel against kinfolk; she had been brought up on the ballad of the outlaw berserker who had slain his brethren and been exiled by his last remaining sister . . . and she had drawn her dagger on Camilla. True, Camilla had first come at her with a dagger. But perhaps the woman had only been trying to frighten her . . . it need not have come to a fight. The slash on her arm smarted and throbbed; no one had troubled to bandage it. *By oath, Camilla is my sister . . . mother and sister and daughter to every other woman oath-bound to the Guild. And I drew my dagger on a kinswoman, the more so because she, too, is Kindra's oath-daughter.*

But Kindra could not help her now.

She does not love me at all! She would not pledge herself to me . . . she loves Camilla better than me!

At last one of the women came and summoned them, and Rafaella saw the pale angry face of her fellow culprit. They stood side by side before the four Guild-mothers, their slashed garments and small wounds telling the tale, and Kindra added that they had refused, before witnesses, to compromise or amend their quarrel. Mother Callista, the oldest of the Guild-mothers, and one of the judges of the Guild, said at last, "This is oath-breaking," and Rafaella trembled.

What will they do to me? she wondered.

Mother Lauria said, "You, Camilla n'ha Kyria, Rafaella n'ha Doria, stand before me. This is no game; I ask you two for the last time if you are willing to join hands, exchange a kiss as sisters, and pledge to amend your quarrel before it is too late. You will have no other chance."

Camilla said, her hands clenched into hard fists, "I would rather you killed me, than apologize without fault and grovel before her!"

Callista said, "Rafaella, will you apologize?"

Rafaella had the craven thought, *If I do, then perhaps they will only punish* her . . . *if I break down now and apologize, they will think I do so because I am afraid of punishment, and they will know I am more cowardly, that she is braver and more defiant than I am! Show myself cowardly before her? Never!*

She said, spitting the words out, "Beat me, then, or kill me if you will! Is this Amazon justice?"

"Kill you?" Mother Callista laughed, not amused. "We are not Guardsmen, to challenge your defiance, and reward you for your stubbornness because you are able to disguise it as heroism. You stand here, then, ready to submit yourselves to punishment? Or will you apologize and pledge to live at peace?"

Rafaella felt her stomach lurch, her knees almost too weak to hold her upright. *What are they going to do to us?* She wanted to cry out, beg for mercy, but before Camilla's cold, defiant face she thought she would rather die there and then, than show herself afraid. Neither of them spoke, and at last Mother Lauria shrugged.

"On your own heads, then, you silly, stupid girls! You have left us no choice. Go and fetch the chains."

Chains! Rafaella thought in horror. *This is worse than I feared. . . .*

Camilla was deathly white; Rafaella wondered for a moment if she would faint. Mother Lauria said, "Make sure neither of them has any weapons."

They stood side by side, each trying to ignore the other's presence as they were searched to the skin. Rafaella was shaking, but before Camilla's iron control she resolved she would not betray any sign of her terror.

Mother Callista stretched her hand out and one of the women handed her a pair of handcuffs, joined by a short length of chain, not more than three inches. She said, "You two have refused to keep your oath of your free will, and will not pledge to live together at peace. Now you will be chained together wrist to wrist; you will eat together, sleep together, work together and live together until you have learned to live in company as sisters must do. When you discover that neither of you can take so much as a single step without her sister's cooperation, then you will learn a lesson that whatever we do of necessity involves another. Most of us learn this lesson less painfully. Camilla, are you left-handed?''

"Yes," said Camilla reluctantly.

"Give me your right hand, then. Rafaella, are you left-handed?''

"Right.''

"That is good; otherwise you would have had to flip a coin, and abide by the lot.'' Her mouth tight with angry distaste, she buckled the handcuffs on their wrists.

Some of the women watching giggled a little, nervously. One of them intoned, "May you be forever one,'' mocking the phrase of *catenas* marriage, and frowned at the Guild-mother's angry look.

"Leave them now,'' Mother Callista said, "and go up to bed, all of you. This shameful episode is finished.''

Camilla said nervously, "What do we do now?''

Mother Callista said indifferently, "That is for you to decide. Together.'' She rose without a backward glance and went out of the room. Kindra looked at them for a moment and seemed about to speak, then she, too, turned and went up to bed.

One of the women who had witnessed the quarrel said, "Maybe now you silly brats will stop keeping us in an uproar night and day—and if you want to fight, you'll have all the time you want to do it where it won't bother anyone else!''

Rafaella sat with tears rolling down her face. *Unfair, cruel, humiliating! How could Kindra have let them do this to me? Why didn't Kindra warn me what would happen? Doesn't she love me at all? They all hate me, they're all taking Camilla's part. . . .*

She moved automatically to wipe away her tears and felt the metal cuff jerk hard on her hand, pulling Camilla's wrist up toward her eyes. Camilla yanked hard on it and said, "Stop that, damn it!"

Rafaella began to cry, sobbing helplessly, her free hand up to her face. Camilla said coldly, "Now you may weep, when it is too late to mend matters."

"And what did you do to mend them?" Rafaella demanded, snuffling.

Camilla's voice was icy. "Nothing. You need not remind me what a fool I am."

For a long time neither of them moved. The fire burned low and the room was very dark. Rafaella saw out of the corner of her eyes that Camilla raised her hand to her face as if she was wiping away tears, but thought, *Her crying? That* emmasca*? I don't think she's human enough to know how to cry!* And indeed, Camilla made no sound or movement.

Rafaella felt weary, incapable of coherent thought. She had never been so tired in her life. How would she stand this? How long would it last? Since the Guild-mother said they would eat together and work together and sleep together, she wondered if it would be many days. How could she possibly endure it, to have her enemy always at her elbow? She shuddered, and saw Camilla turn to stare angrily at her.

She wished she was safely in her own room, her own bed. But how could she go to bed with Camilla chained to her wrist? This was worse than a beating! She would not make the first move, nor ask that they go upstairs.

Although, soon or late, I must go up to the bathroom—sooner, rather than later, since I have been pregnant . . . well, I will not ask her.

And she felt that she had won a kind of victory when it was Camilla who finally muttered, "I suppose we cannot sit here all night. Shall we go upstairs, then?"

"I don't mind," Rafaella said ungraciously, but it was hard to keep pace with Camilla's long steps, and Rafaella stumbled and fell on the stairs, dragging Camilla down; Camilla swore.

"Will you break my shins, too, damn you?"

"Do you think I break my own leg to spite *you*, bitch?"

"How do I know what you are likely to do?"

Rafaella lapsed into furious silence. Even years later she remembered the angry humiliation of having to relieve herself with the other woman at her elbow, and the struggle she had not to cry. *I won't give her the satisfaction!* Camilla herself behaved with complete, calm aloofness, as if she were completely alone. Rafaella wondered how she could accept it so calmly.

(Years later Camilla said to her, "I wanted to scream, to cry for hours, to slap you. But you were so arrogant, so aloof, as if you didn't know I was there. I felt I couldn't behave worse than you did, I had to pretend to be calm . . . then, too, I had had more practice than you in enduring humiliations. You did not know, then, how much I had endured in the way of torment, that I could endure this, too. . . .")

Rafaella said coldly, "Well, are we to sleep on the floor in the hallway here?"

"Where they can all jeer at us in the morning? Not likely!"

Rafaella said reluctantly, "There is room in my bed."

"You would like to wake all your friends, then, to jeer at me?"

Rafaella realized that the three other women who slept in her room knew nothing of what had happened. "Would you rather wake *your* friends?"

"*What* friends?" Camilla asked, "I sleep alone— which I am sure you have never done in your life—and at least in my bed we will not be seen!"

Discouraged, Rafaella muttered assent. In Camilla's room she had to struggle one-handed to get off her boots. Camilla was already undressed, in the slashed, still-damp nightgown she had been wearing. Rafaella decided not to take off anything else.

Rafaella slept badly, in her clothes, and on an unaccustomed side. Every time she stirred, the handcuffs

jerked her awake again. When she woke, she felt
abruptly the surging, uneasy nausea which she had felt
only a few times before, but which the Guild-mothers
had told her some women suffered in early pregnancy;
she sat up, sick and retching, and Camilla grumbled,
waking abruptly, "Lie down! What in the devil—"

"I'm sick," Rafaella mumbled miserably, and hurried off down the hall, Camilla angrily stumbling behind. She knelt over the basin, retching, sunk in
hopeless misery. Devra, there early for kitchen-duty,
came to wipe her face with a cold cloth.

"Poor Rafi, I hoped you would escape this—" she
broke off, staring in angry shock at Camilla.

"What—"

Rafaella was too sick and wretched to explain. Camilla said briefly, "We fought. This is how they punished us."

Devra stared in dismay. "But Rafi, this is terrible,
when you are sick—does Kindra know? Can she do
this to you *now?*"

Rafaella could not answer; she could only think, *I
brought it on myself.* Camilla was standing there, her
face turned away in angry disgust. Stumbling to the
room for her boots, Rafaella found that she was crying
helplessly.

"Oh, shut up," Camilla shouted. "Is that all you
can think to do, cry all the time?"

"I—I can't help it—"

"It's bad enough to be kept awake all night with you
jerking around, and wake up with you throwing up all
over everything, do I have to listen to you bawling all
day, too? Shut up or I'll slap you soft-headed!"

"Just you try it!"

Camilla raised her hand for a blow, but discovered
that the force of the slap threw her off balance. They
fell together in a tangle on the bed. Camilla, swearing,
hauled herself upright.

"Where are you going now?" Rafaella demanded.

"To wash myself, dirty pig, and dress, or don't you
wash? And am I to go to breakfast in my dirty night-
gear?"

Rafaella said shakily, "I'm not hungry." She felt she could not face the room full of women.

But Camilla said coldly, "I am. I'm not pregnant," and Rafaella had no choice but to trail along awkwardly to the bath where Camilla awkwardly washed herself with one hand. She turned her face stubbornly away while Camilla dressed. The room was full of women who stared or giggled or whispered to one another. Rafaella supposed every woman in the Guild House knew the story by now. In the dining room they had to argue again about where they would sit; finally they balanced awkwardly on the end of the bench. Rafaella could not eat, though she drank a little hot milk. Kindra, at a nearby table, turned and looked at them, but, though it seemed to Rafaella that her glance was sympathetic, she did not speak.

"Ah," someone jeered, "so you have wedded *di catenas,* you two?"

"Camilla is a Dry Towner, to put her woman in chains!"

Rafaella began to realize what she had never recognized before; Camilla was not particularly well liked. Most of the taunts were aimed at her; what few expressions of sympathy were spoken, came to Rafaella. But most of the women seemed to avoid them, embarrassed.

It was a miserable day, punctuated with insults and occasional slaps, jerking at the cuffs that bound them, hobbling awkwardly around the house to their assigned tasks. After a time they began to be able to walk without pulling one another off balance, but they still argued angrily over almost every step and when, toward evening, Rafaella began to cry with exhaustion, Camilla slapped her again, and Rafaella turned and grabbed at her throat. They went down together, fighting, clawing, gripping at any part of each other they could reach, sobbing with rage and humiliation . . . they could not, with their hands chained together, even get a good grip on one another's hair!

Abruptly, Rafaella began to laugh. She lay back,

released Camilla, and lay laughing helplessly on the rug.

"What's so damned funny?"

"You are," Rafaella gurgled, "and I am. We are. Can't you see how idiotic we are? Here we are fighting this way and we can't even get *at* each other—any more than we can get *away* from each other!"

Camilla began slowly to chuckle. She said, "And I can't even run away without taking you along." They laughed together till the tears ran down their faces, Rafaella holding her sides with pain.

"My shoulder," Camilla groaned. "I think it's broken—"

"Did I do that? I'm sorry, I didn't mean—oh, this is ridiculous—"

"It isn't hurt, I guess. Just pulled. Did I hurt you?" Camilla asked, "I didn't want—" she helped the other girl to her feet. Rafaella stumbled on the stairs and Camilla reached out and steadied her. Surprised, Rafaella thanked her.

"Don't thank me," Camilla grumbled. "If you fall, I am sure to break my knee!"

In the bathroom, Rafaella looked wistfully at one of the tubs.

"I wish I could have a bath. But I don't see how—"

Camilla began to laugh. "I don't think there is a tub big enough to hold us both."

For some reason that struck them both as funny, too. Camilla said, roughly, "If you will wash my face, I will wash yours."

Weakly, tears of laughter dripping down their faces, they washed one another. As they went down to dinner, Rafaella said shyly, "Before we go in—let us agree where to sit so we don't have to haul on one another before the rest of them—"

Camilla shrugged. "As you will. Where we sat this morning, then?"

When they had found a seat, Camilla said harshly to the serving-woman, "Here, you, we can't chew our meat like dogs. They have not given us back our

knives; we must have something to cut our meat
with!''

Kindra heard them. She said, ''Here,'' and handed
her own knife to Camilla, watching while they cut up
the meat into bites. When Camilla had finished, she
sheathed it again without comment and walked to her
own seat. Rafaella watched her walk away, wondering,
Is she gloating over us?

After dinner some of the women gathered in the music room to hear Kindra and Devra sing ballads; Rafaella and Camilla sat on a cushion to listen, but the
novelty of the sight was wearing off and no one paid
any attention to them. When they separated to go upstairs, Rezi stopped beside Rafaella and nudged her.

''I thought you boasted of never sharing your bed
with a woman, Rafi!''

Rafaella felt hot crimson suffusing her face. She
knew Kindra was watching them. Camilla snapped
''Let her alone!''

''Why, Camilla, gallantry? And after only one night
in her bed? Tell me, what is this magic which a woman
of her kind can cast on you, so that already you guard
her like a lover—''

''Shut up, damn you,'' Camilla said, her voice dangerously quiet. ''I will not always be chained.''

''So now the sworn foes are *bredhin'y?*'' someone
else jeered. ''Like bride and groom, strangers before,
and afterward—''

Camilla said in an undertone ''Let's get out of here.
We don't have to stay here and listen to that.''

They got out of the room hurriedly, to a chorus of
jeers, catcalls, and ribald jokes. On the stairs, looking
at the tears in Rafaella's eyes, Camilla said quietly,
''I am sorry about that, Rafaella. I would not willingly have exposed you to that kind of joke. I know
they do not like me, but I had thought they were your
friends—''

Rafaella swallowed hard. She said, ''I thought so,
too.''

''But they take it out on me because I have brought
this on you,'' Camilla said bitterly, and was silent. ''I

am older than you, and I first drew my dagger. You should have told Kindra that. Why did you not?''

Rafaella bent her head. She mumbled, ''I don't know.''

She had thought of it. And then she thought, *If they send me away, even in disgrace, I have kinsmen and kinswomen, I will not be wholly alone. But Camilla is* emmasca *and I once heard Kindra say that her kin had cast her off. She has nowhere else to go.*

She said instead, ''I must have clean clothes for to-morrow. Will you come to my room while I fetch them?''

''Of course. Though I hope your roommates are not there . . .'' Camilla said, stifled. ''I am afraid of them . . . they all dislike me, and you are so popular—''

Rafaella said, really shocked, ''Why, everyone in the house likes you!''

''No,'' said Camilla, bitterly, ''they are carefully polite to me because I am *emmasca, mutilata* . . . no one truly likes me save Kindra, and now she will hate me, too, because I have brought trouble and disgrace upon you, her pet and darling. . . .''

''Kindra does not love me at all,'' Rafaella said, and began to cry. Camilla looked at her in dismay. ''She took your part against me, Camilla . . . and I thought she loved me . . .'' and all the old hurt surged over her again. Trying to keep back her sobs, she went to her chest and took out a fresh tunic and under-tunic, clean breeches and stockings. She said ''I do not want to sleep in my clothes again. . . .''

''You need not,'' Camilla said, and then, bitterness breaking through, ''unless you are afraid to undress in my presence, knowing I am a lover of women. . . .''

''Don't be silly,'' Rafaella said. ''That never occurred to me; do you think I even listened to their rude jokes?'' Then she realized, suddenly, that Camilla was not joking. ''But you are serious! Truly, I never thought it!''

''If you did not, it is sure you are the only one who did not,'' Camilla said. Rafaella stopped and stood very still, looking at the taut face, the thin mouth. It seemed that she was seeing Camilla for the first time, and something that had been no more than a word, an insult, suddenly became real to her. She thought; perhaps she was even Kindra's lover, perhaps it was for her sake that Kindra would not pledge to me . . . but she was afraid and ashamed to say the words. Finally she said, feeling the words awkward on her lips, "That was not—not necessary, Camilla. I do not care what they say."

What can I say to her? I loved Kindra and I never really understood, and now I do not know what to say to her. I feel like a fool.

And Kindra loved me, too. But if she loved me as she said, why did she drive me into the arms of a man? Shaking, suddenly aware of a thousand things beyond her knowledge, feeling suddenly very young and childlike, she turned her eyes away from Camilla. She said "Will you unfasten my cuffs, please? I cannot reach the buttons on that wrist."

They helped each other undress; but although Camilla did not remove her under-tunic, as she turned to get out of her trousers, Rafaella saw what she had not seen that morning when the other woman dressed, the terrible scars all along Camilla's shoulders and back. She drew a long breath of consternation.

This must be why she never bathes in the common room, why she always sleeps alone. How came she by those dreadful scars?

Camilla said, very low, "Now you have seen. Now you can spread the tale of my—my degradation, of how I am doubly mutilated. . . ."

Rafaella turned away. She said, "Hell, no. I have troubles enough of my own to worry about."

Camilla drew a long breath. "I had thought . . . Kindra would have spoken to you of this. It is told from here to Dalereuth, I suppose, in the Guild Houses; how I had to be stripped naked at my oath-taking because I had nothing like to a woman's form, and—and they would not believe me a woman. . . ."

Rafaella said "You wrong Kindra if you think she would spread such a tale. Nor has any woman who saw you stripped spoken of it to me. But how came you so scarred, Camilla?''

"I—I would rather not speak of it,'' Camilla said. "I was very young, but I do not like to remember it . . . perhaps some day I will tell you. But I—I cannot talk about it.''

"As you like.'' Rafaella was quiet as they climbed into bed and shifted about for a comfortable place. Rafaella woke suddenly, hearing her companion scream aloud, moan, start upright, wildly flailing her hands.

"Don't. It's all right, Camilla—it is only me, there is no one to harm you. . . . ''

Camilla started and shivered, staring at her in the darkness.

"Oh—Rafi—I am sorry I woke you—''

"I am only sorry you cannot sleep without nightmares.''

Camilla said after a long minute, "I was afraid. I—there was a time when I was tied—like an animal—and beaten like an animal, too. Mercifully, I have forgotten much, but sometimes I still have nightmares. . . .''

"Why, this must be worse for you than for me, then,'' Rafaella said, compassionately. *Tied like an animal . . . beaten like an animal . . . what can have come to her?*

"Camilla,'' she said at last, "I am sorry. Our quarrel was my fault; I splashed you with dirty water and I should have apologized and never let it come to this. Tomorrow I will go to Kindra and tell her, and ask that I alone should be punished. You can be freed, then, and need not have nightmares of being tied up.''

Camilla bent her head. She said, "You make me ashamed. I knew you would apologize and I didn't want that, because that would mean you were better than I. I think if you had apologized I would have pretended not to hear, so I need not acknowledge it.''

"Then we are both to blame,'' Rafaella said, hesitating, "Will you—will you exchange forgiveness with me, Camilla?''

"Willingly—oath-sister." Camilla used the ritual phrase, *com'hi-letzis.*

Rafaella leaned over and lightly kissed her on the lips; wondering, touched Camilla's face with her fingertips. No one in the Guild House had ever seen Camilla cry. Even when she had been brought in from the battle in the hills with a great wound in her leg and it had to be cleansed and cauterized with acid, she did not cry out or weep!

Camilla said, "I always wanted to be your friend. You were Kindra's kinswoman, and for that alone I would have loved you. And yet I could not refrain from making a quarrel with you and bringing this upon you. . . ." her voice broke. "And because you are beautiful and everyone loves you, and because you are pregnant."

"But you are the best fighter in the house, everyone admires your courage and your strength."

"I am a freak," Camilla said, her voice shaking, "An *emmasca,* not a woman at all."

"But Camilla, Camilla—" Rafaella protested, dismayed, putting her arms around the older woman; it had never occurred to her that Camilla, who had, after all, chosen to undergo the neutering operation, could possibly feel like this. She was not to know for many years why Camilla had had this choice forced upon her, but she sensed tragedy and it made her gentle.

"I thought you despised my womanhood; you taunted me for being pregnant—"

"Taunted you? If I did, it was only out of envy—" Camilla said, choking.

Rafaella said incredulously, "Envy? Of this insane—insane trouble I have gotten myself into? And I have been hating myself for being such a fool, vulnerable. . . .

"Envy because you are to have a child," Camilla said, "and I never shall, now . . . nor, I suppose, really want to, though sometimes it seems to me hard . . . nor could I ever, I suppose, make myself vulnerable in such a way. Is it worth it, Rafaella? Is it really such a delight to you, what you do with men, enough to make up for all the risks?''

"I suppose you would not think it so," Rafaella said, trying not to remember that her reasons had been quite otherwise, "you who are so defiant about being a lover of women."

"Defiant?" Camilla shrugged. "Perhaps. If you had had my experience, you would not think so much, perhaps, of what men desire of women." She turned her eyes away, but Rafaella, thinking of the terrible scars Camilla bore, guessed at something too dreadful to be spoken. She put her arms around the older woman in silent sympathy, but Camilla was rigid, unmoving. She said, "I did not die. That is what I cannot forgive myself. To live with the memory. That is what none of my kinswomen could forgive me; that I lived when a decent woman would have died." She pulled herself free of Rafaella's arms. "Don't touch me, Rafaella, I'm not fit to live.

"Don't say that, Camilla, don't—" Rafaella said, holding her.

After a moment the older woman shuddered and said "I'm sorry. I get like that sometimes. And when I heard you were pregnant, it seemed I could not bear my hate—that you were young, lovely, cherished . . . but it was myself I hated . . . for all the things I would never have or enjoy. . . ." She smiled, bleakly, in the dark. "It is all born of nightmares. Forgive me, Rafaella."

"I think," Rafaella said, subdued, turning her hand within the chain so that her hand lay within Camilla's, "that I should ask you to forgive me instead, *breda*."

"We will forgive one another, then," Camilla said, squeezing the soft hands. "Come, you must sleep, it is not good for a woman with child to lose sleep this way. Here, will you sleep better like this?" She eased the pillow under Rafaella's side and neck. "Lie quite still, and when you wake up tomorrow, maybe you will not be sick and I can sleep a little longer."

They were chained together for another three days;

but now they had learned to help one another, and it cemented a friendship which was to endure lifelong, and to go so deep that in years after, neither could ever remember why they had quarreled.

Broken Vows

by Annette Rodriguez

Annette says she lives with a "perky little angelfish"
who is an ideal roommate (at least she'd be quiet),
and her reaction to the news that we were going to
accept her story was "WOW!" She'd never been pub-
lished before. She has a degree in biological science—
makes me feel very inferior, since I only managed a
Bachelor's degree from a small college in Texas—I'm
the only person I know without a Master's degree—
and she plans a career in molecular biology and ge-
netics. She is of Cuban birth and has no children,
which follows naturally from being single—or does it?
Unless you're a movie star, probably.

This story deals with what must, from the very first
days of the Renunciates, have been a very vexing ques-
tion; there are always some Renunciates who fall in
love, and from the first, I've received letters asking
what happens then. They can't all follow in the steps
of Jaelle n'ha Melora.

Exhausted, chilled to the bone by the icy wind that
blew from the Hellers, limping painfully on a foot
raw and bleeding from a dog bite, Aleta dragged herself toward the distant light of the Guild House. The
night had been merciless, leaving her no thought but
that of shelter. She picked up her heavy skirts, grateful
for what warmth they gave her, only to stumble again.
It was no good; she couldn't make it. But the howling
wind brought sounds of movement, faint rustlings that
frightened her worse for all that they were unknown.

Bandits? She struggled to her feet. Better to fall down dead than into the hands of such men.

The lights of the Neskaya Guild House flickered tentatively. At such a late hour, with everyone asleep, would her knock be heard? Did Zelda still keep vigil by the door or had the years changed her habits?

But her question only made her shiver from a cold inner fear. Would they let her in at all? Her fingers were insensible as she tightened them into a fist to bang on the door. The seconds seemed like hours as her knock went unanswered.

Then, with a loud click, the door opened slowly. A breath of warmth swept the threshold. Aleta looked up through swimming eyes to see the corpulent shape of Zelda, the doorkeeper. "I crave shelter," she managed to mumble.

But the wide, pleasant face that had at once turned compassionate was now hard and angry, as recognition swept across it. "You!" Zelda uttered like an accusation.

"Please," Aleta begged. "I've nowhere else to go." *I know I should not have come. It was wrong. I should have stayed a prisoner to where my folly led me.* But it was too late. The night grew around her, tightening its hold on her consciousness. She swayed and held out her hands vainly to intercept the hard ground.

A second figure wavered before her. Strong arms caught her before she fell and carried her inside. The door shut with a resolute bang, and all at once the familiar scent of spices mingled with raw leather indulged her senses with the memory of security.

A cup was pressed to her lips and Aleta drank. Sour wine burned down her throat. She sputtered and coughed, but her sight cleared. She took the cup between her trembling hands and finished its contents in several gulps. But when she looked up with words to thank Zelda, it was the tense, lean face of a middle-aged woman with short cropped brown hair that met her glance.

"So you finally found the courage to return," the woman told her with a cynicism that grated upon Aleta's ears. "I would not have thought that much of you."

Aleta put the cup down without a word. The woman walked behind her and pulled back the fine cloak that covered her head, revealing a glossy mantle of chestnut brown hair held by a jeweled copper clasp. "So you not only renounced our vows, but grew your hair and accepted his gifts as well as his protection."

"I knew no better," Aleta replied, forcing herself not to flinch at the harsh words.

But the woman grasped her shoulder, pulling Aleta around to face her, and said. "You dare tell me that. I gave birth to you here in this Guild House. You were raised among us. You took the oath of a Renunciate. You know us and our secrets. And you threw all that away and betrayed our deepest trust because of a man!"

"I loved him," Aleta uttered with a deep cry, tearing herself from her mother's painful grasp. "He would not take Aleta n'ha Kira. He could not accept me as freemate. He is the son of a Comyn lord. There was no other way for us but *di catenas*."

"There is always another way," Kira stated. She took to pacing. "If you had chosen to leave us and bind yourself to a man before you took our vows, I would have been disappointed, but I would have accepted it. But what you did, Aleta, the breaking of our vows, is punishable. Even then, if you had returned to accept punishment and be reinstated, I still could have forgiven you. But you stayed with him and defied our laws. You can expect only one thing from us now."

"I know," Aleta replied barely above a whisper. The last words of the Renunciate oath rang through her memory—*let them slay me like an animal and consign my body unburied to corruption*—. Still the unfairness of it all fueled her response.

"Don't you understand? I was a child when I took the oath. A child of fifteen, awed and blinded by your deeds of bravery. I wanted to be just like you, and like Dana, my oath-mother, who boasted of her battle scars. But I couldn't. I felt out of place. It was differ-

ent with Alan. I could belong to him. He said I was
pretty. He said that he loved me.''

Kira stared at the blank wall as Aleta finished. ''But
in the end he really wasn't so different from the rest
of you. What he wanted was not what I am. I tried to
pretend, but eventually I came to be an unwelcome
stranger in his household.''

''Then you are not yet bound to him *di catenas*?''

Aleta shook her head. ''We were supposed to be at
the last Midwinter Festival in Thendara, but—''

''But here you are,'' Kira finished with a deep sigh.
''Very well. This is a serious matter and not to be
decided lightly in the middle of the night. Though I
should throw you to the dogs and let them gnaw at
your bones, you may stay the night. Zelda will take
you to a spare room and see to your immediate needs.
The morning will be soon enough to judge the merit
of your actions.''

Aleta stood to take a step and winced as feeling
painfully returned to her wounded foot. She caught a
flash of concern in her mother's eyes that was quickly
wiped away. But still Kira forced her to sit again so as
to inspect her foot.

''One of those dogs has already had a taste of me,''
Aleta said, trying to manage a wry grin as her mother
undid the dirty bandage.

Kira said nothing beyond calling for water, oint-
ments, and a clean bandage to dress the jagged wound.
Her quick, efficient ministrations were gentle, and the
sharp, acute pain that had been Aleta's constant companion dulled into distant ache. But as the girl stood
to thank her mother, Kira shook her away roughly.
''You don't have to thank me. I would have done the
same for any animal in distress.''

There was no response to that. Aleta saw Kira go,
and though she longed to run after her and embrace
her mother in a hold so tight as to wipe away the hurt
and sorrow that separated them, she refrained. Kira's
stance was inflexible and unforgiving.

Zelda came beside her with a look on her face as
cold and stern as Kira's. ''This way,'' she indicated

with a wave of her arm down a long hall toward a flight
of stairs. Aleta followed her meekly, trying to find
comfort in the bright memories of days long past. She
stood before the stairs remembering the neck-breaking
races with her girlhood friend, Melinda, running down
the stairs two or three at a time. *Melinda!* Breda, *I had
almost come to forget you.*

Zelda waited for her impatiently at the top of the
stairs, but Aleta had to know. "Is Melinda still here?
Or has she gone to another Guild House?"

"For her sake I wish she had," Zelda replied with
a touch of regret. "She stayed even after we were certain that you would not return. Chance has it, though,
that she is away guiding a party through the hills. It
would have been too cruel for her to be here and witness your coming."

Aleta accepted the harsh speech because she de-
served it, though her spirits fell even deeper. It had
been her one and only true regret, to leave behind her
foster-sister Melinda. Zelda showed her to a room and
closed the door, leaving Aleta alone with her thoughts.
Had she any right to expect Melinda to be waiting with
open arms to receive her as if nothing had happened?
She looked around the room's stark walls. Had she any
right to expect compassion from her mother or her
Guild-sisters?

The walls had no answer. She fell upon the bed, the
fatigue of four days of travel in open country taking
its toll. Sleep was the one consolation that she would
get from the Guild House that night.

But when it seemed that she had barely sunk her
head on the soft pillow, the sounds of frantic steps
running past her door forced her to wake. Pale sunlight was streaming through the windows. Aleta
rubbed the sleep from her eyes, realizing that it was
early morning.

She rose and shook the wrinkles from her wide skirt,
vaguely recalling that she had fallen asleep fully
dressed. Her door was unlocked; she opened it, and
with a glance down the empty hall, walked toward the
top of the stairs.

Confusion reigned on the floor below. Aleta heard voices, and from their tense tones realized that something out of the ordinary was occurring. Several people came toward the stairs and in their midst was a tall girl with short blonde curls who walked with the grace of a doe. Her loose Amazon trousers were dusty and stained, and beneath the scraps of the torn tunic that covered her shoulders were long, red scratches.

Alarmed, Aleta pushed back against the wall trying to hide. But the party came up toward her, and their words became distinct.

"It's a miracle you're all in one piece. A rock slide is a death trap."

"I certainly thought it was all over for me. But the Goddess seemed to have another plans. We were only roughed up a bit and in the end I counted us lucky."

"Well, losing most of your supplies isn't very lucky. You were smart, Melinda, in turning back."

"If only my employer would have agreed with you. He fumed and bellowed all the way back to—"

The silence that fell was deeper than the darkest night. Melinda's words ended as she met Aleta's hastily averted glance, and her face paled in recognition. Aleta turned away and backed into her room, barely seeing anything through the veil of tears that filled her eyes. Melinda had seen her and remembered. And in her frank expression had been the first hint of real welcome. That was until it became obscured by the same cold indifference that had sullied her mother's face, the look of bitter reproach.

She limped to the bed. Kira's harshness she had expected. And the hostility of the other Renunciates was a natural consequence. She accepted that. She could even understand it. But enmity from Melinda was something she had not prepared for. It was too cruel. And it cut her to the bone.

A knock at her door sent her into panic. Was it Melinda? She cringed, unable to face such an ordeal now. Thankfully, it was only Zelda who entered with a tray for her breakfast. "Kira said to tell you to come down after you've bathed and eaten," she stated briskly. "They've reached a decision."

Aleta glanced at the food, the knot in her stomach chasing away any hunger pangs. "I'll be there in a few minutes," she told Zelda. But the woman had left without waiting for her reply.

Aleta slumped back on the bed. *I must find the courage to face this—whatever it is that they are going to do to me. And the sooner it's done, the better. If only Melinda were not here, I could have borne this shame with more resolve.* But her lament had no answer other than getting up and walking into the Guild House meeting room.

The hallway and stairs were empty, all evidence of Melinda's tumultuous arrival erased. Aleta took a deep breath to steady her nerve. She had not been so faint-hearted when she had left. Two years spent among the Domains woman had made her soft. But now that she had to stand before her Guild-sisters she would not quaver and let them see her fear. She would somehow face whatever fate awaited her. But she knew that her courage was like glass and easily shattered.

A figure approached. It was Zelda. "They are waiting for you."

Aleta nodded, not needing to be told. She walked through the doors and into the meeting room. All her Guild-sisters were there. Kira stood as she entered and motioned Dana to come forward. Aleta crossed glances with her oath-mother, seeing once again the blatant glare of reproof.

"A messenger from your lover has come," Kira spoke, bluntly using the vulgar term. "He is here to escort you back. It seems Alan misses you."

Aleta didn't even dare to look up, much less say a word. "At least he is civilized enough to not send an army to fetch his intended bride," Kira resumed in the same bland tone. "That, of course, is inconsequential. His demands have no right over our laws. And our laws strictly say that one who has proven herself false to our oath must present herself for judgment. Failure to do that is punishable by death."

"The matter is not so clear in this case," Dana stated.

Aleta glanced up quickly. How was it that someone spoke in her favor? But she was even more surprised to hear her mother agree.

"That is so, Dana. We have perhaps erred in administering the oath to one who was not mature enough to fully understand its implications. It is late to undo the damage, however. Death is too extreme, but we cannot allow our oath to be taken lightly. Instead we inflict a different punishment.

As quickly as Aleta's hopes rose, they were quenched by Kira's next words. "Aleta, you are hereby consigned to the fate of one who is dead. No Renunciate may approach to speak or aid or comfort you. You are banished from all the Guild Houses and from contact with any of its members. The name of Aleta n'ha Kira is erased from all our records and all our hearts. Return to the man whose household you once took in preference of our own, and never again set foot upon the grounds of this house."

At a gesture from Kira, the Renunciates turned their backs to Aleta. "Leave," she told the dazed girl. "And may you find solace in this love that has caused you to lose ours."

Aleta swallowed, unable to believe the harshness of the judgment. Rigidly, she walked out, barely coping with what had occurred. The front door was open, but slowly it closed behind her. *No, this can't be happening.* Was there no forgiveness, no understanding?

There were several Renunciates in the yard, but they, too, turned their backs to her as she glanced in their direction. She was an outcast, empty and barren, denied even a way to fight back.

Steps neared her and she looked up to see a man, the messenger from Alan, approach with a horse. "My lady," the man said, "you are to return with me."

Aleta nodded. What other choice did she have? What else had been left her? She let the man help her mount, feeling beaten into submission. The man mounted his own horse, guiding Aleta through the trees away from the home of her childhood—her home forever lost.

Somehow the hours passed as the red sun slowly settled below the horizon. The wind started blowing fiercely, but to all this Aleta was indifferent. She was like a puppet whose strings had been cut, insensitive to any more pain.

Noises followed their passage through the misty woods. Noises that, if she had been alert, would have frightened her. Her horse neighed in warning, his nostrils twitching at the whiff of danger. But it wasn't until the messenger's horse reared up, flinging the man from the saddle like a dead heap to the ground, that Aleta awoke from her lethargy.

Shadows separated from the trees. Men, ugly, leering in the darkness, came at her, their knives gleaming like sharp fangs. Aleta would have screamed, but terror tore the sound from her voice. All she could do was kick and watch the man coming at her fall back stunned.

She rammed her heels into her mount's side and felt the horse lurch forward. But someone grasped at her trailing cloak and pulled her off the saddle. She landed on hard ground, the breath knocked from her lungs. A hot, heavy hand muffled her face, and Aleta went limp. There were too many. She couldn't fight them all.

They pushed her down, clawing at her clothes. She was helpless, a pawn to be played with. She didn't care any more. But as a man's vile-smelling breath smothered her mouth, she rebelled. She did care. She would not submit. A hot flash of anger blazed inside of her. Motion slowed. The men's faces became dark blurs. The teaching and training of her early youth took over her movements. She was not a weak, soft Domains woman, nor was she a wide-eyed child yearning to be heroic and yet failing at every turn. She was Aleta. No more and no less. And she would not be pushed and manipulated by anyone else.

Her attacker cried out in sudden pain as her knee slammed into his groin. He rolled on his side, moan-

ing like a baby. Aleta sprang to her feet, released like
a tightly wound coil, and ran. She ran like the wind,
free at last from the weight that oppressed her. The
other men were nowhere in sight. If she could find a
horse, she could ride away and—

A form came at her from between the trees. Before
Aleta could defend herself, she was knocked to the
ground face-first. Her hands were pinned, and helplessly she squirmed beneath the strength of this new
attack.

Savagely, she swung her legs, trying desperately to
dislodge her captor. But a light, musical laugh rang in
her ears. "Whoa, Aleta. Zandru's hells, stop or you'll
knock me senseless."

"What!" Aleta sputtered, sitting up as she was
quickly released. "Who? What's happening?"

"Who? Have you forgotten me so soon? It's Melinda, *breda.*"

Aleta gasped, hearing Melinda use the personal in-
fliction. "But how? I mean why are you here? I've
been banished. No one can speak to me."

"That order has been rescinded," spoke another
voice, an all too familiar voice.

"Mother!" Aleta cried struggling to her feet. "I
don't understand. How are you here?"

Kira put her arms around her daughter's trembling
shoulders. "Easy, *chiya.* You'll know everything in a
few minutes. Tell me, are you hurt?"

"No, but—"

"Ssh," Kira uttered. "I said I would explain. We
learned that you had left the Comyn lord's home several days ago. You were well on your way to us when
two Renunciates found you and followed to keep you
safe. We then faced a very difficult decision. You see,
we all had agreed to take you back, but in order to do
so you had to be punished. You had broken our laws,
after all. Believe me, when I saw you at our door, so
lost and forlorn, it was all I could to stop myself from
taking you in my arms and holding you as if you had
been a small child."

Aleta was dumbfounded. Dare she believe her

mother's words that everything had been a sham, a trick meant as punishment? But that very truth of the matter was like a rigid stick up her spine. Her choice, her life, was being manipulated again. The injustice of it all made her anger flare. "Because of what you've done, I will not go back," she asserted. "You should have let me choose to accept or not accept punishment. It was my right. Instead you denied me my choice, assuming that I would meekly agree to whatever you did and be happy just to return to you."

Kira stared at her without betraying any emotion. "If you will not return to the Guild House, then you plan to go back to Alan?"

"No," Aleta replied turning away to face the dark night, knowing that that part of her life was over. "He is like you, trying to make of me something I am not. I will not be bullied or harassed or intimidated into adhering to anyone else's decisions. I will decide what is best for me. And I choose to be free."

As Aleta came around to face her mother and Melinda, she fully expected to see anger and resentment in their faces. She wouldn't let that change her, though. She would stand fast to her decision. But to her surprise, Melinda was smiling, and her mother's happy face was shining with tears of joy.

"My daughter," Kira said gently. "I am so proud of you. Now at last you understand what it is to be a Renunciate. You have finally fulfilled the oath you took when you were too young to understand."

Melinda came toward her. "*Breda,* don't you see. You've always let others form your life, and that is not the way of a Free Amazon. We choose our fate, as you have just done, and depend only on ourselves for protection. No one may lay claim to us. That's what it's like to be free."

Aleta understood. Her anger abated. It was like finding herself at last, knowing where she belonged. But suddenly the years, the separation, seemed to be traced in Melinda's face. Aleta almost felt her heart break. "*Breda,* can you forgive me for the pain I caused you when I left?"

Melinda smiled. "Take my hand," she said, "and you will see how all is forgotten."

Aleta did and the warm clasp of friendship was like a life-giving balm to her frayed emotions. She turned to Kira as her mother's arm fell across her shoulders again. "But what happened to those men?" she asked looking around. "The one who attacked me."

Kira laughed crossing glances with Melinda. "I'm afraid, *chiya*, that you proved a little too much for them. When we hired them to perform this little show, we told them that you were slight of build and not strong. So when a mountain lion instead fell upon them, they fled back to town. I suppose they'll soon spread more rumors about how dreadful the Free Amazons are."

"No," Aleta chuckled. "They're not dreadful at all. Only perhaps slightly devious, especially certain Guild-mothers and their minions. But still I can think of no other place that I would rather be than in their company."

Kira smiled broadly in reply. "Then, my daughters, home we go. And may nothing ever again tear us apart."

And to this Aleta wholeheartedly agreed.

If Only Banshees Could See

by Janet R. Rhodes

A great many people have asked me if there will be a sequel to CITY OF SORCERY. My answer has always been "No: this is a story of seeking, not of finding, and traditionally the ancient story of a search for Shangri-La always means that the finding is either obvious or impossible." But Janet Rhodes didn't like that answer and provided her own—and this is it.

Janet Rhodes first appeared in DOMAINS OF DARKOVER (DAW, 1990), and has just joined SFWA (Science Fiction Writers of America). She is now working on a novel in her own universe. She lives in Olympia, Washington and works for the state.

Deep in thought, Margali n'ha Ysabet walked the halls of the City of the Wise Sisterhood, her heart heavy. With every few steps, she clenched her hands into fists and released them. The wine-colored rays of the late afternoon sun peered through skylights, spattering the stone floor and seeming to follow her.

Bredhiya, *what weighs on you so heavily?* called a familiar voice, mind-to-mind. The question pulled Margali to a stop. She turned and retraced her steps to where Camilla, her friend, her *breda,* stood at the door of the rough-hewn room that was their home. Tall and lean, Camilla appeared more as a man than a woman. She was an *emmasca,* having undergone the illegal neutering operation known only to the *leroni* of the Towers. Margali and the older woman had not taken the oath of freemates—only once before had Margali made the commitment that bound two women as surely as it bound man and woman. But they were committed to each other in love and friendship.

Margali answered aloud, "Time enough to talk later, when you are done with your study. I do not wish to disturb you."

Camilla widened her gray eyes in surprise and slammed shut the ancient book she held in both large hands. "But I am nearly done, and you are more important to me than that which I can do any time." Camilla placed the leather-bound book on a small stone table, and Margali entered their room, letting the door shut behind her.

While Camilla watched, perplexed, she paced the room. After some minutes Margali spoke, forcing words past a throat thick with emotion, "They want me to go to Jaelle's and my children. . . . They, Kyntha, said—they said . . . I had to, to assist Jaelle's daughter. . . ." Margali halted, finally looked Camilla full in the face, and said flat-voiced, "I cannot go into the world again. I had hoped to stay here forever after Jaelle died and we came into the city. I cannot face Jaelle's child."

"Our oath-mother has requested this of you?" Camilla asked. Margali nodded. "Whatever happens," Camilla continued, "I will face it with you. You are not alone." Drawing Margali to their bed and onto her lap, Camilla rocked her lover as a mother rocks her child awakened from a terrifying dream, close, protectively, caressing shoulders and back.

"*Bredhiya*, the children are symbols of yours and Jaelle's love for each other, even though each was fathered by a Lord of the Domains."

"But I killed her!" yelled Margali, pounding her angry fists against the bed. "I killed her just as surely as if I had thrust a knife in her heart!" And she groaned, rocking her fear-dampened face against Camilla's shoulder. "I was close enough . . . if only that cliff hadn't dropped off. . . ."

"If only banshees had eyes and could fly, they might have the pick of the herdbeasts, rather than screeching all night long in the snowy wastes for want of food," replied Camilla quietly. "Avarra's mercy! None of us fault you for fearing heights."

"But Jaelle was my life. She had so much strength, so much to offer. If anyone should have died that day, it was me!"

"Others were there; none of us could have saved her. Zandru's hells! *I* didn't even try to save her!" Camilla's voice became dangerously quiet. "Who can say, but that it was her time, that the blessed Avarra would have taken her from us even had we not come to this frozen land far from the Domains." Margali stiffened, wanting to deny even the Goddess of birth and death the right to cut short Jaelle's life.

"No. Jaelle would not have wanted you to blame yourself for her death," continued Camilla. "She would not want to see you suffer for her sake. She would want you to go to Dorilys. . . ."

"Cleindori," Margali whispered. "When she was small, her blonde hair and the blue frocks her nurse dressed her in made Dorilys look like the flower of the *kireseth*—with its blue bells all covered with pollen. So we called her Cleindori, Golden Bell." She gave a sad laugh. "There were those who thought it blasphemous to call a child after the herb used to catalyze the powers of the *laran*-gifted."

"Jaelle would want you to go to the child. You are her mother now that Jaelle is gone. The oath of freemates makes you so." Camilla pulled back a stray wisp of dark hair from Margali's clammy forehead. "And your own daughter, Shaya—she carries Jaelle's nickname, does she not?—has not seen you since she was two. I can see how the Sisterhood would want you to—"

Margali pulled back. "If that was all they wanted, for me to see the children, to face Jaelle's death. But, no, they want me to . . . I can hardly speak of it . . . they expect Cleindori to break the rules of the Towers, to free the Domains of Arilinn's hold over matrix work. Camilla, they say she will take matrix work out of the Towers, into the Domains. To do so—even to attempt it—carries risk for Cleindori, Shaya, and all of us from Armida and the Forbidden Tower.

"Even my leaving the city and going to Cleindori is a risk. Who knows how the *leroni* of the Towers will see me now—trained by the Forbidden Tower . . . and by the Sisterhood. Though in their arrogance, the Towers may disbelieve the legends of the Sisterhood's powers."

Margali threw up her hands. "I don't know what to do. I cannot face Cleindori. She must hate me for her mother's death. And Shaya must wonder at a mother who is not dead, but acts as if she is."

"Do you really think they would not welcome you with open hearts? Margali! They would rejoice to have their mother back . . . I think Kyntha is right."

"What?"

"This is not new, what Kyntha asks of you. She has spoken thus before. The Sisterhood teaches we must release our fears, or they become our lives. Right now, Jaelle's death is more real to you than the city or even—" Camilla's voice broke and she had to swallow several times before continuing. "I love you. So much it hurts to see you in such pain. To know you wish yourself dead rather than Jaelle. Yes," she silenced Margali's ready denial with a gesture, "I, too, wish Jaelle had lived. But I have not made that wish my life. I am not filled with self-hatred for it. I have not refused—for *ten* years—to see my child, or Jaelle's child.

"I want you well, Margali. This hate eats at you from within. There are no herbs that will drive it from you. You alone can dissolve it. But I will be with you; I will be a strength for you. If I could do it for you, I would. Please let me help you." Camilla grew silent.

Margali hardly heard the words. But Camilla's love and her deep yearning for Margali to regain wholeness of mind finally reached through the anger. Allowing her fear-charged muscles to relax, Margali fell again into Camilla's arms.

"You'd think," she mumbled, "after years of study and practice at the arts of the Sisterhood," and she sniffled, "that I'd know it all by now. And when we first got here, I thought we'd have all the answers!"

"The journey of the heart must be taken one step at a time with one's own legs and mind." Camilla began one of the chants with which the Sisterhood's apprentices accompanied their daily chores. "A sister cannot travel the path for another, nor can she reach ahead and prepare the stones for the road."

And Margali joined in, "For I am my own person, heart and mind and spirit, and I alone of all the universe know the steps of my path. They are indelibly etched in the core of my being." Camilla kissed the dark crown of Margali's head, hugging her tight.

A scratch at the door interrupted their reverie. "Margali." Taletha's voice carried clearly into the room. "It is your turn in the watching room."

"Uh-h-h-oh," moaned Margali, her hand combing through tousled hair.

"Sh-hh," said Camilla. "I will take your turn. You rest."

"No." Margali propped herself up on unsteady arms. "I will take my turn. It is my duty."

"But you are overtired. And you haven't even eaten yet. Take my watch tomorrow, when you are refreshed." Camilla's concern etched lines on her face as she turned to the door. "Taletha, I will come. Margali is unwell."

"No." Margali's strained voice carried only to the *emmasca*. "I will take my watch. It will help keep my mind off my . . . decision."

"I would take one burden from you," whispered Camilla.

"No, dear heart. I must do this." Margali knuckled both eyes, ran fingers again through unruly hair, and smoothed her tunic as she rose from the bed. "Do I look too terribly unfit? No?" And she was out the door before Camilla could stop her.

Passing the great gathering room the sisters used for visiting, doing handwork and the like, Margali smelled warm bread fresh from the communal kitchens. Its yeasty aroma pulled her in to tear off a handful.

A few minutes later, Margali turned a corner and approached a small table bearing a copper water basin that stood outside the watching room. She licked off the last of the bread crumbs and wiped her hands on her tunic before formally washing her hands of the soil of the world and her mind of unsettled thoughts. The ritual cleansing would prepare her to enter the watching room free of attachments to their daily life, to fear, worry, or the busy-ness of the day. For it was not wise to take one's problems into the overworld where thoughts and feelings had substance. Margali hoped to free her mind of the decision thrust upon her by her oath-mother Kyntha and the Circle of Twenty. At least for the duration of the watch. While on the worldly plane, Margali could block out the cold fear that clawed at her heart. But in the overworld . . . she had avoided for years a dark, murky place that chilled her soul. Margali had no doubt of its source. Once she had passed too close and the darkness had reached out to enclose her heart in a cold fist. The shock had thrown her instantly from the overworld, and she had returned to consciousness many hours later in a pain-racked body.

Margali quietly entered the softly lit watching chamber, noticed Adela sitting motionless on cushions, eyes closed, and mind far away. Taletha, squatting to the left of the curtained doorway, took a deep, calming breath and recited the ritual words that called Adela back. Margali then settled on the floor nearby. It would not take the girl long to return from her watch.

Even in such a short time, Margali's mind wandered. And she reflected on the watching room, where the Wise Sisterhood observed the activities of the people of Darkover, recording the patterns of wisdom and error, of progress and decline. Rarely, after deep deliberation, the Sisters tweaked the mind or altered the path of one or two Darkovans so Darkover itself would survive.

In this way, the Sisterhood had saved Jaelle's and Margali's lives while they were still of the Guild of the Renunciates and unaware of the Sisterhood. Some

eighteen years before—*has it really been that long?*
wondered Margali—a raging flood had held them captive in a cave, Jaelle deathly ill from miscarriage. The
Sisterhood, aware of their plight, had sensed something special in Jaelle. Their inner council, the Circle
of Twenty, foresaw that a daughter yet unborn could
revitalize Towers that housed ever dwindling circles of
trained telepaths. This daughter was destined to become a Keeper, the specially trained woman who directed the psychic energies of the Tower circles at the
expense of life-long chastity; but a Keeper fated to
break the most sacred of taboos and thereby to bring
new life and new ways to the Towers—and to Darkover! For this daughter would bring the science of
matrix work out of the Towers and into the towns of
the Domains.

It was as a direct result of this intervention that Jaelle
and Margali had gone to live for a time at Armida with
Callista and Ellemir Lanart and their husbands and
children. And how they, too, had become members of
the Forbidden Tower—the only circle of telepaths to
function outside Tower walls. The circle at Armida
conducted themselves in ways totally unacceptable to
the established Towers. They survived only because
their circle had successfully defended their Tower in a
laran-battle against Arilinn Tower, whose Keeper had
challenged the Forbidden Tower's right to exist.

Adela shuddered, tossed her tawny hair, and flexed
cold, stiff muscles as she returned from her journey
into the overworld. Taletha, the sister who had sat with
her, had ensured that Adela's body continued to
breathe and her beating heart circulated blood without
distress while she watched from the astral planes.
Margali would do the same for Taletha, as someone
new would for Margali. Two sisters kept vigil in the
watching room at all times: one to watch Darkover and
one to watch the watcher.

"Adela! How goes it?" Taletha's voice was far too
cheery to suit Margali's mood.

Adela started her report as, next to her on a small

table, a candle sputtered—one candle, one watch, one watcher, went the teaching chant. "The overworld is fairly quiet," she began. "Some activity in the Tower relays. But there hasn't been much communication from Tower to Tower.

"I did pick up something odd near Arilinn Tower." Margali perked up her attention although no movement of body betrayed her. "The Keeper of that Tower, Dorilys Aillard, is distressed." Margali shivered, and not because the Sisterhood insisted on using a Keeper's family name, rather than her given name and her Tower. "I do not think her circle knows yet; she is deeply barriered. But she came into the overworld and walked about the Tower marker for some time. The Circle has asked us to remark on her closely."

Zandru's hells, all nine of them, raged Margali silently. *They've been remarking on Cleindori since before Damon and Jaelle conceived her! It is not enough the Circle of Twenty has us spy on her during watches. No! Now they want me to go out into the Domains, to Thendara, and spy on her myself! Oh! Kyntha clothed it in platitudes and talk of final tests. To prove to myself that I am free of the pain of Jaelle's death. Jaelle, my Shaya, my freemate, mate of my soul. . . .*

With grim determination, Margali checked her galloping thoughts, listened as Adela said she would notify the Circle of Dorilys Aillard's activities after recording her watch. The journal was in the recovering room across the hallway, where the sisters retired after their watches to devour sticky sweets, dried fruit, and nuts to restore the energy depleted during their forays into the overworld.

Taletha lit her candle from the one sputtering out, and made herself comfortable on the low couch and cushions Adela had just left. After Taletha refolded her long legs and composed herself for the watch, she trained her eyes on the candle flame, as did many of the Sisterhood-trained. Margali cleared her mind, settled into well-worn cushions, and made contact with her matrix crystal. Then she reached out for the light rapport that would allow her to monitor Taletha's body, making sure it functioned properly while its owner walked the overworld.

Taletha's candle formed dancing shadows on the wall and threw out a comforting glow. Soon, it seemed the candle was but a stub, and Margali sent the watcher a reassuring mental touch, with adjustments to a muscle about to cramp, before she went off to call in the next monitor. She returned with the recently trained Meloran and spoke the ritual words that ended every watch and called the sister back to her body. Taletha came to herself quickly with a start and a big, catlike stretch. Her report was short and uneventful.

Margali lit her candle from Taletha's stub and arranged herself comfortably on the couch. She centered on the candle flame, took several deep breaths, sensed her matrix respond, then sprang into the overworld after Meloran made rapport. It always amazed Margali to see the two figures below become small and fuzzy, then disappear as she entered the gray stillness of the overworld itself.

Each watch she followed the same pattern—Towers and relays, then any unusual activity or *laran* use, with special note of the Circle's "remarkables." Normally, Margali enjoyed the freedom of the watch. It gave her time alone and allowed her to see what befell Darkover outside of the isolated City of the Sisterhood. She could see the expansion to the Terran headquarters in Thendara where she had once lived and worked as Terran Intelligence agent Magdalen Lorne. Or follow the growth of the little ones at Armida, home to the *leroni* of the Forbidden Tower. Except for Cleindori and Shaya. She would find them at Arilinn where they lived as members of that Tower's circle. So many things had changed since . . . since Jaelle. *Ah, Jaelle,* thought Margali. *Jaelle, my love.* In the overworld, a gloomy blackness stirred in response to Margali's sorrow; grief, palpable and real in this place, reached out its icy hand and gripped her soul. Slowly, relentlessly, it tugged Margali toward its mighty maw.

The anguish that enveloped Margali echoed through

to her physical body, a sharp pain and cramping in her chest. In the watching room, Meloran did what she could to calm spasming muscles, ease labored breathing, then winged a frantic telepathic message for help.

Margali, caught in the overworld, all but paralyzed in the numbing grip, wanted to run, to cry out. And yet the thing touched deeply a part of her Margali had all but denied. She struggled. But the more she fought, the stronger it pulled at her, drew her ever closer. Margali tried to visualize a wall between herself and the evil place. She molded thought stuff into a high stone fence—stone fast to stone, higher than she could see, stretching from horizon to horizon. And a door, festooned with chain and lock and bolt. Solid. But as she reached out to touch the wall, to reassure herself of its protection, it vanished: stone, fence, chain and lock, all into the darkness. Margali teetered at the cusp demarking the dark from the gray twilight of the overworld, a knife edge between sanity and terror. And plummeted into the terror, into the sorrow of losing her freemate—Jaelle so much a part of her, the pain was that of having a limb torn from her living body. Margali could drown in the sorrow and pain if she did not act soon.

Terror rapidly gave way to certainty she would die. As the darkness devoured her, the thin thread of consciousness linked to her body in the watching room stretched, threatened to break. And Margali knew with a jabbering corner of her mind it was simply a matter of time until she lost connection to her physical self. Soon she would join her beloved Jaelle.

"Jaelle!" she cried. "Shaya, my beloved!" The call echoed through the overworld, touched two dear to Margali.

The agony in her heart melted as Margali spied her freemate—Jaelle with waves of copper-golden hair dissonant against the crimson of her flowing robes. How odd, Margali thought, for Jaelle to wear the crimson of a Keeper. Alarmed, she realized the vision of hope was not Jaelle, could only *be* a Keeper!

As Margali made the connection, Dorilys, called

Cleindori, Keeper of Arilinn, reached her hand across the gulf of hungry darkness separating them. Within the space of a few heartbeats, Margali mustered her strength and overcame her terror-paralyzed muscles to stretch out and grasp Cleindori's offered hand.

"Who are—?" Margali gasped. Then, "Cleindori," she whispered, shaking anew. A wave of dizziness passed and Margali saw a third person, dark-haired and slender, join her and Cleindori in an island of light . . . "Shaya!"

"Mother!" cried Shaya, throwing her arms tightly around Margali's neck. And though Margali knew Shaya was physically in Arilinn, many tendays distant, she treasured the feeling as if she truly held her daughter. "Mother! It has been so long and we have worried. Not to hear anything, except through Ferrika, since Aunt Jaelle died."

Margali shuddered and Cleindori, with the power of her thought, formed a bench out of the stuff of the gray world. "Come," she said and pulled Margali down to sit beside her.

"Aunt." Cleindori spoke the word that meant, at once, mother's sister, honored woman of my mother's generation and freemate to my mother. "What happened that you endangered yourself so? Why did you not wait after you called?"

At the last, Margali pulled back, the better to see the Keeper's face. "I never called you!" Bitterness hardened her voice. "I called . . . Jaelle." Margali could not look at Cleindori or Shaya who sat at their feet.

"Do you forget that your daughter, my sister, is called Shaya? You called. We heard. We answered." At Margali's shocked look, Cleindori drew back. She looked much older to Margali than a seventeen-year-old should. But, after all, she was a woman, a Keeper, and Arilinn-trained.

"Aunt Margali. Why have you not contacted us? Why have you stayed away? I know the Sisterhood has not kept you from us." At Margali's horrified look, Cleindori continued, "Do not worry, your secret is safe. We know very little. But Ferrika has told us something of the Sisterhood.'' She added as if in afterthought, ''Not enough for us to pass on to those who could hurt you.''

Now came Margali's test—not tendays or months away, but now! She worked her jaw open and closed, soundlessly. She hugged herself. She almost preferred the suffocating darkness to this. And yet, here was Cleindori, full of love, respect and strength, and, yes, she had to admit it, of Jaelle.

Margali sagged forward and whispered, ''I was afraid.'' She reached around and hugged Cleindori tightly, cast an embarrassed look at Shaya, before continuing. ''And I was angry Jaelle was gone. I hurt so much. I wanted it to have been me instead. I should have been able to prevent her death. If not for the cliff—the heights—I could have saved her. She was my life. I felt maimed without her.''

They sat silently for some time, while tears of release flowed unchecked into their laps.

Cleindori spoke quietly, ''I cried, too, when I learned of my mother's death. I cried in hurt and frustration, in anger that she left me. Then Father and Ellemir and the others reminded me of her gifts, of her laughter and joy, her stubborn-headedness, of her love for you and for me, and of her gift of life to me. She is gone, but we are here, to carry on.'' Margali looked up at this child-woman in wonder. ''I let go of the pain of her death years ago, Margali. She would have wanted it that way. You know that. I have work to do. You have work to do. Let Jaelle travel her own path.''

In Margali's mind echoed, ''. . . A sister cannot travel the path for another . . .''

Cleindori withdrew slightly from Margali to see the effect of her words. And into the too quiet space, Shaya, her eyes dark, liquid pools, pleaded, ''Mother, please come home.''

''Yes, Shaya, little one,'' Margali said hesitantly. ''Yes, it is time.'' She stood and gazed into the distance as if thinking, or searching for some thing.

The shaking began as tiny bumps on her skin, a prickling and standing up of the hairs on her arms and legs. Then her limbs quivered and her face paled.

"Margali. Aunt," said Cleindori. "What is it? What is wrong?"

"... so cold. It's been hard ... so many ..." Margali made a helpless gesture.

Cleindori, concerned, made a quick assessment, running her skilled hands over Margali's astral body. "Avarra's mercy, Margali! You're in crisis! What have you— Never mind. We'll get you back to the city. You must return.

"Let me help you," she added, supporting Margali on her left side. Shaya joined them and, quick as thought, they came to a peculiarity in the fabric of the overworld.

"We cannot continue with you," said Cleindori. "But you know the way now. Please return safely and come visit us at Arilinn as soon as you are able. I have wonderful news." And Cleindori sent Margali quick images of her and Lewis-Arnad Lanart-Alton together, in ways a Keeper should not be with any man. At Margali's shocked look, Cleindori and Shaya giggled. "Do not look so surprised!" Cleindori scolded. "You were of the Forbidden Tower long enough to know love should not be forbidden—even to a Keeper of Arilinn!"

She and Shaya pushed Margali toward a misty door forming in the grayness. "Go now—your sisters call."

Margali heard the cawing of crows as if from far away, and realized the raucous heralds of the Circle of Twenty had been gnawing at her thoughts for some time.

Kyntha's voice came to her, "Margali, come back." Many voices picked up the chant that called the watching sister from the overworld. Among them Margali recognized Meloran's and Camilla's. But why? Margali wondered as she stumbled through the doorway and slammed into her body. In a moment of consciousness, Margali recognized that half the Circle of Twenty had jammed into the room and that Meloran

huddled in the farthest corner with wide, terrified eyes.
Then Margali's body twitched violently, throwing her
to the floor before she passed out.

After a time, Margali heard the muted buzzing of
anxious voices. She realized through a fog that her
head swam and her temples throbbed while the rest of
her seemed frozen and numb. Someone—she thought
it was her oath-mother—probed her gently.

"Here, Kyntha." So, it was Kyntha! "This will help
bring her round."

"Margali, drink this," commanded Kyntha, pulling
Margali onto her crossed legs and cradling her head
in the crook of her arm. Margali swallowed. Gahh, it
burned all the way down her throat! Margali groaned
and thrust weakly at the offending vial, managing only
to fall off Kyntha's lap.

"Margali," shouted Camilla. *"Breda!"* And Camilla's strong, knobby hands gathered Margali up and
onto her lap. Margali looked into the *emmasca's* tear-
stained face, then settled into the safety of her friend's
arms.

"Let me monitor her, Camilla, I must see how the
drug is working. With her all clutched up to you,
you're influencing my reading. I must touch her."
Margali felt her oath-mother's mind touch. Then Kyntha withdrew her hands and mind and sat on her heels
with a satisfied sigh. "She has passed crisis now. We
can move her to the healing room. We will monitor
her closely for the next day or so."

Camilla reached out protectively and Kyntha, notic-
ing, gave her an awkward pat. "You may stay with
Margali for as long as you like. I will have Llewellyn
bring soup and bread; the evening meal is long cold."

Sweeping the chamber with her glance, Kyntha in-
cluded all there as she said, "It is time we went to
what is left of our meals. If it meets with your ap-
proval, Mother," she nodded to Mother Judyth, "I
will report to the Circle tomorrow morning, after I
have talked more with Margali." Mother Judyth nodded and Kyntha rose, beckoned Camilla to follow her
with Margali.

They entered the healing room, and Camilla steered Margali to the nearest couch, pulling off pieces of her clothing and dropping them on the floor, more interested in Margali's welfare than where her tunic, house boots, or stockings landed. Margali collapsed on the couch and wished she hadn't. The sudden movement started the room dancing and heaving.

"Margali," cried Camilla, concerned at her sudden pallor. "Are you all right?"

"Yes," whispered Margali through clenched teeth, hoping her stomach would settle. "I'm just dizzy from that potion they gave me. Yeach!"

"What happened?" exclaimed Camilla as she tucked the blankets around Margali. Camilla lowered her voice and whispered, glancing around to see if Kyntha had arrived yet. "They said you were in trouble in the overworld, and that I should be there." She pursed her lips and snorted. "Not that I could do anything but worry, with all those high and mighties scurrying around and not looking as if they knew much either. What happened to you?"

"Yes, what happened?" echoed from the doorway.

Both Camilla and Margali started at the sound of Kyntha's voice, Margali instantly regretting the movement and Camilla covering a sudden feeling of guilt by fussing with the blankets. "I am not sure she can talk to you yet," Camilla said hoarsely, unsure but feeling that Kyntha had something to do with Margali's plight in the overworld.

"Oh," said Kyntha, a slight rise to her tone indicating surprise and irritation. "Margali is sufficiently recovered to tell *you* what happened, but not her oath-mother?"

Camilla frowned and Margali groaned. "It is all right, Camilla, I will talk with her. Just as long as I don't have to move again."

Llewellyn arrived that moment with tuber soup and bread. So they rearranged chairs, blankets, pillows, stools and food, until Camilla sat perched at the end of the couch and Margali reclined upon it with a bowl of soup warming her hands. Kyntha sat in an armed chair near the head of Margali's couch. Llewellyn left quietly, her work done.

Between mouthfuls of soup and bread, Margali recounted what she remembered. When she was done, she could not say for sure what Kyntha thought. Camilla was aghast. "Margali! You nearly died! And Cleindori. A Keeper of Arilinn, with that Alton," Camilla sputtered.

"That is enough, Camilla. Margali, you did well." The *breda* exchanged puzzled looks. "Rest now. I have suspended your work assignments for the next few days. Rest and gather your strength." Almost as an afterthought, Kyntha added, "The Circle of Twenty may wish to speak with you before you leave for Thendara. Do not talk with anyone else about what happened."

Suddenly, the alarm call of crows filled the room. At the alert, Kyntha immediately stood and turned her attention within to receive the Circle's urgent message. She opened her eyes, a worried frown wrinkling her brow, and began moving at the same time. Then she spoke with a sharpness and urgency Margali hadn't heard her use before. "Those-who-are-unnamed advance on the City. We must defend the walls. *Everyone* is needed. Can you walk, Margali?" Without waiting for an answer, Kyntha swirled from the room and strode stiffly down the hall, as Camilla stuttered with objections.

Margali was already pushing back her blankets.

"You cannot go," said Camilla forcing her back onto the couch.

"I must. We must!"

"No, you are not well. You must rest, recover your strength."

Margali, anger growing, clenched her fists until the nails bit half-moons into her palms. "The unnamed ones killed Jaelle! Can you not see? It is time to avenge her death! I must fight."

Shocked, Camilla stopped resisting, helped Margali into her clothing. Going slowly through empty halls to conserve Margali's strength, the two gathered weapons and headed for the city wall.

The Sisters stood calmly outside the walls that encircled their City of Wisdom. From the south, over the ice and snow, approached an army of black-clad women. They were weaponed, for the unnamed ones worked their will with physical and mental strength only. They had never learned to walk the psychic realms.

Camilla and Margali drew their short swords. It had been years since they'd used their weapons in battle. But an urgent shout stopped them before the swords cleared their scabbards; Mother Judyth strode swiftly to the friends' sides. "Children, we must put hatred and fear aside. Weapons of fear, too. Hatred alone draws these evil ones to us. Love and solidarity will keep our city safe and free."

"But they have weapons and they mean to use them!"

"Let them see what little use their weapons are against the Sisterhood." Mother Judyth stood tall and imposing before the *bredhiya*. "Margali, you must empty yourself of any remaining hatred. You must free yourself of the curse that has consumed you these many years. Finish what you began today in the overworld."

Camilla's jaw dropped and Margali looked at the elected leader of the Sisterhood in astonishment and despair. "Mother, I have not the strength."

"You must find it, or we fall. The hate you still bear has drawn this evil to us."

Margali drew a deep breath. She had begun to see the unfairness of what she had done to herself, to Camilla, and to the children. In facing Cleindori and Shaya in the overworld, in facing her fears, she had begun to dissolve them. But hatred for the evil ones who were the direct cause of Jaelle's death still remained inside her. Did she have the strength to return love for evil?

Margali replied, "Mother, I shall strive to do as you say."

"That is all I ask. The blessed Avarra grant you the

gift you desire.'' Judyth laid her hands on Margali's
dark curls, turned, and rejoined the others in the circle.

Camilla and Margali looked at each other. With rapidly beating hearts, they placed their swords against
the city wall. Silently, they joined their sisters.

The horde of unnamed ones continued to advance,
their clubs, swords, and knives held high. At the sight,
Camilla's hands itched to pick up her sword. She said
so to Margali. ''I know. My hands ache, too. And yet
I wish to overcome the hatred. Why is it so hard?''
Stern looks from sisters nearby caused Camilla and
Margali to stop talking and look to the attackers.

The closeness of the evil ones recalled to Margali
the battle in which Jaelle had died. Vainly, she strove
to drive it from her mind. The harder she tried to push
away the vision, to rid her mind of hatred and fear,
the stronger they grew. Even though it had happened
years before, Margali could *see* Jaelle in her mind's
eye grappling with Aquilara. Margali's hand tightened
around the sword that was no longer at her side. If
only she could have saved her freemate! Desperation
rose in her like bile. She had to conquer the women
of evil!

Suddenly, a shout went up, breaking Margali from
her grisly reminiscence. She saw several black-clad
figures approaching the east wall. The line of sisters
wavered as the evil ones began their attack; one, no
two, sisters went down under the blows, lifeless.

Margali cried out silently, *No! Avarra, blessed
Mother, don't let this happen!* as her stomach slowly
rolled over. Urgently, she searched her mind for an
answer, something that would help her fight the evil
ones. And in an odd, altered time sense Kyntha's words
came to her, ''The hatred you still bear will bring evil
to yourself and to the Wise Sisterhood . . . You must
come face to face with . . . the daughter of Jaelle . . .
who is now your daughter.'' And what had Cleindori
said? ''I let go of the pain years ago . . . You have
your life to live. Jaelle would have wanted it that way.''

In taking Aquilara into death's hands with her, Jaelle

had ensured freedom for her friends. Because of her
selfless act, others had lived. And for the gift of life,
Margali had returned hatred and fear. Not an equitable
exchange. The thought forced a groan past her lips.
Somewhere deep inside, Margali felt a sudden tearing
and a searing pain.

Again and again, it tore through her body, forcing
her to the ground. The more Margali resisted, the more
waves of pain engulfed her. She couldn't breathe for the
gut-wrenching pain. She feared she would die from it,
then wished she would, as her stomach tried to leap
into her throat. The pain! The agony! Margali sought
to cut it off, to force it back. Frantically, she searched
for a way. "Blessed Avarra, let there be a way!" she
cried and was rewarded with a vision of Jaelle struggling with Aquilara. Again Margali relieved the horror—Jaelle flinging herself at Aquilara. Margali going
for her, too. Jaelle's "No. No. I'll hold her back. Get
the others away." Margali running to her freemate's
aid anyway, but stopping short at the cliff's edge. Jaelle
and Aquilara grappling, then, clenched together, sliding over . . . and down—

In the midst of the old terror, a glimmer of a thought,
of sanity, shone through. And this time, Margali gave
in to the pain, surrendered to it as Jaelle had to Aquilara.

Abruptly the pain receded, and from some unknown
place within, Margali felt the beginnings of a growing
strength, a blessed relief. As it welled up in her, the
strength pushed out the last of the pain, then surged
powerfully through her unresisting body. The sudden
burst of power thrust Camilla, bent solicitously over
Margali's tortured form, backward. Released from paralysis, Margali slowly rose, stood tall. All the inde-
cision, the "what ifs", were shattered and gone.
Margali looked calmly out at the attackers, reached a
hand to Camilla on her left and to the sister on her
right. They each clasped the hand of another, and on
and on, until the Sisterhood joined in a circle that en-
closed the city. Power flowed freely through the joined

hands until it formed a glowing, protective shield about them.

The first of the attacking women to touch the shield jerked back as if burned. Those who tried to bludgeon their way through the shimmering wall were thrown violently to the ground. Others became confused and incoherent, or insisted that the City of Sorcery had gone up in a ball of fire.

The leaders reformed what was left of their ranks and advanced once more, directly toward Margali! For a moment, the Sisterhood's protective circle wavered as Margali felt the brunt of their anger turned on her alone. Valiantly, she turned again to thoughts of Jaelle, of life and love, focused them inward until the final, black seed of hatred dissolved. The released energy surged outward and upward from the Sisters' joined hands forming the illusion of a wall of fire that engulfed, but did not consume them. The unnamed ones cowered from the flames that seemed all too real to them. Then, in the swirling depths of the flames arose a figure of a woman in chains—the Goddess. The attacking women cried out in terror and scattered like the dried leaves of autumn.

With a collective sigh, the Sisters dispersed. The strength of the circle gone, Margali collapsed.

Camilla sat as she had for hours, anxiety etched deeply in her face, and watched over Margali. Finally, Margali moaned and flailed about. "Camilla. Camilla?"

"I am here, *bredhiya*," said Camilla softly.

Margali found Camilla's hand, clasped it, muttered a few words, and fell into a troubled sleep.

Camilla brushed a strand of hair away from Margali's eyes with her large, gentle hands and whispered prayers.

The second time Margali pushed up through the clouds of unknowing to consciousness, she lay for a time with eyes closed, gathering her thoughts, which flitted about like insects during the too brief Darkovan

summer. Then, slitting her eyes against the light of
candles and lamps, Margali searched the room. Seeing
Camilla slouched down in the chair by her couch, doz-
ing, brought a smile to her lips, a touch of color to
her face.

"Oh, Camilla," Margali whispered, "I have been
untrue to you . . . all these years . . . I hated myself,
hated life without Jaelle. I shared so little of living
with you who have loved me so well—"

Camilla, alert even in sleep to the slightest sound,
came fully awake and to her feet in an instant. "Margali?" she said. "*Breda*, I am glad you're awake! How
are you?"

"Oh, Camilla," Margali said, her voice thick with
emotion. "Kima," she added, stumbling over the af-
fectionate name she used so seldom. Camilla appeared
pleased and concerned all at once.

"What is it?"

"Are we, is it safe? Are they truly gone?"

"Yes," Camilla said. She smiled. "How do you
feel?"

"Tired," said Margali in a small voice. "Tired and,
and empty. It hurt so much . . . Jaelle's death. It did
something to me." Margali looked up at Camilla.
"And now the hurt is gone. It's gone and I'm empty."

"Hush," Camilla whispered, trying to stop the
words with upraised fingers.

"No, let me speak, Camilla. I must," said Margali
and struggled to sit up. "I walled off the pain, and
. . . and, shut off part of me as well. It wasn't fair,
how it hurt you, too!"

Camilla, surprise edging her voice, said, "Margali,
whatever made you think that?"

"But, Kima. When you wanted—while we have been
together, even then, part of me was wishing for Jaelle,
for Jaelle to be—" Margali gulped.

"Camilla, come with me to Thendara." Margali
dropped her eyes. "I know we have talked of it before,
and I wouldn't. But this time, let us go as freemates."

"Margali!" Lights danced in Camilla's eyes.

"Yes, Camilla. If, after all that has happened, you

will still have me. Come with me into the world, to
see Cleindori and Shaya. It is no good to have a city's
worth of wisdom if I do not have a world, and a family, to share it with.''

Exhausted Margali dropped Camilla's hand and
rolled back onto her pillows. "I am so tired. Yet I feel
as if a great pack has dropped from my shoulders.''

Camilla spoke, "Rest now, Margali. I will watch
over you. Rest. Sleep.'' Camilla monitored Margali
until certain she slept soundly, then with a sigh, the
emmasca dropped back into the chair and made herself
comfortable.

A tenday later, Margali breathed ice clouds in the
near dawn chill at the gates of the City. Camilla held
the lead for their pack animal which carried their supplies in bulging packs.

As the bloody Darkovan sun broke clear of the horizon, Margali and Camilla said their good-byes, then
stepped onto the trail leading from the City of the Wise
Sisterhood. It was a long trip to Thendara. But not
nearly as long as the one Margali had already under-
taken.

A Midsummer Night's Gift

by Deborah Wheeler

As I always say in talking about Diana Paxson; one of my greatest pleasures in reading for these anthologies is to get a story I know at once I can use. I love discovering new writers, but in order to discover them, I have to read an overwhelming amount of amateurish and unusable stuff. (I could use a much ruder word; but unless I get another story about a vampire with AIDS, I'm too polite.) I have been known to compare reading slush with pearl diving. You sift mountains of stuff, and sometimes come up with a pearl; most of the time, though, all you get is a cold, wet, soggy oyster that's not even good to eat.

But one of the rewards of editorial reading is to get the occasional manuscript that I know in advance will be good enough to print. I wish they all were; but then it's frustrating, because of the inelastic qualities of typeface.

Deborah Wheeler has appeared in all of the Darkover anthologies since FREE AMAZONS OF DARKOVER (DAW 1985), as well as SWORD AND SORCERESS I–V (DAW 1984–88), SPELLS OF WONDER (DAW 1989), and the fourth issue of Marion Zimmer Bradley's Fantasy Magazine. She is a graduate of Reed College, and in true Amazon style is a black belt in kung fu, a chiropractor, and the mother of two daughters.

Midsummer Eve was not, reflected Gavriela n'ha Alys, the most favorable time to be crossing the dense forests bordering the Venza River. It was warm, almost hushed beneath the canopy of green, even in the occasional wildflower-dotted glades where the massive resin-trees had burned like torches and their successors were not yet full grown. The three Renunciates seemed to be the only creatures moving in the forest, except for an occasional far-off bird. There was no sign of trailmen, who could be dangerous to such a small party. Fiona, their guide, had chosen a route far from their territory to avoid any chance encounter.

If she'd had her way, Gavi would have waited a few days, but Fiona and Maire had jobs in Hali, and Gavi had learned from painful experience never to travel alone. She'd known Fiona slightly at the Thendara Guild House, where she studied midwifery, but now wished she'd never set eyes on the woman. Since they'd left Rosario, she and Maire kept teasing Gavi about missing the Midsummer Festival. Sometimes it was with the condescending tone of adults scolding a child greedy for unwholesome sweets, sometimes their laughing barbs stung more than either of them guessed.

Gavi set her lips together and brushed away the drops of sweat which had gathered on her lank auburn hair. There was nothing contrary to her Oath in liking men, the only thing she had sworn herself from was becoming their property. She could even marry as a freemate if she wished, but there was about as much chance of that happening as her becoming Keeper at Arilinn. Between her Renunciate Oath and her ethics as a midwife—to treat the husband of the laboring woman with scrupulous integrity—she had little enough chance to find a man who might stir her heart. Which left her dreams and, at Midsummer, a single night to hope.

I've never for an instant regretted my Oath. Even if I'd stayed in my father's house, and married at his bidding, nothing would have been different. She wiped her face again, a sudden tear blending with her sweat.

"Let's make camp early and hold our own Festival," Maire laughed. She stood aside for Gavi to pass, and hooked her arm through Fiona's.

"Great idea. I've got a little wine left in my bottle," said Fiona.

Gavi sighed, ignoring Maire's giggle, and kept walking along the thread of a trail. She stepped carefully over a fallen sapling, then paused, listening. Ahead lay underbrush so thick the path seemed to disappear into a wall of tangled green. Her fragmentary *laran*, which gave her such sensitivity as a midwife, shrilled out a warning.

Maire bumped into her and stumbled, laughing, but Fiona came instantly alert. "What is it, Gavi?"

"Something ahead . . . But I don't hear anything."

Fiona slid her long knife soundlessly from its sheath and stepped in front of the two other women. No trace of merriment remained on her stark features. As she and Maire drew their knives, Gavi prayed she would not need to use hers. She was never a skillful fighter, and her midwife's Oath bound her to preserve and cherish life.

Like a liquid shadow, Fiona crept forward on the trail. Leafy branches parted for her as gracefully as if moved by a natural breeze. Gavi and Maire followed as quietly as they could. A moment later Gavi heard the rustle of someone moving through the brush.

Here the trail ran straight and clear for a short distance. Fiona halted and dropped into a fighting stance.

The sense of warning built like a pressure behind Gavi's heart, alarm blending into pain, pain and a cry for help. She stepped forward. "Fiona—"

Fiona jerked her head, commanding her back, just as a young man, barely out of boyhood, came hurtling along the trail. His clothing might be that of any forester—boots, leather vest over an open shirt, and loose trousers—but didn't quite fit him. He skidded to a halt, his eyes on Fiona's blade, and drew the sword at his side. Then he saw her face and threw the sword down, holding his empty hands out in a gesture of appeal.

"I mean you no harm, good women. I was headed to Rosario—for help—my master's wife—is one of you skilled in healing?"

Gavi stepped forward. "I am a midwife."

"The gods have surely smiled upon us!" The man was practically fawning on her. Only Fiona's blade, still raised and ready, kept him from throwing himself at her feet.

"Fiona, a woman needs my help—" Gavi said.

"Maire, pick up the sword. Now, lead the way, boy, and any tricks will get you your own sword in your back."

As they hurried along the trail, the man told his story in breathless snatches. He was, he said, named Felix, paxman to Valdrin, true son of old Lord Caradoc of Sweetwater in the Venza Hills—although that *nedestro* uncle had seized the manor, forcing the young lord to flee for his life—

At this point Fiona interrupted rudely, "I don't give a *cralmac's* fingernail about your local politics. You said some *woman* needed our help." She poked him in the back to emphasize her point.

"Yes, I understand that," Felix raised both hands and jumped forward. "His freemate—Nyssa, she's called—comes from somewhere up by the Kadarin River—she's with child—never been strong—forced from her home and into the forest—"

An image rose behind Gavi's eyes—firelight gilding a woman's rounded, sweat-drenched belly, straw colored hair tossing, eyes wide with pain. "She went into labor too soon."

"Yes, how did you know?" young Felix asked, still keeping a respectful distance from Fiona's knife.

"It's her business to know such things," said Maire grimly. "How did you think?"

They'd camped away from trailside, three sturdy *chervines* hidden behind the thickets. Nightfall had drenched the underbrush with shadows. As Felix hailed the camp, Gavi noticed the rude tent beside the fire of her vision and the clump of bodies beside it. One got up and came toward them—a man, dressed like Felix in forester's garb.

Gavi's knees turned to water. *Not even Aldones himself,* she thought, *could be so full of grace.*

In the failing daylight, his eyes were gray, but full of brightness, like a clearing storm, and his long chestnut hair fell around his princely features like a

mantle. His shoulders were broad but not bulky above
a dancer's hips. When he smiled and spoke, his words
filled her with fire.

"May Evanda bless you, *mestra*. My wife—"

Gavi forced her eyes from the man's face and darted
to the cleared area around the fire. A woman lay on
piled blankets, her head cushioned on a roll of wadded
garments. She wore only a thin sweat-drenched che-
mise, stretched tight over her bulging abdomen. Gavi
knelt beside her and took her hand.

"I'm Gavriela n'ha Alys, midwife from Thendara.
How long have you been in labor?"

The woman licked her lips and grimaced, panting.
Her whole body contorted suddenly, the muscles of
her belly standing out. The young lord—what had Felix called him, Valdrin?—pulled her up to rest against
his body, his hands cupping her shoulders protectively.
Although the contraction still racked her body, the
woman's face softened as she gazed up into his face.
He looked down at her with such undisguised tender-
ness that Gavi had to glance away.

"Since yester eve," the woman said in a low clear
voice. Her pale eyes again went to her husband's face,
and her thin, six-fingered hands clutched his arm.

"But it's too soon," he said. "The baby shouldn't
come for another two months."

"Yet it may live," Gavi said as positively as she
could. "Or sometimes a woman is mistaken in her
cycles. Let me—" Gently she laid her hand on the
woman's belly to judge the size of the fetus.

Sensations flooded through her, momentarily blinding her. The first, overwhelming, was the power and
alien beauty of the woman's mind. *She's chieri, at least
half, or I'm Durraman's donkey! But she looks so
womanly—perhaps because he is so manly.*

And the second was the stagnant, black presence
where the life energies of the unborn child should have
been.

Stunned, Gavi sat back on her heels. This was no
time to indulge in sentimental maundering, not when
the woman's own life might be at risk. Forcing all

awareness of Valdrin's magnetic beauty from her mind,
she took Nyssa's hands in her own. The pale eyes met
hers unflinchingly.

"You know, then?"

Nyssa nodded. "I'd hoped I was wrong."

"It's why the labor is so hard," Gavi said. "The
child cannot help in its own birth."

"Nyssa," Valdrin said in a quiet, shocked voice.
"You didn't tell me—"

"How could I, when you wanted this child so much?
Ah—" She cried out as another contraction seized her,
seized her and shook her like a rabbit-horn in the jaws
of a wolf.

Gavi held her firm. "Nyssa, look at me, look at my
eyes. That's right, don't see anything else. Just my
eyes. Let the pain be a storm, and you a falcon sailing
on its crest. Feel yourself floating on its strength, soaring. Keep breathing with me. . . ."

The contraction ended, and Gavi shouted to Fiona
and Maire to boil some water and find some clean
cloths. She could feel the outlines of the dead baby
through Nyssa's thin abdomen. Instead of being in a
normal head-down position, it lay crosswise. There
was no way it could pass the birth canal, and unless it
did, Nyssa would surely die.

As calmly as she could, she explained what she had
to do. "The muscles of your womb are holding the
child in this bad position, so you must relax, and let
me turn it."

"Relax?" Valdrin asked. "When she's in such
pain?"

"You must trust me, Nyssa, just as you did in that
first contraction. Here, hold Valdrin's hands, and follow my voice."

Gavi talked on, in the soft murmuring tones she had
learned during her years of apprenticeship. She put her
hands on Nyssa's abdomen, and felt the uterine muscle
tense with the next violent contraction. Even as the
spasm raged through Nyssa's body, Gavi sank into the
glowing energy fields, soothing the pain from within.

She felt Nyssa, like a jeweled blossom, opening to her mental touch. . . .

And then another mind joined theirs, like deep-hued silk, smooth and subtle, not as brilliant as Nyssa's, but blending with them both.

Eyes closed, Gavi pressed deeper into the uterine wall and felt the muscles go buttery. The dead baby, stiff and brittle, resisted her. Nyssa gave a high, breathy cry, distracting Gavi for an instant. When she returned her concentration to the stillborn, she felt another pair of hands over hers, not physical but mental, feeding her with vibrant life force. She could feel his heart beating, feel the power streaming from his loins through his body and then through hers, out her fingertips and into Nyssa's womb.

As the baby slipped into the proper alignment, Gavi was deep enough to read the pattern in its dead cells, and realize that no union between this human man and this half-*chieri* woman could be viable. Her midwife trainers had mentioned *lethal recessives* as a problem of the inbred Comyn, but she never thought she'd see one.

A few minutes later, her hands half-scalded by the hot soapy water, she reached inside the laboring woman and began guiding the tiny head outward. The stillborn baby was small, even for its age. Nyssa screamed as it left her, and began hemorrhaging profusely.

Gavi had no time to spare for sadness at the stillbirth. She had to act quickly, or there would be two deaths. Normally, the suckling of the infant would stop the bleeding, but now Nyssa's life blood poured forth in a heavy gush. Fearing again for the woman's life, Gavi began vigorously kneading her uterus from the outside. It took all her skill to stimulate the muscles into clamping down on the broken blood vessels, without causing further injury. She scarcely noticed when Maire wrapped the baby in a bit of torn blanket and gave it to Valdrin.

It was a long, messy business getting the bleeding controlled. By the time it was done, Gavi's shirt was covered in dried blood and sweat, and her thighs and forearms trembled with fatigue. Pale and exhausted, Nyssa lay wrapped in cloaks from the women's packs. Gavi sat back and took a deep breath.

The camp was deserted, except for Fiona and Maire, sitting together just beyond the tent. The two men had disappeared, probably to bury the infant.

"Gavi . . . Gavriela."

Gavi moved to Nyssa's side and took her hand. Her fingers felt cold. "You should sleep now. Your body needs rest to repair itself."

"I won't die now?"

"I don't think so. The worst is over."

"But I mustn't bear another child."

Gavi took a deep breath. She would have preferred to wait until Nyssa was stronger, but she couldn't lie to her now. She looked into the pale, unflinching eyes. "No. Not by Valdrin. Probably not by any man with *laran*."

"There's no other whose child I would want," she said passionately. "And he—he loves me, but it's so *important* to him—to have an heir—to hold Sweetwater after him."

Gavi's thoughts flashed to her Amazon's Oath, "I will bear no child to any man save for my own pleasure . . . no child for house or heritage, clan or inheritance . . ." But Nyssa had sworn no such Oath, and with her *chieri* sensitivity, was completely vulnerable to the depth of her husband's desires.

"I saw the way you looked at him," Nyssa continued. "And I felt—when we were together—your life energy danced with his. When we were in my body— I felt yours. I know—you are fertile now."

Gavi scuttled backward, almost falling. Her voice came out as harsh as a *kyorebni's*. "What are you saying?"

"That you can bear his child for me."

Gavi couldn't see, couldn't think straight for the roaring in her head. Nyssa hauled herself upright with sudden, desperate vigor. She grabbed Gavi's hands in fingers of steel. "On your Amazon's Oath—*no woman shall appeal to me in vain.* That's what you've sworn isn't it?''

The Oath meant another Renunciate, but how could she tell Nyssa that she owed her no allegiance? As a midwife, she had sworn to nurture, to defend, to protect with all her powers, any woman in her care. If she could not bear a child for a man's choosing, what about another woman's? Would she not be saving Nyssa's life?

It would be brief and sweet, a dream to treasure for a lifetime, lying together under the moon-bright sky. Midsummer Festival night, with a god in her arms. She imagined his lips on hers, his graceful fingers curved around her breasts. Her heartbeat quickened and her nipples tingled, sending tiny tendrils of pleasure through her body.

Nyssa's fingers trembled as she held Gavi's. Her breath came fast and light, as if she were drawing on the ragged edge of her strength.

"Lie back," Gavi said gently. "You must rest now."

"Not until you say yes."

"I . . ." Gavi no longer knew what was right. One Oath was pitted against another, and her soaring desire clouded both. She couldn't ask Fiona or Maire for advice, she knew exactly what they'd say.

"Val . . ." Nyssa whispered. "How long have you been listening?"

Gavi twisted and looked up to see Valdrin standing a few feet behind her, shadowed by a low-hanging branch. He moved closer, the firelight burnishing his features. "Long enough," he said tightly. "Have you gone mad, Nyssa? Or do you think because I love you I am your toy, to be given away to any other woman you choose, without consulting my feelings in the matter?"

Nyssa whimpered and fell back against the roll of wadded clothing. He turned as if to storm away.

"Listen!" Gavi cried, suddenly furious. "What she wanted—she wanted for *you*, you blockhead! You and

that heir you want so much—she nearly died trying,
do you hear? And now you turn your back on her—''

Like a dancer, he knelt at her side. "Forgive me,
my love, I didn't understand. But—''

"But if I were pregnant, or ill, and you were in
need, I would send you to the woman I loved best,''
she murmured, reaching up to touch his face. "You've
told me this is the way of your people.''

He brought her hand to his lips and kissed her fingers, his shining eyes fixed on hers. "That was—a sort
of bragging.''

"But true.'' She glanced at Gavi. "This woman can
give you what I cannot. A sister's gift, with my blessing.''

At first Gavi couldn't meet his eyes, not until he
cupped her chin and held her. His touch was like satin,
like flame. His fingers caressed her cheek, brushed her
lower lip. Even in the dim firelight, his eyes held
depths she'd never seen before. "And you, you are
willing?''

"I don't know.'' She clambered to her feet, surprised at how stiff her knees were. *I'm getting old, I
may never have another chance. . . .*

A chance at what? she asked herself. *A night with
another woman's man? A child already promised to
her father, to live the life he makes for her? Why did
I leave my father's house, if not to gain the right to
choose my own life?*

He took her hand, led her toward the woods. "Let's
walk a while, and talk. We need not decide in haste.''

The four moons had gathered overhead, silvering
the tree trunks. The forest seemed unnaturally still, a
fairyland, before some bird, as if thinking it were day,
erupted into song.

"I can appreciate the difficulty of your situation,''
he said.

"Can you? What do you know of my Oath, or my
life?''

"I know you're a woman of integrity. If Nyssa—if
things had been different, if you and I had met on
some Midsummer Festival, and both of us free of

heart, I think we might have found pleasure in one another.''

Gavi's heart leapt within her. He paused, as if measuring her response. She turned away, chewing on one knuckle.

Here is an evening of pleasure, pitted against a lifetime Oath. Is it something I can set aside, simply because I wish it? Am I bound to break my Oath because a woman demands it of me in the name of sisterhood? And if the Renunciate Oath does not give me the freedom to follow my own desires, what good is it?

Valdrin must have taken her silence for assent, for he put his hands on her shoulders and drew her closer. Her body responded to his overwhelming masculine energy, her heart beating like a captive bird, and her loins melting like butter. He bent his head and kissed her.

She almost raised her hands to put them around him. But she couldn't move, not until she knew what she truly wanted.

"Don't I please you?" he murmured, his breath gently blowing her hair.

"You do," she whispered, and then repeated it firmly, "You do. I've wanted you since the moment I saw you. But this isn't a simple Midsummer gift, it's four lives at stake. Yours, mine, Nyssa's, the child's. I have no say over what you and Nyssa do with yours.''

She moved away from him and her body still quivered where he'd touched her. "But I have two Oaths which I must honor—an Oath to live my life to my own pattern, not anyone else's, no matter how beloved. And an Oath to respect my sisters, Amazon or not. What Nyssa has offered me is not something she can share. I would be wanting you to look at me the way you look at her, and that is something not she, not you, not Aldones himself, can give me.''

"But—" he protested, and she cut him off, half-afraid that if he touched her again she'd forget everything that was now so clear to her.

"But I could take what you—and she—offer me, if there were not a fourth life. A life I would be twice sworn to defend. To defend not just from physical danger, but from the same enslavement I ran away from. If I bore you a child, and it was a girl, would she be free to choose her own life—even one such as mine? Or would she be pushed off on the man you thought could best hold Sweetwater?''

"No, what do you think of me?"

"And if it were a boy, would he be any more free, or would he be your heir even if his heart led him elsewhere—to a Tower, to Nevarsin?''

Valdrin hung his head, his face shadowed even in the light of the four moons. "I couldn't promise you that.''

"I know," she said gently. "And if you were not a man such as you are, I would not be so tempted.'' She kissed him gently, a sister's kiss.

"Your wife is waiting for you. Go back, and pray Aldones to make you worthy of her.''

After he'd left, she stood among the trees, wondering how she'd remember this night, and what it might have been. *Talk about sentimental maundering!*

Shadows moved beneath the trees. Fiona and Maire, their knives drawn, stepped into the moonlight. "I see you didn't need any help after all," Fiona said.

Gavi raised her eyebrows. "Fiona, have you still got that wine? Let's get it out and celebrate Midsummer together.''

Fiona gave a whoop of delight as they headed back toward the camp, their arms around each other.

The Honor of the Guild

by Joan Marie Verba

Joan Marie Verba has been with us in these anthologies for quite some time; her first professionally published story was in FREE AMAZONS OF DARKOVER (DAW 1985). This year's story starts out like a classic murder mystery. . . .

Joan Marie Verba was born in Massachusetts, but has lived in Minnesota since the age of four. About all I know of Minnesota is that the climate resembles that of Darkover.

Janna n'ha Cassilde studied the body in front of her carefully. The man should not be dead. There were no marks of violence, no signs of illness. She uncovered the matrix around her neck, hoping her *laran* would reveal something. It did not. Tucking the rewrapped matrix back into her tunic, she turned, thinking to speak to the deceased's wife. A crowd had silently gathered behind her, in this old, dim shack where the body lay.

Janna ignored the staring eyes. "And you say a Renunciate did this, *mestra?*" she asked the woman.

"Ay, ay, no mistake. She had her hair sheared off—wore pants, and a sword just as you have." The woman pulled her head scarf closely around her face, obscuring her features.

Janna scratched an ear. The woman's accent was rustic, not the learned *casta* or the city-dialect of *cahuenga* she was used to, but she could make out the words. The Renunciate turned back to the body, half-expecting it to rise up behind her, but it was as still

and cold as before. "And you say she just looked at
him and he fell dead."

"Ay, ay." The words were slower this time, less
certain.

"And there was no reason to kill him, you say?"

"Nah, nah, no reason. Just out in the field, minding
the crops." The widow glanced nervously from Janna
to another man in the room, named Ruyvil, who appeared to be one of the more prominent men in the
poor village.

"All Renunciates are crazy, if you ask me," he
blurted out. "The Comyn Council should revoke your
charter, and marry you all to men who would whip
you into shape. The Dry Towners have the right idea—
keep the women in chains!"

Janna ignored him. "I am sorry for your loss," she
said to the widow. "I, too, have a freemate, and he is
very dear to me. . . ."

"A sandal-wearer, no doubt," mumbled Ruyvil.

"if your family needs help with the harvest, I and
my Guild-sisters will do what we can."

"Na' thank you, *mestra*," said the widow, pulling
back a little to make it even harder for Janna to see
her face. "I ha' three grown sons to help me, two
unmarried."

Janna reached out to give the widow a reassuring
embrace, but the smaller woman flinched away. Instead, Janna murmured a polite formula and walked
out.

Outside, away from the close air of the shack and
its many mourners—Janna had no doubt that in such a
small town, the whole village must be in there—she
inhaled a deep draught of the cool, fresh air. The ham-
let was in Ridenow territory, almost equidistant from
the Serrais estates, the Alton estates, and the Dry
Towns—which was to say, right in the middle of nowhere. Normally, a town this size would not have a
Renunciate Guild House, but a modestly wealthy ma-
tron of the area had joined the Renunciates in her wid-
owhood, and, being childless, left the Guild a horse
ranch, which was now the Guild House and headquar-

ters for the Guild in this area. Besides keeping the other Guilds supplied with mounts, some of the Guild-sisters were midwives to the women in the scattered villages, traveling the area in circuits, checking on clients. There was also a small barn and plot of land to raise feed for the horses and the dairy animals, and to raise enough vegetables to keep the Guild self-sufficient.

Janna was neither a native nor a resident. Eldest daughter of the Hastur clan, she had served her time in a Tower, but declined Comyn marriage, and joined the Renunciates. She wanted to be her own woman, and her own woman she was. She had taken a cartwright in Thendara in freemate marriage, by whom she had children, and now, grandchildren. In her life, she had ridden as escort and bodyguard for many traveling Comyn ladies, been employed as a tracker, worked on the fire-lines, and, when necessary, spoke with members of the Comyn Council on issues relating to the Renunciates. When Mother Rayna, the Guild-mother here, had sent word to Thendara that a Renunciate had committed murder, and asked for aid, the Guild House in Thendara sent Janna.

"The widow had been beaten by her husband, hadn't she?" Janna said to Rayna as she hung up her cloak in the Guild House.

"Many a time," said Rayna, walking with Janna from the cloakroom to her own room. The Guild-mother was outfitted as Janna was, wearing trousers, a thick shirt, vest, and boots. "She was afraid to leave him, and I doubt she will mourn overmuch at his passing. But this is the second death in two tendays, and I fear that if we do not catch her soon, Comyn Council will make this their business, and our charter throughout the Seven Domains will be in danger." She sat in a chair by her fireplace, and motioned Janna to do the same.

Janna sat, only aware in that act that her muscles were tired and sore from the long ride, the brief stop at the Guild House, and the walk to and from the widow's house. She had not even taken off her traveling

clothes, and had no idea where the other Guild-sisters
had taken her baggage and horse.

"You said that after the first death, you ordered Liriel confined to the Guild House, and she escaped. That
makes her an outlaw among us. You could lawfully
hunt her down."

Rayna spread her arms. "Try to catch her." She ran
a hand through her hair, as gray-streaked as Janna's
own, except Rayna's basic color was black while Janna's was copper. "Liriel was willful and stubborn even
as she came here. She is a *nedestro* of the Ridenow
clan, raised in a village just north of here. She arrived
at our step one day. Usually, kin come to inquire after
the women who join us—either angrily, if the woman
ran away, or to ask after their health, if the woman
came with the family's knowledge. No one has ever
come to ask after Liriel."

"If she was rebellious, why did you take her in?"

"She wasn't difficult—at least, not at first. She was
determined to become a Renunciate, and served her
homebound year with the single-mindedness she had
for every task. There were no complaints about her.
She was a good student at anything we taught her—
especially swordplay. When she completed her year,
she served the house well. But slowly, things began to
happen. She would claim that one of her Guild-sisters
had talked to her, and the woman would deny it. Then
she said that she heard voices coming from the wells.
The midwives told me that when they were in the
woods, Liriel would claim that the trees and the sky
spoke to her."

"What did you do?"

Rayna shrugged. "What could we do? We tried to
keep her busy. That helped a little, but her constant
talk about voices was wearing down the other sisters.
I began to plan to send her to a Tower, to see if the
leroni could help her, as they can sometimes with difficult illnesses. But before I could send a letter, Liriel
went out one night and killed Alaric."

Janna shifted her weight in the chair. "Who was
Alaric?"

"He was a ne'er-do-well who had a reputation in all the villages around here. Most parents would hide their daughters if they saw him. Some of the girls—and Alaric never chased women fully grown—said that he took them unwilling. But he would never stay around any place long enough for anyone to catch him. Liriel came in the door in the morning with blood on her clothes and announced that Zandru had appeared to her and told her to send Alaric to him. She was quite unruffled—changed her clothes, took a bath, and ate breakfast while the others sat at the table, too overwhelmed to speak."

Janna sighed.

"Not many missed Alaric," continued Rayna. "Some fathers of the girls Alaric had used said that Liriel had only done what they were thinking of doing. But I ordered her to stay indoors until I could write to the *leroni*. Before I got the letter drafted, Liriel escaped. That is when I sent one sister to the *leroni* and one to Thendara. You arrived first, and in the meantime, Liriel killed again."

Janna rubbed her forehead. "I served a term in a Tower. They have been sent cases such as this before. I think that you will hear back that they can do nothing. It may be better if she eats some wild poison herbs in the forest and the gods take her. She will endure a lifetime of suffering, otherwise—either chained so that she does not kill again, or out in the open, mindlessly taking lives until someone, at last, murders her."

There was a long silence. At last, Rayna said, "I am sorry. To be honest, Liriel was not a friend, but no matter how difficult the woman, I have never failed a Guild-sister in all my years. I feel that I have failed now."

"Worse," said Janna, "would be to do nothing. Many already have the image of Renunciates as perverts and bullies. Just one case of a murderer among us could ruin the Guild's reputation in the entire Seven Domains. Employers will no longer hire us, people will fear us even more, and there will be calls in Co-

myn Council to revoke our charter. This is something
we must solve ourselves and quickly.''

Rayna smiled. ''Surely you can take time to rest
after your journey, and eat a little?''

''Eat . . . a little, yes. Then I have to go out to find
her before the trail is cold.''

''I don't think she'll stray far,'' said Rayna.

''All the easier to catch her.''

Janna started in the field of the widow's farm. Although the prints were a day old, they were not hard
to spot, in the dried mud. The thick soles of the Renunciates' boots, made by sisters, were scored in a certain way to grip the earth better. The pattern was
unmistakable. Janna looked up, reckoning that it was
just past midday. If Liriel was still in the area, Janna
ought to find her by nightfall. She stood, brushing the
dust from her hands. Once she found the renegade,
she would bring her back and put her in a locked room
until Mother Rayna decided what to do with her. A
nice day's work.

The prints led to the surrounding forest. Liriel was
making no attempt to avoid being followed, judging
by the trail she left behind. Janna reckoned it must
have rained the day before she killed the second man,
for the ground was dry now, but the prints were still
discernible. They led to a place by a stream, well out
of sight of the village, where there was a campfire and
a crude lean-to fashioned out of tree branches and long
grasses.

Liriel was pacing next to the campfire. She had not
spotted Janna; the tracker crept forward, screening
herself from her quarry by circling around from tree
to tree. As she came closer, she heard Liriel talking
to herself. Janna peered around a trunk, trying to make
out the words.

Abruptly, Liriel stopped talking. Janna pulled her
head back. She drew her sword, knowing Liriel was
coming toward her by the sound of the boots swishing
the grasses. When she judged Liriel was just behind
the tree, she swung around, blade raised.

Liriel glared at her. Red curls hung over the other woman's large brown eyes. The face was smooth and unwrinkled, the hair uncompromised by gray. She was taller than Janna by half a head; her frame was sturdy, her expression stern.

"You could be named an outlaw for drawing steel on a sister," Liriel warned.

"It is you who are the outlaw, refusing to submit to the discipline of your Guild-mother."

Liriel straightened up proudly. "I obey the laws of the gods first, the Guild second. So I swore when I took my oath."

Janna altered her stance, although she kept a firm grip on the hilt of her unsheathed sword. Liriel did not rave. Perhaps, thought Janna, there was a corner of rationality that might be reached. "So you killed those two people on the orders of the gods?"

"Of course." Liriel's tone implied that she thought she was stating the obvious. "I admit I made a mistake in killing the first one, using my sword. Zandru did not tell me that there was another way. It was Avarra who told me how to kill bloodlessly, without a weapon—with my mind." She touched her forehead. "She has forgiven me for my error; as a Renunciate, I should not have listened to Zandru anyway. She has given me a new task. May Avarra herself judge me if I fail."

Janna was still trying to figure out exactly what Liriel had done with her *laran*. A telepath with the Alton Gift could kill with a thought—did she have the Alton Gift? Janna did not know. It took an Alton to test another Alton. She herself had the Hastur Gift. If Liriel was indeed a *nedestro* of the Ridenow clan, she ought to have the Ridenow Gift, manifested either in empathic contact or in communicating with alien intelligences. But that did not mean she could not have done what she claimed. *Laran* was a powerful weapon in itself.

Janna licked her lips, considering. "If, sister, your instructions indeed came from the gods, then Mother Rayna may see that she judged you in error. May I speak to them also? Then you will be free. Otherwise, your Guild-sisters will consider you an outlaw all of your life."

"You. . . ? Liriel obviously had not expected that request. Before the older woman could say anything further, Liriel turned her head abruptly, then back to face Janna. "Since you are a Hastur of Hasturs, they say you, too, may see them. Sheathe your sword and come." She walked toward the campfire.

Janna did as she was told, not because she trusted Liriel, but because the younger woman wore only a knife, and Janna had confidence that she could overwhelm Liriel if the two got into a fight.

Liriel stopped at the fire, pointing. "Look at the flame."

Janna saw nothing but fire. But she felt a tickle at her throat. Without prompting from Liriel, she uncovered her matrix, and focused her *laran* through that to look at the flame.

It was blinding. She dropped the matrix. The stone, at the end of its string around her throat, bounced against her sternum. She put her arm up to shield her eyes, but the light was in her mind, not her eyes. It would not rub out. It would not go away when she turned her head or closed her eyelids. It was everywhere, in her head, in her ears. The smell filled her nostrils. Her tongue tasted it. It invaded her very being, and then let her go, into darkness.

Janna opened her eyes. She was looking at stars. The light was framed by a circle of treetops. She was on her back. She turned. The campfire was nothing but dimly glowing embers. Liriel was gone.

Janna moaned and sat up. She felt her legs and arms. They appeared to be all right. Her head was not bruised or ringing. She seemed uninjured. She rubbed her forehead. There was a dull headache, as if a fever had abated, but that was not even a nuisance. She took a draught of the night air and let it out in a sigh. Catching Liriel was going to be more complicated than she thought.

She went back toward the village. Before she reached the first house, she heard a scream. Running to the sound, she saw a man, dead, on a doorstep. A woman stood over him, fingers stuffed into her mouth to muffle her own screams. Janna bent down to examine the body. It was Ruyvil. As with the victim she had seen earlier, there was not a mark on him.

Janna stood and saw Mother Rayna running up. "Did you see who did this, Gwynnis?" Rayna asked the woman on the doorstep.

Gwynnis pulled her hand from her mouth. "Na, na. I heard a thump on the step, and I thought it was Ruyvil, drunk again. I opened the door, and there he was."

A crowd was gathering. "I'll take care of my cousin," said a man who glared at the Renunciates.

Rayna and Janna exchanged a glance and walked back to the Guild House. "No doubt that this was Liriel's work," said Rayna when they were inside. She led Janna to the kitchen. She pulled out some apples and a cold meat pie and set them in front of Janna with a plate and fork. "Here, eat, you look like you just came from Zandru's seventh hell."

"Perhaps I have." Janna related the events of the afternoon while she ate. When she finished her meal, she added, "Either she has the Alton Gift, which she was projecting on me, or she has the Ridenow Gift, and she is in touch with something beyond this world, which she thinks are gods."

"Perhaps she is truly mad, and using ordinary *laran* to pass her delusions to you."

"Perhaps," mused Janna. "When I had my turn in the Towers, someone with unmanageable *laran* was brought to us. The Keeper there burned the *laran* centers from the brain, leaving the victim otherwise unharmed. The kindest thing to do would be to catch her and take her to a Tower."

"But can she be caught without further loss of life?" said Rayna. "She may fight you, and you may have to kill her. She is already an outlaw, according to our Guild rules."

Janna rubbed her eyes. "I don't know. I'd like to go
out right now and find her . . ."

"No," said Rayna, thumping the table for empha-
sis.

Janna smiled. ". . . but I'm not as young as I used
to be. I'll have to get a night's rest, and think it over.
Perhaps morning will bring a solution."

"Good," said Rayna. "Since you are resolved on
that, I have other news for you. While you were out
this afternoon looking for Liriel, a message came to
me from your brother in Thendara. The news of what
has been happening here has reached the ears of Lord
Serrais, and he is coming here with several Guardsmen. There are murmurings about revoking the Renunciates' charter in Council. Your brother is stalling,
but he could not restrain Lord Serrais. If we don't trap
Liriel soon, someone else will undoubtedly do it for
us."

Janna nodded. "If he sent a message to you, he
probably has also sent a message to Mother Margali
at the Guild House in Thendara."

"It is nice to have a brother who supports the Renunciates."

Janna smiled. "Not all men are against us. I happened to marry one who wasn't."

By the time she pulled her boots on the next morning, Janna had a plan in mind. She ate breakfast with
the other Guild-sisters in the house. Some offered to
come with her. Janna thought that a search party would
cause Liriel to run, or make it more likely that the
renegade would kill or be killed. She declined their
help with thanks.

The sisters in the kitchen packed a knapsack with
food for her. She left her horse in the stable, and went
on foot once more. At a distance from Liriel's camp—
Liriel was at the same place she had been the day
before—Janna sat under a tree. A bush shielded her
from Liriel's eyes, but she could see Liriel through the
small leaves. Janna turned, rested against the trunk,
and ate some of the provisions she had brought. Once

more, she peered through the brush. Liriel was still there, sitting by the campfire, mumbling to . . . herself.

Gingerly, as if the whisper of the silk might make a sound, Janna uncovered her matrix. When she worked in the Tower, she did a monitor's work. She knew how to regulate another's body rhythms from a distance. She had also been taught healing, and knew the innermost workings of the body. Most important, she knew where the *laran* centers of the brain were. If she could affect those somehow, perhaps she could free Liriel from the demons that possessed her. It was tricky, and Liriel might die as a result, but Janna was running out of alternatives. If she did not do something about Liriel, the villagers or Lord Serrais and his Guardsmen certainly would.

In the Domains, murder was considered largely a private affair, at least in the abstract, but Janna often found that popularly mouthed opinions were not observed in practice. The three men Liriel had killed would not be greatly missed, Janna suspected, by their victims. But because they died by a Renunciate's hand, rather than that of an outraged father or cousin, public indignation had spread even to Thendara. It confirmed what Janna had long concluded from experience: that killing a person, even a wicked person, often caused more problems than it solved. She was not about to complicate the matter by killing Liriel as well, not if it was in her power to do otherwise. Aside from that, Janna had never once harmed a Guild-sister, not even a renegade. She had a feeling inside her gut that to add Liriel to the dead, now, would be like cutting off an arm to get rid of a birthmark.

She assumed her monitor's posture, which should keep her muscles from getting cramped even if she sat there until sunset. Concentrating through her matrix, she found the network of energons that was Liriel's body. Carefully, so that Liriel would not be aware of it, Janna slowly probed the brain, reaching the *laran* center, isolating the cells. . . .

No.

Janna eased back. Leaning to one side, she spotted Liriel, again, by the fire. The younger woman showed no sign that she was aware of the psychic probing. Janna must have imagined it; it must be her own nervousness. She shifted her weight, doing some breathing exercises to calm herself, and tried again.

There.

She had found the right cell group. Now, cell by cell, she could deaden that part of the brain.

Something grabbed her. No, it grabbed Liriel. No, it was the light again, the blinding light, in Liriel's psyche. Janna set her determination like a hook and pulled, feeling as if she were one of two banshees fighting over a piece of meat, only the meat was Liriel's *laran*. The adversary yanked. Janna saw, as if with her eyes, the forms, the figures, as Liriel saw them. They were bright beings, human in form.

Let her go! Janna said in Liriel's mind.

No, they replied. *We need this one to get our revenge.*

Revenge for what?

We died here, in a war. We have called and called for someone to answer us. This one has. We will use her to seek those who sent us here.

There has been no war here for generations. Those who killed you are long gone. The dead have no claim on the living.

Then we can kill their sons, and their son's sons. . . . Their anger burned like acid.

Janna flinched, but remained steadfast. The Altons were powerful, the Ridenows sensitive, but the Hasturs of legend had bound and banished even the gods. Janna uncloaked her Gift, matching their strength and brilliance. They pounded at her shields; Janna wavered, and then held steady. Something—someone was supporting her. Liriel. Her confidence bolstered, Janna rose over them, surrounded them, smothered them, and sent them back to the oblivion of the dead.

With a gasp, Janna was back in her body. Liriel was at her side, head on her shoulder. Weakly, Janna put an arm around her.

"I am sorry, my sister," said Liriel. "I will submit myself to whatever the Guild requires."

Janna used the last of her psychic strength to probe Liriel's brain. Part of the *laran* center was gone, but not all. "Do you still hear voices?"

"No. It's like I woke up from a nightmare."

Janna smiled. "I think you had the Ridenow Gift, but a far more sensitive one than any Ridenow has ever had. Your mind touched a presence no one should ever see." She kissed Liriel's head. "Don't worry; it's gone now."

"What do you think Mother Rayna will do?" she asked worriedly.

Janna hugged her. "Nothing as horrid as you might be imagining, I'm sure. I think that if you help me back to the Guild House, that will go a long way to erasing your debt." She moaned softly as Liriel helped her to her feet. With Liriel sane again, she had no doubt that the Guild could settle with the affected families, and that she, Janna, could convince Lord Serrais—and Comyn Council—that the Renunciates were in charge of their own. The honor of the Guild had been served.

A Butterfly Season

by Diana L. Paxson

Diana Paxson is, of course, no stranger to Darkover fandom; she's been around on Darkover longer than anybody except me, and is one of the fans whose stories I can count on to be thoroughly professional. As I have said before in these bios, there are a few things I always look for in these stories; and one of them is fascinating or unusual uses of laran.

Diana Paxson is my sister-in-law, and is one of the more successful of those who have followed me into writing; she's been around since the first of these anthologies, and since her vision of Darkover is pretty much the same as mine, I could print her stories unread, because (as in the case of Mercedes Lackey) I know beforehand that anything I get from Diana will be thoroughly professional—and I read so much slush that it's a great relief to get a manuscript which I know will be good enough to print. But I think "A Butterfly Season" is more than that; it contains some of the most fascinating aliens I've ever read about, up to and including those invented by the late A. Merritt—large praise for a large truth.

Diana has also written a series of books—including THE EARTHSTONE and THE SEA STAR—all of which I consider more than readable. She's also created some fine "urban fantasy" novels, of which my own favorite is BRISINGAMEN which is about the only book of which I've ever spontaneously said "I wish I had written that." In addition, she has written a splendid historical novel about the Tristram and Yseult legend, THE WHITE RAVEN, which it would be impossible to recommend too highly; I'd run out of superlatives. I'll just say "read it; if you like my work, you'll love Diana's."

Diana lives in Berkeley—but we're both such busy people we've been reduced to meeting at conventions. She has two teenage sons, Robin and Ian—well, the younger is now 18 so they've been growing (like my own) while I wasn't looking. (It is daunting to realize your youngest child is now 24; my "baby" Moira is now studying music in Long Beach, California. Next thing I know, she'll be making her debut as Tosca or something. . . .)

On Darkover the winter nights are long and bitter, and even in Thendara, folk are glad to gather around a good fire. Winter in the Guild House is no exception. Except for those Amazons who may be snowbound elsewhere or off training with the Terrans, everybody comes home. In the long evenings we sit in the music room, embroidering or mending harness leather and catching up on everybody's news. But by the Feast of Liriel, when the celebrations of Midwinter are a memory and both the old tales and the new are growing as bare as the cupboards in the storeroom, it's time for the strange tales, the ones we tell to allay the boredom or perhaps to deny the fear that perhaps this will be the year that spring never comes.

After twenty years as a Renunciate, I thought I'd heard all the stories, and after fourteen years as Caitrin n'ha Laurian's freemate, I would have said that I knew her life as well as my own, but that night she surprised me.

For two weeks it had been storming, and Thendara was cocooned in snow. The wind was flinging itself against the shuttered windows, and even in the music room we felt the chill, despite the paneled walls and thick rugs upon the floor. For some reason the conversation had turned to the oddities of employers. Kyla n'ha Rainéach was home on a rare visit, and everyone wanted to hear about her adventures with the Terrans. Doria had given us a long and complicated story about

negotiating trade-rights in Caer Donn, and Gilda n'ha
Camilla was just finishing an outrageous anecdote
about a Dry Towner and an *oudrakhi,* when Caitrin
looked around the circle suddenly and said, "I have a
question for you all—"

There was something in her voice that made me look
up from the Terran text on genetics that I was trying
to read, and Kiera, who had finally escaped her Comyn family and joined us, looked at her oath-mother
eagerly.

"Ask it then, sister—" said Kyla in her cool voice.
"And we will do our best to answer you."

Caitrin gave her a quick glance, her sandy hair glint-
ing in the light of the fire. "In our oath, we limit
allegiance to our employers *for the season of our employment . . .* " Everyone nodded. One did not forget
one's oath-taking, even after twenty years, and with
each new witnessing in our hearts we swore it anew.
"What happens to that oath," Caitrin went on, "if
the season of employment never ends?"

"What are you talking about?" asked Gilda sharply.
"I thought the last group you trail bossed went back
to Vainwall last fall—"

"Not them," Caitrin interrupted her. "They're
gone, but they reminded me of the first expedition that
I ever guided on my own. It was a long time ago—the
year after I met you, Stelle—" She gave me a quick
smile, as if asking forgiveness for not having told me
before.

I stared at her, remembering a season of madness
when I had been sure neither of her heart nor of my
own. But living through the summer without her had
taught me how much I needed her. I had never really
dared to wonder what it had taught her.

"Who were they, Caitrin?" asked Kiera shyly.

"Off-worlders," came the answer. "Hastur had just
given permission for licensed guides to shepherd off-
world visitors through the Domains, and for awhile it
seemed as if every bored aristocrat in the Empire
wanted to visit here. There was plenty of work for
everyone, even a newly fledged Amazon with the wax

still soft on her charter. Free Amazons already had a
certain reputation as trail guides—'' she grinned at
Kyla, ''and I was anxious to show what I could do.

''The agent who hired me was a fast-talking fellow
from Vainwall called Genyi Coramne. In those days I
thought all the Empire folk came from Terra, and all
he told me was the number in his party and where they
wanted to go. I asked about dietary requirements so
that I could order supplies, but I didn't think to ask
who the people in his party were.''

''Couldn't you get some idea from the food list?''
asked old Irmelin.

''About Terrans?'' Gilda shook her head disdain-
fully. ''They eat things I wouldn't feed a chervine, and
turn up their noses at good nourishing food.''

''Tripe stew . . .'' came a whisper from somewhere
behind me. I suspected that it came from one of the
women of the Bridge Society who were training with
us this year.

''If I'd been more experienced, I might have been
more suspicious—'' said Caitrin. ''Because all they
ordered was dried fruit and honey. Coramne said they
would be supplying the rest of their provisions themselves.''

''Who cares what they were eating?'' asked Doria
in exasperation. ''I want to know what they were!''

''They were Xerasian Butterflies . . .'' said Caitrin,
smiling faintly at the effect of her words.

I heard a murmur of surprise from the Terran women
behind me, and saw Kyla's eyebrows rise. There had
been something about Xerasus in the text I was reading. I tried to remember what it was.

''Like the ones that come out at Midsummer?''
asked Kiera in the silence that followed. The wind was
changing. In the hush between gusts, snow slipped
with a soft thud from the steeply tilted roof to the
garden outside. Kiera shivered. ''But they only live till
the first snowfall—''

''The Terrans nicknamed the Xerasians Butterflies
because they're winged metamorphs,'' I said briskly.
''Only in the second stage do they become sentient

and grow gliding membranes, but when they have exchanged genes and budded off their offspring, they die." There had been more, but I could not remember now.

Kiera's eyes grew round.

"What your books don't tell you," said Caitrin, holding out her hands to the fire, "is that they are beautiful."

Genyi Coramne brought his clients to meet their guide at a crossroads just outside of Thendara. Caitrin admitted that when he told her about the rendezvous she had wondered if he were doing something illegal, but her contract already bound her, and she wanted the job too badly to question him.

Perhaps, I thought as I listened to her tell the story, she had also wanted to get away from me. Caitrin had been brought up *cristoforo*, and she had fought the idea that what we felt for each other was love.

"It was just past dawn when I got there—" said Caitrin, "one of those early summer mornings when sunrise tints the mists with amethyst and rose and the setting moons glimmer through them like jewels in Avarra's veil. Even with a string of ponies to manage I shivered with the beauty of it, but I was too determined to act professionally to linger. I reached the crossroads before the appointed time, but they were waiting for me. Coramne was pacing up and down, all swathed in furs, and behind him stood three cloaked shapes that made my skin prickle.

" 'Coramne, what's going on?' I grabbed his padded arm. 'Who are they?'

" 'Your clients—' he grinned up at me.

" 'But they're not human,' I began. He smirked and tapped the contract in his hand.

" 'They're sentient beings, *mestra,* and you are sworn to serve them.' He handed the contract to me. 'Let me introduce Xithenith nai'Dorn, who's come all the way from Xerasus to see the hills. I'm sure you'll all have a marvelous time!'

"The tallest one turned, and I saw the rainbow

moons reflected in faceted eyes. For a moment, it was
all part of the beauty of the morning, and then for a
moment I thought I was going to be sick, but my oath
bound me, so I bowed and said I was going to be their
guide.

"The tall one's companions were Kalstith and
Ansth. Their species had no genders and no kindreds,
since each individual reproduced only once. But they
lived a very long time, and adults allied themselves
into Great Houses which sounded a lot like our Guild
Houses—families formed not by birth but by choice
and mutual need."

"How could you communicate?" asked Doria. "I
saw a catman once, and we've all seen *cralmacs*.
They're strange, but you can more or less understand
them."

"Some folk in the Hellers still think the Terrans
have horns and tails!" said a low voice behind me,
and everyone laughed.

"They produced very good *casta,* actually," said
Caitrin, "and although they had to perch in the sad-
dles, they certainly could ride. In hooded cloaks, from
a distance, they passed very well. After a few days, I
learned to tell them apart. Ansth and Kalstith were
smaller, one quick and determined, the other calm and
slow. Xithenith was the tallest, and carried itself like
a Hastur. Up close—well, even though they kept the
cloaks on constantly, I could guess at the strange assortment of limbs underneath them. We had been on
the trail for a week before I could keep my breakfast
down, and at the same time I wanted to sing every
time I saw Xithenith's eyes. It was very odd."

"But where were you going?" asked Kiera. "What
could such creatures want on our world?"

"They had hired me to take them to the Kilghard
Hills. They seemed to live on honey and pollen, and
I thought that perhaps some Vainwall tour promoter
had sold them on our summer explosion of flowers.
That year the season had come on late and swiftly, and
everything that could possibly produce a blossom was
bursting into bloom. You know how it gets sometimes,

when the air goes balmy, and suddenly there's a different scent on every shifting breeze.

"We made camp in the hills above Armida. The first night the wind moved around to the north and there was a brief snowfall. I suspected that the Xerasians were cold, though no one complained. I built up a good fire, and tried to ignore the odd contours that the leaping flames revealed. In the shadow, the swathed shapes next to me could have been anyone.

" 'I am old enough to know that with time, all things, even discomfort, must pass,' Ixthenith said.

" 'How old are you?' I asked.

" 'I have seen more than five hundred revolutions of Xerasus around its star. Do you think me ancient? Even for my people, that is true. All things pass— except our lives. Our maturity extends through centuries, and even our offspring are infants for a hundred revolutions, feeding upon their parents as they grow. We fear to care too deeply, for caring brings attraction, and in giving life, life ends. Now our numbers dwindle, for inevitably some are lost to accident. In ancient times, we responded by budding more than one offspring, but we have learned to fight death too well. Now, many of those who are willing to give up their lives to renew the species find that they no longer can.'

"I shivered, not wholly from cold. Xithenith's voice was too calm. For a moment I seemed to see eternity stretching out before me, bleak as the desert around the Dry Towns, cold as the Wall Around the World. Now I understood why the Xerasians treated each other with such detached courtesy. Even those who were allied in their Great Houses were bound not by love, but by duty, logic, and loyalty. What would life be like if we in the Guild House treated each other that way?" Caitrin paused and looked around the room.

"A whole lot more peaceful!" exclaimed one of the younger women, who had just ended a painful love affair. I remembered how I had suffered in the days when I was afraid that Caitrin would never love me, and did not know whether to be glad or sorry that my own life had become so calm.

"But think how much less interesting!" Doria answered her, and even Kyla grinned.

"I was almost as young as Kiera then, and not nearly as wise," Caitrin smiled at her oath-daughter, then cast an uncertain glance at me. "But when I listened to Xithenith, I wanted to run back to Thendara and laugh or quarrel with you all! What I did instead was to tighten the tent ropes against the shifting wind. We all wrapped up in our blankets and slept, and when we woke the next morning, the world had changed.

"When I climbed out of my blankets, the air was already warming. Morning light glimmered upon the mountains, and every rockface was agleam with melting snow. Mist drifted up from the wet ground in slow swirls as the sunlight warmed it. The air was rich and moist, noisy with the gurgle of water and the ecstatic singing of the birds. I got the kettle boiling and went to see to the horses, thinking that if the weather held, perhaps the Xerasians would like to ride up to the top of one of the peaks to look at the view.

"After a time I began to wonder if one of them was cooking something, for as the wind grew stronger, it carried a rich scent something like bread baking, but sweet. I breathed in appreciatively, and felt my head swim. The sun was high now, and the silver mists had turned to gold. I pulled off my cloak and tugged at the laces of my tunic. As I started back toward our campsite, I saw that the golden swirls were all aflutter with blue butterflies, and I realized that it was not mist, but drifting veils of pollen, through which the butterflies flew.

"I stopped short then, fumbling for the filter plugs I had brought along just in case we found ourselves near some hidden field where the *kiriseth* flowers still grew. I had packed more of them for my clients, but the Xerasians had no nostrils into which to fit them. Perhaps the alien biochemistry would not be affected by the hallucinogen the pollen carried, but I had taken in just enough of it myself to start giggling when I wondered what would happen if they were.

"The three Xerasians were watching the butterflies.

I ran toward them, babbling about tearing up the dish-rags to make filters. Then Xithenith turned and I was silenced. I couldn't tell if it was the Xerasian that the *kiriseth* pollen had affected, or me, but those faceted eyes glowed. I remembered my oath to protect them, and tried once more to explain.

" 'It is not necessary—' the folds of the cloak fell away as Xithenith lifted one forelimb in negation and I saw the glisten of flight membranes below. For the first time, the sight did not trouble me.

" 'It is hoped that the substance will work upon us,' said Ansth. 'It is for that we are come. The drug they call *kirian* stirs us a little, but we are pollen feeders by preference. Perhaps we will be released by the raw essence of the flower.'

"The other Xerasian turned and I blinked, for suddenly the leathery hide beneath the cloak pulsed with quick color. Now they were facing each other, and I knew that I had been forgotten, but Xithenith's rainbow eyes were still on me.

" 'Take care for thyself, small one. There is nothing that thou canst do for them now.'

" 'I took oath to protect you all,' I answered, 'you don't understand what *kiriseth* can do!'

"The Xerasian's body swayed. 'We understand. It may bring death, or the madness that humans call love. Wait and bear witness with me.'

"I took a step backward and then another until I fetched up against a tree. Part of my mind was still gibbering that I must do something, but I was already so dizzy that I could barely stand. Ansth and Kalstith moved a little apart, and their cloaks fell to the ground. For the first time, I saw their forms fully, slightly pointed heads attached by slender necks to a three part body with long, jointed legs, clever three digited hands and a third pair of limbs that supported the wings.

"But there was no time for me to wonder about the details. As the wind grew stronger, color washed ever more strongly through their pale hides. The middle limbs lifted, and suddenly the vestigial flight membranes were expanding, flaring taut as they extended,

shimmering with an iridescence all their own. The two
bright bodies trembled, and then, of a sudden the wind
took them and they were airborne, gliding in great
circles above the meadow like gigantic butterflies.

"I felt a tightness in my throat, for in flight all their
awkwardness disappeared. These creatures had lived
for more centuries than I could imagine, bound to earth
by their ungainly bodies as their spirits were bound by
lack of love. But now the wind embraced them—the
golden, pollen-blessed Ghost Wind that all men feared.
The wind hummed softly through the trees around us;
but from the wheeling forms above me came a sweeter
song.

"Xithenith swayed, narrow neck twisting as it stared
upward. I saw its flight limbs quiver, and the sullen
flickers of color that came and went across the wrinkled hide. It had called itself a witness, but the *kiriseth*
was affecting it, too. Only for Xithenith there was no
partner, no mate to stimulate the metamorphosis that
would give it the freedom of the skies. The courting
song of the pair above us drifted through the enchanted
air, sweet and dreamlike as the pollen's gold. Voices
like twinned flutes intertwined in ascending harmo-
nies. But from the long throat of the one that gravity
had tethered below them came an anguished wail.

"I cried out in sympathy. But there was nothing that
a pitiful four-limbed creature like myself could do to
answer that need. I felt the ecstatic flight of the two
creatures above me in every nerve and pounded my
fists against the soft grass, muscles in breast and arms
and back twitching sympathetically as if any moment
I, too, would sprout wings. I remembered how it felt
to love, and regretted every time I had ever rejected
its comfort and made another ache with this awful
need.

"But at least I had known fulfillment, however hard
it was sometimes for me to accept it. For Xithenith,
there was none nor could there be, and again its agony
skirled across its companions' triumphant song. Then
came a silence. Afraid, I looked earthward, and

gasped, for impossibly, that anguished call had been
answered.

At first, the elongated form I saw facing the Xerasian seemed human, but even as I struggled with recognition, it was changing, its bright body mirroring
the transformations that were at last completing Xithenith's metamorphosis. Music blazed from above.
Ansth and Kalstith were spiraling higher, pale forms
glowing as the light burned through them. Then, at
last, they joined.

But even as they began to flutter earthward, Xithenith and the Other were ascending the amethyst skies.
They soared, and their radiance was too great for my
vision, they sang, and my ears could not bear the song.
Or perhaps my filters were not as good as the outfitter
had promised me and it was the *kiriseth* that was
showing me these visions, for my awareness went beyond the power of human words to confine it, and I
was carried away in a storm of rainbow wings. . . .''

Caitrin's voice faltered. In the stillness I distinctly
heard the sound of falling water. At the time, I thought
it was because my own cheeks were wet with tears. I
wiped my eyes roughly on my sleeve, wanting to put
my arms around her so badly that it made me weep
once more. Her lids were still shut, her expression
closed as if her awareness was still miles and years
away.

It was Kiera who found a way to break the silence,
her undemanding touch that brought Caitrin back to
us again. Clearly her Tower training had some uses,
but it made me want to howl like Xithenith to see. I
forced myself to breathe deeply, trying to understand
why I was reacting this way. For fourteen years Caitrin
had been my lover. What more did I want from her?
*How much more have you done than share a bed these
past few year?* an inner voice replied. *You are getting
older, and you fear that love has fled away.*

"It was a *chieri*, wasn't it?" Kiera asked then. "A
chieri that transformed itself so that Xithenith could
fly."

"I believed so," whispered Caitrin. "If it was not all a *kiriseth* dream."

"But what happened to them?" asked Kyla. "Did they die when the mating was done?"

Caitrin shook herself a little and looked around the room.

"I suppose it depends on what you mean by die. . . . When the Ghost Wind faded and I came to myself again, all three of the Xerasians were lying still upon the grass. I could not rouse either Ansth or Kalstith, but when I came to Xithenith, there was still a little light left in the rainbow eyes.

" 'Find a cave for us—' came the whisper, 'here in the hills. Lay us in a cave and seal it, and send to my people to say what thou hast done. When the time is accomplished, they will come.'

" 'What do you mean?' I gripped that alien flesh without repulsion, feeling the cartilaginous carapace beneath the skin. 'I cannot leave you here—'

" 'My offspring is already beginning to bud within me,' the answer came. 'Very soon now all that I am will pass into sleep, and as the young one grows, body and mind will be consumed. For humans it is otherwise. By the time my offspring is ready to emerge, the body thou dost wear now will be dust. I do not know if you humans are reborn. But for us, this is the final metamorphosis. If thou wouldst serve me, then do my will. . . .'

"The rainbow eyes were dulling already, and Xithenith did not speak again." Caitrin sighed.

"This is like a tale of the Ages of Chaos that nurses tell their children to make them sleep—" said one of the women. In her voice disbelief warred with wonder.

"I have heard stranger stories, though, in the Alpha Colony school," one of the Terran women replied.

"I believe you!" Kiera said stoutly. "For I *know* that what you say is true." The others looked at her ginger hair and remembered that she was a Ridenow. The abilities of the Comyn commanded less awe than once they had, but even now, no one would have dared to doubt her word.

But they were missing the point, I thought as I gazed around the circle. Caitrin had begun this account with a question. And it could not be answered until we knew the story's end.

"What happened then, *breda*?" I asked hoarsely. "What did you do?"

"I could not have got them back to Thendara without help," she started. "And even if I had, how could I have explained? It seemed better to do as Xithenith had asked me. There are surely caves enough in the Kilghard Hills.

"I had enough strength to move the bodies. They were awkward burdens, but lighter than I would have expected, and they were growing rigid already, which made them easier to move. I suppose it was only after I got them arranged in the cave I found that I really began to believe what Xithenith had told me. They did not grow stiff as a dead body does—I could feel the texture of their hides changing even then. When I went back the next day to seal up the opening, all three bodies were encased in a white shrouding like a cocoon. . . ."

"And so you left them there—" said Kyla finally.

"I left them," Caitrin agreed. "But I still have the contract by which they bound me. Perhaps Genyi Coramne could have signed off on it, but he left Darkover as soon as he turned the Xerasians over to me, and as far as I know, he has never returned. I did send a message to Xithenith's Great House on Xerasu, and eventually a draft on the Imperial bank arrived for me, though there was no reply."

"Well, then, you're free and clear," said Gilda briskly. "They wouldn't have paid you if they didn't think you'd done the job."

"That's what I told myself," Caitrin smiled crookedly. "But sometimes I wonder. The contract bound me to take them safely to the Kilghard Hills and *bring them back again*, but Xithenith sleeps there still. So I ask you—am I bound or free?"

"Oh, Caitrin—" Doria shook her head, yawning. "You have surely told us one of the oddest tales ever to be heard within these walls. How can we answer you? You must ask an Arbitrator, or a Hastur! I thank you for the story, but I am certainly too tired to decide!''

"Look, old Irmelin is asleep already, and it's time the rest of us were in our beds as well," added Gilda. And then everyone was laughing and getting up, stretching muscles cramped to stiffness by the fascination of the tale.

I started to get up myself, but my foot had gone to sleep and I stumbled, spilling books and note paper onto the floor. Caitrin knelt to help me gather them, and I reached out and gripped her arm.

"*Breda*—what is wrong?" She lifted her hand to wipe the tears away.

"Nothing! I'm foolish—" I began, but her gray eyes held mine, and I had never been able to lie to her. "Caitrin—" I said finally. "When you described that Xerasian crying out for love I felt that it was me! I'm not young and I've never been beautiful, but I'm still bound to you, and I envy that creature sleeping its cave!"

"Silly, silly Stelle—" Gently she wiped my tears away. "Don't you understand? It's because of what I learned from Xithenith fourteen years ago that I came back to you!"

The books dropped to the floor again as I hugged her. In the silence, I could hear her heartbeat and another sound—the musical sound of falling water as melting snow dripped from the eaves outside.

Misjudged Situations

by Kelly B. Jaggers

Kelly Jaggers says, "I am not really very good at describing myself because I always feel that there are far more interesting things to talk about." However she does say that she enjoys "traveling and learning about people and their different cultures, past and present. This probably has something to do with the fact that I have a B.A. degree in anthropology and archaeology and am currently working on my M.A. degree in archaeology and illustration at the University of Kansas." She says she lives with a stuffed monkey named Murrey and a roommate named something completely different. There's no accounting for tastes.

Mother Mori studied the woman that stood before her. Her wise old eyes seemed to darken with sadness.

"This is an unusual circumstance, Glynis. We have nothing to go on. Murder occurs, but up until now it has never happened within the Guild House." Glynis shifted uneasily under the stares of the women. "We understand that drunkenness does occur and, while we don't approve of it, we accept that it happens. However, to attack and then kill one of your sisters while under the influence is unforgivable."

A murmur ran through the room. Glynis could feel the anger of the Renunciates. It beat at her back until her own heart seemed to throb with it. Mother Mori held up her hand for silence.

"I pity you, Glynis, you must live with this deed forever. I have thought on this and have finally decided on your punishment." Glynis could feel the blood

drain from her face. Mother Mori rose to her feet and
motioned for Keithea to come forward. The swordswoman walked to Glynis and took hold of her arm.
Terrified, Glynis tried to jerk away from her grasp.
"Glynis n'ha Mori," Glynis turned, "I order you banished from this and every other Guild House. From
this day on you are no longer a member of the Renunciates."

A gasp of horror broke from Glynis. Her legs began
to tremble and she started to slip to the floor. At a
signal from Mother Mori, two women moved to
Glynis' side and held her upright. Keithea took hold
of the small golden hoop that dangled from Glynis'
ear and ripped it loose. Glynis bit back a scream of
agony and watched as Keithea took the long knife
Glynis had carried since her initiation and snapped the
blade with a stomp of her foot. Only then did she cry
out as her world shattered with the blade.

For days Glynis wandered the alleys of Thendara;
sleeping in doorways and digging through trash piles
for her food. Gradually the shock that had numbed her
mind began to slip away, leaving her weak and shaken.
As the tear in her ear healed so did her mind. She
knew there was more to the night of the murder, but
she couldn't remember it, try though she might.

Glynis hunched down over the fire that burned con-
tinually at the center of the open market and watched
as the crowd flowed through the square. She paid little
attention to any one individual until one man caught
her eye. He moved through the crowd, pausing occa-
sionally when someone stopped him. Glynis watched
as a young boy, dressed in the uniform of the Cadets,
walked up to the man. She started to look away, then
froze as the boy handed over a few coins and received
a small packet in return. She jerked upright. Gods!
She remembered. *Kireseth!*

They had been out drinking when Moira had pulled
out the small packet and offered it to Glynis. When
Glynis had refused, the girl became belligerent. As the
kireseth took effect, Moira became more violent.

Without warning she had launched herself at the older woman. Taken off guard, her mind dulled by the alcohol, she had barely managed to fend the girl off. Moira had then positioned herself in front of the door and swore that only one of them would leave. Suddenly Glynis was fighting for her life.

The guards had come just as Moira had attacked the last time and as Glynis desperately tried to block the girl's knife. Suddenly someone shouted. Startled, the girl had stumbled forward and impaled herself on Glynis' blade. The last thing Glynis remembered seeing was Moira lying in a pool of blood.

She looked up as a young man in a Cadet uniform took hold of the boy's arm. As the boys began to argue, the man disappeared into the crowd. A shadow followed after him. Together they slipped through the streets of Thendara. He sold his form of nightmares indiscriminately, pausing in doorways and on street corners. Relentlessly Glynis followed behind. By the time they had reached the alley, she felt almost ill. Finally he turned down an alley and walked toward a small gate that was set into the wall.

"Dream-maker."

Slowly he turned to face her. "Ah . . . the Renunciate. Does your friend need more powder?" He sneered as he pulled out a small packet and tossed it lightly in his hand.

"Moira has no need of your filthy potions where she is."

"Is that the way of it?" He smiled slightly. "Perhaps you would be interested?" He drew back as she entered the alley.

"At the moment I'm only interested in one thing, Dream-maker." She drew her dagger as she disappeared into the gloom.

Glynis tugged halfheartedly at her ragged tunic, then gave it up as a bad joke. She leaned back against the wall; it provided a measure of protection from the rain that had begun to fall. Her jaw ached, there was no

question that he'd known how to fight. Glynis lifted
her head and felt a few drops strike her face. She
closed her eyes and thought of Moira. Mentally, she
said her good-bye.

"Hey!" Her eyes flew open.

"You can't sleep here." Glynis almost laughed at
the boy. He was much younger than he looked in the
square.

"How long you been in the Cadets, pup?" She
watched the boy's eyes wander up and down her tattered form. Unconsciously, he straightened his jacket.
Then he gave himself a shake and lifted his head
proudly.

"Two years." His hand searched for the hilt of his
sword as he recalled where he was. "I have to ask you
to move on. There are places to bed down farther in
town."

Glynis grinned at him and relaxed her tensed body.
She crossed her arms and smiled again. "Tell me, pup,
are you always this casual with potentially dangerous
people?"

He leaned back and stared at her. Her grin widened.
Glynis knew just what he was seeing; a woman past
her prime dressed in the cast-offs of some Guild
House.

"Not much to look at, am I, pup?"

Startled by the question, the boy answered her honestly. "No, not really," he admitted. Then he rushed
on. "I know how to take care of myself."

Her eyes narrowed to slits. "Are you taught to stand
around and chat?" She continued to lean against the
wall, her arms and legs crossed, but her smile was
gone. "Where's your partner?" she snapped.

The boy jerked up in fright. Suddenly he didn't feel
so sure of himself. The rain began to splash down
against the walls of the alley. Glynis knew he wanted
to look back. Relentlessly she kept on.

"You came on duty without him, didn't you? He
isn't capable of working, is he?" Uncertainty began
to show in his eyes. "He's off in a dream, right?"
Without warning, she reached out and grabbed his

arm, twisting it up behind his back. The boy tried to block the move, but Glynis had him pinned to the wall before he even fully realized what she was doing.

A small moan escaped him when he felt her dagger prick the side of his neck.

"What do you do now, pup?" She could smell his fear beating against her senses. Tears mingled with the rain on her face; angrily Glynis blinked them away.

"Isn't this exactly why they tell you not to come out alone?" He whimpered and struggled feebily against the hands that held him. "Isn't it?" Glynis jerked him away from the wall. She slid her arm around his throat and lowered her blade. "It wouldn't have been so easy with two, would it?" she asked, her voice heavy with sadness. "You can't help him by ignoring the problem."

Glynis sheathed her dagger and stepped back, her hand reaching up to the small tear in her ear lobe. "He'll have to find a new source now," she added softly. The boy had spun away and pulled his sword as soon as she had released him. Startled, he noticed, for the first time, the body that lay a few feet away, then he looked back at her. His sword sagged.

Glynis shrugged. "He misjudged the situation." She gave him a small grin, then she shrugged again and walked away.

Awakening

by Mary Fenoglio

*Mary Fenoglio lives in Texas and has appeared in these
anthologies twice before, and the update of her bio
says she's "gotten older; smarter is debatable; grayer
is undeniable."*

*Well, aren't we all—older, that is; grayer isn't easy
when you're as blonde as I am. (So when I say in one
of the Darkover books that old Danvan Hastur hardly
appears gray because he is so blond, I know whereof
I speak—from personal experience yet."*

Linzel rode out alone one last time at dawnlight on
her wedding day. Everything had a special poignancy
for her now that she was so near losing it; the smell
of the night-damp meadow, the rich leaf mold fragrance stirred by her horse's hooves, the waking
sounds of birds, the feel of her good horse under her.
She could lose track of time like that, and only her
awareness that the horse was tiring would bring them
home.

She was especially reluctant to turn for home today,
but she knew that her mother would be in a state, and
so she cut her ride far shorter than she wished. As she
came into the stableyard, she saw her mother's serving-
woman waiting there, arms akimbo on her hips and
her face creased with exasperation. She seized Linzel's
hand as the girl dismounted and dragged her toward
the house, scolding, and Linzel sighed, looking back
longingly at the horse being led away.

"Even on your wedding day you have to be dragged
off a horse and chased into the house!" the woman

scolded. "Your lady mother's in a state, and who
knows what your husband-to-be thinks!"

And who cares? thought Linzel rebelliously. *I didn't
ask for this marriage; I was happy just as I was. Mahlon ne Royhann may be a great catch, as mother's fond
of saying, and his Rihannon a beautiful place to live,
but I didn't choose it, or him.*

But of course she didn't speak her thoughts aloud,
then, or during the tedious preparation for the ceremony, and certainly not at the endless ceremony itself.
She smiled as much as she could, but the smiles never
quite reached her green eyes. She was vain enough to
be pleased at the admiring murmurs that followed her,
knowing what a picture she made in her beautiful gown
with her elaborately coiffed auburn hair and her star-
tling green eyes. And she had more than a little curi-
osity about her husband, who stood beside her so stiffly
and who, after his first appreciative glance, hadn't so
much as looked at her again.

But her overwhelming feeling was one of misery;
she had no desire to exchange her home and the rela-
tive freedom she had always enjoyed for the constricting and regimented life of a wife and mistress of a
household. She had observed her mother's life closely
enough to know it was not what she wanted, and yet
here she was, like it or not, expected to make the best
of it. She didn't think she was going to be very good
at that.

There was great festivity once the wedding ceremony ended; food was laid out everywhere and even
the household staff and the people in from the farms
had great groaning tables. Wine flowed in scarlet
streams and musicians strolled among the crowds
playing all the most popular airs. Linzel had never
seen her mother so happy, and she couldn't understand.

I feel like I've been bartered into servitude, she
thought, *and my own mother is delighted about it! I
guess she sees it from a different point of view; I am
nineteen, after all, and I guess she thought I'd never
have a husband.*

That thought made her look around for the man she had married so recently, who had left her side almost at once after a few politely murmured words, and she saw him with a small group of men standing at a wine cask. She lifted the hem of her gown delicately and walked toward the group, only to be stopped by her mother's hand on her arm.

"You mustn't intrude on the men," the older woman said warningly. "They are discussing things of importance, no doubt, things we would not understand. Come, it's time to change and dress for the trip to your new home. Oh, dear, I wish you weren't riding. If only you had agreed to a carriage, you could have had such a lovely going-away gown! As it is, it will seem almost like a riding habit. I mean, the seamstress did what she could, but—"

Linzel allowed herself to be led away, not hearing her mother's nervous chatter. Don't intrude on the men? Her father had always welcomed her company. Discussing things of importance that she couldn't understand because she was a woman? She looked back at the group of men and they were laughing; several of them looked pretty drunk to her. Things of importance?

She did not turn and look back later that day as she rode out the gates of her father's house in her wedding entourage. She rode sidesaddle, as was proper for a young woman of her station, and her back was ramrod straight, her head held stiffly erect on her slender neck and her shoulders squared. Dark auburn hair escaped the confines of her traveling hat in small, untamed wisps, but they were the only undisciplined things about her. The expressive green eyes were blank and unreadable as they fixed on the broad back of her new husband, riding just ahead of her. She had foolishly expected to ride beside him, as she had always done with her father and her brothers, but Mahlon ne Royhann, master of Rihannon, quickly and firmly disabused her of that notion. Cheeks flaming at the rebuke, delivered more in surprise and amusement than anger, she reined her horse into line behind him. It was the first lesson Linzel had in being a wife, and it did not sit well with her to be reprimanded like a naughty child in the presence of the entire wedding party. She almost choked on her fury, but out of deference to her parents decided to postpone telling Mahlon what she thought about his behavior. There would be time on the journey to Rihannon, when they were alone.

Except that on the entire two-day ride, they were never alone, even for conversation. He remained with his men, and she had two ladies for company and assistance. They were kind and deferential, but there to serve her, not to befriend her. Linzel felt an awful loneliness forming a great, dark ball in the pit of her stomach when she saw the two ladies laughing and gossiping together as they went about their tasks in camp. They made her comfortable each night and then withdrew to their own company; it would not have been appropriate to do otherwise and Linzel would not embarrass them by requesting them to stay with her. She could not eat, her throat ached so, but she refused to cry. Lying down to sleep, her mother's face came into her mind and she thought longingly of her airy bedchamber at home.

Only home wasn't home anymore; her home was Rihannon now, and gazing at the great stone walls from across the valley, Linzel felt as if a chill hand stretched out across the sunlit space and took her by the throat. She had the irrational feeling that if she rode through those gates she would never emerge, but she followed her husband steadfastly into the shadow of the walls and through the huge iron gates into the courtyard. The great gates banged shut behind her with a hollow boom and her heart sank as she sat looking up at the gray walls of her new home. There were spots of color at some of the upstairs windows and in spite of her misery Linzel smiled to herself. Servants! They were the same everywhere, all abuzz no doubt about the new young bride and how she would change their lives. She accepted the groom's help to dismount the sidesaddle, wavering a bit as she touched ground but recovering instantly as she felt Mahlon's dark eyes upon her. He held out his hand to her and she placed her own lightly on his wrist as they mounted the wide stone stairs, her light step an echo of his heavier tread. There still had been no private communication between them, and she found herself dreading the moment when they might be alone together.

That moment came at last; directly after dinner, which Linzel could not eat but in which her husband indulged richly, he again held out his hand to her and they mounted the curving staircase together. Looking down, Linzel was surprised to see the expressions on the faces of those watching from below. It was a look she had never seen and could not recognize, but she understood the shout of goodwill they lifted with their tankards as her husband paused at the top of the stairs and stood looking down. She studied him covertly; tall, broad, dark of hair and of eye, smooth-faced as a boy except for his black mustache, his nose straight and elegant, his brow high and chin firm. There was too much arrogance in his bearing to suit Linzel, and she found his silence with her disturbing to say the least, though she had never known a man to talk overmuch with women.

As they passed down the hall her sense of uneasiness increased; the darkness was relieved by guttering torches placed at intervals, but in between the shadows danced and flickered, putting out long, wavery fingers to tangle in her hair. They came to a stop before a great carven door, the torchlight dancing on the carvings, but before Linzel had a chance to look at them Mahlon had flung the door wide and scooped her up in his arms. She gasped with surprise, face flaming at the unaccustomed familiarity, at the proximity of his face to hers. He strode across the threshold, kicking the door closed with one booted foot, and suddenly bent his head and covered her mouth with his. His dark eyes were closed; she saw his lashes in incredible detail as the taste of wine mingled with a sharp, coppery taste invaded her senses. His mouth was hard and demanding; she tried to turn her face away and couldn't, and suddenly panicked. She didn't know what he was doing, what he wanted, what he expected of her, this dark, silent man who held her in a grip that hurt and humiliated, and she couldn't bring herself to ask. With three great strides he reached the huge canopied bed, dressed in snowy linens and scattered with dried rose petals, and deposited Linzel on its wide expanse. She immediately scrambled away against the wall and sat with knees drawn against her chest, watching him with the eyes of a trapped animal as he began to disrobe. Her heart pounded against her ribs; she couldn't draw a deep breath and the room swam before her eyes. She wanted to scream, but she knew no one would come. There was no one tonight except herself and the big, dark, silent man who unhurriedly drew off his boots and breeches, then laid aside his white linen shirt. His broad chest was thickly furred with black, curly hair, drawing into a thin line down his flat, hard belly and blooming out again.

Linzel had often seen her brothers naked, especially the younger ones, and little remarked it, but a mature man in a state of arousal was a new experience for her. Horrified, she closed her eyes as she felt his hand close over her wrist and draw her across the bed toward him. She felt his hands tugging at her clothes, felt the sudden chill air against her body, heard his sharply indrawn breath, but remained aloof and inert, refusing any reaction at all. Dumbly she endured his caresses, barely heard his hoarse whispering, and the pain, when it came, bloomed like a bloody flower deep within her. She never cried out; she had long ago stuffed a corner of the bedclothes into her mouth to prevent it. Neither did she cry when, later, she lay as far from the heavily breathing man as she could get, fearful lest the slightest move should waken him and encourage a repeat of the whole painful, horrifying episode.

Disoriented thoughts chased each other wildly through her mind as the night dragged past. She thought with great longing of saddling a horse and riding away from this nightmare place, but close on

the heels of that thought came the image of being
dragged back to Rihannon in disgrace, her family left
shamed and dishonored because she had broken her
vows. Round and round her mind went until she was
exhausted and she dozed, waking to the sun breaking
over the mountain ranges and her husband turning to
her eagerly. Once again she endured him, and the first
small scar of hatred expanded into a solid calcification
on her heart.

Standing on the stone hearth after he had left her
and gone downstairs, she lathered herself with the soft,
scented soap she had brought from home and scrubbed
until her skin stung. The chambermaid brought her
warm water and she sluiced it over her body, trying to
rinse away the dull ache, the sense of violation she
still felt. A small, hot core of rage burned in her belly;
she might have to endure his eager seeking of her body,
bear his children, run his household, rearrange her life
to fit his image of a wife, but she didn't have to like
it. She didn't have to become suddenly meek and docile; she was who she was, who she had always been,
and Mahlon ne Royhann might as well find out who
that was from the very beginning! When she appeared
downstairs, her thick, shining hair was braided and
bound in a net at the nape of her neck; her dress was
appropriately modest and the long, leaf-green kirtle
she wore over it made her eyes even deeper emerald.
She cared nothing for the admiration she excited
among those at the table, and she took her place beside
her husband with a bland expression, eyes downcast
but stomach churning.

"Good morrow," he said in a formal tone, and Linzel marveled that he should speak so to her, who had
done what he had done, as if things were not changed
forever between them. Truly, men were strange and
alien creatures! Her emerald eyes met his coldly as she
returned his greeting, and except for introductions to
household staff and several men as dark as he whom
he identified as his captains, her husband spoke no
other word to her.

Linzel could not know the pride he felt at her beauty

and bearing before his people, or how eagerly he had
awaited her coming downstairs that first morning. That
their marriage was arranged was a natural thing; he'd
been taken with her from the first moment he saw her,
not the least by her spirit and ready wit. It was only a
matter of getting used to one another, and that would
take time. He had felt nothing amiss in the marriage
bed; he knew her to be virgin. Her fear would change
in time to pleasure; he'd had no trouble along those
lines! And so he awaited their first breakfast together
eagerly, seeing it as a beginning to a life he much
desired.

Mahlon could not know, since few words were exchanged, that Linzel considered the marriage in quite
a different light. She understood that marriages were
arranged for the benefit of all concerned, but there
were obviously many things she had never been told
about living with a man. So far she hadn't cared for
any of them; public rebukes, long silences, and bedding. Living with an arrogant stranger was hardly her
idea of a good life; she had left a good life behind
when she came here, and she didn't intend to enjoy
her new one. Indeed, she had found little so far to
enjoy.

And so, to his puzzlement and her irritation, there
was little conversation at that table or any thereafter.
Time thickened the misunderstandings between them,
and their lives wore away in hours of silence. They
spoke only of matters concerning the estate; he found
her bright and astute in matters of house and hus-
bandry, and would have liked her advice at times, for
he found the farming end of things tedious. He could
never bring himself to let her know he valued her opinion, for she seemed to take a mean pleasure in the
knowledge and he would not bear her contempt. As
for her, she often wished to share her thoughts and
ideas with him, for she found Rihannon and its hold-
ings beautiful and fascinating, the opportunities endless, but she could not consider it as hers and she knew
that the opinion of wives was generally not appreciated. She heard enough talk in the kitchen and among

the other women of the household to know that they all felt great sympathy for Mahlon, married to such a cold and acid-tongued shrew.''

"But that isn't me," she often thought, hearing the tail ends of conversations that stopped abruptly when she entered a room. Her temper grew short and her tongue even sharper; the servants feared her and the other women of the house avoided her. She lived virtually alone in the midst of a great estate, and she was desperately lonely. In her mind Mahlon became the enemy, the cause of her misery, and as she grew to despise him, the silence between them deepened. Sometimes she surprised a look on his face as he watched her, a genuine puzzlement in his eyes as if he would ask her why, how things had come to such a pass. He still came to her in her bed, though he had left the chamber to her and moved into one of his own. Rage sustained her through what she saw as his assaults, and she prayed, she who had been so lax at prayers before, that she would not conceive his child.

And in three years of marriage, she did not conceive. They had long since settled into a routine of bitter conflict; the strain at times grew unbearable and Mahlon rode out hunting with his men. Only then could Linzel drop her guard and relax, but there was no one left to talk to. She lay sometimes at night, cold sweat beaded on her face, heart pounding and breath short, her mind circling round and round and back on itself, desperate for a way out where she knew there was none.

After one such night, when Mahlon had been gone for several days and the illusion of peace had come to her, she descended the stairs to find the Great Hall in an uproar. There was a visitor, it seemed, weary and hungry, and the captain left in charge in Mahlon's absence would not admit the traveler to the hall. Linzel was appalled; hospitality to travelers was an understood in this harsh country. She herself was anxious for news from the outside; a traveler would talk to her, at least. She strode to the door and pushed it open firmly, green eyes blazing as she opened her mouth to

flay the captain. It stayed open in speechless surprise,
for standing on the wide stone steps, stood the travel-
stained figure of a woman. She was tall and angular,
dressed in breeches and riding boots like a man; her
cloak was flung back and her short-cropped hair caught
the morning sun like a cap of gold. She had one foot
advanced a step above the other, her forearm resting
on her thigh and her riding gloves gripped in that hand.
Trailing from the other hand were the reins of a very
tired horse, who stood with hind foot cocked and head
drooping. She seemed to be arguing more for the horse
than for herself, but the captain was adamant, his voice
rough and angry.

"We want none of your kind here!" he snarled.
"We've decent women to think of and protect!"

"I'm no threat to your women," the stranger said
calmly. "I ask only a few hours' rest for my horse and
some food for us both. I will be most content in the
stable with him, if that's what you want."

"What I want is for you to be gone from here at
once. I'll set the dogs on you if you're not."

The traveler seemed about to speak again when Linzel recovered herself and stepped into the fray.

"You forget yourself, captain," she snapped, and
the woman on the steps turned her eyes on Linzel. "I
am mistress here, and while I am, we turn no one away
from this door! Have the horse tended at once!
Please," she addressed the woman directly, "come in
and share what we have."

"Thanks, mistress, but I'll see to my horse myself
first, if someone could show me the stable?"

"Of course. The captain will," Linzel said sweetly,
and met his furious gaze directly. He ducked his head
at last and flung himself down the steps three at a time,
and Linzel grinned. The eyes of the two women met
and they shared a smile; Linzel felt a sudden warmth
in the pit of her stomach. Their thoughts were the
same, she was certain of it, and it was a new feeling
for her.

She was plagued with anticipation all day as she
waited for the woman to awaken; bathed, fed and

shown to a bedchamber, the traveler had slept away
the day in her exhaustion. Linzel had gone about her
routine with a light step, her sharp tongue curbed for
once as she focused on something outside her own
misery, and had retired late in the day to the small
chamber she called her afternoon room. It was here
the stranger found her.

"I do apologize for my rudeness, mistress," the
woman said. "But I haven't slept in a bed like that
since I left my Guild House three months ago. I'm not
exactly welcomed with open arms everywhere I go."

"Certainly our captain seemed to fear you," Linzel
said. "I see nothing so threatening about you myself,
but he was terrified."

"He—and others like him—fear what they don't understand," the woman said good-humoredly. "And
they never understand a woman who prefers to be on
her own, responsible for herself, rather than under the
slightly questionable 'protection' of a man."

" 'We'?" Linzel asked wonderingly. "Are there
others like you?" She colored at the rude sound of her
remark, but her guest only smiled.

"I have forgotten my manners entirely, I fear. My
name is Alane; I'm a member of the Renunciates. You
may never have heard of us."

"But I have heard of you!" Linzel exclaimed, leaning slightly forward in her eagerness. "There were
tales told when I was a girl at home!"

"I probably know the stories," Alane said in a wry
voice. "We are lovers of women, unnatural, and we
lure unsuspecting young girls away from their natural
calling as wives of men to serve our own desires."

"That was mentioned," Linzel agreed. "Are you
lovers of women?"

"Some are," Alane said calmly. "Some only love
their self-respect and seek to keep it, along with a
measure of peace in themselves and a sense of their
rightness in the world. And no, we do not lure anyone
away from anything; any allegiance given is given
freely. Of what use would it be otherwise?"

Linzel's green eyes sparkled, her face flushed with

excitement, and in the next hours, as she and Alane
ate and talked and laughed, it seemed as if a great
weight lifted from her chest bit by bit until she felt as
light as she once had as a girl. Her face, glowing with
delight, turned toward the sound of the opening door.
Her hair had come loose and tumbled down her back,
her cheeks blushed peach and her emerald eyes shone
like great gems between thick black lashes; the grim
line of her mouth had relaxed and softened into the
sweetness it once had, her whole body bespeaking
pleasure and relaxation. Mahlon stood in the doorway
and saw his fantasy of Linzel before him, bathed in
fireglow and more desirable than he had ever seen her,
and his heart leapt wildly. His dark eyes were suddenly
alive and shining and a smile Linzel had never seen
curved his stern mouth to gentleness. As her own smile
died, smothered in confusion, he saw Alane sitting in
the chair opposite Linzel, a goblet of wine in her hand
and a serene expression on her face. She looked comfortable and at home there, far more as if she belonged
with his wife than he himself had ever felt he did, and
a killing rage swept him.

With a hoarse cry he sprang at Alane with all his
soldier's strength and fierceness; the chair went over
backward and he fell heavily on top of the startled
woman, locking his great hands about her throat. She
struggled wildly, but he had her at a disadvantage and
was fast choking the life out of her. Alane reached for
the knife she wore at her belt, but she had come un-
armed to Linzel's chamber; the world turned fuzzy and
gray, and she heard the sound of her own lungs strain-
ing against the constriction of his hands tightening in-
exorably as she lost awareness—

The blast of oxygen was welcome agony; she filled
her lungs again and again. The man was a dead weight
on her body, constricting the flow of air into her starv-
ing lungs. Weakly Alane rolled out from under him
and sat up groggily. Her throat felt on fire and she
knew she had been minutes from death.

When her eyes cleared she looked up at Linzel,
standing over the pair of them with an andiron from

the hearth trailing from her hand. Quickly, Alane felt
Mahlon's pulse, pushed aside the thick hair where the
blood made a sticky pool beneath his face. His heart
was strong and steady, the wound deep but not inva-
sive of the skull.

"He would have killed you," Linzel said tonelessly.
"I couldn't let him kill you. I'd have killed him myself, first."

"It's all right, Linzel," Alane said, struggling to
rise. With Linzel's assistance she made it to a chair
before dropping; her head was one enormous throb.
"I'll have to be gone before he comes around. It will
only make things worse if I'm not."

"Let me come with you!" Linzel cried. "I hate it here!
I hate him! I've been so miserable, so lonely—"

"And yet he loves you, little one," Alane said quietly, and Linzel backed up a step or two, disbelief
filling her eyes. "It's true; I saw it in his face just now.
Would a man do what he has just done for a woman
he cared nothing about? He'd never agree to let you
go with me."

"I didn't mean to ask him!" Linzel said sharply.
"He doesn't love me! You don't know—you can't know
what—"

"I can guess. Listen to me, Linzel, it isn't just him,
it's you as well. You're not ready to come with me,
not ready to join us. Perhaps you will be, one day, but
now is not the time for you; there is much in your life
that you don't understand. There is too much unfin-
ished here for you to leave without a word. You must
make a good decision, when you make one, and you
cannot do that now."

Alane rose heavily, Linzel instantly at her side, and
they went downstairs into the great hall. Swiftly, Linzel dispatched a captain upstairs to see to Mahlon,
ordered that food be prepared for Alane's journey, directed that her horse be saddled and brought round.
And all the while her heart grew smaller and colder in
her chest, anticipating the return of silent, lonely hours
once Alane was gone. On the stone steps Alane turned

and looked into Linzel's eyes, great pools of misery, and smiled a bit.

"Come, *breda,*" she said; to cover her own dismay she drew on her gloves and cloak briskly. "We'll meet again. Something has brought us together, sent me to you for a purpose, and we'll know one day what that purpose is. Until then, we must live our lives one day at a time, as well as we can. If ever you need me, send for me at Harvest Guild House in Galmannorr and I promise you, if I can respond, I will."

Linzel could only nod as she watched Alane swing lightly into the saddle; she stood on the steps watching horse and rider grow small with distance and disappear. Turning slowly, she walked into the great house with a tired, defeated step and closed the door behind her.

But she couldn't close the door on the results of Alane's visit. Mahlon replaced his silence with cruelty and Linzel with a pretty young wench from below-stairs. She cared not at all if he took another woman to bed; she was indeed relieved. But when he replaced her at the table in the Great Hall with the simpering wench, that was more than Linzel could take. Her pride was at stake, if her feelings were not.

She faced him down one night at dinner, when he sat with the girl, feeding her tidbits from his plate and nibbling her neck like some adolescent fool. Linzel allowed her full fury to surface as she stood before them.

"I have maintained the dignity of your station in all things," she said coldly, "and I do not deserve your shaming me now, here, with the likes of her! Have all of her you want, but keep her where she belongs—out of sight."

Mahlon didn't turn to look at her, but his voice was low and dangerous." You deserve whatever I choose to bestow, and you've been lucky so far that it hasn't been a killing stroke!" He lifted his head and looked straight into her eyes and in spite of herself she felt shocked. His eyes burned with inner fire, the whites bloodshot, the lids swollen and inflamed. Almost out of control, he was not a man to be reasoned with. "I was deceived from the beginning by that clever sire of yours. Did he know you're one of Them?"

"Them?" Linzel said, dazed by the hatred in Mahlon's voice. "Them? I don't understand what you mean."

"Of course you don't," he hissed, half-rising, the girl forgotten in his rage. "You never plotted to have that witch come here, did you? Is she your lover, or did you only hope to make her so while I was away? How many other times has she been here when I was not?"

"My lover? What are you talking about?" Linzel asked, scarce believing her own ears. "Alane rode in a stranger in need of shelter; it is your own decree that such are never turned away. Do you think she could have been here ever before and you not be told? Your captains would kill one another for the right to be the first to whisper scandal against me in your ear!"

Even in his rage Mahlon saw the truth of that. He sagged suddenly into his chair and waved his hand in a vaguely dismissing gesture, and Linzel turned on her heel.

"Until you come to your senses, husband, I shall take my meals upstairs alone," she said as she marched away. She heard him mumble something she took to mean 'good riddance' as she mounted the stairs with as much dignity as she could muster. At the top she turned to look over the railing and stopped, startled to see him leaning forward in his chair, elbows on his knees and his head dropped into his hands. She was almost sure she saw his shoulders shaking as if he wept, and the silly young girl was looking around her uneasily as if she knew she did not belong there but had no idea how to leave. Mahlon weeping? Never!

"And yet he loves you," came Alane's voice to her as she proceeded down the hall to her chamber. Once inside she leaned against the door and considered what had just happened. If he loved her he had a strange way of showing it, and it didn't matter, in any case. She wanted only to be free.

She even hoped, in the long empty days and nights
that followed, that he would set her free. Certainly he
hated the sight of her; he never failed to make that
plain. She practiced speeches to give him pleading for
her freedom, demanding her freedom; reasoning with
him, begging him, bullying him, all in the solitude of
her bedchamber. When she faced him, she realized
that he would hear no word as she spoke, and he would
never voluntarily let her go. And shortly it became a
case of being unable to go, for a siege was laid against
Rihannon by a lord from over the mountains to the
west. With his army of mercenaries he cut them off
from all outside contact, and every messenger Mahlon
sent for help was captured, killed, and sent back tied
to his horse. Battles raged for days, the wounded lying
about the Great Hall and the kitchen, all available
women tending them. There would be a lull during
which they could at least sleep, and the assault would
begin again. There were nights when no one slept and
the whimpering of terrified women and children, cou-
pled with the cries and moans of the wounded, almost
drove Linzel mad.

Through it all she moved almost as if in a dream,
tending wounded, feeding children, comforting frightened women, following Mahlon's directions. She kept
thinking that it was some awful nightmare in which
they were all caught up, and it would end soon. Food
was rationed, though water, thanks be, was plentiful
since there were springs in the great walled compound. When the food was gone— But help would
come long before then, Linzel was sure of it; she clung
to that belief even in the face of undeniable facts.

Mahlon himself was running on nerve and little else;
only the knowledge of what they faced if they were
overrun kept him going. In spite of the bitterness between them, Linzel admired his devotion to his people
and his determination that they should be victorious.
It was a side of him she'd had no occasion to see, and
at last she understood why his captains were so de-
voted to him.

They came at last to the edge of desperation; fierce

fighting had raged for several days, and casualties were high. Starved and exhausted men have little reserve on which to fight, and the house had settled into the silence of despair. Linzel was in her chamber taking a few moments alone; a tiny fire guttered on the hearth, giving only the illusion of warmth in the night chill. She sat almost in the ashes, wrapped in a woolen cloak and allowing herself at last the luxury of retreating from reality into a dreamworld. She rode again with her brothers out into the bright dawn, astride a good horse and holding her kestrel balanced on its glove. That dream receded sharply as Mahlon came in, closing the door firmly behind him as if to shut out the world for a time.

Linzel marked his weariness as he crossed to a chair that had so far survived burning; he lowered himself into it heavily and leaned his head back, the dark eyes closing. The long legs in their scarred boots stretched out before him and his arms lay along the arms of the chair with his big hands dangling loose over the ends. He was grimed and filthy, sweat-matted hair and blood-streaked face, a half-dozen wounds and cuts on his throat and arms and chest staining his jerkin. Not all the blood was his, Linzel knew; some belonged to fallen comrades, and some to the enemy, who had twice now breached the wall at unprotected places. They had fallen back, but she knew they smelled victory, and the respite would not be long. She felt a terrible ache for him, knowing how desperately he had tried and how much of himself he had given, to have it end like this. There was little she could do now for Mahlon, but she moved to do what she could.

"How does it go?" she asked, throwing off the cloak, pulling the small pot hanging at the back of the fireplace toward her and ladling hot, thin broth into a mug.

"Poorly." His voice was thick and raspy; she could feel how sore his throat must be from dirt and smoke and shouting. "I've never doubted that we'd beat them back, and we did. But we've lost so many, and there are none to replace them. The men have gone on past any rights or expectation I might have had of them, but they cannot last much longer. We are at the end. I am sorry, Linzel. I have failed them—and you as well.''

The dark eyes regarded her steadily and she knew he spoke of more than the siege; for the very first time she allowed herself to see love in his eyes. She placed the steaming mug in his big hands, and the same simple compassion that let her see the trembling of those hands allowed her to set a basin of clean water on the low table and wipe his face clean of bloody grime. He lifted that face gratefully, like a tired child, and her touch was as kind and gentle as if he had been a weary little boy. He buried his nose in the mug, drinking deeply, and by the time she bent to tug his boots off it was empty. It rolled from his hand to the floor and she saw that he slept.

Covering him with a throw from the bed, she tidied up and resumed her seat, putting a few small twigs on the feeble fire. Her thoughts were no longer of past days; she focused on the here and now, her agile mind considering their circumstances. Alane came into Linzel's mind so strongly that she seemed to stand in the room, her clear voice saying "I promise, if I can respond, I will.''

Linzel came to her feet in one smooth motion, fatigue and despair forgotten in the rush of adrenaline. She glanced at Mahlon, but he slept so soundly that she feared he could not be wakened were it needful. Dragging a wrinkled bundle from the bottom of her clothes-press, she shrugged out of her gown and into the riding clothes she had never given up. She let herself silently out of the room and slipped downstairs; keeping to the shadows along the wall of the great room, Linzel slid out a side door into the darkness.

She met no challenge in the courtyard, and none in the stable. As she moved down the row of stalls to the end, where Mahlon's tall bay racer, his pride, stood with his head over the low door. His blazed face turned to her, his nostrils belling as he took in her scent. He snorted softly, pawed with a forefoot.

"Want a run, do you?" she asked almost gaily as she led him out and cross-tied him. "I think I can oblige, and run you must, faster than you have ever done, or I will be no longer of this world and you will have a new master!" In moments he was saddled and she untied him; he stepped lightly to the side, blowing, and she went with him, using his momentum to swing her slight weight up. He stepped lightly over the cobbles, testing her hands on the reins, puzzled by the light weight he carried. When he would have headed for the main gate, Linzel turned him toward a small postern set into the wall far at the back of the compound. Her plan was to slip out the postern gate and move as silently as possible through the enemy ranks. She counted on their weariness and arrogant confidence that all was won; they just might relax enough for her to get through. If she could get even a small lead, they'd never catch her on this horse!

It worked more smoothly than she'd hoped. There was a guard on the inside, but as he reached for the horse's reins, shaking his head as he refused to allow her to go on, Linzel squeezed the horse so hard he grunted and jumped forward, crowding the guard into the wall. Leaning down, Linzel drew the bar and swung open the gate; she was through it in a flash and out in the unfriendly darkness. The horse tugged at her restraining hands as he smelled the open air, but she moved close under the shadow of the great granite cliff. They passed watch fires so close that she smelled the men sitting around them, and her mouth watered at the rich aroma of stew cooking. The horse wanted to go, and he didn't like the unfamiliar scent of strange men and horses and smoky fires. She kept him quiet by the force of her will until they were almost clear, and then he stopped suddenly, throwing up his head. She felt him go rigid, his nostrils testing the night wind, his great barrel expanding as he sucked in air. She knew what was coming next and leaned forward to grasp his muzzle, but she was too late. The loud, ringing neigh began back at his flanks and pushed out-

ward, shattering the night as he called to the mare
whose scent rode the breeze.

"Now you've done it, you miserable crow-bait!"
Linzel hissed, looking frantically around. The mare
had answered, along with about sixty of her picket-
mates, and the whole camp was instantly in a frenzied
uproar. "We were doing great!" Linzel said furiously;
she jerked the horse around and headed him down-
slope. "We're caught out now, might as well take the
easiest path," she said as they plunged down toward
the camp. She drove her heels into the horse's ribs and
gave a wild yell. "Go!" she screamed almost exul-
tantly, and go he did! His great body coiled and
stretched beneath her, over and over, tremendous
hindquarters driving him forward incredibly with every
leap. They thundered down into a chaotic melee and
rode right through it; Linzel drove the racer straight
at the center campfire and lifted him over it with her
hands and her voice. They hung suspended over the
roaring orange heat for what seemed an eternity and
then he came down as light as an autumn leaf and
Linzel's heart almost burst with love and pride. The
darkness welcomed them, swallowed them up, hid
them from pursuers as they thundered over the hard-
packed road toward Galmannorr and Alane.

At midday next day the watchers on the walls saw a
dust cloud boiling in the distance; their shouts of alarm
brought Mahlon running. He had been pacing the
walls, blaming himself for sleeping, and Linzel for
being so headstrong, but at the same time feeling a
strange stirring of pride in her. Peering at the dust
cloud, his heart sank; it couldn't be Linzel, the cloud
indicated many riders. It must be reinforcements for
the attackers. His face grew grim as he considered his
options and came up with very few, none pleasant. A
shout from one of the captains brought him to the dust
cloud again; two riders had detached themselves from
it and were pounding for the gates, lying low on their
horses' necks, hidden in the streaming manes. Mahlon
recognized his racer and he ran down the steps three
at a time, yelling for the keepers to open the gates. In

a cloud of choking dirt the two riders thundered in the
gates and pulled up short, the horses rearing and pitching a bit, stiff-legged. Linzel, grinning like a fool,
leaned over to stroke the racer's sweaty neck. Her emerald eyes, alive with excitement, sought Mahlon in
the group of men. He came forward and grabbed the
reins as she sprang down, agile as a boy, standing
beside the great horse with a grimy, dirt-streaked face;
her braids had loosened, and there was lather in her
tangled hair. She took Mahlon's arm in both her hands
and shook him gently.

"They're coming, Mahlon! Your kinsmen and mine!
They'll be here by tomorrow night! We have only to
hold out until then!"

"And that dust cloud? Two riders never made that!
We thought it was reinforcements for the attackers."

"Oh, that?" Linzel said with an airy wave of her
hand. "That's just some mercenaries we hired in town.
They're riding back and forth pulling branches behind
them; looks impressive, doesn't it? It might be five
hundred men out there, who knows?"

"Linzel, I'm impressed by your ingenuity, but what
good are a few mercenaries and a dust cloud?"

"Mahlon, you're not listening to me! A courier left
the Guild House not ten minutes after I arrived there,
headed for your kinsmen and then to proceed on to
mine. They could be here tomorrow night at the earliest, the next day for sure. We can hold out that long!"

"You're right!" Mahlon said, the fire of new hope
shining in his eyes. "We've had the worst of it, knowing help wasn't coming. We can fight twice as hard,
knowing it is!" He looked at Linzel and would have
said more, but she held up her hand, silencing him.

"We'll talk later," she said quietly. "When all danger is truly past and we can think clearly."

And so it was that the two of them sat in her chamber a few nights later, clean and well-fed and relaxed.
The attackers were driven off, many killed, and Rihannon safe again. Linzel had talked to Alane at great
length, and the understanding they reached filled Lin-

zel with such peace and joy that all bitterness dropped away. In truth it had been ebbing slowly, and her discussions with Alane wiped away the last traces. She faced Mahlon now with something almost like regret for what she had to say.

He listened to her quietly as she dashed the hopes that had come to life again in his heart. She wanted nothing from him except his goodwill and good wishes, and her freedom. She asked him to free her willingly, that they might part as close to friends as they could ever be, but if he would not, then she would leave regardless. It was wrong for her to stay; wrong for her and for him.

"You are a good man, Mahlon," she said, taking one of his hands in both of hers. "I missed that entirely, and I'm sorry. We just didn't understand each other."

"And if I promised to—" He stopped as Linzel shook her head sadly.

"I don't want that, Mahlon. I always wanted to go free in the world, but I never knew that it could be. I know now, and I have to go. Let it be over gently, Mahlon, please."

Dark eyes held green ones long and deep; tears trembled in both. He nodded at last.

"Go, then, in peace," he said, "and you may as well take that damned horse with you. He's spoiled for anyone now but you."

"Oh, Mahlon, what a lovely gift!" Linzel cried, halfway between tears and laughter.

"And will you cut your hair?" he asked, lifted a shining auburn strand in his fingers so it caught the firelight. "I always loved your beautiful hair."

"I don't know," Linzel said gently. "But I won't do it here." They fell silent, sitting handfasted and looking into the fire for a long, quiet time.

Mahlon was not in the courtyard when they rode out the gates together, Linzel astride the tall racer and Alane beside her. She knew he watched them from the bedchamber high above; her auburn hair floated free in the early morning breeze, shining lustrous copper-gold in the first sunlight. Linzel rode straight and tall, her shoulders squared and head up, into the waiting world, and she did not look back.

Carlina's Calling

by Patricia D. Novak

One of the things I look for when accepting stories for these anthologies—and I should emphasize that every year I get about twice as many good stories as I can use, and I have to choose the ones for the anthology on some consistent basis (though, after all, the ones too amateurish to use have been returned, I could choose the rest at random, and probably have an anthology just about as good)—is something about a popular character in one of the books . . . "filling in the gaps" as it were. Those of you who are familiar with the Darkover novels will remember Carlina from TWO TO CONQUER.

About this story Pat says that she made the assumption that the King Carolin in this story was the same King Carolin mentioned in TWO TO CONQUER, and that he could be still alive.

Pat Novak is an assistant professor of agricultural economics at Auburn University, is 33 years old, and lives in Opelika, Alabama, with her husband, Jim, three cats and two dogs. She is expecting her first child before this anthology comes out. (Yes, anthologies have longer gestation periods than humans.) Her first published story was "Clingfire" in DOMAINS OF DARKOVER (DAW 1990).

Mother Liriel, who had, in the world, been called Carlina di Asturien, slept and dreamed. In a vision, she saw a bush of flowering red *vallaria* flowers entwined with a vine of dark *robinia*. The black leaves encircled the crimson petals, blending and molding into a single glory.

The young priestess smiled in her sleep. It was good, the joining. Natural and right. The Goddess Avarra would be pleased.

With unmerciful suddenness, the pleasant image shattered, and Carlina sat bolt upright in her bed, her heart pounding, her mind awash in a terror that could not have been her own. She was dying, she felt it, brought down with child-bearing fever. She clutched her slender, unimpregnated body and cried for the child who would never live to its birth.

"Jandria, help me," she moaned aloud, but she knew she had no right to call on any of the Sisterhood of the Sword. She was forsworn.

The nightmare held Carlina so tightly that at first she did not see Anya, who had come running to her aid at the sound of her cries.

Anya set her lamp down upon the solitary table and took Carlina's thin shoulders firmly in her own broad hands, shaking the other woman gently. "Liriel, Liriel, wake up. You dream, my sister. Nothing more."

Carlina stared blankly into Anya's eyes for a moment before coming to herself. She shuddered. "It was so real," she whispered, "so very real."

She swung her thin legs over the side of the bed. Gently refusing Anya's assistance, she walked to the window of her small house, her bare feet cold against the floor. In the autumn sky, only pale Mormallor remained above the horizon; the other moons had set.

"That was no dream," she said at last. "That was a calling, and I must answer."

Wiping the last traces of sleep from her eyes, she turned from the window and took a black robe from its hook on the wall. "First, I must find someone named Jandria who dwells with the Sisterhood of the Sword at Serrais. With her aid, I will find the one I seek."

"You cannot mean to leave now," Anya protested.

"If you wait until sunup, a proper escort can be mounted."

Carlina shook her head. "I cannot spare the time."

"Then I must go with you."

"You are generous, sister, but the calling is mine alone. I shall be fine, I promise you." As she spoke, she knew the words were true, although she did not know how she knew.

She finished lacing up her gown and kissed Anya lightly on the cheek. "Tell Mother Luciella I have gone." She slung her cloak across her shoulders, picked up her pack, and walked alone into the night.

The fire had burned down. Mirelli Lindir was cold, bone-achingly cold, but she had not the strength to rise and rekindle the flames. She pulled weakly on the threadbare blanket, trying to make it cover her shoulders, but it was too small. She curled up as tightly as her bloated abdomen would allow but found little relief.

She did not think she could survive another tenday. Ankles and wrists were already swollen to three times their normal size, and this morning her vision had gone gray and hazy. She was no midwife, but she recognized the signs of child-bearing fever. Without a skilled healer, she would die. And there was no one to help her, no one at all.

Her flame-colored hair, dull and brittle now, tumbled about her face in snarls. With unsteady fingers, she pulled at the worst tangles for a moment, before giving up in disgust. What did it matter now, with no one to look at her, how she appeared? Rafael was dead. A million tears would not bring him back.

She had given up her honor and her place in the Sisterhood of the Sword for love of a *laranzu* from Neskaya Tower, and he, for his love, had sacrificed his own place. They had come to this hut, this humble stretch of nothing, and they had been happy for a time.

But love, she thought bitterly, had not kept him out of the endless quarrels of the tiny kingdoms. When the Duke of Hammerfell, his cousin, had needed a *laranzu* to repel an attack from Aldaran of Scathfell, Rafael had gone willingly—never to return.

He had left her nothing. At fifteen, she had renounced her family and her noble heritage to join the Sisterhood. For Rafael, she had forsaken those vows. Now, she had nothing, no clan, no family, no allegiance. Perhaps, months ago when first she learned she carried Rafael's child, she could have gone to his family in Hammerfell, but the time for traveling was long past.

She moaned and tossed, at last falling into a fevered sleep. And in her dreams, she called for Jandria of the Sisterhood, who had been her oath-mother.

A dozen or more pairs of eyes focused inquisitively on Carlina as she entered the dining hall of the Guild House at Serrais. All conversation ceased; not a single spoon clattered against a wooden bowl.

Inwardly, Carlina flinched, dismayed at being the object of interest, but outwardly she retained the dignity befitting the dark robes of a priestess of Avarra. "I seek one called Jandria, Guild-mother of the house."

A woman, well on in years but straight of back and clear of eyes, rose from her place and faced Carlina. "And what do ye want with her?" the woman asked, country accent so thick that Carlina almost did not understand.

"I bear a message from Mirelli Lindir," Carlina answered, "one that I must deliver in person."

The older woman's face creased briefly into an expression of pain. She moved away from the long bench, toward Carlina. "Ye've found who ye seek," she said. Then she turned back to her crimson-clad warriors. "Finish your supper, daughters. I will attend to this."

It was with a sense of relief that Carlina followed Jandria out of the crowded room, away from the staring eyes. "Mirelli is dead to us," Jandria said when they reached the privacy of an empty room. "She is forsworn."

"She is dying in truth," Carlina replied. "She reached me in her dreams, but it is you she calls for. She will not live out the moons-span without help."

"Ah, that is hard." Jandria ducked her head. "But still, the lass left of her own will, an oath-breaker. She has no right to our aid."

Carlina's temper, so seldom evoked, flashed. "Do not speak of rights when one who loves you lies dying. What good is honor without compassion? Are we not all Avarra's daughters?"

Jandria remained silent for a moment, her dark eyes unreadable. "Your voice is harsh, but your heart is gentle, daughter," she said at last. "And you have come all the way from the Isle of Silence to petition me. I can nay refuse you. Tell me what ye need, and ye shall have it."

Carlina smiled; her narrow face became, for a moment, almost pretty. "I will need a midwife from the village to assist me," she said.

Jandria blushed. "You cannot mean—" she began, but Carlina cut her off.

"And you must come as well. That is, if you are not too old to ride."

Jandria swore. "I am nay so old that I cannot outsit a priestess of Avarra! I will not turn eighty before Midwinter night!"

"Well, then," Carlina answered, another of her rare smiles lighting her features, "we will be off in the morning. My horse should be rested by then." And she thought, with a detached amusement, that she had at last found a reason to be thankful to Bard di Asturien, her foster brother. It was he who had gifted the priestesses with a dozen good horses, including her own mount.

Mirelli heard the sound of horses' hooves against the rough stone of the walkway leading to the hut. Her heart pounded in fear. *Merciful Avarra! It's bandits come to rob and kill me, for no others would be abroad so late.* With a desperation that surprised her—she had believed herself resigned to death—she rose unsteadily from her pallet and looked about wildly for a weapon. She spied Rafael's short sword, the only thing he had left her, and tried to pick it up. In her enfeebled state, the small sword was almost too much for her to lift. She balanced it precariously across her swollen belly, grasping it firmly with one hand. With the other, she clung to the wall, so that she would not fall.

"Mirelli," came a familiar voice from just outside the door. "I am here, *chiya.*"

A surge of relief so strong it brought her to her knees flooded through Mirelli. The sword fell with a dull clunk onto the packed-dirt floor. "Oh, Goddess be praised," she whispered, "but am I dreaming?"

If it was a dream, Mirelli hoped it would not end. Three women—old Jandria, a young peasant woman Mirelli did not recognize, and a dark-robed priestess—came swiftly through the door. They lifted the fallen Mirelli and carried her gently to her bed. They wrapped her in warm blankets, and the priestess kindled a fire with a wave of her hand.

"Oh, Jandria, Jandria," Mirelli whispered, tears streaming down her cheeks, "how I prayed for you to come."

Jandria laid a wrinkled hand on the girl's hot brow. "Hush now, *chiya.* I am here. You must lie quietly and let the priestess do her work."

Carlina came forward and bent down over Mirelli. "I am called Mother Liriel," she said gently. From the neck of her gown, she pulled starstone on a silken cord. "You have *laran,* little sister, you can help me. Concentrate on your child." Mirelli closed her eyes.

"I can help you, too," Jandria said softly, "I do not have strong gifts, but I am not entirely head-blind."

Carlina surveyed the older woman in quiet surprise. Yes, now that she looked closely, she could see the traces of red in the faded hair, could feel the aura of mental presence that only one with *laran* would have.

The midwife, whose name was Maura, laughed softly as she put a kettle of water on the fire. "You are too modest, Lady Jandria. Everyone in Serrais knows you are King Carolin's foster sister!"

"I renounced such things when I joined the Sisterhood," Jandria said firmly, "but some *laran*, aye, that I have. I will monitor you if you wish, Mother Liriel."

Carlina nodded, then turned her attention back to Mirelli. "It is short of your natural time," she said, "but the babe must be born now, else both you and your child will die."

Mirelli weakly nodded her agreement. "Then I will begin," Carlina said, and motioned to Maura to be ready.

Dawn came before the babe was born. At last, as the blood-colored sun rose high in the gray sky, the child, alive and healthy, emerged and took its first breath. "A fine lass," Jandria murmured as she helped Maura clean the baby. "May she grow up strong and well."

Carlina wiped her sweaty brow with a clean towel. "Sleep now, little sister," she said to Mirelli. "Maura will tend the babe." Mirelli, exhausted beyond endurance, fell at once into a deep slumber.

"Well, that is done," Jandria said, joining Carlina at the hearth. "If you will come back to the Guild House with me, I will arrange your escort back to the Isle."

"Done is it?" Carlina's voice betrayed her own exhaustion. "And what is to happen to them?" She jerked her head in the direction of Mirelli and her child. "It will be Midwinter before Mirelli is healthy enough to provide for herself. She cannot be left alone."

Jandria shrugged. "Perhaps she has family who can take her in, or perhaps she can go to the Isle with you."

Carlina sighed. "She has no one. I would that I could take her to the Isle, but our rules will not allow."

"Then we have saved her life for naught," Jandria said with bitterness. "For a hostel of the Sisterhood is no place to raise a babe. We are warriors, not nurse-maids."

Carlina's face clouded. "Our rules. Your rules. We are as trapped in a net of our own making as any maids sent unwilling to their marriage beds." She stared moodily into the fire, and it seemed, for a moment, that she saw a vision in the flickering flames, a scarlet *vallaria* flower entwined with dark *robina* leaves.

Carlina gasped and laid a trembling hand on Jandria's arm, the meaning of her odd vision suddenly clear. "You and I, we can change the rules." Jandria shook her head and looked as if she would speak, but Carlina hurried on, spilling out her dreams for the future. "I tried some years ago to get our priestesses to go more into the world, but the older Mothers would not hear of change. I am sure there are many in your Sisterhood who would also object to any departure from what has been."

Jandria nodded. "There are many and many who would scream loudly if the smallest rule were broken."

Carlina looked deeply into the other woman's eyes. "You are Guild-mother. You can convince enough of the Sisters at Serrais. Those who do not like change can go elsewhere, to another Guild House. And I will bring from the Isle of Silence those priestesses who will follow me. Together, we will forge a new order, with humane rules, so that no woman will be forced to make impossible choices."

Jandria did not answer for a moment. She turned troubled eyes toward Mirelli, who still lay fast asleep, and toward the baby, who snuggled contentedly in Maura's arms. "Aye," she said softly. "We lost Mirelli because she fell in love, and there is no place for the love of a man in our Sisterhood." She shook her head. "The lovers of women are not forced to go against their nature, but we force other women to give up too much."

"Will you do it, then? Will you take Mirelli to Ser-

rais and then welcome those priestesses I can persuade
to follow me?''

Jandria shrugged. "I do not know if it can be
done." She sighed and continued in a low voice, "But
I, too, would like to see a refuge where any woman,
no matter what her skills and inclinations, could find
a home—a true alternative."

At this, Maura, holding the baby in her strong arms,
came forward. "Excuse me, my ladies. I could not
help but hear you talking. You do not know what such
a refuge would mean to the likes of me." She turned
beseeching eyes on Jandria. "I am no warrior like you,
mestra." Her earnest gaze traveled to Carlina. "Nor
would I wish to seclude myself from the villagers who
need my skills. But, oh, how I have longed to live free
of my stepfather's domination. As it is now, to be free
of one tyrant, I must bind myself to some other man
and hope that he is not too harsh. Please, *mestra,*"
she turned to Jandria again, "please try what Mother
Liriel has suggested. I would work hard for the privilege of belonging to your order, and would give all my
wages to the house."

Jandria's old face creased into a smile. "Oh, surely
not all, child. A portion perhaps." She threw up her
hands in resignation. "Well, I am old, but not yet set
in my ways. And I cannot leave Mirelli to die. We will
try this new order of yours, Mother Liriel, but if we
are both run out of Serrais at sword point, don't say
you weren't warned."

Maura squealed with excitement, waking the child
who cried feebly. She grinned apologetically and left
the two other women to their conversation as she strove
to comfort the baby.

"We would need a new charter," Carlina said
slowly, her initial euphoria at Jandria's concession giving way to a worried appraisal of the very real diffi-
culties that lay ahead. "The king might not approve."

Jandria chuckled. "Nay, lass. Carolin will not be
an obstacle. I am in truth the king's kinswoman, and
he owes much to the Sisterhood of the Sword. He will
grant me any reasonable request."

Carlina took Jandria's hands in her own and squeezed them briefly. Mentally, though, she was already miles away, counting the priestesses who might follow her. Anya, of course, and Buartha, maybe a dozen others. Not many, perhaps, but it would be a start. And with a certainty born from the strength of her determination, she knew it would be enough.

A Beginning

by Judith Kobylecky

Judith Kobylecky has a new baby, so this story is a beginning in more than title. Congratulations; I wish I did—my honorary grandson is already seven—they do grow fast, don't they, though you never believe it when they're driving you nuts being small and noisy. You turn around twice and they're six foot four!

She says this story "was written immediately after Emma was born, which accounts for its very short length. The story kept wanting to expand, but newborns are very wonderful and difficult to tear yourself away from." Aren't they just. "Also I was tired." Babies do that—especially when you have other children, like Judith, who, with her husband John Orr, also has Ian, age 3, and Anna, age 6. I wrote my first thirty books with kids yelling all over the house—and about being a writing mother, there's nothing to be said—nothing fit for public consumption, that is—except, take heart; they grow up faster than you'd believe. My youngest is now almost 25—and I am convinced that I ought to be carrying her around on one arm.

I could write pages and pages about the delights of being a full-time housewife and mother and trying to write and support a family with two babies—but I don't use that kind of language in public.

The settlement was still burning as Ailain picked her way around its smoldering timbers. Almost hidden in the smoky haze she could see three figures slowly searching through the ruins. Ailain was too numb to wonder who they were or for whom they were looking; she had already found her dead. Cradled in her arms she carried her beloved's sword wrapped in the banner it had been his pride to carry into battle. For the clan's honor generations had fought a blood feud, the cause forgotten. Both sides had finally perished at this battle. All were dead now, except Ailain and the others moving wraithlike through the smoke, searching, searching. A wail of grief told her that one of them had found what she was looking for; the sobbing broke through the wall she had built around her own pain and drove her to the banks of the river. As she knelt to wash the soot and blood from her hands, she was careful not to drop her burden; she alone was left to uphold the clan honor and she feared to put them down for a moment.

At the sound of quiet footsteps she turned to see that the other survivors had been drawn to the river as well. Ailain knew who they were; the clan symbols braided into their long hair identified them as plainly as if they had spoken. The woman with the bandaged hand wore the symbols of her ancient enemies; she was as dirty and tired as Ailain herself. The other two were members of traveling merchant families caught in the fighting; they had had no part in the feud but had lost their people as well.

As Ailain stood up, the others eyed her warily. "I have done with fighting today." Her voice was heavy and flat in her ears.

The older merchant spoke quietly, as if to herself, "We never had any interest in fighting, but it did not seem to matter. How will I live with no family, no clan? Winter is coming and all the shelters and food stocks have been destroyed."

The girl began to cry. To Ailain's surprise the older woman put her arms around the child and murmured comforting words. Their clan symbols were of rival families who would never offer each other a kindness. For the first time Ailain found herself questioning the code that had determined every action of her life. There was a rightness to what the woman had done that she could not deny, even if it was against all she had been taught.

Ailain found herself speaking. "The feud is ended. If we can agree to work together, we can survive."

The rival clanswoman looked skeptically at the banner and sword that Ailain held so carefully in her arms. "How can you say that when we all wear our own people's tokens? Our clans have been enemies since before our parent's birth. How could we ever come to trust one another? Family honor continues as long as one member lives."

Ailain stared at her betrothed's sword and banner a long moment, and then flung them into the river. Drawing her own sword from her belt she saw the others step back apprehensively, the child stifling a scream and burying her face in the older woman's arms. Ailain held up her long braid in her other hand, clan ribbons and emblems woven through its strands. Only that morning her beloved had given her a string of beads in the clan colors and had watched as she plaited them into her hair. Deliberately she cut off the braid and threw it into the water as well. "I renounce my clan and my old loyalties. We are a sisterhood and you are my people now, by my oath."

She watched with growing hope as one by one her new sisters cut off their long hair with the dangling symbols and cast them into the fast flowing water.

Set a Thief

by Mercedes Lackey

I had the singular pleasure—well, not entirely singular because it's now happened to me many times—of presenting the very first story by a writer who would go on to achieve status in my very own field. Mercedes Lackey appeared for the very first time in FREE AMAZONS OF DARKOVER, followed by stories in SWORD AND SORCERESS III, IV, V, VI, and VII, stories of two women, sorceress and swordswoman respectively, who were in all but name, Free Amazons, and she also has a story in DOMAINS OF DARKOVER (DAW 1990). But she's also developed an independent career with the excellent "Herald" books—which I like, paradoxically, even though they deal with a herald corps in communication with sentient horses. As an ex-farm woman, I have no romantic illusions about horses—but I like Lackey's work even when it deals with horses. In general though, I'd even prefer dragons—another over-used fantasy cliché.

She's also written a couple of very fine urban fantasy (Tor Horror) novels, so I can no longer think of her as protégée but as an independent writer on her own. Which makes me think of the time the late beloved Catherine Moore spoke to a group of women writers in the last year of her sentient life. (A victim of Alzheimers, she lived far too long not knowing herself or anyone else.) Looking at us, young writers, some of us forty or more, she murmured bemusedly, "You're all almost young enough to be my daughters! Whereupon, every woman in that room—not only I who thought of it at once—spontaneously cried out, "We are your daughters, Catherine."

So, I tend to think of many young writers—not only those I've personally sponsored—as being my daughters. My friend Sandi once accused me during one of our many differences, "Oh, Marion, you just want to be everybody's mother!" Whereupon I replied, "It's hard not to when the whole world comes and crawls into your lap."

But—I admit it—I'm as proud of Lackey as if she were my daughter.

In this story, Mercedes Lackey deals with a problem which has often exercised my mind; considering the Compact, which prohibits any weapon "beyond the arms' reach of the one who uses it" are arrows lawful? And upon what grounds?

This could have been pleasant; Tayksa enjoyed leatherwork, even when it was mending. The common room of the brand new Guild House was finally *warm*—for the first time since the beginning of winter. Virtually every member of the newly-formed Guild of Renunciates had found some reason to be here, and unlike her partner Deena, Tayksa enjoyed crowds. She was a child of the city, after all, and walls and people were her element.

But things stopped being comfortable the moment one of the other former Sisters of the Sword brought up politics. . . .

Tayksa sighed, kept her head down over her leatherwork, and hoped forlornly that she wouldn't get pulled into this particular argument with her Renunciate sisters.

"Bows don't kill people," Leanna said stubbornly, her jaw set at an angle that betokened trouble with anyone brave enough to nay-say her. "*People* kill people."

That's an oversimplification if I ever heard one, Tayksa thought, but she also remembered that Leanna was newly-oathed, a rawboned shepherd from the hills below the Hellers, and mightily partial to *not* risking her hide hand-to-hand with a wolf or a catman. Her folk hadn't even seen a fraction of the warfare that had been tearing land and people apart until the Comyn Lord Varzil—now called "the Good"—had begun putting a stop to it by conquering the quarreling factions himself.

She hasn't seen clingfire, *Avarra save us,* Tayksa thought bitterly, recalling all too well the sight of those of the Sisterhood who had gotten a taste of the evil stuff at a venue much closer than "sight." *Much less* deathdust. *On the other hand, she has a point. How in the seventh hell are shepherds going to protect their flocks, or farmers their families? They don't have* time *to learn swordwork; they've crops to get in. Huh. Come to that, it's only the rich and highborn that have the time to learn sword and knife— them, and those like us, that make their livings at it. And besides—*

"If you take bows away from the common folk they'll be helpless to defend themselves—if you make it a crime to have a bow, then only criminals will have them," Leanna continued, her voice rising, saying the very words that had been in Tayksa's mind. "Would you mind telling me what good *that* will do you?"

She looked about for reinforcement, and her eyes lighted on Tayksa. The young woman groaned inwardly, sure of what was coming. She'd be drawn into this tangled controversy whether she liked it or not—

And if truth were known, she really had mixed feelings about the whole damned mess. She could surely see the wisdom in Varzil's Compact, that decreed that no one should ever use or own weapons that could strike at a distance. Surely any price was worth that— worth knowing, too, that the Towers would see to it that never again would *clingfire* or *deathdust* be created and used for *any* purpose.

But where did that leave shepherds like Leanna's folk?

For that matter, where did that leave her?

"Sister," a soft voice interrupted from the hearth,

before Leanna could drag Tayksa into the affray. "Sister, you see only the restrictions of the Compact. You do not see the freedom it buys us all."

Tayksa sighed with gratitude. Maira n'ha Joyse had come to this newly-created House of the Renunciates from the ranks of the other Sisterhood—that of the gray-robed Ladies of Avarra. She still wore her dust-gray robe, though shortened to just above the knee now, and belted over breeches of the same gray. And she wore the long knife of the Renunciates proudly, though she hadn't a clue how to use it.

Leanna subsided meekly. Tayksa wasn't sure if that was out of respect for the gray robe, or the red hair of the Comyn that blazed above Maira's pale face.

Doesn't much matter, she thought with relief. *I'm out of it before anything starts. Trouble is, too many of the Sisters remember what I was and forget what I am . . . and anything I say is suspect.*

Then again, I can't ever stop being what I was. It's part of me.

A part I'm not ashamed of, to be honest. Evanda and Avarra know I saved old Copper-Top's head a time or two. To catch a thief, set a thief. To catch an assassin—

Maira stretched out her maimed, clawlike left hand, and Leanna winced away. "This, *breda,* is the work of a drop of *clingfire* no larger than the head of a pin," she said in the same soft, gentle voice. Firelight made the hand seem worse than it really was, and Tayksa had a shrewd notion that Maira knew that. "Imagine the stuff raining down from the sky, not only on fighters, but on helpless farmers and herders, women and children—*that* is what the Compact will save us from. Is that not worth the sacrifice of a few bows?"

Leanna looked sick—but she was made of sterner stuff than Tayksa had supposed. "Maybe," she said slowly, "but—"

Out of the corner of her eye, Tayksa caught a hint of movement in one of the doorways. She looked up automatically, and just as automatically recognized who it was—that lanky, dark-haired shadow was her partner Deena. Tayksa nodded to show that she'd noticed; Deena jerked her head sideways and in the direction of the staircase, then vanished.

Tayksa gathered up her things and shoved them into her mending kit, loath to leave the warmth but *not* reluctant to escape being pulled into an argument. *So the Guild-mother wants me. Huh. Wonder what for?*

Deena was waiting, halfway up the staircase. "Somebody should sew that girl's lips together until she learns some sense," the skinny brunette said shortly. "Zandru's hells! I'd take up stable-sweeping for the rest of my life if that's what it took to get rid of *deathdust!*"

Tayksa only shook her head and took the stairs two at a time. "She's never seen it, so she can't imagine it, Dee; the poor girl hasn't much more imagination than a lump of dough or one of her sheep—"

Deena muffled a giggle with the back of her hand.

"—so what's the Guild-mother want with us?" she continued, just as she reached the door to the Mother's room and opened it for her partner to step through.

"It isn't the Guild-mother that has need of you, you infuriating young woman," said a voice warm with amusement and two octaves deeper than the Guild-mother's.

Tayksa quickly closed the door behind her.

Zandru's bloody hells! What's he *doing here?*

Lord Varzil smiled at her from the depths of the Guild-mother's second-best chair. He smiled—but Tayksa didn't need *laran* to know that something was wrong. Just his being *here* was evidence enough, but he looked like a man with too much on his mind and no solutions for any of it. The candlelight that gleamed from his coppery hair was enough to show her the lines of strain around the edge of that smile, and around his eyes as well. She crossed her arms and leaned back against the door.

"Any why'm I infuriating, m'Lord Copper-Top?" she asked, as the Guild-mother winced at her complete lack of respect.

"Because you are either blessed with *laran* that evades testing, or you're managing to see consequences that *I* cannot," Varzil replied, a little ruefully.

Ah. So that's it. I told him he'd better watch his back. Sounds like somebody's tried to stick a knife in it.

"Somebody already made a try for you?" she asked.

He shook his head, slowly. "Not yet. But one of my fellows has foreseen the incident; or rather, has seen the image of myself most certainly dead—and far too many of the futures hold my death. But she has *not* seen the agent, only the consequence—there seems to be a kind of blurring about the killer that she cannot penetrate. And even more distressing, we cannot seem to pinpoint either the agent or the one behind the agent in the here-and-now."

Tayksa pursed her lips, and drummed her fingers on her upper arm. "So somebody can block you out?" she hazarded. Then shrugged. "No matter. They can't block us from seeing that it doesn't come to pass."

"Us?" Varzil repeated, one eyebrow rising.

"Us," Tayksa replied firmly, and Deena moved a little closer to emphasize it. "We come as a team. Dee's a tracker; she does the outsides of the places we guard, I do the insides. She'll see things your guards will never catch. And that's something I *can't* do; I'm no good at anything outside of walls. I need Dee; I need what she can do. I told you the last time, you do things my way, or I don't play."

"So be it." She gave him credit for that; Varzil gave in to defeat with a good grace. "Then let me tell you the little I know. . . ."

The hum of conversation in the long hall silenced for a moment as Tayksa and Varzil entered, then picked up again with a certain sharpness added to the collective tone. Tayksa fluttered her long eyelashes and clung to Varzil's arm like the helpless little creature she looked to be. It was a role she had played many times before joining the Sisterhood, though never in the position of being a guard against *another* assassin.

Males of every rank and station smirked or winked slyly at one another as she passed. Females frowned at her; some coldly, some with anger. Varzil's young and gentle bride—who was now pregnant as well—was popular with the women of his estate. No few of them resented this "entertainer" who—they thought—had replaced young Ambria in Varzil's bed.

Praise the gods, Ambria's as quick-witted as she is sweet, Tayksa thought, managing her skirts as gracefully as any lady of the Comyn born. *She's maintaining the illusion of the neglected wife beautifully. Zandru's hells, but she'd have made a good assassin! I'll have to tutor her a bit before this is over. Never know when she might need a trick or two.*

Tayksa certainly didn't *look* anything like the tough little fighter Varzil had spoken with in the Guild House. Her long blonde hair—unlike most of the Sisterhood, she braided it rather than cut it—was caught up in an expensive copper clasp that matched the copper pendant at her throat. Her heavy wool dress was dyed a rich and costly red, and was of the softest and finest weave obtainable—and was cut so low as to border on the obscene. Physically, she looked as if a harsh word might break her in two; fragile and acquisitive, and not overly bright, just shrewd.

And there was a knife up either sleeve, a third strapped to her thigh where she could reach it through a slit in the pocket of her skirt—and in direst need, that expensive copper hairclasp broke into two nasty clawlike weapons that Tayksa had used on more than one occasion.

Outside Deena was prowling the gardens and grounds on an ever-changing route; looking for anything at all out of the ordinary. She hadn't found anything yet—but Tayksa had an uncomfortable feeling that she and Varzil were being watched, this past day and a half. Which meant they probably *were*. Which meant the assassin was somewhere in the building and beginning his—or her—final preparations.

That was why Tayksa had insisted on maintaining the fiction that she was Varzil's *barragana*, even to sharing his bed, though the "intercourse" that took place there was of the conversational variety. . . . *She* had often spied on her targets in their most intimate moments; these grand estates were often riddled with passages and hiding places their owners knew nothing about. It would have been incredibly revealing for them to act as lovers in public and conspirators in private.

She clung to Varzil's arm all the way to the table, and only loosed him to take her place at his left. Ambria's chair, at his right, remained empty.

Tayksa dropped down into her seat with a lithe grace that called up another frown from the women nearest her. *It's a good thing that I'm not really Varzil's* barragana; *the atmosphere around here is chill enough to freeze the hottest of passions.* She smiled at the woman; a superior smirk calculated to infuriate her that said wordlessly, "You may hate my insides, but I'm the one with the power, and you'd better remember that."

Exactly the way a very expensive whore would be *expected* to act.

The tables filled, and the room warmed with the buzz of conversation and the scent of cooked food. Servitors lined up at the service hatch to take steaming platters and bowls from the lift. As the dishes arrived at the table, Tayksa kept a close watch on all the servers for any furtive movement that might signal sleight-of-hand. There had been no one new in the kitchen staff since the conclusion of the wars—and at any rate, they'd all opened themselves to Varzil's *laran* willingly when the threat first presented itself. But not only did the ranks of the servants change constantly, it would have been very easy to slip someone into their midst and out again before anyone noticed the extra set of hands. At the height of dinner, attention was on the food, not the hands that served it.

Most of the suspicious movements would prove to be nothing of consequence; Tayksa was not looking to prevent a poisoning, she was filing it all in her memory for later, if a poisoning did take place. By knowing the dish it came from, she would know who had brought it, and whether there was any point at which it might have been tampered with.

This had been going on for several days without results, but Tayksa knew better than to relax her vigilance. After all, she had played this game herself. . . .

Which was why Varzil was eating his meals cold.

He *had* to eat with the rest; anything else would have been a danger signal to the assassin. But Tayksa had a solution to that; he would allow his server to give him a portion of a dish, but he would only eat it after everyone else had devoured the course. Including Tayksa, who had acquired at least a partial immunity to every poison she had ever handled. If a dish was poisoned, Tayksa would feel its effects—hopefully in a milder form—before Varzil had even tasted it.

Of course that meant Lord Varzil was eating cold and congealing food most of the time.

"I fear your methods of keeping me safe are as unpleasant as a poison," Varzil whispered to her as she chattered to the deaf old warrior at her side. She was keeping up a steady stream of inane conversation in order to keep track of the servants without appearing to watch them.

"Hardly, my lord," she whispered back dryly. "You have no familiarity with the subject if you think—"

Her throat spasmed, choking off her last words. And halfway down the table someone stood up abruptly, and just as suddenly collapsed.

Garbena-seed, she recognized absently, forcing her throat to relax even as it tightened again. *Causes paralysis of the respiratory system*—and even as she was identifying the substance, she was sweeping Varzil's plate to the floor with one hand before he could take a single bite, and drawing her knife with the other.

The crash of Varzil's plate on the stone went unnoticed in the general pandemonium.

The effect of the poison on both those who had eaten it and those who had not was spreading. Already other diners were collapsing, blue-faced and gasping. The rest were in a state of panic; some were actually trying to do something, but most were acting like frightened sheep.

Had to have been the rabbit-horn; it had a sauce of fennel seed. Tayksa remained exactly where she was, scanning the mob for any movement out of the ordinary. *That was the girl with the big hips and nothing-face. But I don't see her—she's—ha!*

Varzil had left her side and was on his knees beside the nearest victim, starstone in his left hand, his right on the man's forehead, his face taut with strain. And just beyond him, Tayksa saw the girl in question edging her way along the wall towards a doorway. *Not* fainting or screaming, like about half of the other servants. *Not* trying to help the fallen, like the rest. Purposefully and quietly making her escape.

Not this time. The knife was already in Tayksa's hand. In an eyeblink, her knife was flashing across the room.

And it missed.

Somehow, the girl saw it and managed to duck out of the way, squirming into the shelter of the doorway with an agility Tayksa had only seen in two other people. Herself, and the thiefmaster who had taught her.

No matter. Even as the knife clattered against the wall, Tayksa was out of her chair and crossing the room in a swirl of fabric. As she reached the doorway she heard the faint sounds of running feet ahead of her. She followed, her own leather-soled felt boots making no sound at all on the stone.

The corridor made an abrupt turn to the right just ahead; Tayksa stopped just short of the turning. The corridor ahead was dark—the girl must have put out the lights to delay pursuers.

Just as I would have.

In fact, she was probably back there even now, waiting for anyone following her to be silhouetted against the light as he rounded the corner.

The muscles of Tayksa's chest spasmed painfully for

a moment, doubling her up with the need to breathe. Then they relaxed, though she didn't straighten.

Do I call out to her—try and get her to surrender to me? Tayksa wished she could see around that corner; she fancied she could hear someone panting softly from the dark. *I was in her shoes once . . . the Sisterhood took me in. Shouldn't I offer her that chance?*

Then she recalled the moment of her own capture; she'd had plenty of opportunities to take her target— she could have killed him and been gone days before. But every opportunity would have meant she'd have had to take someone else along with her victim; an innocent who might have little or nothing to do with the quarrel that had led to her hire. She'd never killed anyone but her target before. She'd sworn she never would.

This girl had been willing to do that. Who could predict how many would die tonight of the poison she'd intended for Varzil?

She doesn't deserve consideration, Tayksa thought, a cold rage making her jaw clench. *She's a mad dog, and she should be destroyed.*

She threw herself into the darkened corridor, sliding across the stone floor. As soon as she moved, a knife flashed out of the darkness to rebound from the stone of the wall.

That gave her direction—and Tayksa thought she could see a hint of white; an apron, perhaps. She gathered herself and leapt blindly for it.

She was very nearly too late; one of her outstretched hands caught the trailing edge of a skirt as the other tried to resume her escape. Tayksa jerked sideways as hard as she could, tumbling the girl off her feet, and threw herself on top of her.

Only to find that she was outmatched.

Tayksa landed atop her, and began trying to pin down the assassin's arms and legs. The girl was bigger, heavier, and possibly stronger than Tayksa—and although they were both hampered by long skirts, the assassin's were of a lighter fabric. She was striking out

with hard, open-handed blows. Tayksa couldn't see to
block them; the best she could manage was to try to
keep the girl more-or-less pinned. Gradually it became "less"; the girl had gotten loose from every hold
Tayksa had put on her. Struggling blindly in the dark
like this, there was only one thing Tayksa *could* do,
and she began as soon as she realized that she was
going to lose.

She screamed for help at the top of her lungs.

The other woman cursed her viciously, tried to get
a hand over her mouth, but Tayksa only bit it as hard
as she could, and the girl pulled it away with another
curse as loud as Tayksa's cries for help.

Then the girl got both hands loose and around Tayksa's throat. In a second, she'd managed to flip both of
them over, trapping Tayksa beneath her. And she
started to squeeze. . . .

Tayksa tried three times to break her hold, and
couldn't even get her to loosen her grip. Then her chest
spasmed again; stars began to dance in front of her
eyes—

Not stars. Light. Torchlight. Tayksa blinked, and
felt her throat; it was sore, but it could have been
worse.

Sure. I could be dead.

She blinked again; the one holding the torch was
Cemoc, Varzil's paxman. Varzil himself was kneeling
beside her, taking his hands away from her chest.

Zandru's hells. Maybe I was dead.

She struggled to sit up; rather than prevent her, Varzil gave her a hand. "She got away," Tayksa croaked.
"It was one of the serving-girls, and—"

Varzil shook his head. "She didn't get away," he
replied bitterly, "Though she might just as well have.
Your partner Deena caught her trying to climb out over
the walls, and shot her with that damned bow of hers.
So we have foiled the assassin, but we still know nothing of—"

"Maybe not." Tayksa ignored the dancing lights
in front of her eyes, and the way her head spun as

she struggled to her feet. The dress was ruined; both shoulders ripped out, and a long tear in the skirt. Tayksa ignored the damage. "I want to see the body."

"There's nothing to see," Cemoc protested.

"I don't care; I want to see it."

Varzil shrugged. "So be it. It's in the chapel."

Tayksa turned to look at him, aghast. "That—*bitch*—poisoned more than a dozen innocent people tonight. She *tried* to kill you! And you put her in your *chapel?*"

Varzil only shrugged again; clearly he didn't expect her to be able to understand his motives.

And I don't, she thought grimly, following Cemoc to the chapel.

She understood even less when she found the body laid out as if the assassin had been an honorable member of Varzil's household. But understanding didn't matter. All that mattered was if the girl bore a certain small brand.

Sure enough, there it was, a match to Tayksa's own. What Tayksa had *thought* she'd recognized—that the girl had been taught to use Tayksa's old master's techniques—was indeed true. Both she and this now-dead assassin bore an identical three-armed brand on the inside of their right wrists.

Both had been owned by Benno Macarter; thief-master with ambition.

"What makes you think he'll be *there?*" whispered Rafael, the head of Varzil's personal guard.

Tayksa smiled in the darkness, then remembered that Rafe wouldn't be able to see it. She kept her eyes fixed on the door and both windows on this side of the inn as they waited for the signal to move in.

"Because Benno's like me—he's a *city* man. He's not used to the country, or to big estates like Varzil's. He doesn't think of the countryside as a place to hide, he thinks of it as a place to avoid." She shifted a little; there were bruises all over her body that she was only now beginning to feel. Her throat ached whenever she tried to swallow. "There's only one inn for miles around, so that's where Benno will be. That's why I suggested to Varzil that he pack up and move onto his estate until the danger was over; any ally or employer of the assassin would have nowhere to hide."

And in Thendara you could look for a hundred years and never find one of these rats when he'd gone to ground.

"Huh." Rafe stared thoughtfully at the inn door. "Even if he plans on bluffing his way out, he's got no way of knowing *you're* with us."

"Exactly." A group of five stag ponies trotted up the road to the inn; Varzil and his party. That was the signal to the watchers that all was secure. The riders dismounted; Tayksa left Rafe's side and took her place in the back of the entourage next to Deena. Both of them were now wearing their Sisterhood dress of red shirt, leather tunic, and loose breeches. Both of them wore knives just a hair below the length that would qualify them as swords. Tayksa had every intention of making sure that both Benno and Varzil remembered who was responsible for catching the assassin and the assassin's master.

She was expecting a lot more trouble, but Benno had gotten careless, soft, and fat in his old age—when they came in, he was actually seated at the fireplace, mug of beer in one hand. In a way, Tayksa was disappointed. It was hardly a challenge at all.

Benno's eyes widened in his puffy face when he saw Varzil. They widened even farther, though, when Tayksa stepped out from behind the Comyn Lord, pointed her finger, and said, simply, "Him."

"You know, this reminds me of the story about the child that caught the catman by the tail," Tayksa said, packing up her things while Deena lounged on the great bed in Varzil's chambers.

"You mean, now that he's got it, what's he going to

do with it?'' asked a voice from the doorway behind her.

Since she hadn't heard anyone approaching, the deep voice made Tayksa jump; her heart raced for a moment, and she stared at Varzil with dark accusation. ''I think you do that on purpose, Copper-Top,'' she said sourly. ''You want to see if you can make me drop dead of a heart seizure just so I won't be around to embarrass you.''

Deena scrambled self-consciously off the bed and stood at stiff attention. Varzil ignored her. ''These *are* my quarters,'' he reminded her mildly. ''I'm curious; what about this situation reminds you of having a cat-man by the tail?''

''You know why Aldaran hired an assassin to take you out.'' She folded a shirt neatly after removing all the hidden throwing spikes, and stowed it in the backpack. She glanced over at him; he had taken the most comfortable chair in the room, and while he wasn't exactly sprawled in it, his posture was a little less than regal.

''The Compact,'' he replied.

She nodded. ''I'm telling you, Copper-Top, it's not going to work. Where do you draw the line? At *cling-fire* and *deathdust*? If you do that, someone will invent better projectile weapons. At bows and arrows? Do that, and the herdsmen and the farmers will think you're singling them out for persecution. One of the Sisters said something very trite, but true for all that it's trite, just before we left—*Bows don't kill people; people kill people.*'' She folded a pair of breeches and turned to face him. ''Think about it, man. That girl was just as truly a 'weapon that strikes at a distance' as any bow! Did Benno need to be in the same *room* with her? Did Aldaran?''

Varzil frowned. ''The Compact remains. I can re-define 'weapon' if need be—''

''That's not the point. The point is that you need to change peoples' attitudes. As long as there's no stigma attached to pulling your enemy down at a distance, that's *exactly* what the intelligent man will do.'' She turned back to her packing, shoving the last of her weaponry in on top of everything else and lacing the pack shut.

She slung it over her shoulder and prepared to leave; he reached out and prevented her with a hand on her sleeve. "I owe you a great deal, *vai domna*," he said softly. "For food for thought, just now, along with everything else."

"Back the Guild," she replied, some of her sourness fading. "That's all the Guild-mother asked and that's all I ask. But I'd ask you one other favor, for the sake of a Sister who's seen too many wolves in her time—"

"Speak."

"Before you manage to change peoples' attitudes, have your people use a little common sense when you're dealing with those poor farmers and shepherds." She sighed.

He looked at her thoughtfully. "Perhaps it would be best if there were an understanding—that unless a weapon is used to harm another human being—"

She nodded vigorously.

A sly grin began to steal over his face. "And if the *next* generation should decide that using a bow is *dishonorable*—"

"And you *laranzu* decide that guarding farmers from Ya-men and Catpeople is as honorable as any other work—" she shot back.

He sobered. "You truly would have me be my brother's Keeper, wouldn't you?"

She paused in the doorway. "I would. If you're going to take away someone's means of defense, it seems to me you have a moral obligation to replace it with *something*."

Deena squeezed past her as he gave her a sour look. "So this is what it has come to: being lectured on my moral obligations by an assassin."

"My Lord Varzil, I, the humblest of your subjects, wouldn't presume to lecture you on *anything*. I merely remind you."

"Oh?" One eyebrow rose. "Of what?"

"That if you won't protect the farmers, there won't be anyone left to *feed* all us city folk and Comyn," she said, as she slipped out the door. "Remember, m'lord—the hand that holds the ladle rules the world!"

Shut-In

by Jean Lamb

Jean Lamb is well-known in fanzine circles, having written many short stories for same. She lives in Oregon with "a science teacher husband, two children, a cat, and a computer." She is active in the Jaycees, in her church, and is a director in the National Fantasy Fan Federation. She has written a novel, in her own universe, which is now making the rounds of publishers. She has written fan fiction not only in the Darkover universe but also for Star Trek and Blake's Seven fanzines. She has been a strawberry picker, a nurse's aide, a USAF officer, a free lance auditor, and an encyclopedia salesperson. That's about par for the course for a writer; I was a waitress, a dress saleswoman (door to door), a vegetable saleswoman, a peddler, a folk singer, a telephone counselor, a choir teacher, and a fortune teller before I was a full-time writer. Some people wonder why writers have so many funny little jobs. It's simple; it's because writing, in the early stages, doesn't pay much; but you can't take a full-time job without giving up writing, so you do anything and everything to turn an honest buck till your break comes.

Looks as if Jean qualifies.

Larissa screamed as her parents thrust her into the closet and slammed the door. She beat against it even as the bolt dropped home. She clawed at the musty clothes hanging on pegs, as caged as any wild beast.

At last she slumped down to the floor in the darkness. She hated being closed in like this, ever since her sister Shazel had accidentally closed the lid of the clothes chest on her when they were both five. Why were they doing this to her? Why couldn't they love her the way she was?

The door cracked open and a ray of light sliced through her fear like a sword. She clawed at the edge, but it wouldn't budge. A trembling, delicate hand reached through, holding a large mug. "Mama?" Larissa asked.

"*Chiya,* I want you to drink this," she said. The girl could almost taste the odd lemony smell of it. "Darling, please do as your father wants."

"That's *kirian,* isn't it? It made me so ill the last time." She felt sick to her stomach just remembering it, though she was so thirsty she was almost ready to drink it anyway.

"That's all I can give you. Oh, I'm so sorry, sweetling. But you know your father only wants you to be whole. It's not as if we were kin to the Lanart clan. It is truly for your own good, don't you see?"

Larissa closed her ears to the lying, loving words. If Mama really cared, it wouldn't matter what her father wanted. Then the heavy door swung shut again, and she was alone in the dark again with only the mug for company.

The girl shook with panic. The fumes of the stuff made her head ache, though she hadn't drunk a drop. Oh, merciful Avarra, her mouth was so dry. Even if it made her ill, at least the *kirian* would satisfy her thirst. Maybe it would just put her to sleep, the way it did the last time. Maybe then they'd see it was no use, and stop this torture in the mistaken belief that her greatest fear would break her *laran* free.

Of course, she knew better than that by now! Everyone else in the large Sisberto family had *laran,* and none to a greater degree than her flame-haired sister Shazel, now being trained at a Tower. No matter what she herself did, Shazel always did it first, and better. Larissa truly did not grudge her sister anything, and didn't even mind that her own hair was only a dark auburn, but was it too much to ask that her parents love her, too? Yet when she became a woman just after her fourteenth birthday, and still had no *laran,* no telepathic powers of any kind by a year later, she knew it was hopeless.

After all, it was *Dom* Moran's ambition to become a great power in the land through marriage and other means. The Gift of far-seeing was invaluable in war, so her other sisters, who had it, had easily found noble husbands, while Shazel might someday become a Keeper. That left only her, as worthless as ever. Despite the visiting *leronis'* conclusion after examining her with all the deep insight and trained skill from years of Tower work, *Dom* Moran was convinced Larissa was holding out on him just to be stubborn, no matter what loving lies he wrapped it in. Her mother Clarinna was too exhausted to interfere. She had little reason to hope for better treatment in the future. Her cousin Robard, supposedly her promised husband, had already demanded twice the dowry offered for any of her other sisters to compensate for her obvious lacks.

The darkness pressed in on her. She couldn't think. She hated being shut in like this. Why couldn't Father understand how badly she had to be out in the open? Why did he torment her like this? She held her hands over her eyes. That helped. She could pretend she was playing hide-and-seek when she did that.

But that only helped for a little while. She sighed, and swallowed the *kirian* down in several gulps. Her head began spinning, as it had before, only this time she thought it would never stop. The darkness kept closing in on her. Her starstone felt cold and lifeless in her hands, as it always did, but for once it glowed with a light of its own.

Though it had no powers, she could still imagine it was the sky, and that she was under it, not hopelessly caged up by her own family. Yes, it was the sky, and she was free. . . .

She must have fallen asleep from the *kirian* and started dreaming, for now it seemed as if she floated through the wall to the halls of the small hill-castle that was her home. Everything looked different, some-

how, but she couldn't put her finger on what had
changed. As she passed by a storeroom, Larissa saw
two people—one a tattered lordling plainly gnawing
his fingernails wondering how to see everyone fed
through the winter, and the other an old, sick woman
giving him what comfort she could. No—they couldn't
be her parents! *They* were cruel, heartless people who
loved nothing better than to hurt her! She didn't like
this part of the dream at all.

She fled out a window. As long as she could pretend
she had wings, she might as well go where she pleased.
Ah, that was better. She floated over the snowy countryside, and giggled as the softly falling flakes tickled
her bare toes. Then Larissa followed the course of the
small river near her father's holding down to a bustling
small city on its banks. Nes'sky, she thought it was
called. Then she dreamed she saw Shazel's Tower, as
tall and as beautiful as her sister had described it on
her one visit home.

Larissa even let her imagination conjure up women
of a strange sort with cropped hair who carried swords.
They walked as freely through the town as she once
had through the woods, before she'd grown too old.
Yet they looked grown, too, and some of them even
looked Mama's age. If wishes were horses, then banshees would ride, but Larissa felt it could do no harm
to imagine herself one of them. She may as well enjoy
this while she could—the *kirian* wouldn't last forever.

Yes, there she was in front of the gates where the
women in tunics and breeches walked in and out. If
only she could be there for real and not only in heart's
desire! Then she could almost feel the cold street-stone
on her soles. In this wonderful dream she stumbled
toward the gate. Oh, it was glorious how kindly they
spoke to her, how gently they lifted her when she began to sway on her feet, how glad they seemed to be
to see her . . . it even felt as if they were putting her
into a bed piled high with warm quilts.

It didn't matter that it was all fading out now. She
knew the river was real. Once she woke up, her family
would have to let her out of this horrible closet even-

tually. Then she would leave some night on one of the stag ponies and follow the river. Maybe she would find that place for real. For now it was pleasant to pretend to lie back and sleep. She didn't fear waking up in the dark any more.

A few years later, two Free Amazons camped near the crumbling ruins of a small holding. The wars of the Compact had passed over it and left it empty. Gwennis n'ha Ysabet held forth at length at the folly of some lords who thought themselves too secure to ally themselves with one of the seven ruling clans of Comyn. "Why, this is the fifth heap of rocks I've seen like this! It doesn't matter how brave the *vai dom* of the place might have been if he chose the wrong side, or none at all."

"I know," Larissa n'ha Clarinna said softly. Oh, she knew all too well. None of her father's ambitious connections had been any help when it mattered. "I'd rather not talk about it anymore," she said, swallowing back the tears. "I used to live here."

DANILA'S SONG

by Vera Nazarian

This is a story scenario which must have happened many times on Darkover, if only in legend. Vera Nazarian made her writing debut in SWORD AND SORCERESS II (DAW 1985) and is another writer I regard as a protégée, though she is no longer so very young— I believe she is approaching her mid-twenties. She is employed at a college somewhere in Southern California and is working on a novel. Vera is a natural stylist, and her work tends to be overwritten in first draft; she submitted this last year, and it was somewhat too long and too flowery; but this year it fits right in. I can only suggest if her novel, too, meets this fate first time out, that she cut it to the bone and try again. Writing is one profession where less is definitely more . . . in spite of many early markets which paid by the word. I made my first sales by being concise—in spite of having written one novel which was so long it has taken some people longer to read it than it took me to write it. Yes, literally.

"Do you think it at all possible for one man or woman to have two *donas*? Not one but *two*?" Janisse Ridenow was aware that again, she was mostly talking to herself, while her brother Erlend rode sullenly at her side, lost in his *laran*-guarded privacy. Much of what she said lately went almost completely past his ears, and this worried her further because he had good reasons to react thus. More and more, he was becoming a bitter introvert. And this process, the *leronis* at Serrais had said, was almost surely irrevocable. It came as a direct result of what he had gone through, both physically and psychologically, during the horror of the fire—the same fire that had destroyed their father, and left Erlend, despite all ministrations, a lame cripple for life.

Janisse had taken *Dom* Valentine's death better than Erlend, but not because she had loved their father any less. It was that Erlend had always felt the need for a special bond with the reserved Lord of Serrais. Even more precious it had seemed to Erlend now, looking back, for he had fought all his life to have that bond, to break through his father's difficult and subtle alienation. And it seemed, in the final two years he had indeed accomplished it. *Dom* Valentine at last accepted him for himself, as his son, and no longer merely the cause of his wife's death in childbirth. How brief and sweet it had been, these two years. . . . And then came the fire in which his father died, while he stood by helpless, useless, a cripple.

Their party, consisting of six, and on its third day on the road, headed in a very roundabout way to the Hastur lands, and from thence, to Arilinn Tower. Janisse-Lynn Serrais-Ridenow, her brother Erlend-Damon-Valentine Serrais-Ridenow, and Bethan-Rhys Aillard, all had their own private dealings at Arilinn. Bethan, a long-time friend of Erlend, joined their party at the edge of Alton lands, traveling north from Valeron. Erlend's paxman, Arlin, rode at his side, and was to serve as steward if need came of it. Finally, their two guides, hired by Janisse herself, were what they called Free Amazons, or Renunciates. Janisse wasn't exactly sure how proper of her it had been to personally visit the Guild House and request help from this odd sort, but then, she had always been the slightly unconventional one.

Besides, with Father dead, what did it matter now. . . ? she thought.

One of the Renunciates was singing. What was her name again, Danila n'ha Liraya? A sharp-featured but oddly beautiful woman of about thirty, dark-haired and

pale-eyed like an albino *verrin*-hawk, she was warm
and energetic, obviously the superior of the two, and
hence in charge of the party. Her *bredhyia,* or whatever she was, the younger, fairer one who gave her
name as Ysabet n'ha Alla, followed her orders silently, perfectly, and said nothing much. Her smile
however, Janisse noticed, followed the older woman upon occasion, appearing so intimate and in
rapport, that Janisse suspected there might be a
laran link between them. No matter—it was none
of her business anyway. These Renunciates—she
did not know half as much about them as she felt she
should.

Danila was singing:

> *I was a seafarer in Valeron*
> *With only a river to float my boat on,*
> *Dah-rih-rah! La-ha-a-ah!*
>
> *The Lady Aillard stood on the shore,*
> *And beckoned me to her Castle's door.*
> *Dah-rih-rah! La-ha-a-ah!*

Erlend, almost with a jerk, started, shaking his
copper-red head, then muttered in his own low musical voice: "That damned singing, again. . . . She
drives me mad with the sound."

"What was that?" Bethan's cheerful firm baritone
came from the side, and Erlend almost winced at the
equally good mood apparent in it.

"Nothing."

Bethan, warmly handsome, with his short-cropped
straw beard and ready grin, had always made Janisse
feel like he might, if he were with Erlend long enough,
bring her brother around. But then she had to remember how hopeless an illusion this was, and that such
deep depression as his could only be cured by a *laranzu* specialist. That's why they were going to Arilinn
after all.

"Don't you like the song?" asked Bethan. "Frankly,

I do. I've heard it before, a long while ago. Some-where. . . ."

"Maybe in your head, Bethan, together with all the other annoying tunes that one picks up, and then can't get rid of for days. It rings in your head. . . !"

"Ah, come, my friend, nonsense. Really, I do like the song. And I think she sings it not half badly. How does that go, dah-rih-rah—"

"Please! Can't you see it makes him ill," said Jan-isse, but only because she felt Erlend might expect her to say something.

Abruptly, the song stopped. The woman riding ahead of them on the firm pony, seemed to have somehow understood or heard them. The easy slump of her shoulders in itself spoke of her manner, a sort of nonchalance, an ease, and a certain disdain of the Comyn.

"How much longer until the next inn, *mestra?*" said Bethan loudly to the one ahead, to change the subject.

"By sundown. No earlier," came the curt answer of the Renunciate, not unfriendly, but somehow re-moved. She did not turn her head. Janisse observed the earring flashing in her earlobe, seeming blood-crimson, like the sun.

The well-traveled road they followed from the low-lands was entering hill country, lightly forested on both sides. Hawks circled in the lilac skies, and Jan-isse watched their flight with a momentary wistful-ness. The horse under her was strong, probably bred in these very hills. She could sense its presence, sub-tle and clean, as she could *feel,* without having to see, the blue matrix veiled in the hollow of her throat.

I am Comyn. . . .

Even riding a docile old mare, Janisse Ridenow would never diminish the feel of Comyn about her.

Bethan was trying to engage her brother in conver-sation. "Have you heard," he was saying, "news from Caer Donn, of those strangers—what did they call them, the *Terranan?*"

"Yes, I did, vaguely." Erlend's answer was automatic.

"They are supposed to have come down from the stars, can you believe that?"

"Zandru only knows. But then, maybe. Stars, I have heard, are only very faraway suns, like our own. They seem so small because of the distance."

"Ei. . . !" Bethan lightheartedly gestured away with his hand. "I don't know what to believe, friend."

"I believe it," said Janisse. "I remember, Lerrys said it is so, and I believe it."

Erlend gave her a penetrating glance of his pained hazel eyes, but managed a half-smile. "You believe everything Lerrys Aillard tells you, *breda*."

"Not everything!" Janisse's cheeks flared in a crimson blush. "I simply know that in this case he is right."

"Ah, Lerrys, Lerrys," Bethan sighed. "Lerrys, I suppose, would know. The Keeper of Neskaya could not make up stories about such things to one of his circle."

"I am no longer one of his circle."

Bethan looked at the suddenly too serious pale face of the girl, and thought he knew why.

"When did you leave, *damisela?*" he questioned politely. "I don't recall knowing about this. . . ."

"Last spring. My—father—needed me here, and I—"

At her words, Erlend darkened, and Janisse almost gasped at her own carelessness. *Dom* Valentine was never to be mentioned, unless they wanted to see Erlend in an even blacker mood for the rest of the day.

And indeed, as she looked on, appalled, there came a sheen of wetness to Erlend's eyes, while the face remained stoically unmoving. Without a word, he turned away from them and spurred his mount on, racing far ahead, graceful and gaunt, with not a hint of his lameness.

"Cassilda support him. . . ." muttered Bethan,

feeling that already he had said too much for all. He and Janisse fell back into uncomfortable silence.

Janisse wanted to reach out with her mind, envelop her brother with a warm protective veil of an empath, but something about his very being, cold and harsh, made her hold back. She could marginally feel his dark cloud of anguish, had flashes of his sensation, racing wind, an odd ache in his ruined leg, and the thunder-cloud of pain and madness that was his *presence*. Beyond this darkness, she knew, there were impenetrable barriers of solitude.

Ahead of them, Danila again broke into a song. Her voice, clear and ringing, rode on the wind, and there was an odd neutral quality to it, natural like a paradox, full of joy and life, and yet carrying a haunting quality. But to Janisse in that moment, it was the most reassuring thing of all. Somewhere far ahead, she felt Erlend's *presence*, felt him flinch at the sound, but for once, perversely, she was rather glad.

Let him listen—he broods, turning away from life. I can no longer—do anything for him. Therefore—let him listen!

And then, by an odd impulse, she urged her mare on, and neared the woman guide riding alone and leading one of the three pack horses.

"What are you singing, *mestra*? May I call you Danila, by the way?" asked Janisse, reaching her side, and matching the other's gait.

Still keeping eyes ahead on the road, the woman gave a quick smile, and simply shrugged. "Whatever, *damisela.*"

For a while they rode in silence, the country around them becoming more thickly wooded and craggy.

"Ever been here before, lady?" Danila spoke suddenly, simply, and her hand moved to encompass the landscape in a sweep. "These are called the Kilghard Hills. Actually, we're at the very foothills. It gets steeper as we go."

"It's beautiful. No, I've never been here. . . ."

In the back, Janisse could hear Bethan talking to Arlin who led the second packhorse. Farther back yet, completing their party from the rear, rode Ysabet, silent and leading the last of the packhorses. The red sun rode high overhead, slipping in and out through the tops of the great evergreen trees all along the road. The road itself was gradually narrowing, resembling a trail.

"You really love this *Dom* Lerrys, don't you?"

The sudden statement and the very audacity of it caught Janisse completely off balance. She reddened, then was about to reply harshly, but there was no smile or mockery in the older woman's face. Her albino-pale sharp eyes looked on with sympathy, and then she added: "It might be none of my business, *damisela*, but I noticed how silently pained you have been for these last two days since we began the trip. It is when you speak of Lerrys that your eyes first light up and then cry out."

For some reason, Janisse no longer wanted to lie. Riding with her head lowered, she spoke: "I had to leave Neskaya Tower. Because of him. Actually, probably because of myself and what my feelings were stirring up. The circle was no longer properly balanced. I was at fault, my feelings—Zandru's hells, why am I telling you this?"

Again, oddly enough taking no offense, Danila shrugged. "Why tell me, indeed. Only—you must tell someone, is it not true, *damisela*? I *know*."

Janisse could only stare ahead.

She has laran. *She must be part Comyn.*

But in that instant, Janisse saw something dangerous stir in the pale eyes, a memory not to be brought to the surface. The woman Danila had either read her thought or else it was the bright red sunlight in her eyes, but her right eyelid twitched and she turned away.

"I have thrown all that out to the wind, since having taken my mother's name as my own." Danila spoke in a measured remote voice. And then, after a while, she brightened and looked again at Janisse, saying, "What does the past matter now?"

"To my brother, it is his life. . . . The past haunts him with darkness." spoke Janisse softly, musingly.

"Yes, your brother. He should let go of it, I say, throw out the darkness and bitterness from his heart. And then he'll breathe. . . . But you, *damisela*, you think your running away will help?"

"By the Lord of Light, what could I do? He is a Keeper, inviolate! I was destroying myself, him, all of us!"

A moment of silence, as Danila seemed to chew on the thought, and then, "Are you so sure?"

"What?"

"Are you so sure that you would indeed destroy him or yourself or anyone, by staying? Don't you think a Keeper would have enough inner strength to know what is right for himself, for you, and your circle? You just ran away, and never allowed yourself to look, instead, deeper into your soul and ask: 'Does he love me?' And then, to ask, 'Do I really love him? Or is it that I'm just in love with love, and my own personal needs?' "

Janisse's eyes sparked. "What are you saying? How can you presume to know any of this? How dare you?"

A gentle sadness crept into Danila's eyes, but she blinked it away, then again simply shrugged, saying coolly, "I am sorry, *damisela*. I believe I did say too much. It is your business, then, and it's wrong of me to think you might want a sympathetic ear or advice. I am nobody—your guide to Arilinn, only. I'll be still." And with an oddly proud humility, she turned her eyes to the road.

Janisse rode silently by her for several moments, then fell back to where Bethan and her brother rode (Erlend having moved back to his former place).

It was late afternoon along the narrow wooded trail, when they finally took a rest stop. Arlin and the two Renunciates busied themselves with the care of the horses, the collecting of wood, and the making of a small, careful fire, while Janisse helped Bethan unpack the road supplies. Soon the stew was boiling.

Having dismounted with only light difficulty, Erlend

stood watching the woods about them, all the while standing well clear of the little cooking-fire. It was only when he took a couple of steps that his pronounced limp and the special boot made to hold his right foot became apparent.

Danila and Ysabet whistled as they worked. Dressed in masculine leather tunics, they moved about deftly and silently, with not a single creak of a boot over the pine-needled forest floor. Danila seemed to have forgotten the strange intimate interlude of only an hour ago. She addressed Janisse cheerfully, ladling the stew, and offered her a bowlful.

"Eat up, *damisela*, or you'll 'pine' away, and be like this little thin needle here." She winked.

And involuntarily, Janisse could not help smiling back at the peculiar albino eyes, and she took the food, finding herself ravenously hungry.

The conversation somehow returned to the earlier topic of the afternoon. "What do you suppose, Bethan, can there be two *donas* in one man or woman?" asked Janisse.

Bethan wiped his mouth and beard with a sleeve, then proceeded to give her his opinion on the subject. He argued interestingly, they all had to admit.

"Let's say a man has both the Ridenow and Alton blood. He might then be expected to have a little of both empathy and forced rapport. Or he *could* have a lot. Who knows, *damisela*? In any case, theoretically I think it could be possible for the psi energy to be doubled and split, due to an odd gene mutation— although, there hasn't been such a case discovered yet. I mean, why shouldn't there be?"

"Why not? I can give you one good reason," said Erlend sullenly: "A *dona* is a thing of genius. It is a certain *level* of psi power, a high level. Everyone has psi energy, but only in the Comyn is it so concentrated and focused that it amounts to significance. Now, just imagine, supposing the presence of the right genes, the possibility of that *high* level happening *twice* in a single person! Is that at all conceivable?"

"I don't know," said Bethan, "but I can give you

a non-*laran* example. A man or a woman can be talented to the point of genius in two different areas—a great craftsman can also be a great musician! I myself have seen it. Take, for example, the Ridenow *nedestro*—what is his name, the one who is a harpist and also a dancer. Remember how he impressed everyone last Festival Night?''

''Whatever.'' Erlend shrugged stubbornly. ''Only you cannot compare the genius of *laran* to any other genius.'' His voice had risen several notches.

''Hold it! Why not? I think *laran* is a talent like any other! You develop it and—''

Janisse again saw the dangerous turn of this argument. ''Bethan,'' she said, ''never mind. We hardly know enough to discuss these things properly.''

''Oh, and you think *Lerrys* does?'' said Erlend bitingly.

Bethan realized that it was time indeed to change the subject. ''Well, I suppose I am not an authority in such things,'' he winked at Janisse, ''but regarding the two *donas* idea, specifically, there have been rumors that Carcosande Hastur has both the Hastur and Alton *donas*.''

Again Erlend shrugged, firelight on his now blank face, his expression settled for the moment.

''There are too many rumors altogether about Carcosande. I wonder if her Regent brother suspects even half of it, half of what has been going on between her and the Alton clan,'' began Janisse, glad to have a specific topic, to leave the argument.

''Oh, these Zandru damned rumors!'' Erlend's neurotic face again flared, took on a thin sarcastic look, ''I don't want to hear it. Enough foolery.'' And he turned away, then got up from the fire, stretched, and walked farther off the trail into the woods.

''I think the fire bothered him.'' whispered Janisse. ''Ever since you-know-what, he's been like that. Never admits it, but even the sight of a cooking-fire makes him uneasy. I mean—you can't even talk to him.''

''I understand. I've heard how everything was,'' Bethan nodded quietly. "How he had to hold and carry *Dom* Valentine's charred corpse—"

Danila meanwhile, while her helpmate cleared the cookware and food, was busy stamping out the fire.

"We'll ride soon," she announced in her brisk clear voice, and then began to sing:

I was a seafarer in Valeron . . .

Erlend whirled around. "Stop it!" he cried, and there was a great psychic disturbance in the air, "Stop singing, damn you!"

He stood straight as a post, staring at her, his eyes dilated in pain, suddenly maddened. Everyone became silent.

Janisse took a step forward. "Erlend—"

"No." It was Danila who had spoken. And then she slowly looked Erlend full in the eyes. She saw hate there. And darkness. And somewhere, in the deepest part, an ancient burning fire. . . .

"Why, *dom?*" was all she said. "Why?"

For a cold moment he was silent, And then, "Do I need to have a reason? It disturbs me. . . . Therefore, being in my—in our employ for the duration of this trip, you, *mestra*—" and he spat out the word *"mestra"*—"are under our full command and obedience— even if I am but a cripple. I command you to stop! Be silent for the rest of this accursed trip!"

The albino eyes narrowed for an instant, as though a spark flared and had to be put out quickly, before an inferno raged. *"Vai dom,"* she said. "Not a cripple. . . . You are but a stripling before me. You could have asked me. But no, you are, by Aldones, hardly in full command on me, or my Guild-sister here. No man is! In fact, from this moment on, we return to you the unearned part of our pay, and we depart, leaving you to do whatever Zandru might do in his seventh hell!" The last words were said in a voice so powerful it almost seemed to be a *laran*-based command voice.

Without another word, Danila n'ha Liraya dropped

a pouch of coins at their feet and, silently followed by
Ysabet, began to ready their two horses.

"Wait, please, Danila!" exclaimed Janisse, and
made a move to follow her. Danila glanced blankly at
her, then resumed her business.

"Leave her be," said Erlend harshly. It was a command.

"Erlend! Why speak thus? Was it really necessary
to insult her? To tell one of her kind, and in such a
manner, that she is under your full command, is like
telling a wolf that he is born to herd sheep," said
Bethan, shaking his head. "I'm afraid we're now stuck
in a bad situation. And surely, even if you apologized,
it would be useless. Renunciates, from what I know
of them, are damn proud. Damn. . . ."

"What will we do? We don't know the trail!" said
Janisse, as the two women mounted and quickly
rode away along the trail. "By Aldones, maybe if I
try—"

"We ride on our own," Erlend cut her off sharply.
Anger apparent, he began collecting their things, moving about with an even more sharply pronounced limp,
while his face was like ice.

The sun was beginning to sink to the rim of the
purple sky when they finally had the things readied
and rode once more on the trail. "We'll never find the
inn," lamented Janisse. "And even if we do, it'll be
too dark to know it! Lord of Light!"

Erlend, grim as a thundercloud, rode in silence.
There was something wrong, it seemed to him, wrong
with these woods, although he'd never admit it. It was
true, he could probably find their way, for as a boy he
had been an excellent tracker of animals, using both
trail-skills, and *laran* to do it.

But now, something seemed not quite right.
Not quite right.

There was an odd silence to the woods, Janisse
noted, as she rode with tiredly downcast eyes. Not a
bird sang, no hawk circled high above. There came
no rabbit-horn to jump from the horses' hooves

and scatter in the brush. A dead silence filled it all.

Silence, and something on the wind. Suddenly, with a sickening premonition born of *laran*, Janisse felt it from far away, rapidly approaching. A crackle and roar, and a black ash stench on the wind. . . .

Forest fire!

Before she even could react, she could hear Erlend's anguished psychic cry, and frenzy was in his eyes.

Father! My father!

And notwithstanding that the fire was at least several miles away, Erlend suddenly spurred his stallion, and broke into a gallop up the narrow trail, his bright copper hair visible from behind the trees, as he raced by toward the fire.

Gods! Stop him! she cried in her mind before her vocal cords could form the sounds, and then, like a whirlwind, was after him. During that single moment of mind contact, she knew the truth of what he was about to do.

"Bethan!" she cried to her back, "Help me, please. He wants to die!" And then the world was but one flashing forest before her eyes as she raced after her brother.

Erlend was indeed mad. She could see his red hair flying far ahead, while from behind came the pounding of Bethan's horse.

The stench was getting worse. And then, from almost a half-mile away, the roaring thunder. . . . Erlend raced on, getting off the road, and making his way, weaving, past the sparse trees toward the approaching blaze.

"*Damisela*, wait!" Bethan's cry came from behind, "Stop, *damisela*. He won't go on. There are people there, can't you see?"

And indeed, as Janisse allowed herself to glance where Bethan pointed, she could see a large group of local villagers lined up, digging trenches, and otherwise preparing to make a barrier to stop the advancing blaze. Breathless, and wiping her scratched dirty face, she slowed her mare to a walk, falling behind to where Bethan rode.

Erlend, ahead of her, also seemed to have slowed. His thin figure did not slump in the saddle, but was arrow-straight, although she knew he held himself up only by sheer willpower. And yet, he was unreachable, his barriers like a fortress of granite.

What will he do? her pulse raced. *O blessed Cassilda . . . and I can do nothing! He will not hear me, or even want to listen! If Lerrys were here, oh, if only Lerrys—*

Erlend approached the fire-lines, still mounted. It was odd to see his solitary figure moving as in a dream, while all around action boiled.

"Ho, you there, come and help!" someone cried out, seeing him. But as in a daze, he sat in his saddle, while the horse came to a full stop. And then, slowly, with some difficulty, he dismounted, and limping, took a step forward.

A sickening image was in the mind of Janisse, and yet, she was so far away! So far! If only she hadn't listened to Bethan, and had raced straight on behind Erlend, she would've been close enough to reach—

She saw his actions, the very movement of it, take place before the actual event.

Lerrys would have done something . . . her one thought managed to race by, *he would have—*

Erlend's body, only feet away from the fire, lunged forward. At the same instant, a figure disengaged itself from the fireline, a familiar flash of dark hair, the single earring, the pale albino eyes. As Erlend rushed, lunged, catching fire like a straw doll, Danila fell on him, dragging with her body, then both rolled on the ground, only a couple of feet into the safety line of the cleared brush. As some bewildered onlookers stared, the two bodies struggled.

. . . Fire . . . scorching pain . . . Father! Erlend's mind was a mad inferno of light and pain. He saw himself rush forth, trying to bring his father back from the blazing depths of the room into which he had dis-

appeared just a second ago. . . . A highly sensitive new bond of *laran* made him experience double vision, seeing the burning room out of his father's eyes, and just as his father knew then, realizing suddenly that there was no escape, that this was one false move that couldn't be corrected.

His father's last thoughts, peculiarly he remembered, were: *Erlend! How odd that he would leave me here now.* . . . And was there an old tinge of mistrust also?

But Erlend had not left him. A sudden mindless fury in his blood, he rushed forth into the flames (seeing himself through *Dom* Valentine's eyes, emerging as though out of a radiant sea), and then, in a life-death embrace, took hold of his father. . . .

Whatever happened during those instants of horrible eternity of light and flames, he did not know. Something had fallen on them, he recalled at one point, something pinned his father, and himself, by the right leg. . . . He pulled, feeling himself (or was it *Dom* Valentine?) begin to burn, an agony almost holy, so acute was it. But then it was his body, its life instinct, that had gotten the best of him, and screaming in madness and pain he let go, and having freed his leg, then plunged forward and *out,* while his leg burned, and his mind—also burning—cried for him to stay behind and die. . . .

Danila, having pinned him down, was slapping him hard across the face, meanwhile calling his name. All around, a small crowd had gathered, and Janisse and Bethan were leaning over him. Janisse was sobbing, dripping great dirt-stained tears, while Bethan's eyes had a spark of horror in them.

But it was to the pale colorless albino eyes, that Erlend turned now, the only calm and gentle ones, as if she did not remember, or care to remember what had taken place earlier that day.

"At last, *chiyu,* you are yourself . . ." she muttered, with an odd look of something undefinable in her eyes, as though forgetting herself, and then took

him close to her, in one somewhat rough, almost uncomfortable hug. Her leather-clad body was warm and
strong in the instant that they touched, and he thought
he could catch traces of thoughts, and the smell of
smoke and raw leather. . . .

She released him and then stood back. A thin, once
again neutral but cheerful smile played about the corners of her lips, and the pale eyes were clear. He
watched those eyes for a long time, while Janisse came
to take him into a loudly weeping familiar embrace,
and Bethan helped him rise.

"I am only a damned useless cripple." His parched
lips barely mouthed the words. And still he watched,
his mind in a half-daze, supported by Bethan and
limping away from the fire-line, while folk went back
to work, and she did also.

Later that evening, when the fire was reasonably
contained, Janisse sat around a safe and small cook-
fire, and watched her brother talk himself hoarse,
spilling months of repressed emotion before an almost
uncomfortable audience of herself, Bethan, and Arlin.
A few feet away Danila and Ysabet were downing their
soup and porridge. They were once again a part of the
company, Danila herself having reassured Janisse that
most was forgiven and oddly enough, forgotten, and
she and her Guild-sister would once more consider
themselves in their employ.

"I had forgotten," Danila had said when Erlend was
too far to hear, "forgotten what I am, and what *he,*
your brother, is. And how insignificant and mean of
me was it to take a sick youth's words to heart, when
I should have known what he felt, what he *knew.*"

"I'm not sure I—understand." said Janisse quietly.

Danila shrugged. "Ei! There's nothing to understand." And she turned back to sip her bark-tea.

"You are—" suddenly ventured Janisse, "so ex-
traordinarily sensitive. To me and to Erlend, to all of
us. You did not hold a grudge, when you had every
right to do so."

"You, all of you Comyn," said Ysabet, sitting next

to Danila, "we don't usually talk so openly with the
likes of you. But Danila here—she's the odd one, even
among us. She *knows* what anyone needs, when
anyone's hurting. And she never grudges. Anyone. She
can talk to the Hastur himself, if need be, and pry into
his very soul, without offense. Only—that thing your
brother had said earlier, that had really touched her in
an ill way."

"What way?" asked Janisse. "Mestra, again, I still
don't quite understand."

"Maybe sometime she'll tell you. She's—"

"Ysabet." Danila's voice came in warning, silencing the other. She turned to Janisse then and said,
simply, truthfully: "The past is past, *damisela.* Never
dwell on it. But one of the things, if you must know,
is that I, too, knew the pain that your brother had
known, and with it, the self-humiliation, the sense of
oneself being a useless cripple."

As she was speaking, she began unlacing the tall
leather boot on her right leg, deftly moving with her
fingers, while Janisse watched, under the flickering
light of the fire. Underneath the leather and a thin covering of sock, Janisse saw the leg end, just an inch
below the knee, in a stump. The rest—a cleverly made
wooden device, made to the rough shape of a human
calf and foot, old and polished from much wear against
the leather of the boot.

Janisse stared, in slowly growing shock. It was almost as if, together with the unrolled sock, old
thought-memories came flickering in the albino eyes,
and Janisse could just barely catch them, touch them,
as they flickered by.

The sock and boot were replaced, and then, in a
neutral wooden voice, Danila spoke curtly: "I lost this
leg of mine in a fire, together with the life of my
daughter, whom I—couldn't—save."

And then, with equal curtness, she was silent. She
sipped her bark-tea.

"Gods, *mestra,* I think my brother should know of
this indeed!" exclaimed Janisse. "He should see how

undeservingly he had wronged you, when you yourself—''

"Erlend knows already," said Danila. "He had
known for a long time, and it drove him insane because I was so much like him, and yet so—*unlike* . . .''

*And only later, when he read it again in my eyes,
after the confrontation with this fire in which he did
not quite succeed to punish himself, later did he really
know me and understand. And it no longer hurt him,
to compare. . . .*

"Who *are* you?" whispered Janisse, "Who are you
really, *mestra*? You are Comyn, too, I know it! You
have *laran*, otherwise—''

In reply, Danila's eyes clouded over, she got up
abruptly, and walked several feet away.

"No, *damisela!* Forget the past! Otherwise, there's
no life for any of us. I am only my mother's daughter,
Danila n'ha Liraya."

Janisse suddenly stared. "You mean, daughter of
Liraya di Asturien? And of *Dom*—''

But the flashing eyes caught her, held her by the
sheer force of their pale depths.

"I think it's time we get ourselves to bed, all of us,
now," said Danila through gritted teeth. But then, her
mouth relaxed. "It is still some while until we get to
Arilinn, and although your Erlend is probably no longer in dire need of Tower help, he should still be
checked. An early night's sleep would do us all good."
And then she began to unpack her bedroll.

Nearby, Janisse, still under the strong impression of
her thoughts, watched the flames, and thought. She
thought of Lerrys, and her feelings, and of Erlend, and
his release, and of their father, burning—eons ago, it
seemed—in the flames. . . .

And she thought of Renunciates, and who they were,
of the strange *Terranan,* and of faraway stars, and of
women and men having two *donas,* and . . .

The small fire was put out, and Janisse suddenly
remembered how, back at Neskaya, when the circle
was done with the day's work, how they would all go
down next to the warm fireplace and . . . Lerrys Ail-

lard's warm impersonal eyes on her—they were impersonal, weren't they, really? And did it really matter, now? And maybe, just maybe if she were to go back there *now,* and look him truly, deeply in the eyes, she—

In the twilight, came Danila's clear, living voice:

I was a seafarer in Valeron
With only a river to float my boat on . . .

And in the darkness, thus she sang.

A Proper Escort

by Elisabeth Waters

I found, when I began doing these Darkover anthologies, that more than half of the stories I received fell into the category of what I came to call Subject A: A woman (all too frequently a Free Amazon) giving up her freedom for the sake of a man she can love and trust. Of the stories that didn't fall into that category, half the remainder seemed to be Subject B: Dyan Ardais finding a woman he could love and trust. After a few years of this, my secretary Lisa started threatening to write what she dubbed "Subject AB: Free Amazon meets Dyan Ardais." This year she finally did it; and before everyone starts screaming, I should comment that this is the earliest chronological appearance of Dyan Ardais in the out-takes, presenting him as a child of ten.

Dyan has been so consistent a figure in these out-takes—chronicling his "unofficial" adventures—that I have begun a novel about him, presenting him as a major character, where now he appears only as a minor one in HERITAGE OF HASTUR and SHARRA'S EXILE, and a walk-on in THE BLOODY SUN. The background of the novel will probably deal with the events of the rebellion where Rafael Hastur was killed; it's still nebulous, though I've given it a tentative title of CONTRABAND.

But I still have two other Darkover novels to finish first: REDISCOVERY, whose main characters are Elizabeth Lorne and a very young Leonie Hastur; and the third of the Regis Hastur books, tentatively titled RETURN TO DARKOVER. Both of these now exist in incomplete form in my files—but need some work.

Elisabeth now has her own place as a novelist; she has written a novel, currently titled CHANGING FATE, whose heroine made her debut in SWORD AND SORCERESS III in the story "A Woman's Privilege." The novel won the 1989 Gryphon Award given by Andre Norton, and DAW will be publishing it— probably in about two years; Lisa wants to rewrite it first. She wouldn't be the first author to graduate from these anthologies to her own work; Mercedes Lackey, Diana Paxson, and Jennifer Roberson have all done so. (Then what'll I do for a secretary?) But I still encourage Lisa to do her own work; what will I read when I'm ninety—and Lisa a mere infant of seventy?

Linnea n'ha Marilla sat quietly in the gatehouse at Nevarsin under the disapproving eye of the porter. She wondered whether it was Renunciates the monk disliked or simply women in general. The sun had shifted noticeably to the west during the time she had been sitting there, and she hoped that the Abbot had by now at least received the message she had carried in such haste from Ardais. Lady Rohana of Ardais had sent Linnea to fetch her grandson, Dyan Ardais, home from his studies at Nevarsin so that she could bid him farewell before she died—an event which was expected to occur within the tenday. Linnea had been three days on the road from Ardais—although "road" was a rather generous description of the route she had taken, and she wanted to collect the boy quickly and start the journey back before dark and the threatening snowstorm arrived.

Sandaled footsteps scraped along the stone pathway, and a stooped white-haired monk entered. "You are *Domna* Rohana's messenger, *mestra?*" he asked politely. Linnea nodded, and he continued. "I am Brother Harrel, the guest-master. Please forgive me for not having come to welcome you sooner, I only

just learned you were here. If you will come with
me, I'll find you some supper and a bed for the
night.''

"That is most kind of you, Brother," Linnea replied, matching his polite tones. "But I am afraid that
you may not have been informed of the urgency of my
errand. Lady Rohana is failing rapidly, and Dyan and
I must leave as soon as we possibly can. I had hoped,''
she added, ''that he would be ready by now—surely
he doesn't have that much to pack.''

Brother Harrel looked distressed. "But, *mestra,* it
will be dark in less than three hours! You can't drag
a boy of his age out on the trail this late in the day—
and you may not realize that it is going to snow tonight.''

"I do indeed realize that it is going to snow tonight,
Brother," Linnea said grimly. "That is precisely why
I wish to leave immediately. "I grew up not a league
south of here, and I know the signs of a storm that
will undoubtedly block the pass for at least the next
three days. We do not have that much time to spare;
we must leave immediately.'' He looked dubious, so
she added, ''Lady Rohana's order does say to bring
Dyan with all possible speed.''

Brother Harrel looked even more unhappy. "I shall
go to Father Abbot about this," he said, hurrying away
to dump the problem of this stubborn woman in someone else's lap.

"I can't imagine what the boy's father is thinking
of,'' the porter grumbled *sotto voce,* "not to be sending a proper escort for the boy.''

Linnea ignored him, firmly suppressing her first
impulse to retort that the only thing on *Dom* Kyril's
mind was the nearest bottle of wine. She hoped that
Dyan did not resemble his father too much—if he
did, he would prove a most unpleasant traveling
companion.

Brother Harrel must have run all the way to the Abbot's office. In a surprisingly short time Linnea heard
his voice in the hall, protesting to the Abbot that journeying in this weather was madness. The two men en-

tered the gatehouse together, the Abbot holding Lady
Rohana's order in his hand, and while he looked no
happier about it than Brother Harrel, he did not seem
as disposed to dismiss it out out hand.

"Mestra," he gave her a brief courteous nod, "is
this really necessary? Can't you wait until the storm
passes?"

Linnea shook her head. She had seen Lady Rohana
herself when she received the order, and she prayed
the woman was still alive even now. Her order was
clear, and she was going to obey it. "The Lady of
Ardais has sent for Lord Dyan, and she wishes him
to travel with all possible speed. Spending three or
four days here waiting out the snowstorm that's coming does not fit my definition of 'all possible speed'—
and the longer you delay our departure, the greater
our chances of getting trapped in the pass. I'm not
asking for your blessing, Father; I have a job to do,
and I intend to do it—with your blessing, or without
it!"

"And if the Lady of Ardais has sent for me, it is
my duty to obey her summons." Linnea started; she
had not seen the boy come through the archway. By
his speech, this must be Lord Dyan Ardais, but he
bore no resemblance to the rest of his family—or
indeed, to most of the Comyn. Instead of the red hair
common to his caste, his was dark, his eyes were a
steely gray, and he was slight in stature. Linnea knew
him to be ten years old, but he appeared younger,
except for the calm graceful air of the born noble-
man.

"Dyan, my boy," the Abbot began, "we all appreciate your desire to attend your grandmother in her
illness, but you do not have to rush out into an oncom-
ing storm," he gestured to the window, which now
showed only overcast sky with barely a hint of the
sun's position, "with only a single woman to escort
you. We can provide a suitable escort of lay brothers
and guards for you as soon as the storm passes."

Dyan regarded him with a carefully expressionless
face. "Lady Rohana has been ill for months, Father

Abbot,'' he said politely. ''If she sends for me now in haste, she is dying; and I shall leave at once with her chosen escort.'' Another boy, this one with the red hair of the Comyn, appeared behind Dyan, carrying two saddlebags.

''Kennard,'' said the Abbot, ''you should be at your studies at this hour.''

''Yes, Father,'' the boy agreed meekly, handing the bags to Dyan and embracing him. ''Safe journey, *bredu.*'' Dyan returned the embrace without speaking, and Kennard left them.

The Abbot sighed. ''If, as you say, *mestra,* the storm is almost upon you, I suppose you had best leave at once. And if you are determined to go—with or without my blessing—you shall go with it.'' He rested his hand first on Dyan's head and then on Linnea's. ''May the Holy Bearer of Burdens bless and strengthen you in your journey.''

''Thank you, Father,'' Linnea said formally. Then she turned to the boy. ''If you're ready, Lord Dyan, the chervines are in the courtyard. Dyan nodded briefly, shouldered his bags, and preceded her out the door.

They mounted and rode at their best pace through the pass, but even so, the snow was thick on the ground and beginning to block the way by the time they won through.

''Do you have *laran, mestra?*'' Dyan asked abruptly as they started down other side of the pass. It was the first remark he had addressed to her, and Linnea suddenly realized that he probably didn't even know her name—in the haste of their departure, she had neglected a proper introduction.

''My name is Linnea, Lord Dyan,'' she said, ''and you may call me that if you wish. And no, I don't have *laran.* Why would you think I might?

Dyan looked faintly embarrassed; apparently he disliked being in error. ''You told Father Abbot that the pass would be blocked, and he accepted your word for it—and you were correct.''

''That's true,'' Linnea said, conscious of a seemingly irrational desire to spare the boy's feelings and help him maintain his dignity—as if this self-possessed Comyn lordling needed much help in that direction. "I can see how such foreknowledge would look like *laran*, but in truth it's the result of years of experience watching the weather patterns in this area. I grew up near here, and when the sky is a certain color and the wind smells a certain way, I can tell that a storm is coming and when it will arrive. And Father Abbot has doubtless been at Nevarsin long enough to recognize at least some of the signs himself, so he didn't have to take my word entirely on faith."

Dyan smiled faintly. "And, besides," he said, "if you have *laran* you wouldn't have to be a Renunciate; you could have gone into a Tower instead."

"To give me equal protection from the men in my life, you mean?" Linnea inquired ironically.

"You shouldn't need protection from the men in your life," Dyan said primly. "They are supposed to protect you."

It would be cruel indeed, Linnea decided, to mention Dyan's father in this context, but she was developing a lively interest in how Dyan's mind worked. And since they would be spending several days on the trail together, it would help to know how far she could trust him. So she confined her response to a simple "Why?"

"Because men are stronger than women."

"And you feel that it is the duty of the strong to protect the weak?"

"Of course it is," Dyan replied matter-of-factly. "Why have strength if you are not going to use it?"

"Some people seem to feel that strength should be used simply to get them what they want," Linnea remarked.

"No." Dyan shook his head definitely. "I'm not a *cristoforo*, but I have noticed that strength and burdens go together. And if you waste your strength on selfish gratification instead of doing the tasks your station in life lays upon you, then you become an object of pity at best, if not of contempt."

Presumably, Linnea thought, *he's thinking of his father, but he could just as well be describing mine. Well, at least he doesn't appear to share his father's tastes and weaknesses, and he isn't complaining about the trail or the pace we're setting. Still, I think it's about time to call a halt for the night.*

They made good time the next day and a half, and their journey was uneventful until they reached the bridge over the chasm that lay a half-league from Castle Ardais. But their luck ended there; the bridge was out, apparently collapsed under too much weight.

Linnea bit back a curse, not that she thought Dyan didn't know the phrase, but she had scruples about corrupting the young and supposedly innocent.

Dyan scowled at the chasm. "This wretched bridge falls about twice a year," he grumbled, "but did it have to be now?!"

He sat silently on his chervine for several long minutes, chewing on his lower lip and looking pale. Then he sighed. "*Mestra,*" he said slowly, "are you afraid of heights?"

Linnea, about to return a flip answer about the impossibility of living in the mountains and fearing heights, took a second look at his face. Heights didn't bother her much, but she strongly suspected that the same could not be said of her companion.

"I can handle them when I have to," she replied. "Why? Do you know another way across?"

"There's an old fallen tree trunk up that way a bit." Dyan gestured off to their right. "The tenants' children walk it on dares." From his tone of voice, it didn't appear to be a sport he participated in willingly.

"Well, we may as well go take a look at it," Linnea said. "There's no guarantee it's even still in place, but if it is, it could save us several hours—the next bridge over the chasm is at least two leagues downhill, isn't it?"

"Yes," Dyan said, turning his chervine and heading uphill. "And if we can get across the log, we come out right behind the castle. It's no particular military risk; it will barely hold an adult, and certainly not an armored man." He looked appraisingly at her. "It's a good thing you're small. We'll have to leave the chervines and packs on this side. If we get across, we can send the servants back for them."

They reached the log, and Linnea eyed it dubiously. It was about a foot in diameter and looked fairly sturdy, but its top was covered with snow, and there could easily be rot hidden under it. She considered roping Dyan and herself together and decided against it—too much chance of her dragging him down if the tree broke under her. She must outweigh him by a good thirty pounds.

"You'd best go first, Lord Dyan," she said. "You're lighter and have a better chance of making it— although I trust," she added, forcing a smile, "that if I fall, you will send out a search party after me."

Dyan's answering smile was even more forced than hers, and his skin had a distinctly greenish tinge to it.

"Remember," Linnea said bracingly, "we are not children playing 'I dare you.' Style and grace don't count; the object is to get across in one piece. I intend to straddle the trunk and crawl across—it may look silly, but I'm much less apt to get blown off or lose my balance that way."

Dyan considered that approach and his color returned to normal. "We'll get wet, of course," he said, "but it's only a few minutes' walk to the castle and dry clothes." He tied the ends of his cloak around his waist, straddled the trunk, and shimmied across, dislodging a good deal of snow in the process.

"It seems solid enough," he called back from the other side. "Come ahead."

Linnea hiked her tunic a bit higher through her belt and started along the trunk. Halfway across however, her tunic slipped and caught on something just behind her right hip, snagging her firmly into place. She twisted to try to free herself, and almost overbalanced into the chasm.

"What's wrong?" Dyan called from the bank.

"My wretched tunic appears to be caught," Linnea said, trying to sound calm. "Why don't you go ahead to the castle and send somebody back to free me."

"Somebody like a big, heavy adult?" Dyan asked skeptically. He took a deep breath and with a resolute expression on his face started crawling back across the log to her. In a moment he was practically in her lap. "Lock your ankles around the tree, brace yourself, and hold my waist," he ordered. "If you can hang onto me, I think I can reach back to where your tunic is snagged."

Linnea locked her legs tightly around the tree and clung to Dyan's wriggling body for dear life—both his and hers, if anything happened to him. After several uncomfortable moments, there was a sound of ripping cloth and she was free. Dyan inched backward to a stable position and said carefully, "I think you can let go of me now."

Linnea cautiously loosened her grip, and Dyan pulled slowly free and wriggled backward to the other side of the chasm. As soon as he was across, Linnea followed slowly, being very careful not to get her clothing snagged again.

Once on solid ground again, Linnea dusted the snow off herself and checked the damage to the tunic. Fortunately, it was just a rip in the hem. "It's a good thing I wasn't wearing long skirts," she laughed nervously.

Dyan started to giggle. "And it's a good thing that I didn't have 'a proper escort'—can't you just see them trying to shimmy across that tree while holding their banners at the proper angle?"

Both of them burst out laughing at the picture that called to mind.

"Come along," Linnea said, as soon as she could speak again. "We'd better get indoors and into some dry clothes, and we need to send someone for the chervines."

"Follow me," Dyan said, "the path is this way." After a few steps he turned and looked back at her.

"Linnea? When I return to Nevarsin, will you escort me?"

"With pleasure, Lord Dyan," Linnea replied. "You're a good company on the trail."

Lesson in the Foothills

by Lynne Armstrong-Jones

Lynne Armstrong-Jones proves, in her own person, what I always say about writing: that it's 10% inspiration and about 90% perspiration and persistence; that sometimes you simply have to wear the editors down; bombard them with stories till they get tired of sending you rejection slips. When I started the magazine—Marion Zimmer Bradley's Fantasy Magazine—for a while every mail brought me a story from Ms. Armstrong-Jones—or so it seemed; and I predictably got sick and tired of rejecting them. Fortunately, after a while, I didn't have to.

Lynne lives in London (Ontario, Canada, not England), and is "pleasantly non-employed; pleasantly because finances haven't yet reached the danger zone" and she has time to write. Well, that's sometimes what it takes.

She has appeared in Marion Zimmer Bradley's Fantasy Magazine, SWORD AND SORCERESS VI and VII, and in DOMAINS OF DARKOVER. She has also sold to WEIRD TALES and to various fan publications. She is "the mother of a four-year-old son whose imagination and ability to fantasize seem intact." Like mother, like son, we'd say.

Ostensibly, Jenna was looking downward at her facts and figures, checking over the month's income and expenditures. In reality, however, her eyes had strayed once more to the sight of Kali, Dorel, and Gwynnis as they prepared to head into the mountains.

Another mission.

How exciting it must be to work as mercenaries, mountain guides, and the like!

But Jenna sighed, returning her attention to her work. After all, she, too, had a very important function to perform here within the Guild House. They all did, for that matter. Imagine what life would be like without Saris' delicious baking!

And inside, Jenna knew well that they depended on her precise and detailed bookwork in order to ensure that no debts were accumulated. Yet still sometimes she wondered what it would be like . . .

She chuckled, admonishing herself. Why even dream about it? A tiny thing like herself, who looked more like a young boy than a woman! The Renunciates who did the "physical" things were long and tall. And very strong.

I should be happy with my lot, Jenna decided.

Her usual frown of concentration returned to crease her forehead as her thoughts once again focused on her work. She had not been at it for all that long, though, before she was interrupted by a knocking at the door. Her frown deepened as she struggled to concentrate, wondering why Saris had not yet responded to the summons. Suddenly, she recalled that Saris had ventured out for more supplies.

With a sigh, Jenna pushed her chair back from the table, running a hand through her short, dark hair, and headed to the front door.

"Yes?"

She'd seen the woman in town but didn't know her by name. She looked to be one of those whose family businesses were successful, judging by the fine silky material of her gown. And she was obviously distraught.

"Oh, please," the woman sputtered, blue eyes brimming with tears, "you must help me! It—it's my daughter, Innana. She's wandered off! Someone said they saw her climbing in the foothills! You people know the area—you've got to find her for me! There are bound to be banshees nesting up there now! Please, please!"

No matter how Jenna tried to explain that she was *not* one of the guides, the poor woman continued to beg and sob.

What can I do? thought Jenna, the frown once again leaving creases between her brown eyes. *I can simply tell this poor woman that the guides have gone, and close the door in her face—or I can try.*

She sighed, feeling the shiver of fear crawl up her spine. But she prepared the little pony, ensuring that bandages, water, and rope were packed. She felt for the knife one more time, just to make sure that it was securely tucked into her belt.

She mounted the little creature and looked down at the mother. "I shall do what I can," was all she could say.

It was spring—but still there seemed to be a hint of winter chill in the air. There were mists in the foothills of the great mountains. From somewhere came the terrible cry of a banshee and Jenna found herself shivering again—but not from the cool temperatures.

She tethered the pony in a sheltered area and, after securing the rope to her belt, prepared to take a look around. From up here she'd be able to see much of the surrounding countryside, as well as the depths of the ravine.

Whatever shall I do if I find the poor child dead at the bottom of the gorge, she wondered—then admonished herself. She must *think,* not worry!

She saw a rocky outcropping and prepared to step onto it, searching for a suitable vantage point. But she stopped, gasping in horror—

A banshee nest! Just past the rise in the outcropping. She couldn't see it from here, but she'd caught the sound of the horrible creature as she murmured to her chicks. Even at the level of a murmur, the banshee had sounded awful!

Jenna backed slowly away and onto the cliff once more, thanking the Goddess for giving her good hearing. She'd try another spot—and hope she didn't find another one of the things there, too!

Carefully and quietly, the young woman stepped toward the edge of another area of the gorge—and nearly fell over the edge at the sound.

No, not a banshee this time, but something just as fearsome.

A *catman!* She'd heard that snarl before. Quickly she turned, knife in her hand.

What good will this little weapon do me against a monster that size! she thought in despair.

The thing hovered at the edge of the wooded area, its fangs catching the sunlight as it eyed her. It was a huge, fearsome thing, with whiskers that bristled as it growled once more.

"I'm no match for *you*," whispered the small woman, her heart pounding hard inside her narrow chest. *Zandru's hells! Why am I not big and strong like my sisters? But no,* she decided. *I do have one thing. I've always been told I have a good mind. It's all I've got. I'd better start using it!*

The vicious creature still eyed her, growling quietly, seeming to wait for her reaction.

Jenna turned, stepping away from the ravine's edge. She moved until her back faced the direction from which she'd originally come. And she continued to back up. . . .

The cat-creature stepped after her, picking up speed as did the woman. Finally, Jenna turned and began to run, praying that her timing was not faulty. With the cat in hot pursuit, she raced along the outcropping, to the rise, and quickly dropped to her knees and eased herself over the edge, clinging to the rocky side of the narrow thing.

Right behind her but unable to stop came the cat. Jenna was grateful she couldn't see it from this vantage point. Hearing it was enough, as the cat was surprised by a huge, gaping beak, just over the rise of the outcropping—

The sounds were awful as the mother banshee screamed in delight, proceeding to rip the cat to shreds and offering morsels to her hungry offspring.

Jenna was enormously thankful for the distraction,

though, as she heaved herself back on top of the out-cropping. Even though she knew the banshee was well-occupied, the sound and stench of the bloody meal were incentive enough to have her crawling slowly, carefully, quietly, back to better ground. It was just as she reached the edge that she saw something else.

The girl! There she was, just down and to the left of the outcropping, trembling on the little ledge.

She's lucky she's there, thought Jenna; *there's been no breeze coming from behind her to tell the banshee of her presence.*

She put a loop in the rope and dropped it down to the child, who secured it around herself as Jenna instructed—all the while glancing back at the still-munching banshee family, just in case. Finally the child was close enough that Jenna could ease her, too, onto the top of the outcropping. Together they crawled onto the edge of the ravine—

And, together, they raced down the hill as quickly as they could and onto the little pony's back.

Jenna counted the many-colored coins once more, still not quite believing the total amount. So absorbed was she in entering the total—*her* total—into the book of accounts, that she did not hear the arrival of Kali.

She looked up at the sound of Kali's voice. But this time she was not admiring the long, muscular build of the brown-haired woman.

"So . . . what did you do today that was exciting, little Jenna?" Kali was asking with a grin.

"Not much," came the customary reply as Jenna returned to her bookwork.

But this time, though she was concentrating, a small but satisfied smile had replaced the usual frown.

Summer Fair

by Emily Alward

Emily Alward was born and grew up in West Lafayette, Indiana—"the home of Purdue University" and says "possibly the science and technology ambience there affected me at an early age, because I have liked science fiction for as long as I can remember."

She says of herself that she has two daughters and two young grandsons, both of whom say "to my delight . . . that their favorite stories are those with 'wizards and dragons and magic swords.' "

(I guess I'll have to finish that story about the last dragon on Darkover one of these years).

She has sold one previous story with a science fiction setting; and has had many printed in various fan publications. Like Maura in her story, she makes stuffed animals to sell at science fiction conventions and craft fairs. And, like most writers, she has held down a series of outright weird jobs: "typist, proofreader, nanny" etc., and is currently working as a librarian. That's just par for the course.

Sunlight warmed the cobblestones of the Trade City that summer day, but worry chilled my heart.

Since the disastrous year of the World Wreckers, nothing had gone well. The fleecy woven capes and droll hand-sewn animals which earned me a fair living in better days no longer sold. Even the *Hali'imyn* were too overextended repairing fields and forests to spare money for luxury goods. I still kept my cozy little cottage, but only the Goddess knew how the rent could be paid next month. I thought of the herb

pots on its windowsills with a foreboding sense of
loss. My dogs could not go with me if I had to move
back into the Guild House. My sisters might allow
one dog the run of the kitchen-yard, but certainly
not all three. How could I ever choose which of them
to abandon?

Another dread, even stronger, bore down on me that
summer afternoon.

*Child of my heart, daughter of my body, how can I
save you without the money—?*

People had told me the Terrans would buy my goods;
they were always looking for handmade "souvenirs"
to show how many worlds they'd seen. So I paid a
hefty fee and came to this trade fair, which had been
organized to promote native crafts. The Terranan liked
my goods, all right. A steady stream of people had
walked past, complimented me on their quality, and
then strolled on. Admiration is enjoyable, but it doesn't
pay the rent.

Two gawky adolescents came up and staged a mock
battle with four of my delicate rainbirds. I bit my
tongue and kept a pleasant countenance. It never pays
to scold a potential customer. They walked off and I
struggled to hold down panic. The day was ebbing,
without a single sale so far.

"I see you like to make beautiful things," a new
voice said.

"Yes." I looked up into eyes of forest green. The
speaker was a woman, not a Terran, but with an air
of assurance that hinted lofty breeding. Her
strawberry-blonde hair cascaded down from the
butterfly-clasp into a soft exuberance of curls. The
gown she wore was the violet of a dawn-streaked
sky, and it fell about her body with infinite grace.
Though she appeared about my own age, a no-longer-
young thirty-nine, there was something about her that
shone. A frisson of envy for the soft life of a *vai
domna* went through me. I shook it off. I was a little
embarrassed that she had seen so far into my heart.
"Yes, I do."

"So do I." She smiled at me. "Do you mind if I stay here and rest a bit?"

"Of course, you're welcome to, *vai domna*." I took my box of yarns off the extra stool and motioned for her to come behind the table. She sank down with a tiny sigh which carried the echo of relief after long journeying.

"Please stay as long as you like," I added. A noblewoman she might be, and privileged, but the Oath required succor to any woman who requested it. This small amount of succor was easy to provide.

Another group of people stopped at the table. I watched them anxiously; the lady watched me. When they turned away without buying, she said, "All looking and no buying, is that the way it's been?"

"That's about it," I replied bitterly.

"I know things have been hard this year," she said. "Is it so very important that they sell?"

"Goddess, yes!" I said. It's bad form to admit your desperation, but I was beyond caring. At any rate my listener seemed an aristocrat, not a fellow craftsperson familiar with the code. Tears welled up in my eyes; I fought them back.

Still I am not clear how it happened, but suddenly I started telling her my worries. Not the little ones, about the herbs growing on the windowsill and my fear of losing the comfort of my modest home. The story of my daughter poured out. Carlinna had married well—or so folk thought. I, a woman long-ago made wary of both marriage and men's promises, had no credibility when I asked her to defer the bracelets for a while. She married a minor lording and moved far up into the Kilghard Hills, where catmen prowled and the *vai dom's* word was law. Six months of bliss she had, followed by an introduction to hell. When *Dom* Felix's soil turned poison, he started beating his wife.

Now Carlinna was pregnant, and the beatings had grown more savage. The baby had been monitored and proven to be a girl, and *Dom* Felix's rage knew no bounds.

"And can she not seek shelter somewhere? Perhaps with some of your sisters?" my visitor asked gently.

"Oh, there are no Renunciates so far up in the hills," I snapped. "No one else will take her in. They all fear the *vai dom's* wrath too much. I—" I bit my lip, fighting the guilt that clung to me. It was undeserved guilt; I knew any rescue attempt of my own was futile, but what honor has a mother who cannot protect her daughter? "I would go for her myself, but I am no match for *Dom* Felix's paxmen. Besides, she cannot travel so far by horseback. She is very near her time. Her whole pregnancy has been precarious. She could not ride the mountain trails far enough to get outside *Dom* Felix's lands."

"I see." The woman gazed across the crowded square. She wore serenity like a veil. She seemed a woman who could solve any problem she might meet. My own powerlessness shamed me. I felt impelled to show her I was trying.

"There is one chance. The Terrans have a camp not far away. They poke metal instruments around in the ground there. They go back and forth in machines that are like huge flapping birds. That's how Carlinna sends me messages, with them. The Terrans are willing to bring her out in one of those birds, if—if I can pay a fee for her passage. I have tried to borrow it, but no one with funds to spare will trust a woman whose livelihood is so uncertain. I have even thought of stealing it—I shuddered; such thoughts always ended with me caught and dragged before the magistrate, having betrayed the honor of the *Comhi-Letzii*. "So I need very much to sell my goods . . . to save my daughter."

"Strange people, those Terrans, who make a pregnant woman's safety depend on money," the lady mused.

"Well, at any rate they are willing to help, *Dom* Felix or no. The man said they had a noninterference rule about local customs, but if a passenger paid they assumed she came as a free agent." I was surprised to hear myself defending the *Terranan*. My life had

brought little contact with them, but those who carried
Carlinna's messages did not act so full of themselves
as the men I commonly meet. When I went to their
project-leader's office this morning, he said Carlinna
could fly out—what a strange idea!—tomorrow if I paid
for her passage tonight. I was so near to rescuing my
daughter—

"Ummm." The *vai domna* seemed abstracted. Had
she even heard me? "What is your name, *mestra*?"

"I am Maura n'ha Caillean."

She did not give me back *her* name. She leaned
over, her shining hair brushing the tabletop, and
reached for a woolen cape. I watched her silently
stroking it. Her fingers seemed to draw into the cape
the very essence of the colors and the warm sheep's
fleece. All the bright hues of Evanda's springtime pal-
ette began to glow in the design I had woven in. I
could almost feel a little lamb's playfulness and joy
spreading out from the fabric.

Then she picked up a fuzzy, dusty-brown stag-pony
doll. It was appealing enough to begin with, or so I
thought. I always put much care into the making of
my animals. But in her hands it changed from a mere
toy to—something else. The shy pony's eyes sparkled
with love; trust and steadiness radiated from its body.
The lady turned her attention to a little rabbit-horn.
She cuddled it against her cheek, and all at once I read
the creature's watchful impulses and the gentle soul
beneath its downy fur.

She handled item after item. Each one seemed to
blossom into a new level of perfection when she
touched it.

Or was I just imagining things because of my own
tension? After hovering over my merchandise all day
in so much desperation I could no longer clear my
thoughts. The lady was standing back now, looking
at the table with an appraising gaze. I wondered if
she had just been searching for something to buy.
I did not want that, not if she purchased out of
pity.

"How much is this?"

A boy was holding up a large, comical-looking chervine-doll, one of my most expensive creatures. I told him the price. The boy dropped coppers into my hand and darted away with his purchase.

"You see? It isn't hopeless." The *vai domna* smiled at me.

"Yes," I said, heartened but not optimistic. Twenty sales like that one could pay for Carlinna's passage. Barely. There was hardly enough time left to hope for twenty sales of any size.

A couple in Terran uniforms stopped, and began unfolding the capes. The woman flung one over her shoulders.

"It looks beautiful on you, Margot," the man said.

"It *feels* beautiful on me. It makes me feel—mmm, warm, sheltered. Like the horrible winters here would never bother me," the Terran woman murmured.

Her companion pulled out a leather folder and plunked down a large denomination Empire credit slip. I looked at it, hastened to count out change, but they were already gone.

I started to turn to the *vai domna* with an exclamation of triumph on my lips. Another customer interrupted.

"This is the most adorable stuffed animal I've ever seen in my life," the girl said. Her rosy cheeks and open manner recalled my own Carlinna. She hugged the bear. "It wants me to take it home, I can tell. Oh, I have to have it!" Another sale.

"Something is happening!" I whispered to my visitor when the tablefront cleared of people for a minute. "Did you make it happen?"

"Me? How could I?" Her green eyes lightened and danced with amusement. "Perhaps I bring luck, *Mestra* Maura. One of my lovers said I did. But now, I will go and look at the rest of the fair. Many thanks for your kindness."

I bid her good-bye but had no time to wonder at my change in luck. Customers kept stopping at my table. They cuddled my animals, clucked at them, bought them and bore them away, saying the little creatures had captured their hearts. Other people snatched up the capes and cloaks, declaring them the warmest and most beautiful garments they'd ever found. I sold steadily. The next two hours were a craftswoman's dream.

Only when the square emptied at a day's end did I catch my breath. A mere two items remained unsold. In twenty years of selling my handwork, I had never had a better day. And never needed it more desperately.

Could the mysterious lady have used some form of *laran* to enhance my animals and capes? The more I pondered, the more implausible it seemed. A comynara might be kind, but she was not going to work her sorcery for some poor Renunciate craftswoman's benefit. And if—as I was beginning to suspect from her unusual habits and demeanor—she were *not* of the Comyn? I knew of no one else in *this* world who had such powers.

No, I had just been incredibly lucky. Perhaps my plight had reached the Goddess' notice, and she decided, tardily, to give me a good day. It didn't matter how it happened. Copper coins and credit slips spilled out when I opened the cash box. I had enough money to save Carlinna, to pay my rent and food for many tendays; even enough to buy a treat to take home to my dogs—

I grabbed up the money and ran to find the project-leader before the gate to the Terran Zone swung closed.

She was waiting by my table when I returned to pack up. Happiness still bubbled in my veins.

"I've had such a good day!" I burst out.

"I'm glad, *chiya*," she said.

"Oh, and— You're tired, aren't you? Do you have any place to stay tonight?" It seemed impossible that such a grand lady would not have a town house in Thendara to go to, but that appeared to be the case. Else why would she return to my table when she had met me only this very day?

I offered the hospitality of my home; it was not a

hard thing to do for another woman. My only hesitation was that she would not find it fine enough. We started toward my house. She borrowed my sole remaining cape, and carried the folding table while I brought the stools. The nightly frozen rain was falling; we picked our way carefully along the slickened streets.

When I unlocked the door, Callie jumped up joyfully to greet me. Callie's soul brims with love, but her fur usually hides burrs and her huge paws can knock a person back a few paces. As Callie jumped at my visitor, I called her down.

The *vai domna* protested. "Please don't. I like beautiful real animals, too." She scratched the dog's ears, and Callie stretched in contentment. The little dogs pranced around the lady's feet like excited gnats. Before the borrowed cloak could be shrugged off, she was down on the floor playing with all three.

Well, I have never spent enough time around noble ladies to know how they behave at home. I decided if she was happy romping with my dogs, why should I worry? A woman who cares for animals is generally a woman who can be trusted with human matters, too.

We shared cheese and nut-bread and herb tea. The logs had to be poked and nudged till they caught fire. After the fire burst into cheerful celebration, we settled down at hearthside. My visitor seemed satisfied to relax, asking no more questions of me. *We're secure in sisterhood,* I thought, *whatever her elevated status in the rest of life.* She told a joke—a very funny joke— about Durraman's donkey, and soon we were giggling like little girls, thinking up ridiculous variations on the beast's dilemma.

Finally the hour grew late, and I went off to make up my bed for her. The cot on the back porch would do well enough for me for the night; I certainly could not ask such a gracious woman to sleep in half-freezing quarters.

She was standing at hearthside when I came back out. Her hair gleamed in the fire's reflection—not like burnished copper, not the strawberry-gold hue I had seen in it earlier. It was the very color of luscious apricots from the orchards of Valeron in my girlhood. The little eye's-edge wrinkles that trail womanhood were clear on her shadowed face, and she looked very tired. But those eyes held the secrets of forest glades in their emerald depths.

"Breda," she said, and held out her arms.

I fell into them. Her skin had the scent of the little valley-bells that bloom in hidden places. She cupped my breast in her hand, and I kissed her.

We went in to my bed together.

I snuggled closer, not wanting to leave the comfort of her arms. It didn't work. The red sun was halfway up the sky, and Callie, who'd sneaked in sometime during the night, was stirring at the foot of the bed. I sighed, and got up to heat water for tea.

The lady did not come out to join me for a long time. When she appeared, she carried two blossoms from the sheltered garden outside my front door.

"Flowers for a sister of my heart," she said.

I had forgotten that today was Midsummer's eve. "Thank you," I said, embarrassed again for not thinking of this touch myself. I poured the tea, and we sipped it in silence. She picked up her travel-pack.

"Breda, I would be glad for you to stay with me. As long as you like," I told her.

"I would like to stay, but I cannot."

"Well—" I fumbled around, the pain of parting so soon stabbing me with quiet grief. "Let me wish you good journey, then. And thank you again for every-thing—for your help with the stuffed animals, too. You *did* do something to them, didn't you?"

She laughed. "I could have done more, but—" She glanced fondly at Callie and the smaller dogs, waiting patiently for tidbits from the table "—I doubt you need any additions to your menagerie."

* * *

Long after she'd left, long after my granddaughter's baby smiles began to fill my life with another kind of joy, the faint fragrance of Evanda's flowers still lingered in the little house.

Varzil's Avengers

by Diann S. Partridge

Another of the characters who turns up fairly regularly in the stories I get is Varzil, a legendary Keeper of the Ages of Chaos who has been mentioned many times in the Darkover books but who appears, I believe, only a few times in the series: in TWO TO CONQUER and THE FORBIDDEN TOWER.

I'm always happy to learn something I didn't know about my characters. Diann Partridge is no newcomer to Darkover stories, having appeared in my original fanzine of Darkover stories (now long out of print), and being a winner in at least one of my contests. For those of you who have followed Darkover from the beginning, I should mention that she is the writer who was published in various fan publications as Patricia Partridge. On the cover of this story I scribbled a little note—it was one of the first stories I got—to the effect that "the idea of a Renunciate with laran was basically untenable," but the story was good enough that I meant to use it anyway. That was before I knew (or guessed) how popular the "Renunciates with laran" idea would prove to be with the better writers this time.

Ms. Partridge lives in Wyoming and has three children, two of whom are now teenagers. My sympathies.

Aislinn Aillard limped up the Guild House stairs, hanging on to the banister and swinging her stiff leg up to the next step while giving a hop with her right. *Avarra,* she swore to herself, *it's hell to get old.*

As if in answer, there was a dull rumble and the

whole building shook. Aislinn stumbled near the top step. She grabbed the railing with both hands, twisting around to sit down. Just in time, for the next jolt felt as if Avarra herself had grabbed the house with both hands to give it a hard shake. There were screams and shouts accompanied by the sounds of crockery breaking. Outside in the street someone yelled FIRE! Then the high ding ding ding of the fire bell took over.

Suddenly hands were grasping her under the arms, helping to pull her up the last step and across the landing. She scooted backward until she was under a doorway. Her rescuer and cousin, Lucie Valeron, crouched beside her. Again the ground trembled and everything shook.

"Almost like the old days, huh, *cara*," whispered Lucie, wrapping both arms around Aislinn. Aislinn made a rude noise and swung her stiff leg to a more comfortable position.

They waited. When her galloping heartbeat returned to normal and there were no more quakes, Aislinn pushed herself to her feet. Now the other Renunciates were calling to each other, taking stock of the damage.

Aislinn scooped up the tunic Lucie had dropped. The tiny metal sliver she used for a needle was tucked neatly into the hem. Her latest creation was a series of exquisite little horses cavorting across the yoke. She handed it back and Lucie tucked it under her belt.

Amidst all the confusion, someone yelled at them from the bottom of the steps.

"Lucie, there's someone to see you. He's waiting outside."

Aislinn looked at her cousin. "It has to be Fergus. No one else would arrive in the middle of an earthquake."

Lucie offered a shoulder to help Aislinn down the stairs, but she shrugged her away. "Go ahead. Don't wait for me."

Lucie moved unerringly to the banister and started down. Aislinn bit her lip, watching the embroidered strip that was tied around Lucie's neat gray braids to hide the ragged holes that had been her eyes. Over the

years, Lucie had taught herself to use her *laran* to
compensate for her lost sight.

She hopped back down the steps as quickly as possible, clinging to the rail. The young Renunciate who
had called them was still standing at the door. She
looked on curiously as Lucie walked out and turned
her head toward the man who waited in the street.

He came up the four steps in a rush and threw his
arms around her. Their embrace was much more than
just that of kinsmen. The girl backed up a step, feeling
as if she had intruded on something extremely private.
Aislinn pushed past her and was swept into a similar
hug.

The girl turned away, shaking her head. "You would
think," she muttered to herself, "that he is the blind
one. He acts as if he can't see how old and scarred
those two are."

There was nothing the two women could do to help
clean up. The quakes had been occurring regularly
over the past few tendays, so by now there was a routine to the recovery. The fire alarm had not been serious. A street vendor selling hot pasties had panicked
when his grill spilled out onto the floor of his cart.

As they rode toward Thendara Castle, Aislinn surveyed the damage to the houses and shops. The closer
they came to the castle the easier it was to see the eerie
blue glow that encircled the North Tower. The glow
seemed to throb along with her heart. Lucie reached
out and touched her hand, breaking her fascinated
stare.

It was bitterly cold here in the streets and she pulled
her fur-lined cloak tighter about her shoulders. Lucie
sat in front of Fergus on his horse and his patched
leather cloak covered them both. The same menace
that was causing the quakes was also affecting the
weather. This was supposed to be high summer in
Thendara City and they were still shoveling knee-deep
snow from the streets each morning.

A young page swallowed hard when Aislinn announced who they were and that they were to see Ca-

van Hastur. Lord Hastur stood only one step below the king. The boy's eyes darted from Aislinn's pockmarked face and cropped gray hair to Lucie's bandaged eyes back to the deep jagged scar that ran from under Fergus' eye up across the top of his bald head.

"Quick now!" Aislinn barked and the boy fled. Fergus chuckled. Lucie turned toward the fire to warm her hands, shaking her head.

"You shouldn't have scared the child like that, 'Linn. It isn't fair."

"The twit shouldn't stare. You would think he'd never seen battle scars before."

"He probably hasn't," added Fergus. "At least not on women."

Aislinn snorted in contempt and moved to stand by Lucie. She held out her hands, then quickly tucked them back under her cloak. She had been the finest ryll player in Dalereuth Tower in her youth, but you couldn't play the ryll with just five fingers on one hand. Lucie's heightened *laran* caught her cousin's memory. She put her arm around Aislinn's waist.

A young man stepped into the room and the three turned as one toward him. Aislinn felt rather than heard the gasp that Lucie concealed. He was foppishly dressed in clothing rich enough for a prince. But it wasn't the clothing that stunned them; it was all the metal he wore. His short red cape was caught at the throat with a large silver clasp etched with a hawk's head. Two rings adorned one hand, three the other. The lacing holes in his silk jerkin were metal, as was the buckle on his belt. His boots were buckled just below the knee and his spurs jingled with ugly metal rowels.

He strode into the room. "Lord Hastur has no time today for the likes of you," he announced without ceremony. "You will have to make an appointment with *my* secretary in order to see him."

Fergus was across the room in a second, his large rough hands tangling in the silk shirt as he shoved the young man back against the wall.

"I'm Fergus MacAran, you insolent young pup. And

this is the Lady Aislinn Aillard and her cousin, the Lady Lucie Valeron. Do the names mean nuthin' to ye, laddie?" he snarled, his brogue taking over in his anger. "We're here at the express command of him in yon blue tower. Now, ye go and find Cavan for us or Ah'll see if Ah can't divest ye of some of this fine metal ye're awearin'."

The young man controlled his fear, letting his anger support him. *How dare this old man lay hands on me!* Aislinn could hear his thought clearly through her link with Lucie. Automatically, she raised a protective shield around the three of them. It went up as easily now as it had when they were in the midst of battle. The young man's *laran*-shaped bolt of energy bounced harmlessly off Fergus and would have splattered back into his own mind if Lucie hadn't diverted it away from him.

He's one of the genetically-altered Altons, Lucie, Aislinn thought swiftly at her cousin. *You should have let him have a taste of his own medicine.*

Before Lucie could answer, Cavan Hastur filled the doorway. His very presence dispelled the tension and Fergus unhanded the young man and stood back.

"Ah, my friends, you are here," said Cavan easily. He spoke as though nothing were wrong. "I see you have met Falan Alton, my aide. Falan," he turned to the young man, "please bring my friends some refreshments, if you would."

The young Alton smoothed his shirt. "Yes, my lord," he answered in a tight controlled voice.

"And Falan," continued Cavan Hastur quietly, "I want you to see to it personally."

Falan's lips tightened, but he bowed to the Hastur lord and with an obvious second thought, turned and bowed toward the other three as well. Then he left the room.

"You must forgive his boorish manners, Fergus. He is new at court and very young."

"And very full of himself, Cavan," answered Fergus grimly.

"That, too. And he is the only one of old Rimal Alton's grandchildren to survive threshhold."

He moved across the room and enveloped Fergus in a tight kinsman's embrace. Lucie was next. As he put his arms around Aislinn, years of tightly shielded emotions threatened to break loose for both of them. They had been fostered together as children in the low sprawling castle at Dalereuth; had served their time in the sea-pearl Tower there, then fought side-by-side in the last days of the wars and lived to see the Compact enforced from the Valeron Plains to the Yellow Forest.

Two of their original group that had become known as Varzil's Avengers had died in the last days before the Compact. Now, their leader lay imprisoned in the North Tower. They had come together once again to try to free him.

In the hectic days following the Compact their group had disbanded. Fergus MacAran had gone north, Varzil had returned to Neskaya Tower, Cavan had taken his place beside the king, and Aislinn and Lucie had joined the newly formed Renunciate Guild. There were hundreds of homeless, clanless women drifting into the city; women who had fought men in battle and could not or would not go back to being mere chattels again. Most were scarred and hardened and too unladylike to appeal to the men of the now peaceful Seven Domains. It had been a relief on both sides when the king signed their charter.

Aislinn and Lucie had lived with the other Renunciates in Thendara until their numbers were just too many for one house. At the end of the first decade, two groups split off. One group went northeast toward Neskaya and Aislinn's group went southeast to Dalereuth. She wanted to live near the sound of the sea in her old age.

And now, fifteen years later they were back in Thendara. The cold made her leg ache. But Varzil needed their help. Aislinn thought of him as she had seen him last, blonde hair from his Ridenow mother flopping over his forehead and his dark blue Alton eyes sparkling with mischief. He had been the greatest Keeper of his time, both at Neskaya and later at Dalereuth. Together they had destroyed the giant matrix weapon screens and forced a lasting peace on the warring clans from the Kilghard Hills clear to Nevarsin.

Some remnant of that terror had come back to haunt him now. For it was Varzil that lay in that blue enshrouded Tower, trapped there in body—locked within his own mind. The battle he was waging by himself was threatening to destroy the whole city.

"There have been more than two hundred people killed in the last forty days," Cavan explained when Falan had returned with a wooden tray full of neatly arranged meat and cheese. There was also a bottle of fine Cathon wine and four intricately carved stone cups.

"How do you stand him, Cavan?" Aislinn asked with a shudder when Falan had left. "Wearing all that metal."

"I have grown accustomed to others wearing metal again, *cara.* While I am not able to wear it myself, I can understand why the young people don't share my aversion."

The back of his right hand bore a deep twisted scar that extended up under his shirt sleeve. There was no metal in the room. Even the grate in the fireplace was carved stone. No metal to attract the matrix-generated lightening. No metal to attract the splattering bursts of *clingfire* dropped by the enemy. Aislinn's face was distorted by *clingfire* scars and it had taken Lucie's sight. *Bonewater* dust had killed Fergus' brother Angus and Cavan's only sister had died in his arms from a breath of *lung rot* gas. After twenty-five years their clothing was still laced and tied with leather or buttoned with wood.

It had only been in the last few years that Lucie could bring herself to use a metal needle again. Her *laran* enhanced sight brought about some interesting variations on established embroidery patterns.

There was a shuddering beneath their feet. Everyone froze. A second tremor, harder, shook them. Cavan

rose, motioning for the others to follow him. Fergus
finished off the wine in his cup.

"If you are not too tired, my friends, I think now
would be a good time to begin. No one else has been
able to get through to contact Varzil since he barri-
caded himself inside the Tower. When I could think of
nothing else, I sent for you."

They walked quickly down the hall and went up
more flights of stairs than Aislinn cared to count. Cavan guided Lucie and Fergus supported Aislinn. Even
so, her leg soon began to throb with pain. They
stopped three times to wait for the tremors to subside.
Dust from the stone walls drifted down like white rain.
The closer they came to Varzil the harder the quakes
became.

The Tower door was blocked by a thick, roiling blue
haze. It was the same color the air turned just before
a blob of *clingfire* would burst into the open. Aislinn
shuddered as Cavan led them into a small room several
doors away.

Here instinct took over. She had been under-Keeper
with Varzil, so she directed the others to their places
on the thick, padded couches. When they were ready,
she took out her matrix and focused her attention on
it. One by one, their breathing slowed as their hearts
began to beat in rhythm. Hands joined hands in a mental circle and with a tiny audible *snap!* Aislinn took
them into the overworld.

It had been many years since she had done this. Her
overworld body was a delight after years of pain,
standing straight and tall. She put her hands to her face
in wonder. The skin was smooth and soft, no longer
something that made small children run screaming
with fright.

Turning slightly, there was Lucie beside her. The
embroidered band was gone and her eyes glowed a soft
green. A happy smile broke across her face as she
touched her eyes. Fergus, too, was taller and slimmer
with a full head of curly auburn hair and no scar to
mar his features. Cavan stretched both unscarred hands

delightedly. Aislinn looked at her own hands. Twelve fingers flexed easily and she grinned.

Far ahead of them was the sickening blue glow. it was brighter and stronger here in the overworld. They moved forward. The closer they came, the harder it was to move, like dragging their feet through stiff thick mud. *Avarra,* Aislinn prayed, *we need Angus and Roa more than ever now.*

The fabric of the overworld quivered. From far away came the sound of hoofbeats. Aislinn stopped and looked back. In the wavering distance she saw two horses. In a matter of seconds they had covered the space that divided the two groups. It was a joyful surprise to see that Angus MacAran and Roa Hastur rode the horses.

The reunion brought the strength needed to push ahead to the blue light. Close up, the light pulsed in a ragged rhythm. It was tinged around the edges with black. They stood in a half-circle just outside the glow.

"Varzil!" shouted Aislinn. The ether shuddered. She called his name again.

From deep inside the Tower Varzil Alton-Ridenow answered.

"Aislinn, foster-sister, you are finally here. You must destroy the ring, *chiya,* destroy it before the evil breaks free."

"If we destroy the ring, Varzil, you will die, too. There must be some other way."

"I am already dead, *cara,* no matter what happens. Better to go by your hand than to let this evil take over my body. I am too weak to hold the forces at bay any longer. If an opening is made, the Chaos will be free once again. Please, if you love me, you must. . . ."

He was cut off in mid-sentence. Aislinn snarled in frustration and imagined a window looking inward through the haze, channeling energy into creating it. A tiny little square in the center of the virulent blue cleared and they could see him lying on a cushioned divan in the tower. His hands were crossed on his chest and the enormous blue matrix ring blazed on his hand. It was his personal stone, the one he had supposedly

used to destroy the giant matrix screens so many years
ago. Only now they could see he hadn't destroyed them
so much as captured the powerful essence that made
up each matrix into this one stone. He had held that
power there, locked away for over twenty-five years.
Now he was losing the battle.

The power surged up again, struggling. It knocked
them back and they felt Cavan Hastur falter.

"We must wait, my friends. I cannot hold out much
longer."

Aislinn felt Cavan drop out of the link, sliding back
into the real world. His heart was very weak, something he had kept hidden from the rest.

"NO!" shouted Lucie. She fed energy into Cavan,
strengthening and steadying his heart; literally dragging him back into rapport with them. His shadowy
form solidified beside them again.

The ravenous evil roared again, fighting to escape.
Varzil's control was slipping. Since Varzil had physically destroyed the giant screens, the power sent out
tendrils searching for a new place to occupy. It was
beyond the little circle's power to control. It was drawn
toward each of the large lattice screens in the Towers
at Dalereuth, Neskaya, the new Tower at Arilinn, Corandolis, Hali, and Ashara and finally the deserted
Tower at Tramontana. At each one it probed, sending
out a blast of psychic shock that sent the Keepers and
their circles scrambling to protect themselves.

There was no resistance at Tramontana. It hovered
there, searching hungrily for any sort of entrance
into the closed screens. Varzil screamed, a heart-
rending sound of fear and loss.

Lucie came forward, pulling the tiny sliver of needle
from her pocket. It glinted gold as she took the edge
of her cape and using a tiny strand of energy she
threaded the needle and began to sew.

More and more of the old matrix screen power
slipped free. Varzil's screams turned into wails. The
silent screens at Tramontana began to vibrate into life
again. Lucie continued her stitching, the rest focused
their energy on her. The design spiraled ever outward.

In a matter of seconds it was enormous, totally obliterating the cape until Lucie held in her hands a gigantic net of pure energy.

Cavan faltered again, slipping out of rapport and back into his dying physical body. There was a tiny *pop!* and he was dead. But in the next instant he stood beside his sister and Angus MacAran. Lucie handed each of them an edge of the net she had woven and together they turned to contain the escaping evil.

Spreading out, they dragged the net forward. When it touched the blue, sparks flew and they staggered in shock. Aislinn felt their physical bodies spasm in pain. She gritted her teeth and *reached* with her *laran,* fighting to bring everyone in Thendara with the barest scrap of *laran* into contact with the overworld and their struggle. Time stopped in the city as young and old alike, Comyn or commoner, fed energy into the net.

It grew larger and larger until it encompassed the evil. They swept it up like a blanket and brought it swooping downward over the pulsing stone. When the ugly glow was hidden under the sparkling blanket, Lucie took her needle again and stitched the net tighter and tighter, until it was drawn down close around the ring. At the last the net was a shining brilliant silver-green. And it was now of a size to fit into two cupped hands. It pulsed for a few moments along with Varzil's faltering heartbeat, then they both went out.

Aislinn's control over the City snapped in that instant and they were thrown back into their real bodies in the room near the Tower.

"Damn and blast!" Aislinn swore with a groan, struggling up from the couch. Her whole body ached and her leg felt as if it was locked in a vice. Cavan Hastur lay composed as though asleep, with a slight smile on his lifeless face. Lucie sat up slowly while Fergus awoke with a snort.

They knew without having to see that the Tower at Tramontana lay in ruins. There were several dead at Hali and Corandolis; Neskaya's young Keeper lay in shock. Aislinn did not want to know how many had died from *her* desperate act.

The North Tower had been severed cleanly away from the rest of the castle. In his last act Varzil had tried to protect his friends. When his body was dug out of the rubble, the stone in the massive ring was dull and cracked. His body, along with that of Cavan Hastur, was carried in state to Hali. The king himself took it past the veil into the Temple. There it would rest for eternity.

The three remaining Avengers departed the city in silence. Aislinn wished she were brave enough to try the overworld again, to see how Varzil fared there. But she knew the temptation would be too great to remain. It would be better to return to the Guild House by the sea and await her turn as the gods had decreed.

Several of the younger Renunciates offered to escort the old people home, which caused Fergus to roar with laughter as he swung into the saddle. Aislinn just swore and shook off the helping hand as she clambered stiffly onto her horse.

"Avarra!" she snarled, "it's hell to get old."

TO TOUCH A COMYN

by Andrew Rey

We get about one usable story a year from what I'm beginning to think of as token males; the writership of these anthologies is pretty overpoweringly female, although there's really no prejudice involved; I just get more good, readable stories from women. This story features Peter Haldane, known to readers of THE SHATTERED CHAIN, THENDARA HOUSE, and CITY OF SORCERY. Come to think of it, Peter was pretty much of a token male himself.

Andrew Rey is 28 years old and a graduate of Pomona High School in Southern California. He also has a degree in physics from the University of California in Santa Cruz. Like many writers he has held down a variety of eccentrically described jobs: electronics assembler (huh? How does one assemble electronics?— no, don't tell me—), technical writer, and production manager, though he didn't say of what. He says, "I currently plan to be a teacher, but that plan is subject to change without notice." (My son Patrick studied physics, and dropped it, saying the choices were among working for the government, in nuclear power, or teaching high school physics—none being his idea of much of a career.) But with that array of jobs it sounds as if Mr. Rey is planning to be a writer; and judging from this good beginning, he's qualified.

"As dumb as a Ktoller"—*Galactic saying.*
"As crazy as a Ktoller"—*Darkovan variation.*

"Damn compression pump!"

Mellis, the new mechanical technician, leapt to one side as the pump went flying through the starship's repair hatch. He watched in shock as the pump skittered across the concrete, coming to rest about twenty meters away.

"That does it!" Mellis yelled into the hatch. "Rakk, if you want someone to help you, get one of those stupid Darkovan natives. You're a menace to anyone around you."

"Go ride a Ronga," the voice from inside the hatch replied.

Mellis tramped over to another technician who was replacing the electronics on a motor. "That crazy Ktoller. One day she's gonna kill someone . . . and what are you smiling at, Davia?" he asked sharply.

"We were wondering how long it would take you to realize that it isn't safe to work with Rakk," Davia said. "You've lasted longer than most."

"What's eating her?"

"Oh, Rakk's always been a hotheaded one. Been getting into fights since her first day here. But since she lost a fight to a native about a month back, her temper's been hotter than an exhaust funnel. Personally, I think she is afraid to go back into town and is getting cabin fever. The natives are too tough for her."

"The day I'm afraid of those wimpy natives is the day you beat me arm wrestling," Rakk said. Mellis gasped as the tall, brawny woman grabbed hold of Davia's collar and lifted him off the ground. No strain showed on her round face, and she breathed evenly through her large nose. Her small breasts were not even heaving. "Now, Davia, why don't you mind your own business for a change?"

Davia managed to choke out a yes.

"Good," Rakk said, releasing him. "I've got to get a new compression pump from supplies. Can you keep the ship from falling over until I get back?" Without waiting for a reply, she marched over to a groundcar and sped off toward the other side of the spaceport.

As she drove the small car, Rakk noticed that she

was slowly bending the steering wheel. *Calm down, Rakk,* she told herself, as she turned to go around the administration buildings. *Those Booze Cats just talk because they're afraid their jaws might rust shut. They don't know what happened, and couldn't care less. They . . .*

An image flashed through her mind, of a red-haired man sitting at a rough-hewn table, with a beer pitcher sliding toward him.

With a screech of tires, Rakk suddenly swung her vehicle to the left, racing between two buildings. *Why should I always have to drive around these stupid buildings anyway? If the planners were too dumb to build a roadway through them . . .* she thought, as she maneuvered along the twisting walkway.

When she emerged into the central plaza, Rakk glanced at the main gate. Two black-clad security guards were already staring at her. *Ah, who gives a hoot about reprimands, anyway?* she thought as her eyes swung back to the plaza. She was looking for a walkway out when she noticed a red-haired man in a Darkovan costume walking toward the main gate.

Rakk slammed on the brakes. *I'd recognize that head anywhere,* she thought. Smiling broadly, she leapt out of the car and called out, "Sean!"

The man, apparently lost in thought, did not turn around. "Hey, Sean," Rakk cried as she ran up to him, "why didn't you tell me you were here?" Rakk grabbed the man's shoulder. "Sean . . ."

With a loud cry of surprise, the man spun forward and faced Rakk, his sword half drawn. The thin, long face showed anger and surprise—a face Rakk did not recognize.

It took Rakk a moment to recover her wits. "Hey, I'm sorry," she began. "I thought you were—"

"*Vai dom,* are you all right?" Another red-haired man, but wearing a Federation uniform, interposed himself between Rakk and the Darkovan.

"I'm well," the Darkovan said, sheathing his sword. "He—she just startled me."

"I'm very sorry, Lord Gabriel. I should not have

left you for a moment. Some of our people are not familiar with Darkovan customs.''

"It's nothing," Gabriel said, regaining his composure and turning back toward the gate. The Federation man began to follow, but then turned to Rakk. "I want you in Room 127 of the security building in ten minutes," he said. Before Rakk could answer, the man turned away to accompany Lord Gabriel.

Rakk sat quietly in the office, slowly twisting a metal pen in her hands. She was attempting to straighten it out when the red-haired official entered.

"Stay seated," he said as he sat down behind the desk. "I'm Peter Haldane, head of Darkovan relations. And you are?"

"Rakkaloaliquadarose Olbidavaroulacu, Mechanic First Class. People usually just call me Rakk."

"I see," Peter said. He leaned forward onto his desk. "I'm not going to ask what you were doing driving across the plaza. It's not my department, and in fact, I really don't care. What I want to know is, why did you grab Lord Gabriel?"

"I thought I recognized him," Rakk said.

"Really? Do you know many red-haired Darkovans?"

Rakk just stared at him.

"Never mind," Peter said, brushing away the question with a wave of his hand. "The person you grabbed is one of the Comyn—a ruler of this planet. Now, as you should know from the orientation lectures, there are certain customs regarding these rulers. One is that you don't just come up to talk to one of them; they first must recognize you. The second is that you never touch a Comyn. For some reason, they often find it painful to touch the skin of another person."

Rakk leaned back in her chair. "Really? And where do you get your information—Fordi's Galactic Travel Guide?"

A flame shot through Peter's eyes, but he spoke quietly. "I am this base's expert on Darkovan culture. I grew up here, and I've made a career of studying their society. And the first thing a Darkovan child learns is that he must never disturb, and *never* touch, the Comyn.''

"Just how sure are you?'' Rakk asked. "I've been in the Trade City many times, and I've talked to, and even touched—''

Peter slammed his palm on the table. "I lived with the Comyn for six months, and I *know* what I'm talking about! No one, not even their servants, touched them. The Comyn hardly even touched each other, and then only with the lightest and briefest of touches. It's an act as intimate to them as—well, as sex is to us.''

"You're kidding!'' Rakk said in disbelief.

"Do I look as if I'm kidding?'' Peter asked, thrusting his flushed face at her.

"No,'' she whispered.

"Good.'' Peter sat back into his chair and brushed his hair back with his hand. "This had the potential to be far more serious than it turned out to be. But since Lord Gabriel decided not to make anything of it, I'm not going to hold it against you, *if* you promise never to repeat this stunt, and if you remind the other workers that they are not to talk to, or touch, the Comyn. Make that any red-haired Darkovan, just to be safe. Do we have an understanding?''

"Yeah, sure,'' Rakk said. She had a slightly glazed look in her eyes, as if her thoughts were far away.

"Good. Thank you for coming in.'' Peter stood and indicated that she could leave.

Outside, Rakk leaned against the corridor wall. Peter's words echoed in her mind. *It's an act as intimate to them as sex is to us.* . . .

"Sean. Oh my god, Sean,'' she whispered to herself.

Days later, Rakk sat in a Trade City bar. She was about to order another drink when she realized that it would be her fifth. *Damn it, I only needed one for courage. All right, maybe two. But four? I'm braver than that. Besides, I think I'm out of practice,* she thought, as the chair next to her slowly swayed in the nonexistent breeze. *I haven't had a drink since I met Sean.*

Oh, Sean. . . . she thought, remembering.

* * *

She remembered that she had just finished her fourth tankard, too, the night she had met Sean. It had been a rough day, working on two starships that were down, trying to find parts reasonably quickly, and punching her supervisor in the jaw because he had started yelling at her for some reason or other. *But that was the day,* she thought, *and now it's the night, and Chucky will probably forget the whole incident by firstday. That is, if I didn't break his jaw, and it really felt like I didn't.*

She drained her mug and called out for another, looking around the bar for someone who might give her a bit of physical entertainment. So far she had no luck. She had seen only regular-sized people, huddled around candles in small groups or hiding in the shadows alone. *Just normal Terran-types,* she thought. *You bump one, he just falls right over. No fun at all.*

She reached for her mug, and discovered that it was not there. Annoyed, Rakk looked up to find it sitting, half-filled, under the keg spout. The bartender was out on the floor, hovering over the table of a young, red-headed man who was just sitting down. "How may I serve you, *vai dom*?" the bartender asked.

"Hey, you, how about my *firi*?" Rakk called out.

The bartender jumped. "A moment, *mestra,* please," he said, and turned back to the newcomer.

Rakk could feel the hackles on the back of her neck rising. "My drink, mister!" she said again.

The bartender glanced pointedly behind her. Rakk turned, and saw the bouncer emerging from the shadows at the end of the room. He was big, over two meters of blond hair and muscle. Rakk smiled. *Just about my height and weight. He looks like fun,* she thought. *But a few more drinks will make it really good.* She turned away from him and tried to simmer down.

By the time the bartender had served the young man and had brought her drink, Rakk was smiling again. She had come up with a better plan. She took a swig for luck, and went to the young man's table.

He was swilling down his drink when Rakk slid into the seat across from him. The man was in his early twenties, with a thin nose and thinner lips. He was wearing an elaborately embroidered cloak, and a pouch hanging from his neck which Rakk assumed held money. Rakk noticed him survey her over the rim of the tankard, his leafy-green eyes widening slightly. *Let him look,* Rakk thought. *Let him see what a woman from a high gravity planet looks like.*

The man put down his glass and licked the ale from his lips. "To magic," he said, raising his glass.

Rakk drank to it, then deliberately said, "There's no such thing as magic."

He smiled back. "I wasn't talking about *Terrani* magic," he said, his voice slightly slurred. "I was talking about matrices and the Towers, Darkovan magic. Potent stuff, you know?" Rakk noticed a slight edge on the last two words.

"Magic is either a stupid trick for stupider people, or science that fools don't understand," Rakk said. "You backwater people think that everything you can't fathom is supernatural. I work with the star drives, the data bases, the piloting systems. They do amazing things, like flitting at speeds faster than light, from one incredibly small point to another. It may look like magic, but it follows the repair manuals. Now, if we could get a five-year-old from a real world, like Ktoll, to look at your 'magic,' why, he'd know exactly what makes it tick, and be improving on it in a week."

The man's eyes blazed, and Rakk knew she had hit home. "You are stupid, arrogant, and don't know *reish* about it," he replied.

Although she was not fluent in the local language, Rakk always made it a point to learn the curses first. So she responded with a *cahuenga* saying that implied that his carroty top came from a union between his grandmother and a red-maned stallion.

He bolted up, revealing a shade less than two meters of good, solid muscle. *Loads of fun,* Rakk thought.

He also revealed over a meter of sharp, cold steel belted at his side. Since swordplay was not her expertise, even if she had brought one, Rakk decided that she had best make the first move. She upended the table on him.

He leapt back, almost slipping on the spilled ale, but recovered his balance instantly. Rakk grinned. *Quick, agile—this is going to be a* good *fight.* Then the bartender shouted something and the red-haired man dived at her, fists clenched.

Rakk's memories were pretty confused after that. She remembered taking some good punches from the redhead, while only getting in one or two good shots herself. She remembered getting hit on the side of the head with a pitcher, and later throwing off the bouncer who tried to get her in a full-Nelson hold. Finally, she remembered rolling in the dirty slush outside the bar. Staggering onto one arm, she called out a few good-natured curses after the bouncer, who was limping away with the bartender. She then looked around, and saw the young man sprawled in the muddy street next to her. He was trying to stand up, but not quite making it. Rakk got up and lifted him to his feet with one hand.

"Kid, that was one of the best bar fights I've ever had the pleasure of being in!" she said. The young man stared vacantly ahead, then slowly focused his eyes on her.

"You know, you shouldn't let bouncers throw you into the wall like that," she continued, wiping off the worst of the mud from his shirt. "You can get hurt that way. Hey, let me buy you a drink, all right?"

The man nodded his head. "Tavern . . . over there . . ." he said, pointing up the street.

"Great." Rakk helped him walk the first few steps, until he was steady. "Say, did you see who that moron was who kept chucking tankards at me during the fight? Every time I looked, no one was there. The guy must have moved like lighting."

"That wuz me," he said.

"What?" she asked, wondering just how hard he had hit that wall.

"Me, me," he repeated. "I am . . . my name is Sean. . . ."

"Pleased to meetcha, Sean. I'm Rakk, from the planet Ktoll . . . oh, yeah, I remember this place," she said as they reached the tavern. "I haven't gotten thrown out of here in at least, oh, three weeks. They probably won't even remember me."

Sean smiled lopsidedly, gingerly touching his cheek. "I think I will remember you for a long time, *me-mestra.*"

At the door, Sean hesitated, then straightened his cloak and collar. He extended his arm to her. "Shall we enter, *mestra*?" She proudly accepted his arm, and together, half-supporting each other, they staggered through the doorway.

It seemed to Rakk that they spent hours at that bar, sprawled out on a large oaken table, drinking *firi,* trading stories, songs, and poetry. She learned that Sean really loved poetry, from all across the galaxy. Terran poetry especially, when he could get his hands on it. She remembered him reciting several poems, one that ended, " '. . . boundless and bare, the lone and level sands stretch . . . far . . . far away.' "

Sean smiled happily, and leaned forward on the table. Rakk smiled, too. He had managed to finish his recitation without forgetting more than three lines, and starting again only twice.

"That was beaut'ful," Rakk said, trying to remember what he had been talking about. "Who wazzat? Tha' Shakerspear fellow?"

"Percy Bysshe Shelley," Sean said, articulating each word like some holy name. " 'Nother ancient Terran bard. One of the shining lights of human history." He tried to point out the shining light, but his hand got caught on one of the pitchers on the table and knocked it to the floor. Rakk decided that his lights were about to go out, and so quietly nudged the half-full pitcher away from him.

"Tell me, Rakk, why do you fight so much?"

The question took her by surprise. "Hell, I dunno, Sean. Probably 'cause I'm good at it, like drinking and fixing starships. I also got a bit of a temper, I su'pose."

"You're telling me," he said, gently touching a swollen eye.

"I get so angry when I see people smirking at me behind my back. Or ignoring me, or jumping to conclusions about what I'm like. Hell, they all think we Ktollers are stupid 'cause we're so big. Even my instructors in school thought so—they graded me harder than the rest. Now I can fix a problem that has stumped the ship engineers for weeks! But do I get respect? Hell, no! So when I see some fool making fun of me, I get their attention, and show them that it isn't in their best interest to think that way. Works real well, too."

"Believe that," Sean said. "But why attack me? I didn't do anythin' like that."

"Oh, I thought that you were some local high-head who was throwing his weight around. Thought I'd do some commun'ty service and bring you back from orbit. I guess I was wrong. Y'aren't sore, are ya, Sean?"

"No, no. Not any more. You weren't much worse than my swordfightin' instructor. Besides, I wouldn't have got to know you. I like you, Rakk. You're one of the few people I've met who treats me like a person, and not just a Comyn. Maybe that's why I keep coming to these Trade City bars, to meet people like you—even if it does cause a few bruises."

"Ah, Sean, you're sweet," she said. She leaned forward and gave him a quick kiss on the forehead.

He pulled back, startled, and then smiled. "That, *mestra*, calls for another," he said, and leaned toward the pitcher.

"Ah, no," Rakk said, and moved the pitcher farther away from him. "You've had enough, m'friend."

Sean lay across the table in the direction of the pitcher. "Robert Browning, he was another great ancient poet, and he said, 'A man's reach should exceed his grasp, else . . . else . . .' "

"Else it's time to go home, Red," Rakk said, holding the pitcher closer to her.

" 'Else' . . . ah! . . . 'else what's a heaven for?' " he said proudly, and squinted at the pitcher.

The pitcher quivered. As Rakk watched, it slid from her hands, inching across the table in short jerks. Sean peered at it, an intent, predatory look on his face. The pitcher suddenly skipped, flying the last few inches into Sean's hands.

As Sean gazed at the pitcher, Rakk slowly stood up. Sobriety had returned to her in an adrenaline-charged rush. Slowly and steadily she made her way to the door. Sean lifted the pitcher with both hands and, trying to take a sip, upended it over his face. Rakk slipped out the door and took off running down the street.

She did not stop running until she reached Terran headquarters. All she remembered after that was stumbling into the barracks, throwing up in the bathroom, and falling into bed. She curled up in the blankets like a little girl.

* * *

Rakk took a swig of her fifth *firi,* which she had ordered while reminiscing. "Pitchers don't fly, even when you're very drunk," she muttered to herself. "Well, that doesn't matter now." She called over the bartender.

"Hey, you remember that red-headed guy who was here the last time I was here? You know, the *vai dom*?" The bartender's eyes widened when she mentioned the title. "Do you know where he lives?"

"If you do not know his residence, you do not need to know," the bartender said, moving away. Rakk's hand shot out and grabbed his wrist.

"I asked you a question," she reminded him as she squeezed. The bartender grimaced, then glanced to her left. The blond bouncer had stood up at the end of the room.

Without letting go, Rakk also stood up, sending her bench flying. The bouncer hesitated, glancing at Rakk and the bartender, and then headed for the lavatory.

Rakk turned back to the bartender, smiling. "He remembers the last time I was here, which means that you do, too. Now, where can I find Sean?"

Confusion and fear swept across the bartender's face. Finally, he said, "At Comyn Castle."

"That tells me a lot. How do I get there?"

"Follow the road until you reach the other side of the valley. . . ."

It was a long trek up to the castle, but the air was cool and Rakk was feeling quite good. She had taken a brisk stroll through Thendara, admiring the quaint cobblestone streets, the rustic wooden shops and houses, the antiquated stone wall around Thendara which she found easy to jump, and the delightful glass jaws of certain Darkovans who thought she belonged back in the Trade City. So when she met the castle guards, Rakk decided to try being polite.

"Hello there," she said, raising one arm in greeting. "I've come to speak with Sean—he's one of your Comyn lords. Could you tell him that Rakk is here? I'll wait outside, if you'd like. I wouldn't want to barge in on anything."

The two young, green-clad guards looked at each other, and exchanged words in a dialect that Rakk did not recognize. Then one of them turned to her and said, "*Terranan,* you are outside of the restricted zone, and so under arrest."

"Now wait a minute," she said. "Let's not complicate things. I just want to speak with Sean. Send him my message; he'll understand."

"We will not bother the Comyn with any messages from a *Terranan grezalis,*" the guard said. "Come with us." The guard drew his sword, and motioned Rakk in the direction of the guard's entrance.

Rakk backed off, her temper rising quickly. "Look, just send my message to Sean, will you? He'll understand."

"Move!"

Rakk bunched up, readying to tear the sword from the guard's hand. Then she suddenly relaxed, and smiling, said, "All right, but let me tie my bootlace first." She squatted down and began to fiddle with her shoe.

The guard lowered his sword and looked at his partner in puzzlement. Rakk ignored them. Finally, the guard poked at her with his sword. "I said, *Terranan*, move!"

Rakk jumped—right over the two startled guards. She landed in a tuck-and-roll, came out onto her feet, and dashed for the main gates. After a confused moment, the two guards were running after her, shouting. Rakk rushed through the gates, and collided with a guard who had come around the corner. The guard went flying back.

Rakk surveyed the wide parade ground of the castle, with stables to one side and a pile of lumber on the other. Directly opposite the gateway were a series of broad steps leading up to two heavy oaken doors. Beside the doors were two guards, who were beginning to run toward her.

"Sean!" Rakk yelled, while sprinting toward the lumber. "Sean, I want to talk with you!" She reached the lumber pile and grabbed a long, thick beam. Swinging it by one end, she checked the onrush of the five guards. "Sean! Please hear me, Sean!" Her voice echoed off the stone walls. A guard to her far right tried to parry her swing with his sword, and got his weapon knocked out of his hand.

Then the two middle guards rushed her. Rakk hit the sword arm of one of them and heard the crack of breaking bone, but she had no time to stop the other one. Dropping her makeshift weapon, Rakk darted between the disarmed guard and his injured colleague, and sprinted for the doors of the castle. "Sean it's getting awfully busy down here! You'd better answer now!" From an upper window, Rakk saw a blue glint, like light reflecting off glass, and for a moment thought it might be Sean. The next instant she felt a presence pushing into her mind. "Sean!" she screamed one last time, and clutching her head, collapsed.

Rakk walked into the coordinator's office the next day, still suffering from her headache despite the painkillers the medics had given her. She had awakened in the Terran hospital, with no idea how she had arrived there.

Montgomery, Darkover's coordinator, looked up from a report he had been pretending to read. "So you're Rakk," he stated.

"Yes," Rakk replied, feeling a little groggy from the drugs.

"What the hell did you think you were doing?" Montgomery shouted. Rakk winced. "Going outside of the Trade City, beating up the natives, attacking the Comyn Castle guards, threatening one of the Comyn—"

"I wasn't threatening him," Rakk interrupted. "I just wanted to talk with him."

"Not threatening, huh? How can you say that when you almost killed one of his guards?"

"They wouldn't let me see him!" she shouted back, then groaned as her head throbbed. "I tried to talk with them, but they just kept pointing swords at me."

"Of course they wouldn't let you see him. Even I can't just walk in and see one of the Comyn." Montgomery pushed back his hair and shook his head. "Lucky for me you didn't kill anyone. You were drunk, right?"

"Well, maybe a little . . ."

"You were drunk," the coordinator stated. "And what the hell did you want to talk with him about, anyway?"

"It's . . . private."

"Private. Well, it isn't private anymore. Do you have any idea what you've done to relations with this backwater planet? Thank God that person you threatened was out hunting at the time, and thank God that Lord Hastur likes us; he's agreed to ignore this incident, with only a *few* concessions. My God, you could have thrown relations back a decade or more!"

Rakk stared at Montgomery. "You mean Sean doesn't know that I was there?"

"Of course not, and hopefully he never will. You certainly won't tell him. For one thing, the castle guards have orders to arrest you on sight. Personally, I'm surprised that they hauled you back to us at all. For another, they're not going to get the chance. From here on, you are restricted to base, and if you try to leave, I've ordered our guards to use whatever force is necessary to stop you."

"But . . ." Rakk said, wordless.

"Oh, don't look so worried," Montgomery continued. "You won't have to suffer through this long. Because I've also sent a request for your transfer. In a month, you'll be out of my hair and be somebody else's problem."

"But, but . . ." Rakk flailed.

"Just be thankful I don't slap seven demerits on you and get you kicked out of the service," Montgomery said. "You've certainly given me more than enough reason to. Now get out of my office! If I'm lucky, this is the last I'll see of you until you board the ship."

Rakk silently turned and left.

In the female barracks, Rakk slammed her fist into the wall, easily penetrating the thin board over the insulation. She sat down on her bunk, and put her face in her hands.

You stupid cow, she thought. *You can't do anything right, can you? You can't even contact one stupid person on a dumb, backwater planet. You're useless, to yourself and everyone else. Useless.*

Hearing the barracks door open, Rakk quickly composed her face. "Rakk?" she heard someone behind her ask.

"Yes," she replied gruffly.

A man with red hair sat on the bed opposite her. "Remember me? I'm the guy who bawled you out for touching Lord Gabriel a while back."

"Oh, yeah, Mr. Haldane," Rakk said, shaking his hand.

"I've heard about the Old Man reprimanding you for trying to see one of the Comyn."

"Yeah."

"Bawled you out pretty bad, didn't he?"

"I've had worse."

"I doubt that. Montgomery may not be good at much else, but he certainly knows how to chew a person out. He's done it to me often enough. But that's not what I came here to talk with you about. What I was wondering is, do you know Sean?"

"Yeah," Rakk said. "We met at a bar about two months ago."

Peter looked surprised, but said nothing. He waited for Rakk to continue, but she just stared at him, expressionless. "Well, do you know Sean well?"

"No. We only met that one night."

"So why do you want to talk with him?"

"Why, is there something weird about wanting to talk with a person?"

Peter looked uncomfortable for a moment, then said, "Look, I may be seeing Sean in about a week, so if you have a message for him, I *might* be able to give it to him."

"Could you get me to see him?" Rakk asked, suddenly enthusiastic.

"No, that I couldn't arrange," Peter said. "Some of the high ranking Federation officials have been invited to the Comyn Castle for the Midsummer Ball. Since Sean is one of the local Comyn, I should see him there. I can't guarantee that I'll be able to talk with him—I'd need to be recognized first, which sometimes isn't easy. But if he does speak to me, I can give him your message. But as for getting yourself invited to the party, forget it. We're lucky to have been invited at all."

Rakk sat for a long time, staring at nothing, her brow knitted. Finally she said, "I don't think I can give you a message. It's too personal. I have to see Sean myself."

A disappointed look crossed Peter's face. "I'm sorry to hear that," he said. "Frankly, I think this is the only chance you will have to get a message to him, short of sprouting wings and flying." Peter stood up to leave. "Tell you what—if you are able to find the words, let me know. All right?"

"All right," Rakk mechanically said.

"Fine. Well, it was good talking with you," Peter said, and left.

Rakk lay back in her bunk, closed her eyes, and tried to imagine ways to sneak past the guards. She thought about dressing up as a native woman, but then she considered the number of two-meter-tall, one-hundred-thirty-kilo Darkovan girls there were. She considered dressing as a castle guard, but wondered how she could talk her way past the gates without knowing *casta*, the lowland's dialect. Then she suddenly sat up.

"Yeah . . . flying," she muttered.

For the next week Rakk threw herself into a secret project. She ordered a bizarre range of items from the parts requisitioner, and would not allow anyone to see what she was working on. She kept the doors closed to the hanger she was using, and even slept there to keep trespassers out. Her supervisor, wondering what the mysterious project was, asked her about it. She just assured him that it was approved. Rubbing his jaw, he decided that it wasn't worth worrying about, since Rakk would be gone soon. He didn't find out how big a mistake that was until the night of the Midsummer's festival.

"They must be having some party out there tonight," said Albaine, the security guard, as he lounged against the main gate of the Terran spaceport.

His partner Elac listened to the distant cries and singing from the city. "Yeah, sure sounds like it. Wish something interesting would happen over here. Except having to stand at attention to let the bigwigs out."

In the compound, a high, whining noise arose.

"Well, just remember that old Terran curse," Albaine said, " 'May you live in *interesting* times.' "

"Personally, I think those old Terrans were hopeless pessimists." Elac glanced at his watch. "Well, we only have a half-hour more for this shift. Someone else will get to greet the returning dignitaries when they come home drunk.''

The whining grew louder.

"If they come home," the other guard said. "I've heard that some of them stay with the natives all night, having fun. Things get pretty wild out there.''

"They'd be a lot more wild if *I* had the night off.''

Albaine laughed. "Sure, just like the time you said you . . . hey, Elac, what is that noise?''

"I don't know," Elac said. "Sounds like an electric motor. Seems to be coming this way. . . .''

From behind a building a streamlined silver ground-car suddenly appeared. Tires screaming, it turned and headed straight for the guards. "What the—'' Elac began as he reached for his gun. Bright lights erupted from the vehicle, blinding the guards for a moment. The next second, the car sped past them, and Elac caught a glimpse of the driver.

"Damn it!'' Elac yelled. "That crazy Ktoll woman is in that thing. And she's heading into town.''

"Interesting times,'' Albaine muttered.

Rakk crouched down in her modified groundcar as she raced through the streets. *Crashing the gates was easier than I expected. Poor guys didn't even have a chance to shoot at me. If I'd known that, I wouldn't have put so much ship hulling on for protection. Now,* she thought, swerving to miss a startled pedestrian, *my only problem is getting to the castle without hitting anyone. Pity I never learned how to fly.*

Rakk was happy to note that the Darkovans in the Trade City were highly cooperative in getting out of her way—typically by throwing up their arms, screaming, and diving for the side of the road. A pair of young, short-haired women she found particularly entertaining. One leapt behind a pole, while the other cowered behind a skinny man. Rakk heard the one behind the pole start screaming at her companion, but she did not have time to hear what the young woman said.

After passing the startled gate guards of Thendara,

however, driving became more difficult. The Darkovans there were not as quick to clear the way. Most
barely moved, causing her to swerve several times.
And often the men would throw their swords at her,
which bounced harmlessly off the hull but made seeing
the road difficult. One man even tried to attack her,
standing right in her way and drawing his sword. A
load blast from the air horn fortunately sent him running.

The worst obstacles were the animals. On one narrow street, a panicking horse went galloping straight
at her. She thought she was going to hit the beast, but
at the last second the horse hurdled over her ground-
car. Another horse, harnessed to a cart, bolted across
the street in front of her. Rakk had to drive straight
through the cart, sending wood pieces flying everywhere. Between these obstacles, the fainting women,
the icy cobblestones, and the buildings crowding the
winding streets, Rakk thought it remarkable that she
made it safely to the road leading up to Comyn Castle.

A few hundred yards from the top of the hill, a
horseman came riding down. When he saw Rakk, he
gave a short cry, reined his horse, and rode back up
the road at full gallop, shouting something in one of
the Darkovan dialects.

"That does it," Rakk said to herself, as she floored
the accelerator. Stones flying behind her, Rakk pursued the shouting horseman.

She reached the top just as the rider entered the
castle courtyard. Wide-eyed guards were frantically
setting the barricades in place.

"No you don't!" Rakk yelled, and shifted gears.
The car jumped forward, and flew past the barricades
before the guards could close them.

With a whoop of joy, Rakk aimed her cart toward
the main doors. As she hit the steps, an image flashed
through her mind, of driving her small car into the
center of the dance floor, screeching to a halt, standing up on the seat and announcing, "Sean, I've come
to speak with you, and this time no one is going to
stop me!"

The sight of herself standing there, hair blown about, grease and mud on her face, was imprinted on her mind's eye as she went over the top step. There she faced the large, heavy, closed oak doors of the palace. She heard a heavy bolt thud into place the instant before she hit.

Images fluttered in and out of Rakk's consciousness. She saw Montgomery's face, red and angry; green uniforms, when she felt herself lifted up; Sean's face for an instant, making her want to cry out; red canvases of pain; and finally, a blue crystal, which she saw clearly, minutely, each facet sharp and precise, as if she were staring at it through a jeweler's glass. Then it was as if she were inside the crystal and part of it. She could almost feel the crystal course through her, and she through it. She could sense it finding her pains and injuries, and mending them. She saw faces behind, or within, the crystal, she was not sure which. Young and old faces, alert and weary, ageless and aged, but all worried, all concerned. She wanted to ask them what they were doing, but one gentle face looked at her and smiled, and she relaxed. Then she slept.

She awoke suddenly. Automatically, she tried to sit up, but simultaneously felt a sharp pain in her lower back and a slap across her chest. She dropped back down, and looked around the room while lying down.

Rakk found herself in a stone room, with sunlight streaming through a small, high window onto a tapestry hanging on the opposite wall. Six fine chairs circled her wooden bed. The bed itself was of finely carved wood, with several layers of cotton bedding and six straps which firmly held her, although she could still move her arms. She shook her head. *If this is a Darkovan prison*, she thought, *I'm surprised the crime rate is so low. Especially if they rely on cloth manacles.*

A servant glanced into her room and said something Rakk did not understand. He then hurried off before

Rakk could say anything to him. Feeling annoyed, Rakk examined herself. *Well, it appears that the worst I did was to bruise my back, which is damned surprising. I could have sworn that I sent part of those doors into space.*

"I thought that I would see you again someday, but I never expected you to storm the castle to do it."

"Sean," Rakk said, as the red-haired man strode in and sat down on one of the fine chairs.

"Hello, Rakk," Sean said. "How are you feeling?"

"Like I fell two stories down an access stairwell," she replied, "but so far, no serious damage."

"No serious damage anymore," Sean said. "You were lucky we had a few healers here last night, else I'm afraid you might not have walked again. You broke your back, you know."

"What?" Rakk asked, slowly.

"Yes, in the lower back. You must have been thrown over your vehicle when you hit the doors. The lower part of your back bore the brunt of the impact. Fortunately, we had invited most of the local matrix technicians for the festivities, so we had no trouble getting a first-rate circle together. They were able to mend your injury in a couple of hours. But they suggest that you don't get up from bed for at least a week."

A chill swept up Rakk's back when Sean had finished. *A broken back?* she thought. *Mended, mere hours after the accident? Impossible. It doesn't fit any of the laws of physics. It's like saying that a starship could travel in hyperspace pulled by flying horses. Or that a pitcher of beer could slide across a rough table by itself.* Rakk closed her eyes, and tried to control the shivering that was welling up inside of her.

"Anyway, you are safe now," Sean continued. "I've talked with Lord Hastur and your Peter Haldane, and they've told me about your previous attempt to see me." He smiled and shook his head. "If I had heard about it, I would have guessed that it was you. Who else would have been crazy enough to try a stunt like that?"

Sean's face turned serious. "In fact, you could have

been killed both times. Peter said that you had a message too confidential to be sent by courier. To be honest, that scares me a little. So tell me, what is so important that you risked your life to tell to me?''

Rakk opened her mouth to speak, and then shut it, horribly embarrassed. She groped with her thoughts, but she still could not find the words.

"I don't know how to explain it," she said. "That night we met was a really good night. Something special. People usually don't open up to me. And I certainly don't open up to others. But for some reason, we touched each other that night. You told me about your loves, your dreams. I told you about my fears. We were close, closer than I've been to anyone in ages.

"But then I saw that pitcher move. I don't know how it happened, or why I thought that you were responsible. God, I'm not even sure it really happened anymore."

"It happened," Sean stated.

Rakk looked at his calm, attentive face. "Yeah? Well, anyway, I saw it, and . . . I panicked. I ran. I abandoned you, rejected you. At first, I told myself, 'Hey, he's just some guy I met at a bar one night. No big deal, nothing really happened between us.' But then I heard how you Comyn don't touch . . . how intimate an act it is . . . and I remembered the kiss I gave you. How you didn't recoil, how you just smiled. And I realized just how real the feelings were that night. I . . . I just couldn't live with myself doing that to you.'' Tears began to form in her eyes, and she turned away, hiding them. "I'm going to be shipped off planet soon, but I wanted you to know, Sean, that . . . I'm sorry. I never meant to hurt you *that* way.''

Sean stared thoughtfully at the back of her head. "You couldn't have sent a message to tell me this?''

"No," Rakk said, her voice muffled by her pillow. "I tried, several times, but I couldn't do it. I couldn't write the words down where anyone could see them. The only way I could say it was to see you, personally.''

Sean rose from his chair, and paced the room. Rakk

could hear his muffled footsteps on the carpet, feel his glances. Finally, he stopped. "Rakk, I want to show you something."

Rakk slowly turned her face from the pillow. She saw Sean taking the sack from around his neck and opening it. Inside, Rakk saw a blue crystal, precisely cut like a diamond. It seemed familiar to her; then she realized that it was the crystal she had seen in her dream right after the accident. Ribbons of light ran inside of it, in a complex pattern she could not follow.

"What is it?" Rakk asked.

"This is a matrix," Sean said, as he carefully wrapped it again in silk and returned it to the pouch. "It's a natural jewel of Darkover. It amplifies certain powers of the mind. Power to move objects by the force of will, or to read minds, or to locate objects in other rooms. We Comyn have these powers more than other people do; we've been bred for it. This is how I moved that pitcher on the night we met, and how we healed your broken back. The matrix. It's what I meant by Darkovan magic. And I bet it isn't in any of your technical manuals."

Rakk smiled, but then frowned. "You can read minds by physical contact, right?"

Sean smiled. "Yes, when we make contact, it's very difficult to block out the other person's thoughts. That's why Comyn don't touch very much."

Rakk's frown grew deeper. "That means you read my mind when I kissed you."

"Well, I suppose I did," Sean said. "But I was so drunk that night that whatever I read was forgotten by the next day. Assuming that there was anything to read after the fifteen pitchers we had."

"Eighteen," Rakk corrected him. "But why are you telling me this? Even Peter Haldane doesn't know about this."

"Why?" Sean said. He sat down next to her and leaned forward. "Why? You, who have turned two worlds upside down, who have risked her life and career, simply to apologize to me, asks why? You, who single-handedly have caused more commotion in one

month than I have in my entire life asks why? You've
risked more for me than anyone ever has, for a slight
anyone else would have ignored." Smoothly, Sean
reached out his hand and brushed Rakk's cheek. "By
Zandru's hells, if you are an example of what the *Terrani* are like, then you're the best thing that has ever
happened to this world. And Sharra take me if I let
you go without a fight. And you ask why?

"Well, I'll tell you," he said, leaning back. "I need
a drinking partner, and you're the only one I know
that I can drink under the table."

"Liar!" Rakk screamed, throwing her pillow at him.
She knew this was one fight she could not win, but for
the first time in her life, she did not mind losing.

ABOUT TIME

by Patricia B. Cirone

One of the pleasures of editing these anthologies is to welcome back old friends. Pat Cirone has appeared before in these anthologies, and says about her writing that she has now arrived at the stage of "personalized, sometimes glowing rejection letters," but has not yet sold to anyone but me, except for one story to the anthology YANKEE WITCHES. Well, the personalized rejection slips mean you're on the way. Every word an editor writes beyond a printed slip is meaningful. (I can't emphasize this too much; editors are chronically overworked.)

We also had the pleasure of printing her very fine story "A Flower from the Dust of Khedderide" in Marion Zimmer Bradley's Fantasy Magazine. Her full-time job is that of a children's librarian and she "dabbles in poetry."

"Where *is* she?" Delaa demanded in a grunt as she cinched the chervine's belly strap tighter. "When she goes to the market for one hour, she takes three. If she says her trip will take five days, it's six or seven before she arrives. She's *never* on time!"

"Relax, Delaa. We're going no farther than the beginning of the vale tonight. It doesn't matter if we start a little late," Sharyl said placatingly.

"That's not the *point*," grunted Delaa as she slung the saddlebags into place. "If you say you're going to start two hours after dawn, that's when you should start. Octavia is no true Amazon."

"I never heard punctuality was part of the oath,"

Sharyl replied in a voice tinged with laughter. "And don't let Mother Anna hear you saying *Amazon*."

"Being responsible *is* part of being a Renunciate. And not being on time is irresponsible."

"Delaa, Octavia is hardly irresponsible. She does the work of two women, even three. So, sometimes she does so much she's late. That doesn't make her irresponsible," Sharyl chided.

"Oh, I know," muttered Delaa. "She always has a good *reason* why she's late. But if she were truly so wonderful, she'd organize herself so she was on time. *I'm* busy, too, and I don't like being kept waiting for her to show up." She swung her tall body up onto her chervine and held her reins as if she were prepared to depart any moment.

Sharyl signed. It was no use. Delaa and Octavia were chalk and cheese. She had told Mother Anna that pairing them for a journey would never work, but Mother had said skills were what were important, not personalities. Until the newly established Derin Guild House built up their numbers and their members learned the skills, they needed the loan of a midwife, a swordswoman, and a guide. She, Octavia, and Delaa were them. And since Derin House would likely think it a favor to house the three of them together, they would be cheek by jowl not just for the journey, but for the entire six months of their stay. Sharyl sighed and wondered if she could persuade the Derin Guildmother to give them separate quarters without revealing the shame of two Guild-sisters who could *not* get along.

Quick footsteps sounded down the overgrown path.

"Hello. Sorry I'm late," Octavia said cheerfully, shaking her brown hair out of her eyes. Her wide, mobile mouth curved in a bright smile. "I heard Tavish was coming in to market, so I waited for him to arrive. I got that rope you were unable to find yesterday, Delaa. Good herring weave," she said with satisfaction, giving a tug on the end of the thin, strong rope. "Here."

She handed several lengths of it up to Delaa, who was still ensconced upon her chervine.

"Thanks," Delaa grunted ungraciously, a twinge of guilt making her expression even more sour. It had been her job to get the rope; she was the guide. It would be needed for breaking horses and chervines for the fledgling Guild House, and possibly on the trip itself. They would be traveling through some pretty rugged foothills, and you never knew when you might need extra rope. She *had* gone to the market yesterday to purchase it, but she'd found only a weave good enough for hanging wash or belting a pair of trousers, but worthless under the demands she would put on it. She could have searched further, she supposed, but she hadn't wanted to be late for her before-dinner chores.

Delaa got down off her chervine and stowed the rope away properly.

The three of them left the Guild House behind, made their way out of the busy city and traveled along the road that crossed the plains. They were not far from the foothills, and well before sunset they turned off the main road onto the beginning of the trail that would lead them up into them. Delaa fussed about, rejecting first one and then another possible campsite as unsuitable. At last they found one that met her acceptance, and Sharyl settled in gratefully, spreading blankets upon the ground and starting a fire. Delaa gathered the chervines together and led them over to the stream to drink.

"I'm going to go check out this trail," Octavia said, loosing her sword from the back of her pack and oversetting it in the process. She didn't bother to straighten it, but moved off down the path. Delaa, coming back with the chervines, noticed and tightened her lips.

She proceeded to groom the chervines and then, her back rigid with annoyance, straightened and arranged all three packs as neatly as guards at attention.

The fire was stable; a pot of water above it was already softening the dried trail meat when Octavia returned. Sharyl looked up in relief. She had begun to worry.

Octavia smiled and held up a rabbit by its hind feet.

"What a perfect time to return!" Delaa said sarcastically. "When all the work is done!"

"Yes, I see *you've* been busy," Octavia snapped, looking at the packs. "And checking the trail for rock falls and markers is work, too, not to mention getting us a rabbit for the stew!"

"Thanks, Octavia," Sharyl intervened. "The stew's ready, but we can split the rabbit and roast the pieces."

They did so, and ate them, the hot fat from the rabbit running down the sticks and over their chins. No one complained: hot, fresh rabbit tasted *much* better than any trail food devised.

Soon after finishing, they turned in: trail hours. Sharyl grumbled a bit as she had to get up and remove first one and then two acorns from under her blanket. Despite the most careful cleaning, one or two rocks or acorns or whatever was indigenous to an area always waited for you to lie down before making its presence felt.

In the morning pine needles stuck stubbornly in their hair as they brushed it, and limbs were achy from the cold ground. It would have been surprising if no one grumbled, but usually, Sharyl thought, it was more good-natured than what Delaa and Octavia exchanged. Sharyl was thoroughly out of sorts by the time she had stowed her blanket and saddle bags on her chervine.

"You have to go to the stream *again?*" Delaa asked Octavia.

"Some people care about cleanliness," Octavia muttered as she rummaged through her bag, looking for her small face cloth. She found it and stomped back to the stream.

"Are you saying I didn't wash my face? I just didn't make a big deal out of it!" Delaa shouted after her.

"Hush!" Sharyl said wearily. "There's no need to announce our presence to every creature between here and the Hellers!"

Delaa made a face but kept her silence as Octavia

finished up, cinched her pack together, and clambered up onto her chervine. At last they were off, and Sharyl took the lead. Although Delaa was a guide and Octavia a swordswoman, it was Sharyl who was most familiar with the foothills. She had grown up in them.

Usually the moment her chervine started climbing, she relaxed into total enjoyment of the trees of her childhood and refreshingly thinner air. But this time her peace was destroyed by the two behind her. First would come an observation, about anything from a rock to the sky, that Delaa would manage to turn into an insult. Then from farther down the trail could be heard Octavia's answer.

When their bickering halted the song of a thirene, Sharyl, her patience exhausted, turned in her saddle. "SHUT UP!" she screamed.

That produced silence, but Sharyl, with a throat raw from the scream, gained no peace. Her enjoyment of the foothills had been destroyed by the two, and it wasn't to be won back.

That night the three of them prepared their campsite in silence. In silence the tough trail meat was softened, the chervines readied for the night, and the meal eaten. Sharyl lay on her blanket as it was, annoying stones and all. She didn't have the energy, or the interest, to get up and make it more comfortable. She stared up at the stars through the dark branches, and it wasn't until Idriel had begun its pass that her thoughts faded into scattered dreams.

She was thoroughly grouchy and achy the next morning. Octavia also moved without her usual zip, and Delaa's eyebrows didn't bother to rise even once. Sharyl registered that they were feeling out of sorts also, but she, usually the peacemaker, didn't care. If it kept them silent, then she would count it a blessing.

As usual, Delaa was ready well before the other two. Sharyl, trudging back up from the stream to the hairbrush she'd forgotten, decided she would make herself a small pouch for morning necessities as Delaa had. Having everything together was a big convenience on the trail; it would come in handy in the Guild House, as well. Guests usually got whatever rooms were free, and that usually meant the ones farthest from the bathroom.

Sharyl was still musing on this, and wondering what their accommodation at Derin Guild House would be when she creaked into her saddle.

"*Finally* ready?" Delaa asked sweetly. Sharyl silenced her with a murderous look and slapped her reins gently against her chervine's neck.

"You lead," she snapped at Delaa. "You're the guide."

Delaa opened her mouth to protest that Sharyl had *asked* to lead before, because of old familiarity, but she changed her mind after a second glance at the other's face. Quietly she took the lead.

Octavia moved into her usual position, protecting their rear from unwelcome two-footed and four-footed beasts. That left Sharyl in the middle, which she hoped would foil Delaa's attempts to badger Octavia. It was only partially successful. By midday, her mouth was grim and her head was pounding.

Octavia nudged her chervine forward to talk to Sharyl. "You know what she was at me about this morning?" she demanded in an exasperated voice. "If I put all my morning necessities in a small pouch and carried it to the stream instead of walking back and forth to my pack two or three times, I would save a minute and a half every morning! I ask you!"

"It is a good idea," Sharyl said, congratulating herself on the mildness of her tone, considering what her head felt like.

"Of course it is! But who but Delaa would measure exactly how much time it would save! The time it takes to do this! The time for that! Does she ever stop worrying about time long enough to *live?*"

Sharyl shrugged. Each person had their foibles, and after thirty-five years in a Guild House she had learned to ignore or accept most of them. Couldn't these two? "She enjoys being precise as another might like pretty festival clothes."

"Precise! She's . . ."

"Enough," Sharyl said firmly.

Octavia bit back the rest of her reply. "Yes. Sorry." She let her chervine drift back behind Sharyl's again. The next time any of them spoke was near the end of the day, when Octavia suggested they start looking for a good place to camp.

"There's a small town on this path, I believe," Sharyl said, dredging her memory.

"Valan," Delaa, always prepared, replied. "About twenty families, mostly trappers, hunters and hide-sewers. There's a small inn."

"An inn!" Octavia said. "No rocks and acorns! No prickly pine needles! *Real* food! I will enjoy it to the utmost!"

"It won't be an inn like you're accustomed to," Delaa snapped. "Probably just one room in the corner of someone's home."

"I don't care," Octavia declared fervently, her anticipation only slightly dampened.

Delaa made a face. "Probably lark about talking to everyone and take two hours to say good-bye in the morning," she muttered under her breath.

Octavia snapped her elbows against her sides, and straightened her back parade rigid, the picture of disdain. Sharyl sighed. She had known the quiet would end soon. But she *had* hoped it would at least survive the journey.

The town of Valan was small, the inn low-beamed and dark. But it was bigger than Delaa had said. *Two* rooms over where the family lived. Plus a small common room for eating, drinking, and whatever conviviality this town had. The common room had a fire. After dumping her packs in the room they had engaged, Sharyl came back down the stairs and settled down beside it gratefully. She had forgotten how chill even foothills could be this time of year.

Octavia walked over and engaged what appeared to be the innkeeper's daughter in conversation.

Delaa, coming back from seeing their chervines content in the stable, harrumphed when she saw Octavia chattering away and stomped up the stairs to the room.

Good riddance, Sharyl thought. She was tired of Delaa's sulks and her ill-considered remarks. She was tired of Octavia's quick offense. She was tired of riding horseback, tired of living out of a pack, tired of woods and rock-studded trails and rabbits that thumped mockingly away, leaving them to dried trail meat. She was especially tired of companions who were anything but. She leaned back against the bench and let her eyes drift shut.

Delaa's touch awakened her. "They're serving dinner."

"Oh. Where's Octavia?" Sharyl asked, looking about.

"Who knows?" Delaa asked with an edge to her voice. Sharyl bit back a shrewish retort of her own. A few days in the undiluted company of these two and she was ready to behave like them!

Delaa and Sharyl sat down to hot plates of stew and small, fresh-baked loaves of bread. Sharyl would have enjoyed her first good meal in three days a bit more if she knew where Octavia was. Even more than in the cities, Renunciates were regarded with suspicion in these remote areas. She thought of Octavia possibly being set upon while they ate, and the soft, sweet-smelling bread turned to straw in her mouth. She debated searching for Octavia, but knew, if everything was all right, the other woman would resent it as only a swordswoman, proud of her own ability, would resent a midwife mothering her. Sharyl chewed some more and wondered.

When they were almost done, Octavia, carefree and smiling, walked in.

"Ah, this looks good."

"Sure you wouldn't rather eat it with your new friends?" Delaa snapped.

Sharyl lay her fork down with a snap. "Enough," she said, low-voiced and angry. "I've listened to the two of you peck and prick at each other for months now, not to mention your behavior on the trail, and

I'm not going to listen to any more of it. If you don't have the maturity to accept each other as you are, or the loyalty to the oath to honor your own Guild-sister, then have the courtesy to keep your squabbling to yourselves!''

"I'm sorry," Octavia said sincerely.

Delaa looked down at her plate. "It's mainly my fault," she said in a low voice.

"It's *both* your faults," Sharyl said. "Octavia, Delaa *has* a point. You shouldn't go wandering off in a strange town, with no word to either of us. I don't care *how* good a swordswoman you are, it's not wise. Nor is it considerate of your fellow travelers. I barely tasted what I ate, I was so busy worrying about you. If it weren't for your constant habit of behaving this way, I would have been out scouring the town!''

"I'm sorry . . . I didn't think . . . I *am* a grown woman. . . .''

"We're *all* of us grown women. But there's a *reason* Renunciates don't travel alone. It's because we're none of us invincible. You, especially, with your sword and breeches, are a challenge to most men, and even some women. Someone might decide to better the world by removing you from it.''

"Yes. I know. I'm sorry. I was just . . . Jayla, the young woman I was talking to, has a half sister who's in the Neskaya Guild House. She asked if we were from there. And,'' Octavia shrugged guiltily, "one thing led to another. I got to helping her in the kitchen, and then we kept talking even after you were served. I'm sorry.''

"Accepted," Sharyl replied. "But *do* think of others. *You* knew you were safe, but we didn't. And Delaa, stop carping at others. If you have a legitimate grief, discuss it reasonably, but this habit you have of snide remarks is juvenile and unbecoming. And stop busying yourself trying to reshape everyone else to your way of doing things; you're not perfect, nor is your way the best for everyone. There's strength in differences. If everyone were best suited to be a guide, the horses and chervines would be well-cared for, but there'd be some pretty lonely birthing tables. Not to mention ill-cooked food.''

"Yes, Sharyl.''

"Octavia is quick to explore new surroundings, quick to see new possibilities, quick to change her mind. You see that as a fault to be expunged, but don't you see that it's that quickness that makes her such a good swordswoman?''

Delaa stared back at Sharyl confounded. "I . . . I . . .''

Sharyl pressed on. "Just like your attention to details, your care in planning, your memory, make *you* a good guide.''

"And your compassion and insight into people makes you a good midwife,'' Octavia said, low-voiced, in something of a cross between an apology and a compliment.

Sharyl shrugged it off. "Some would say that's a fault, that I'm too 'womanly' to be a Renunciate, that I act too much as men would have all women act. All I can say to that is I hold the oath as dear as any Renunciate, but all I can be is me. That's all any of us can be—and despite what men say or believe, we're *not* all the same. What's more, we *need* our differences. It's what makes the Renunciates strong. It's what makes any group strong.''

The rest of the meal passed more pleasantly than any they had shared yet. Still, Sharyl felt too exhausted to enjoy the peace.

By the time they were finished, some of the townsfolk had started to gather in the inn's common room. With a touch of apprehension, Sharyl noticed none of them were women. The three Renunciates gathered not a few looks.

"Come on,'' she said, low-voiced, to the other two women.

"Right,'' they agreed as swiftly, and left the common room for the privacy of their own chamber. Sharyl eyed the plain door that had no lock or latch. She wedged the wide platform bed against it.

Delaa started to arrange all of their packs as she

always did, then stopped and stared awkwardly at them.

"It does make sense," Octavia said, realizing the other was wondering if this was another of the annoying habits she should stop. "It certainly speeds up the morning."

Delaa smiled at her gratefully, and the two of them lined the packs up, ropes and other gear neatly bestowed, fresh clothes for the morning on top of openings nearly cinched shut, the short swords they prudently carried propped neatly in the pack loops, ready to hand. In the morning, all they would have to do was thrust used clothes and morning articles inside, cinch tight, lift and be off. It made Delaa feel good to see them ready like that, and Octavia felt better for having given a little. She walked over to shutter the windows.

"No, leave them open," Sharyl yawned. "We might need the light of sunrise to wake us up."

"But even if we wake up, will we want to get out of our first bed in three nights?" Octavia asked with a smile.

"Another bed tomorrow," Sharyl replied, happy at the thought their destination was so close. She stretched a little and settled down on the bed. She punched her rolled cloak into a comfortable shape for a pillow and drifted off to sleep as the others blew out the candles and did likewise. For a few hours the only movement in the room was the drift of the light of the moons across the dark wood of the floor.

The pounding sounded like thunder and Sharyl's dream wandered confusedly between rain and trees falling before she realized someone was knocking on the door right next to their heads.

"Huh. Wumph?"

"Octavia!" a voice hissed through the thick wooden door.

"Whazzat?" a voice muttered grumpily from under the blanket next to Sharyl.

Sharyl's instincts had come fully awake now, and

something about the utter darkness of the night and the far-off murmurs of angry voices had her feet moving out of the bed even as she shoved Delaa and Octavia awake.

"Octavia!" the voice on the other side of the door implored.

"*Jayla?* It's the middle of the night . . ." Octavia's voice trailed off as, like Sharyl, she noticed the unnatural darkness of the night beyond the unshuttered windows.

"You've got to get *out* of here! They're saying you're witches! Quick, before they come back in the inn!"

"Great!" muttered Sharyl, as she started to haul the bed away from the door. Delaa helped her.

Octavia dived over to the wall and cinched the packs shut, silently thanking Delaa that they were both ready and easy to find in the dark. Where *was* the moon Liriel? Or Idriel either, for that matter?

The door opened. Jayla motioned to them. "Quick. We can go down the back stairs."

Octavia, Delaa, and Sharyl hoisted their packs and all three, not just Octavia, grasped the hilts of their swords in their hands.

As they stepped into the hall, a sudden increase in noise signaled the arrival of a mob at the foot of the stairs.

"There they are!" someone shouted and began the rush up the stairs.

Sharyl jumped back, crowding Jayla, Octavia, and Delaa behind her. Quickly they slammed the door shut and heaved the bed back across it.

With one thought, they sprang toward the window. "It's too high!" Jayla protested.

In answer, Delaa thrust her sword through its loop on her pack and unwound one of the lengths of rope Octavia had bought. Sharyl flung open the window. As if they had rehearsed it, Octavia leapt onto the sill, crouched like a frog, and threw out the loose end of the rope Delaa handed her. She disappeared down its gray length. Delaa grunted as the rope pulled taut under Octavia's weight.

"Jayla!" Sharyl hissed.

The girl darted forward in a flurry of skirts and Sharyl helped her over the sill as the pounding on the door changed to a shudder.

"You next!" Delaa said to Sharyl. Sharyl jumped, grasped the rope, and slid.

Down in the inn's dark yard the three women peered upward, trying to see Delaa come out of the window.

"Hurry!" Octavia whispered under her breath.

The window stayed a dark hole. At last Delaa appeared. She slid down, jerking as the rope jumped with a life of its own. There was a creaking, sliding sound as the bed to which she'd tied it pulled away from the door. From the room above came angry shouts, but Delaa was already down.

As soon as her feet met the ground, the four of them ran.

"This way!" Jayla hissed and darted around the pigpen, under wash ropes and down the path behind the stables. She turned and darted into the woods.

"The chervines!" Delaa protested.

"Guarded," Jayla hissed tersely. "Don't *talk!*"

The three women followed her blurred gray figure, stumbling and fetching up against trees in the unnatural dark. Sharyl snatched quick glances upward, wondering what had happened to the moons. All four should be out tonight, but the only one she could see was Mormallor. Yet the sky wasn't clouded over; she could see stars between the thinning branches of the trees. She shivered superstitiously, remembering tales of her childhood of places of enchantment where a night's sleep took months or even years from your life.

She ran into a soft body in front of her. Gasped.

"I have to go back," Jayla whispered from the side of a large boulder. "Just climb up by the side of this boulder and follow the crevice on up to where it joins the high trail. That's a longer way, and more dangerous, but it will take you to Derin. You do have more rope, don't you?"

"Yes . . . thanks to Octavia, we have plenty," Delaa said, a bit galled that it was the other woman's

preparedness and not her own that they had to thank
this time. She was glad Octavia didn't rub it in, knowing *she* would have. She felt ashamed of herself, and
knew Sharyl was right about her quickness to criticize.
She was far from perfect, and . . . maybe she didn't
even need to be. Maybe that was a legacy of her father's demands that should have been shed with her
long hair.

"Sorry, Octavia," she whispered so low the others
didn't hear her. *And sorry, Delaa,* she apologized to
herself.

"Good luck," Jayla was wishing them.

"But you can't go back there," Sharyl protested.
"They'll punish you for helping us."

"If anyone saw me, I'll say I was bewitched by
you."

"But why did they think us witches? Just because
we're Renunciates?" Octavia asked, bewildered.

"No. Well, yes. I mean, it's because of the moons."

"Yes, where *are* the moons?" asked Sharyl low-
voiced.

"Shadowed," Jayla answered briefly.

"*Three* of them at once?" Sharyl asked in dismay.
At least one moon would fall into shadow every six
months or so. It would last a few hours and then the
errant moon would creep back out again, a bit at a
time. It wasn't unheard of for two to be shadowed in
the same night, though Sharyl had never seen it herself. But three? No wonder the townfolk of this remote
village thought them witches! Were she still a
mountain-girl, she might have thought it a spell herself, instead of merely the natural movement of Darkover's moons into the planet's shadow.

"Yes. Well, you see. You were strangers. It could
have been anyone, but you being Renunciates . . . I
don't think even I would have helped you if I hadn't
talked to Octavia . . . I mean, strangers . . . and this
happening."

"You've risked much for perfect strangers," Delaa
said. "Why?"

"Well, I knew Octavia was no witch, and you're her

sworn sisters, so of course . . . It must be wonderful, the three of you always having each other, and all the other Renunciates as well.''

There was an awkward pause. Then Delaa broke it. "It is wonderful," she said. "Not that all of us deserve it.''

Octavia's hand came up and rested on Delaa's. Lightly she gripped the other woman in the traditional gesture of comradeship. The two of them smiled slightly at each other under the dim glow of Mormallor.

"I have to get back," Jayla said with a rush.

"Yes, of course. And thank you," Sharyl said gratefully.

Octavia gave Jayla a quick hug, barely seen in the dimness, and Delaa murmured her thanks as well. Then the three Renunciates were alone.

"Well?" Sharyl asked after a pause, eyeing what she could see of the boulder.

"You first," Octavia said, a grin in her voice.

"Yes," Delaa agreed, and the two of them moved as one to help Sharyl clamber up the steep, ankle-wide "path" next to the boulder.

"It gets worse," she groaned down to the two of them.

"We'll make it," Octavia said.

"Together," Delaa agreed.

Six days later, three battered Renunciates knocked at the door of Derin Guild House. One of them was missing her pack; none of them led chervines. All of them had tears in their clothes that, to the knowledgeable, spoke of scratches and bruises on the flesh beneath. Still, despite their appearance, they did not seem angry or upset. Indeed, they seemed oddly triumphant. The tallest of the three was joking, pretending to crown the brown-haired one with a length of rope, while the older one rested weary bones against the side of the building and smiled.

Still, even in the face of such good spirits, the young Renunciate who answered the door did not expect her brief admonition that their arrival was long overdue to reduce all three of them to helpless laughter.

"But we had a good reason!" the tall one named Delaa gasped over her laughter, as the three of them entered arm in arm.

Family Visit

by Margaret L. Carter

*Margaret Carter says she wrote this story "about phe-
nomena that I have some personal acquaintance with—
midlife crisis, the career-family conflict, and the clash
between masculine and feminine attitudes." She
should know; she has four sons aged 8 to 23, and has
published six books, the latest entitled A STUDY OF
THE VAMPIRE IN LITERATURE. However, she's still
awaiting her first book-length fiction sale, even though
she's appeared in four of my anthologies. Her agent is
trying to place a (vampire) novel called SEALED IN
BLOOD. Sounds like fun—I love vampires . . . if
they're good. (What a semantic conflict! What's good
about a vampire? As my co-editor on my magazine
says, "How gross!")*

*Margaret Carter now lives in Annapolis but is re-
turning—with her husband, a career Navy man—to
California in 1991.*

Water dripped from Renata n'ha Jamilla's gray-
streaked brown hair, in spite of her hooded cloak. Her
muscles slackened with relief at stepping from the
spring night's steady rain into the shelter of the Guild
House. But she tensed again at the expression on the
face of the hallkeeper.

Setting down her midwife's bag, Renata said,
"What's wrong, Tani?"

Tani, a plump blonde half Renata's age, said, "A
messenger asking for you, sister—he's waiting in the
Strangers' Room."

"In Avarra's name, not another baby to deliver? One

is quite enough for a night!'' Renata feared some graver problem, though, from the anxiety in Tani's eyes.

"No, it's a servant of your—the man who was your husband." Renata felt her throat tighten at the words. "If you don't want to see him, I can get his message and send him away."

Renata forced a smile. "Why shouldn't I see the man? I've no reason to fear Geremy or anyone from his household."

"I thought—since you did leave him—" Tani blushed.

"I'm not afraid to speak of it, either, but the tale is very dull. The old saying that every Renunciate's story is a tragedy isn't true of mine." Indeed, Renata had broken away from a life many women would have considered ideal; she remembered a training session, during her housebound time, when a girl scarred by a father's beatings had taunted her with that truth. Nevertheless, Renata felt an inner chill at the idea of communicating with Geremy. She had seen neither him nor her former home since the day she had left, over four years ago.

Well, the sooner she found out what the messenger wanted, the better. *One of our children must be ill. Why else would Geremy stoop to send me word?* She strode rapidly into the Strangers' Room.

The wiry, leathery-skinned man seated on the straight-backed chair stood up as she entered the room. "Good evening, Dame Renata. I pray the gods all is well with you?"

Up close, she recognized him as one of the chief servants on her former husband's prosperous horse-breeding ranch. "Very well, Davin." She offered him her fingertips. "What trouble brings you here?"

Davin swallowed, shifting his eyes from hers. "My master asks you to ride back with me, and he sends you this." He thrust a message-tube into her hand.

Removing and unrolling the letter, Renata stepped a few paces away to read it. Her husband's rough handwriting said: "Our daughter Lanilla is to bear twins at

Midsummer, and she has had a difficult pregnancy. She has come home to rest until the birth. She asks you to visit her. Even after forgetting all your other obligations, surely you will not deny the claims of your youngest child.''

With a sigh Renata rolled up the parchment. Her efforts to part from Geremy without bitterness had done no good at the time, and clearly his view had not changed. She anxiously searched Davin's face. "Is Lanilla very sick?''

"Not now, Dame Renata, but the children weigh heavily on her, and the midwife has ordered her to keep to her chamber. She has lost all the others—" Davin caught himself. "These things are not for me to speak of.''

Renata knew that Lanilla had miscarried twice during her first year of marriage. She had not seen her daughter since three Midwinters ago, when she had visited the girl's new home at Festival. The holiday, begun in cold formality, had ended in a quarrel. Lanilla resented Renata's leaving as much as Geremy did. As for Renata, she had failed to hide her irritation at seeing Lanilla, apparently content, chained into the same limited existence she herself had fled. "Then we have time for you to be refreshed with a hot drink,'' Renata said, "and me to pack. I'll be ready to ride in less than an hour.''

While bundling a compact assortment of clothes into a pack, she tried to hold at bay her anxiety over returning to her old home for the first time since taking the Oath. A mere three days' ride, yet it might as well have been the far side of the Hellers. Lanilla, youngest and last-married of five daughters—Renata and Geremy had produced no sons—was the only one who lived near her father's home, and the only one to invite her mother's company. *And once was enough for her! No doubt all of them still think I've gone mad.*

Renata visualized Lanilla at the age of sixteen, on the afternoon of her wedding, dumbfounded at Renata's announcement of her plan to leave for Arilinn Guild House the very next day. The girl had taken the announcement as a personal betrayal. How could Renata explain that only the wait for her youngest child's marriage had kept her with Geremy so long? Now, with Lanilla safely wedded to a younger son of a minor noble—a proud triumph for a horse-breeder—Renata had felt no further obligation to limit her own freedom.

She closed her pack and glanced at her midwife's bag in the corner, filled with the instruments of her craft as well as drugs, both traditional herbal remedies and potions borrowed from the *Terranan*. She decided to leave it behind. Why exacerbate the inescapable tension by flaunting her choice that way? She would not need her supplies, since Lanilla was not acutely ill and had a midwife nearby anyway. Renata's typical Renunciate tunic and trousers would cause enough of a sensation in her husband's household.

Should I wear skirts instead? No—it was one thing to avoid provoking a fight, another to appear ashamed of her sisterhood. *Besides, I could hardly grow my hair down to the middle of my back in three days*, she thought with a wry smile.

No external change would make any difference if Lanilla still harbored bitterness. But surely, Renata thought, this summons must mean the child wanted to resume a loving relationship. The thought hastened her steps as she went down to rejoin Davin. In the absence of an emergency, she could have waited until morning to depart, but she longed to get the journey over with as quickly as possible.

Apparently he felt the same way, for he did not object to mounting up and setting out in the rain. They could make several hours before weariness forced a halt for the rest of the night. Renata noted with rueful amusement that Geremy had sent one of his finest mares for her to ride. The man had never been less than courteous to her, even after his mild affection had turned to scorn. Davin still seemed embarrassed to meet Renata's eyes or speak to her, though. No doubt he felt uncomfortable, caught between his master and his former mistress.

"Can't you tell me anything more about Lanilla's condition?" she asked him as they rode down the deserted street away from the Guild House. "I've missed her." Renata felt a twinge of sadness at the memory of her last-born as a baby at her breast, then a flash of Lanilla at twelve, helping her attend the birthings and illnesses of the ranch-hands' wives. *Stop that,* she commanded herself, *you're not old enough to melt into a puddle of sentiment.* "Why has she come home, instead of staying at her own estate for the birth?" she prompted Davin.

"From what I've heard the *damisela* say," he replied, "she was lonely. She wanted to give birth under the care of her old nurse." Annelys, who had tended all of Renata's babies. "She's frightened, I think—she has lost so many before their time, and this is the first she has carried even this long—" He trailed off, clearly uncomfortable at being urged to step outside his place. He would not say anymore, replying to further questions with polite nothings.

At the moment of riding up to the gates of the respectable stone house where she had spent most of her adult life, Renata felt little more than relief at the prospect of getting out of the drizzly night and under a dry roof. Rain, light or heavy, had hung over her all the way from Arilinn, and judging from the mountains of gray clouds that had preceded sunset on this third day of travel, a storm might break before morning. Davin showed her into the Great Hall and quickly withdrew to care for the horses.

Before Renata stood a slender young woman with hair of pale gold. Dori, the *barragana* Geremy had taken the year before Lanilla's marriage. If his behavior in Renata's bed the last few years was any indication, he had sought a mistress more for the status befitting his wealth than for sensual pleasure.

And one other purpose. As the girl crept timidly forward—*why, she's far more self-conscious about this meeting than I am!*—Renata noted the incongruous heaviness of the girl's bosom in contrast to her other-

wise slight figure. Davin had let slip the fact that Dori
had recently borne Geremy a son. *So now he has the
male heir he always wanted.*

Dori ducked her head in a half-bow. "Welcome to—
to your house, Dame Renata."

Some of Renata's tension dissolved in the impulse
to relieve this child's anxiety. She stepped up to clasp
Dori's hand. "It's your home now, and I don't intend
to come back and usurp it. I bear you no ill will."

Dori acknowledged the gesture with a shy smile.
Why had Geremy never married the girl? Probably because that would imply that Renata was no longer his
wife, an admission he would feel as a defeat.

Before Renata could protest, Dori unfastened her
cloak for her. "Let me call someone to bring you a
hot drink. You must be exhausted after such a journey."

So Geremy would not greet her himself. Well, she
had hardly expected it. Could she avoid meeting him
throughout her stay? And how long was she invited to
stay, anyhow? "Later, perhaps—I'm anxious to see
Lanilla. Is she awake?"

A moment later Renata stood at the door of Lanilla's
chamber, the same room the girl had occupied as a
child. Old Annelys opened to her knock—a small
woman, but still straight-backed, her black hair shot
with silver. Renata interrupted Annelys' half curtsy
with a hug.

"We've missed you, Dame Renata. Could it be that
you've come back—"

Renata cut her off. "Only to see Lanilla." She knew
better than to try explaining her decision. Annelys
would only react as she had four years ago, shaking
her head and clucking as if her mistress' wits had taken
flight.

Renata hardly heard the door close behind the de-
parting nurse. Lanilla, in a heavily cushioned chair
next to the bed, started to pull herself to her feet.
Renata hurried across the room and clasped her
hands. "Don't get up, *chiya.*" She bent to kiss her
daughter.

Lanilla turned her head to catch the kiss on her cheek. "So you did come, Mother. I wasn't sure you'd be able to spare the time."

A pang of mingled hurt and annoyance went through Renata. She swallowed the impulse to point out that Lanilla, not she, had ended their last meeting in anger. *She wanted me to linger nearby to help tend my grandchildren. Young people always think their parents are put in the world for their convenience.* "Leading my own life doesn't mean forsaking you," she said as mildly as she could manage.

"What's wrong with the life you had? Oh, let's not go into that again." Lanilla shifted restlessly. Pulling up a smaller chair for herself, Renata noted with dismay the changes in her daughter. Lanilla's deep auburn hair looked dry and lifeless, her skin the color of pale clay. Renata's trained eye fixed on the swollen ankles, the bloating of the face in contrast to the slender arms.

"I was told you're not well. What does the midwife say?"

Lanilla cupped her hands around her oversize belly. "She insists I must spend the next two and a half moons in this chamber, moving from bed to chair and back again. Merciful Goddess, I'm sick of it already!"

"If that is necessary to save your health and your babies' lives, you must do it," said Renata. Inwardly she raged at the unnecessary pain and hazard. The *Terranan* had drugs to neutralize the poisons this disorder produced in a pregnant woman's body. But Geremy, always conservative, would never allow his daughter to be treated with such innovative methods. Probably Gareth, Lanilla's husband, was just as tradition-bound.

Seeing Lanilla rub her forehead, Renata, with her rudimentary trace of *laran,* caught a flash of the chronic headache the girl endured. "I'll do anything to bring this pregnancy to term. I've lost so many—" Wiping her damp eyes, Lanilla gulped down a sob. "This is the first one I've carried past the third moon. But I'm so tired."

Renata patted her shoulder. "Then that's a good sign; you may well keep this one. But you mustn't upset yourself, it's bad for your babies." How could Lanilla put herself through this ordeal over and over, year after year? And why did she stay with a man who forced such suffering upon her? Surely there were plenty of neglected children in need of fostering that she could adopt. Knowing better than to voice these thoughts aloud, Renata said, "And I'm here now. I'm so glad you sent for me."

Resentment smoldered in Lanilla's eyes. "That's hard to believe, considering how you were in such a hurry to leave us. At least you might have warned me, instead of disappearing the day after my wedding."

Surprised, for she had never thought of her decision that way, Renata said, "*Chiya*, I thought it better not to say anything ahead of time. I didn't want to spoil your marriage preparations."

The spark in her eyes fading, Lanilla said, "Well, that was not how I saw it. I felt you couldn't wait to get rid of me, so that you could begin your 'own life.' "

"Oh, my dear!" Renata started to embrace her, then drew back when Lanilla stiffened. "That didn't make you any less a part of my life. But after all those years, I came to realize Geremy was not allowing me to be a whole person. How can I explain to you?" She couldn't; she had tried before, pouring her thoughts into closed ears. None of the family could understand Renata's discontent as Geremy's brood mare and household manager. After all, what else should a woman expect from marriage? She had her husband's confidence and the respect of his servants. Why would she want to study midwifery at Arilinn—even, scandalously, nurturing what little *laran* she, though a commoner, possessed—and earn a few coins of her own, instead of remaining satisfied to deliver foals and servants' babies? Why should she waste time reading books about scientific horse-breeding methods and urging her husband to adopt those outlandish views, when such things lay outside a wife's legitimate

sphere? Too many occasions of having her suggestions
dismissed with a vague smile had convinced her Geremy would never acknowledge that she had a mind of
her own. But Lanilla, like Renata's other daughters,
found these complaints frivolous and incomprehensi-
ble.

Lanilla did not invite explanation. "My back hurts,
and I want to go to bed. Send Annelys to me, please."

Leaving the bedchamber, Renata suppressed a sigh.
Maybe tomorrow, rested, the girl would be more open
to her mother's affection.

Striding briskly through the great hall, Renata inter-
cepted the maid carrying a pot of steaming herb tea
toward the stairs. "I'll take that in the back sitting
room. And I want to see Master Geremy—right now."

A few minutes later she sat on a familiar worn couch
before the hearth in the small parlor, sipping her tea.
Faintly, through the stone walls, she heard the howl
of a rising storm beat against the house. She forced
herself to greet Geremy with a cool nod when he
marched in to take a seat opposite her.

"So, Renata." He cleared his throat. "I thank you
for coming. No doubt you are quite—busy."

Her suppressed irritation bubbled over. "Gods, do
you all think taking the oath has turned me into a monster? Did you really think I'd ignore my own child's
suffering?" She thumped her mug down on the table,
sloshing tea out of it.

"Gareth and Lanilla have been through so much
grief, trying over and over to have a child," he said.
"Thank the Goddess, it looks as if this time the birth
may take place."

"Gareth—!" Renata caught herself, knowing that
berating Geremy about men's insensitivity would do
no good. "Geremy, how could even you let this go
on? Can't you see how bad off Lanilla is? She needs
more help than a country midwife can give."

He sat up straight and said in a frosty tone, "That
kind of help was good enough for you."

Renata shook her head in exasperation. "I gave birth
like a sturdy plow mare. Lanilla is different. She needs

special food supplements, and medicine to purge the poisons from her system. When the twins come, it might take instruments to deliver them safely, not to mention equipment to keep them alive if they're born too early."

"Enough! You know how I feel about those *Terranan* customs."

"Does keeping tradition mean you have to be blind to simple common sense?" Renata choked down her anger. True, Geremy had a grain of common sense on his side, too; even some of Renata's teachers questioned the wisdom of using complicated techniques to save infants the Goddess would have allowed to die. *But not my daughter's babies!* More quietly Renata said, "At least, if you'd warned me how ill she was, I could have brought my supplies. Some of the medicines in my bag could—"

Geremy flushed. "She doesn't need the kind of tricks you learned from a pack of women who seduce wives to desert their husbands!"

So Geremy still held that grudge. He could have understood, had his wife left him for a younger or wealthier man—but for a *pack of women?* He had never begun to grasp Renata's motives.

"I don't care what you think of me, but your feelings shouldn't keep our daughter from getting the best possible treatment."

Geremy stood up. "I don't wish to speak of this again. You are welcome to stay as long as Lanilla wants you, but don't upset her with your wild ideas."

Renata gritted her teeth to keep from screaming at him. "Believe me, Geremy, I would never think of bringing *ideas* into your house."

In the depths of the night, a crash of thunder woke Renata. Sore from three days of riding, she groped her way to the window and looked out. A flash of lightning showed a curtain of rain and a flooded stable-yard.

Had the thunder alone awakened her? For some reason a chill clung to her limbs, despite the heavy nightgown, and her heart scampered like a panicked rabbit-horn. Mere nervousness after a rough day, or a genuine warning from her embryonic *laran?*

Lanilla! she thought. *Something is wrong!*

At that instant, a thin shriek split the air. Grabbing a house gown and shrugging it on over her nightdress, Renata scurried into the corridor. The scream sounded again.

She raced to Lanilla's room, where she found Annelys massaging the girl's back, trying to calm her. Geremy paced near the door. "It's too early—far too early. I've sent one of my men for the midwife—"

"Have you seen the storm out there?" Renata cried. "Do you seriously think she can get here in time? If your messenger even gets through in the first place?" Hurrying to Lanilla's bedside, she clasped the girl's face between her hands. "Hush, *chiya*, you must be calm. Take a long, deep breath—that's it—let it out slowly. Good girl." She held Lanilla's eyes with her own and compelled the girl's breathing to slow and deepen. With a glance at Geremy, Renata said, "I'll take care of her. This is what I'm trained for."

Fists clenched, he retorted, "You think I'll allow your meddling—"

"Fool, what choice do you have?" she raged. "Do you care more about your prejudices than your daughter's life? Now get out and let me do my job."

Lanilla clutched her shoulder. "Yes, Mother—I want you to— Please don't let my babies die!"

"Work with me, darling, and I'll do my best." She said to Geremy, "If that midwife ever gets here, send her up." He stalked out of the room.

For the next two hours, Renata guided Lanilla's breathing, while Annelys stroked the girl's distended abdomen. Renata felt an echo of Lanilla's squeezing, tearing pain in her own body. She pushed it to the bottom layers of her mind, knowing she could not help her daughter if the contractions drained her, too. After the amniotic sac burst, Lanilla whimpered like a wounded animal while Annelys gently removed layers of soaked sheets to replace them with dry ones.

Renata stroked Lanilla's fingers, clenching and un-
clenching on the hem of the quilt. "You must relax,
chiya, and save your strength for pushing."

"I can't go on, I'm too tired," Lanilla moaned.
"Mother, make it stop!"

Annelys whispered in Renata's ear, "I'm afraid for
her. Pain this hard shouldn't go on so long." Lanilla,
submerged in the contractions, paid no attention.

"You're right," Renata murmured back. How she
longed for her small cache of *Terranan* drugs, to
smooth and quicken the labor and control bleeding.
She molded the shape of Lanilla's womb with her
hands. "It's too early for the babies; they haven't
turned yet. They are both lying head upward." At the
Guild House, she would probably deal with such a
case by surgery, rather than exhaust mother and infants
in an attempt at vaginal birth. Or, at the very least,
she would use forceps to ease the delivery. Here she
had only the skill in her mind and hands. "I'll have
to try turning them. Lanilla, darling, breathe deeply—
Annelys will help you—I must move the babies' heads
into the right position."

Renata's fingers flowed over her daughter's abdomen. While Lanilla gasped for air between shrieks,
Renata shifted the first infant's head, a fraction of an
inch with each stroke. Her wrists ached with cramps
by the time the baby finally slid into position, its head
nestled in the pelvic cradle. And none too soon—
Lanilla's cries changed to husky groans, and she
clutched Renata's arms in a crushing grip.

"Annelys, hold her up!" The nurse knelt behind
Lanilla to support her curled back. Freeing herself,
Renata stuffed the edges of the quilt into Lanilla's hands.
"Yes, *chiya,* push now! Stop—pant for me,
that's right—now take a deep breath and push again—"
She continued her litany, as automatic as her own
heartbeat, while monitoring the infant's progress by
touch and *laran.*

A moment later she saw the wet shape of the head
crowning. With a cry of triumph she caught the tiny
body that slipped into her hands.

"A girl," Annelys murmured. "But so small!"

"Thanks be to Avarra, you have a beautiful baby girl," Renata said to her daughter. She did not mention the baby's bluish skin. Handing the infant to Annelys, Renata whispered, "Breathe into her mouth—get air into her." She packed rolls of clean cloth under Lanilla's thighs to catch the gush of blood that followed the afterbirth. "Now the other baby. Take another deep breath."

Again her hands traced the outline of the infant's body. Too late to turn this one. Contractions accelerated again. More blood, followed by a shriek from Lanilla.

Renata's probing fingers touched a small foot and leg. She worked her hand up inside the birth canal, keeping up her soothing mutter of instructions. "Stop pushing—take fast, shallow breaths—" Gradually she managed to coax the other leg out. "Now push again." Renata gave a gentle tug as the contraction bore down. With a final keening cry, Lanilla expelled a blood-streaked baby boy. She collapsed on the pillow, her eyes shut.

Renata snatched up the baby and blew into his mouth. No response. Pressing on the fragile breastbone, she breathed another puff of air into the blue lips. Still nothing. The tiny limbs hung flaccid over her arm, and she felt no heartbeat. Wrapping him in a strip of swaddling cloth, she laid him on the nearby chair.

When she turned back to deliver the afterbirth, she found that a tide of blood still gushed between Lanilla's legs. Renata placed an open palm on her daughter's clammy forehead. "Listen to me, Lanilla! You're bleeding badly. We have to stop it. Help me—listen to me, concentrate!"

Lanilla opened her eyes to stare dully at her mother. Gazing at Lanilla, compelling her attention, Renata imagined swimming up the river of blood to its source, damming it with the pressure of her will. She took long, deep breaths, guiding Lanilla's breathing to ebb and flow in rhythm with hers. Calmed, Lanilla lent her will to Renata's, and the hemorrhage ceased.

"My babies," Lanilla said in a hoarse voice.

Renata clasped her hand. "You have a daughter. But the boy was stillborn." She glanced at Annelys, still blowing into the baby girl's mouth. At that moment the infant emitted a weak cry. To Renata's relief, the blue tint began to fade. Renata reached over to take the baby, bundled in a blanket. "Annelys, get more blankets, and have stones heated. We must make a warm bed for her in a covered box. Hurry!"

With deft speed Renata cut and tied the cord, then laid the little girl on Lanilla's breast. Her face damp with tears, Lanilla hugged the baby fiercely. "Thank the Goddess! If only Gareth were here!"

Renata was thankful that Lanilla was too preoccupied to notice the grimace of disgust that she could not quite suppress. Doubtless Gareth wanted a son, like all men. Lanilla would probably oblige him by getting pregnant again as soon as her milk began to dry up.

Renata smoothed the baby's hair, then her daughter's chilled hands. "I'm so happy for you, that you have a baby at last. But, my poor dear, you need not go through this again. If Gareth wants you to wear yourself out by year after year of childbearing—at the risk of your life—you need not stay with him. He can't force you to make that sacrifice."

Lanilla's eyes blazed through her exhaustion. "Can't you understand, Mother? Stop trying to make me into yourself! I *love* Gareth. I *want* his children."

Stunned, Renata stared at her daughter. *She means it! Have I really understood her as little as she does me?* "Forgive me, *chiya*. The choice is yours. Be happy with it." She kissed her daughter and granddaughter.

The door opened, admitting Annelys with the warming-box, followed by Geremy. Almost timidly he walked over to the bed.

Renata straightened up to face him. "Meet your grandchild, Geremy."

He kissed Lanilla's hand and ran a tentative finger over the baby's cheek. Catching Renata's eye, he quickly looked away and said gruffly, "Gods be praised." He swallowed hard before continuing. "I hope you'll return for the child's naming ceremony."

She smiled through the soreness of her back and arms. "I wouldn't think of missing it."

Dalereuth Guild House

by Priscilla W. Armstrong

*Priscilla Armstrong says of this story that she has of-
ten wondered what became of the community of Dalereuth when the Compact stopped the manufacture of
weapons. The loss of the* clingfire *industry must have
wrought considerable economic hardship. Since both
Rohana and Kindra claimed Dalereuth as home, it
must have been an unusual place to have produced
these two—one from the Tower, the other from the
Guild House.*

*Priscilla says of herself that she has a daughter and
two grandchildren and that her husband is a consul-
tant in housing for the elderly; her son is a psychiatric
social worker in San Francisco (and survived the 1989
earthquake "quite nicely"). Her professional credits
include a story in* ELLERY QUEEN's *and articles in*
THE GERONTOLOGIST *and* ACTIVITY DIRECTORS
GUIDE.

*With this background one would expect a story con-
cerned with the realities of social work, and it is.*

Ginevra n'ha Rina and Rina n'ha Rina rode quietly
along the old Thendara to Dalereuth high road, now
reduced to a grassy track through disuse and lack of
care. They had been on the way nearly two days, and
absolutely nothing had happened. Ginevra was constantly alert to the woods which bordered the road,
casting about for signs of the bandits who were reported to infest this forest. She saw nothing but the
burgeoning spring, and that she dismissed. She sighed
and checked her long knife again to be sure it was

loose and ready to hand. Her handsome face was grim, gray eyes narrowed, and even her short auburn hair seemed alert. In contrast, Rina rode relaxed, smiling and commenting on all the beauties surrounding them. In addition to her knife, Rina carried her small *rryl*, and strummed as she rode. Ginevra shook her head in despair. Rina was too inclined to enjoy the moment rather than to expect and be ready for sudden attack. *Had she had been too easy on her little sister? She'd been harsh enough getting them out of the hands of the Dry Town traders, but that was necessary. Winter in Darkover woods was bad enough, but in the silks and satins they had been decked in for the pleasure of their purchaser it was nothing short of brutal and if she hadn't driven her they would have made food for scavengers instead of coming to the Thendara Guild House.*

Ginevra had not been happy with this assignment from the start and had only agreed to it in the hope that there would be work for her knife on the way. It had been far too long since she been out of Thendara Guild House on a journey, and even longer since her short sword had had proper exercise. It was really her sword that Mother Carla had wanted on this trip, but she was expected to be a diplomat when they got there.

She reviewed the interview with Carla. "It is time to consider reopening the Dalereuth Guild House. Thendara House is too crowded, we're getting stacked in like winter's wood. Women are coming to us nearly every week who need shelter and protection, and we can't turn them away. I want you to go to Dalereuth to see if our old House there can be put into proper condition and whether the town will tolerate us coming there again."

"Why us?" asked Ginevra. "There are surely others who can do this better than we can."

"The journey is dangerous. You know what happened to Marla Hastur, just a couple of weeks ago. Your skill as a fighter is necessary for the journey itself, Ginevra. There is no point in sending anyone if they can't get themselves there safely. This is not a journey for one of our midwives or merchants."

"Then let them come and Rina and I can ride guard for them," said Ginevra.

"No. Two is the largest number I want to send. I have no idea what their reaction will be to us in their midst after so many long years. You two together can do it. You are both good with your knives, and if Ginevra is uneasy about talking with the people there, especially with the Tower, Rina can do the talking." She smiled warmly at the silent Rina.

And so it was arranged, and Ginevra found herself off on a diplomatic mission. Carla was right, of course, Rina was nearly as good as Ginevra with a knife.

"Rina, what are we going to do when we get there?" she fingered her knife.

"We really can't plan what to say or do until we have some information."

"You always want information."

"Yes, and you always want action. We are a well-balanced team *breda*, you must admit."

Ginevra smiled at last and clapped her sister on the shoulder. "Right. I keep my knife sheathed while you do the talking. How soon do you think we should approach this Helena at the Tower? Carla seemed most insistent that we have an interview with her. How do we arrange that? Does one simply walk up and ring the doorbell and say, "Oh, your eliteness, listen to your humble subjects'?"

"Ginny, Ginny! The *Domna* Helena will know we are there, Towers always have information, and she will probably send for us. Or, yes, we can ride up and ring the doorbell."

Ginevra growled something. Rina could feel Ginevra's anger under the surface, and sighed.

Am I jealous of those Comyn? thought Ginevra. *Or I do just hate them for what they are that they do not allow the rest of us to be? But if I have laran, as Carla says, and Rina, then our mother must have been with a Comyn Lord, not with our father, Zandru take him. If Rina wants to think that, let her, but I know she was virtuous though foolish, in love with him all those brutal years.*

* * *

The sun was sinking into the west and casting deep purple shadows as they rode into Dalereuth. Lights were appearing in a few houses, and they looked with surprise at the numbers of sturdy stone houses of all sizes which were evidently uninhabited. Off to their right they could hear the steady crash of waves on the shore.

"Tomorrow, we will go and look at that ocean," said Rina. "I can't wait!"

"Let's go now," said Ginevra, to her own and Rina's surprise. She was not one to want to go and look at things like natural wonders or views.

They followed the sound, and soon found themselves on a coast road which followed a sea wall, and beyond the sea wall, the ocean.

They dismounted and sat on the sea wall in wonder. There it was. The sea, the ocean. Wave followed wave on the beach and beat against the long wooden piers, tossing the fishing boats at their moorings. The air smelled crisp and salty. As the sun sank lower and lower, the foam became deeper and deeper pink and rose, and the water as far as the eye could see tossed and moved restlessly, blue and purple and pink under the setting sun.

"Let's find a place to sleep," said Rina when the last of the red sun disappeared and left a rose afterglow in the darkened sky.

"We could camp here," said Ginevra, "the sand looks comfortable."

"I don't think so," said Rina. "Look at the marks on the sea wall and the beach just at the sea wall. The water must come up this far sometimes. We'd get wet."

So they made their way back into the main part of the town and found an inn at the edge of the market square.

They were pleasantly surprised to find good stabling for their horses and pack animal, and wonder of wonders, a woman groom to care for them. Inside, they found not the rough bar or travel shelter they were accustomed to, but an orderly, clean common room with a polished bar, freshly scrubbed tables, and com-

fortable chairs. The tables were filled with family
groups as well as groups of individuals. It was a
peaceful and comfortable sight. As they came in, people looked at them, and then back to their table groups,
commenting on the strangers.

A fat, cheery-faced man hurried toward them drying
his hands on his white apron.

"Enter, enter, illustrious strangers!" he boomed at
them in a voice that rivaled the crashing waves. His
blue eyes disappeared into the folds of his cheeks as
his mouth split in a giant smile of welcome.

"We seek shelter for the night, perhaps longer,"
said Ginevra.

"You lend us grace, *mestras*," he said. "We will
prepare rooms for you on the upper floor. Had you
horses? Did the groom take them?"

They assured him that their horses had indeed been
taken by the groom, and followed him to the stairs at
the back of the room. The old man told them he was
Jock o'the Inn, and that every innkeeper in this inn
had been Jock o'the Inn since the beginning of time.
Chattering nonstop, he led them up the stairs and to
adjoining rooms which even then were being made
up with fresh linen by a tall thin woman with gray
hair.

"Jock, my love, you talk too much," she said, smiling as broadly as he. "My name is Judy. We'll shoo
my goodman down to his duties at the bar, and then I
will show you our bathing arrangements. You have
been on the road, and you will want to freshen up
before you come down for dinner."

They introduced themselves, and followed Judy to
the baths at the back of the inn. Judy flung open doors
and showed them not one bath, but four, and these, if
the signs were to be believed, were reserved for
women. Seeing their surprise, she smiled, and said,
"The baths for the men are on the other side, up a
different stair." She busily picked up piles of used
towels, and from a cupboard took fresh ones for them.
"This is surely wonderful!" said Rina.

"Is it? We are the only inn here now, so we don't

have anything to compare it with. Does it truly please
you?"

"Oh, yes," said Ginevra. "It is one of the best we
have seen. But I had thought you have few travelers
here?"

"Oh, the people downstairs? They aren't travelers.
They are townsfolk. Most of them are fishers, and after their day's work, they come here to bathe. We have
the hot springs, and most of them don't have baths in
their homes. After they bathe, they stay and have their
dinner. It saves the women cooking, and after a hard
day's work they can use a rest. They are off at dawn,
you know, and now that it is spring dawn comes very
early."

Bathed, relaxed and changed, Ginevra and Rina
came down to the dining room where they found a
table prepared for them with fruit and bread. A young
girl who was a miniature Judy served them local ale,
fresh water, and brought the main dish, baked fresh
fish with sauce and vegetables.

"Have we died and gone to the Blessed Isles?"
asked Rina.

"I don't know what to think. Dalereuth is not at all
what I expected. At least not yet. Tomorrow we will
know more."

They were aware that the other diners were watching
them, lingering over their meals, waiting until Ginevra
and Rina had finished eating. As soon as they had
pushed their plates back, and leaned back in their
chairs, there was a scraping of chairs on the floor and
people, both men and women, began to approach. Two
little girls ran through the adults and brought up at
their table.

"I am Elena. Are you truly Free Amazons?" asked
the one with the short-cropped red hair.

"Do you really sword-fight?" asked the little
blonde. "Oh, I am sorry, *mestras*. My name is Jess."

"I am Rina, and this is Ginevra. We are sisters and
also Guild-sisters, from the Guild House in Thendara.

That means we are part of the Guild of Renunciates, which you call Free Amazons.''

"Ohhh, you really are," said Elena, with the light of hero worship written all over her freckled face, "Are you Free Amazons? Really and truly?''

"Yes, really and truly. What do you know of us?''

"You fight with swords and you answer to no man, and you do real things, and you can choose for yourselves. My mother Molly MacArran took her midwife training at Arilinn Guild House, and she told me. This is my mother, and my father Dikon." Elena spoke with pride as she introduced her parents. "And this is my friend Jess MacArthur and her parents, Kate and Arthur.'' Having performed these duties, Elena dropped into a chair and hitched it over to the table.

At Rina's invitation, the others pulled chairs around and sat with them.

"Elena, if your mother trained at Arilinn Guild House, she is the best there is." said Rina. "The Guild House at Arilinn is famous for its training of midwives.'' Rina smiled at Molly.

"If you trained there, how is it that you did not take the Oath?'' Ginevra could not imagine a woman who, having lived with Guild-sisters could leave and not become a part of the Renunciates.

"I like Dikon and the children too much to be separated from them.'' Molly said.

"And a good thing, too,'' said Dikon, ruffling Molly's dark hair. "I don't know what I'd do without my Molly. Or the village, either. She is not only a midwife, but has some healing as well. It was to our cottage they brought the young *leronis* who was nearly killed by the bandits.''

"We saw the whole thing,'' said Jess, her blue eyes wide.

"How could that be, that you saw a bandit raid on the road?'' Ginevra asked.

"We were going to walk to Thendara to be Amazons,'' said Elena. "We cut our hair, and walked all afternoon, and stayed behind a boulder to sleep where nobody would find us, and nobody did. We want to learn to sword-fight; we could have helped.''

''Yes, and got yourselves killed or worse, too,'' growled Dikon.

''Do you girls understand you can't take the Oath of Renunciates until you are at least fifteen years old?'' asked Ginevra sternly.

The two children looked at Ginevra, eyes wide. ''Listen, Elena and Jess. If you came all the way to Thendara, Mother Carla would only send you home. You are too young. If you still feel this way in a few years, you can talk to us again, but not now.''

''But we have another idea,'' said Jess. ''We want to go back and be fostered at the Guild House until we are old enough to take the Oath.''

''Not possible,'' said Ginevra. ''We do not go around taking people's children off to the Guild House. Unless there is a very good reason, and unless your parents very badly want us to take you, we won't do it.''

''Their parents want them right here in Dalereuth, in their own homes,'' said Kate.

''Then that is settled,'' said Ginevra. The two little girls looked at them with sad and sulky faces.

''Now, see here, Elena and Jess. You are far too young, you have good homes right here. Obedience to the rule of the House is important to us, and if you can't learn obedience to your parents the Guild won't want you under any circumstances. So stop sulking, obey your parents, and learn all you can learn. If you still feel this way in a few years, you can ask again. But not now.''

After further reassurances that their little girls were not going to be scooped up and carried off, the two families left, the parents relieved, and the children sulky.

It was late when the two women climbed the stairs to their rooms. They were tired, confused, and bewildered.

''It's too easy, Rina. I don't trust anything this easy,

nor this luxurious either. They live well for a town where they claim to be so poor.''

"Maybe tomorrow will bring wisdom.''

Tomorrow dawned clear and cool. Ginevra realized that the sound which had haunted her troubled dreams was the constant motion of the ocean. She wondered how people could grow accustomed to this purposeless restlessness. *How could they deal with these smiling people? Rejection she understood, hostility she understood, the society within the Guild House she understood, but this friendliness was beyond her. Had they known in advance that they were coming? Had they planned together a kind of drama to disarm them? If so, why?*

After a sturdy breakfast alone in the common room, they went outside and to the Guild House. As Judy told them, they could not miss it; it was almost directly across the street from the inn, with massive oak doors opening onto the pavement. A wide gate led into the grounds at the side of the house, and here they entered. They found themselves in extensive grounds with stables, a paved stable yard and large paddock where their animals had been turned out to graze. Behind the house were small walled gardens, one of which was being used as an herb garden.

"Could this be Molly's, I wonder?" said Rina. "It has all the right herbs, and some I don't recognize.''

"Probably. Maybe that's why they were friendly; they don't want us taking away her little herb garden.''

The rest of the grounds were overgrown and the orchard needed care. The back of the grounds were walled also, but through the gate there they could see the coast road and the sea wall, and the sound of the water came more clearly to them.

They toured the house itself and found it in reasonably good condition. Furnishings were scarce, however, and everything movable had been taken. "We'll need to buy nearly everything," said Ginevra. "They have carted off every dish, every piece of cloth, and most of the furniture.''

"Everything but the chairs in the meeting room. I

wonder who is using the meeting room," answered Ginevra.

They found the market square drab and nearly empty. Only a couple of dozen women and children were shopping. Most of the stores were boarded up. The baker was open, and doing a little business, and the glass-maker, potter, and weaver were busy. There was one stand selling fresh farm goods, and a dairy with good looking cheeses displayed. They recognized Jess' mother tending the bake shop, and bought some of her honey cakes.

They wandered around the marketplace, visiting the few open shops, talking with the shopkeepers, asking where they could buy the things they would need for the Guild House. They were told that most of what they wanted would have to come from Thendara, or they would have to make them themselves. "We don't have such things any more, and the last trader came through at least five years ago," the weaver told them.

They strolled back toward Kate's shop, licking the last of the sticky honey off their fingers. A small group of women had gathered there, and Ginevra knew Kate was telling them about their meeting last night. As she was about to mention this to Rina, the clatter of hooves alerted them that a carriage was approaching. They jumped out of the way as it rushed past.

"Who was that?" asked Rina.

A woman in the crowd turned to her. "You must indeed be a stranger, *mestra*, not to know the carriage of the Lady Helena, Keeper of Dalereuth Tower. She is going to Molly the midwife to tend the *leronis* who was nearly killed by the bandits."

"We knew about the injury to Marla Hastur, yes, but we did not know the Tower would send to help her. Because she is one of their own, no doubt. They wouldn't bother else.'

The woman raised an eyebrow in surprise at the sneer in Ginevra's voice.

"The *Domna* Helena has been there every day, and others from the Tower have helped Molly with the nursing," said the woman. A small group of women and children had gathered around them to hear the discussion.

"The Tower always comes when we need them," the woman said stiffly. "It is one of the things they are there for, after all."

"So you say, and perhaps it is true here. Myself, I have no use for the creatures. Aristocrats, elites, and they spend their time in meaningless chatter across the miles, keeping their skills to themselves. The rest of us can just get on as well as we can." said Ginevra harshly. Rina tried to signal her with her eyes. This was not diplomacy!

"You don't understand our Tower, *mestra*," a tall, elderly woman said. "Years ago, before the Compact, everyone in Dalereuth worked for the Tower; many of us worked in the Tower itself. Every child was tested for *laran*, and everyone with *laran* was trained. We worked in the sheds below the Tower, packing the *clingfire* and *bonewater* dust which was shipped out to every Lord of the Domains for the wars. Dalereuth was prosperous then, you can see by our houses, and if you go into the countryside, you will see the fine estates which are now only farms. After the Compact, our work was gone, and we became a poor fishing village once again. Some blame the Tower, because the Compact came from Tower work, far to the north, and the Tower became poor, too. But the people of the Tower, the *leroni*, have not forgotten us, nor we them, and they still bring healing for any serious injury. They will train our children in the skills of *laran*, any who wish it."

The old woman took breath and fell silent after so long a speech.

"Margali, you have always defended the Tower folk. Some of us don't feel quite that way," said one of the younger women, leaning on a crutch. "If they had never made the weapons at all, I would not have been born thus. Anything they do for us is trying to make up for hundreds of years of destruction while they pursued their science."

"Your leg is nothing compared to what used to happen, Lori," said the old Margali. "Even in my time, grotesques were born often, and had to be destroyed, and before the Compact, it was even worse. The materials they used for the weapons and for some of the sciences gave our women miscarriages and deformed babies. There is a valley in the hills full of infant bones where they were left to die after birth. I should know. Some of mine went there years ago. Before Molly the midwife had her training and came to us."

Ginevra heard all this through the red haze of anger which sometimes enveloped her. *Were they all Comyn here that they tested everyone for* laran? *If they were, of course the Tower was friendly, they were their own, elite above the rest of the world.*

She heard Rina say, "Then you have been most fortunate in your Tower, that they still carry an interest in the village. Tell us, what is Dalereuth like now?"

Ginevra could feel Rina calming and quieting her, draining off the anger as she listened to the voices around her, telling about the fishing and farming, the new industries of glass making and pottery and the training of women. Alert, she looked around her. "Women? You train women here?"

"Oh, yes, *mestra,*" said Margali. "Every woman learns a useful trade. The men, you see, are out fishing all day ("or farming," someone else added) or they are in the Guard, and there were too many widows and children to be fed, so now the women choose a skill and learn it when they are very young. Then if their men are lost at sea, or in battles with the bandits that roam the hills, they can support themselves and their children without becoming some man's whore or serving wench." Old Margali shook her gray hair proudly. "I, myself, became a scribe. Now nearly everyone learns to read and write. I teach the little ones their first letters. I also make paper from wood with my women workers. I am considered a woman of substance in the community. I sit on the Council, too."

"If there are so many more women than men, how do you marry?" asked Rina.

"Many of us don't marry. At first, the men were careless of us, they thought if this one doesn't suit me, I can get me another, but they soon learned that if they didn't suit their wife, no one else would have them anyway. It keeps them decent to us. And when a woman has work to do, she doesn't need a man to take care of her. You of all people should know that!"

Ginevra could not contain her astonishment. "This is unheard of! We never thought to see it outside a Guild House."

"You can see, then, that we don't need you here," Kate said firmly.

"You have no need of a Guild House, then?" asked Rina.

"The old one still stands, and we keep it repaired," answered Lori. "Do you and your sister want to live there?"

"Our Guild House in Thendara is overcrowded. So many abused women come to us and we can't refuse them. We had thought to open the Dalereuth Guild House for some of our sisters in Thendara," said Rina.

"We don't need you here," said Kate again.

"So long as everyone does useful work and contributes to the community, you will be welcome," said old Margali.

"Only if you don't take trade from us," said Kate. "I don't want to see another bake shop, and Lori doesn't want another weaver, and Molly doesn't need another midwife or healer."

"I will talk with the Council," said Margali. She strode away, her long skirts swirling around her boot-clad ankles.

They may not need us here, but we need this Guild House for our sisters in Thendara. Perhaps another Guild House in Thendara would be better. Renunciates trained in Dalereuth might not be able to function in the rest of Darkover. The town is too soft, too compliant, too . . . easy. The culture is as different here from Thendara as the culture of the Dry Towns.

I wish there were something to fight, something to come up against. This talking is getting us nowhere.

"What was all that in aid of?" Ginevra said.

"We got a lot of information, Ginevra," said Rina placidly.

"You and your information! But we haven't done anything. Nothing but listen to a lot of sweetness and light about how the whole of Dalereuth is a big Guild with men added for fun. Do you believe all this?"

"You are exaggerating, Ginevra, and you know it. I think Dalereuth is just what it pretends to be. This afternoon we must go to the Tower and find out what the Keeper says; it may be that they don't need us here and we would have trouble reopening our House."

They had just finished their noon meal when the summons came. A messenger informed them that the Lady Helena of the Tower wanted to speak with them.

"Why should we jump just because some Comyn leronis wants to talk to us?" muttered Ginevra.

"Carla wants us to talk with them. If they hadn't sent for us, we would have gone, you know that. If the Tower doesn't want the Guild House reopened, that will change things," said Rina, well aware of Ginevra's temper.

A tall woman with graying red hair greeted them when they were shown into the visitors' room of the Tower.

"Please be seated," she said. "I am Helena, Keeper of the Dalereuth Tower."

"I am Ginevra n'ha Rina, and this is my sister, Rina n'ha Rina."

"You are, then, blood sisters as well as sisters in the Guild?"

"Yes. What did you want with us?"

"I want to ask you to take young Marla Hastur with you on your return journey to Thendara. She will be ready to travel in another day or two. She was raped. She is no longer fit to be a Keeper, for we must be virgin. Arilinn Tower where she had her early training will not take her back. We have no place for her here. Her family will not accept her at Comyn Castle. There is no alternative for her but the Guild of Renunciates. She must become a Free Amazon."

Ginevra was stunned into silence. She looked at Rina. Rina's mouth hung open. She closed it with a snap and looked at Ginevra. Ginevra took a deep breath. She knew her voice would shake with anger if she spoke too soon.

"That's right," the Keeper said. "You will need a moment to consider. I realize this is a surprising request. But you will leave tomorrow or the next day and I want Marla to travel with you."

"Vai leronis." Ginevra was in control again. "It sounds as though you have made a decision for Marla."

"That is quite correct. It is my place to do so." The Keeper was calm, almost icy.

"Domna, you must understand that we do not bring women into the Guild of Renunciates at the request of others. We only accept women who come to us themselves to ask to be accepted. We cannot take Marla Hastur to Thendara at your request. Only Marla herself can make the decision and the request."

"You dare to question my judgment?" Helena of Dalereuth was clearly angered. She fingered the pouch she wore on a thong round her neck.

"Lady Helena, it is my understanding that those who live and work in the Towers are subject to vows, and that one of those vows for those in your position is the vow of virginity. You must also understand that we also have vows, and that we take a solemn oath when we become Renunciates. Our order has a set of rules; I am sure you also have rules which bind all members, not only the leaders. If we acceded to your request we would break our oath, as well as the rules of our House. Therefore we cannot say that we will take this woman to Thendara Guild House. If she wants to go with us, she can accompany us to Thendara under our protection. More than that we cannot promise you." Ginevra felt her insides shaking, though she could see that her hands appeared to be quite calm and relaxed on her knees.

Helena turned to Rina. "And you? Are you in agreement with your sister? Hmm?"

Rina raised her brown eyes to the Keeper. "Yes, *domna,* I agree. What she says about our rules and our oath are true. We refuse to be oath-breakers. Your own rules and vows must give you some understanding of this. Unless this woman requests the oath, we can't take her to our Guild House as a member. We can accompany her to Thendara. That is all."

"And when she reaches Thendara—what will she do then, may I ask? The Hastur refuses to have her returned to him, and no respectable man will accept her as wife. What is this woman to do?"

Ginevra sensed for the first time that desperation and deep concern for this Marla person was motivating the Keeper. *She is trying to be kind and good to this woman,* Ginevra thought, with a mental sigh.

"Perhaps we should speak with Marla ourselves?" suggested Rina.

"Perhaps if you see her, you will have compassion on her," said the Keeper.

More compassion than you? Who won't bring her here? Virginity is only required of Keepers, not every leronis, *or* laranzu *either for that matter. Where is the compassion of your Tower, or of Arilinn, or her family? We are supposed to be more compassionate than all of you? You flatter us. You in your safe Tower, Marla Hastur with her wealth and family, nothing can change her Comyn blood, some man would be glad to connect with the chief clan of Darkover.*

"*Domna,* we will talk with this Marla Hastur," said Rina. Mother Carla of our Guild House wants us to ask you a question." At her nod of assent, Rina continued. "Our order considers opening the Dalereuth Guild House again, after many years, because our Houses in Thendara and in other places are becoming crowded. We would send women from Thendara to reopen this house, put it in order. What would be the attitude of the town and the Tower to this?"

"If you bring your Guild here, will you also bring dissension? Or will these women have useful skills to offer?"

"Our women all have useful skills which they use

in any lawful manner in the community. We do not recruit members, as you know. Nor do we lure children like Elena and Jess into our House. Women who come to us must have a better reason for taking the oath than they presently have. It is said that for every member, there is at least one tragic story. We do not recruit.''

''Then I think that there need be no worry about the town. They are different, I think, from Thendara or any other town in the Domains. The Compact destroyed their chief source of employment and they have not forgiven us for that. But the town is coming back. So long as you do not compete with local work, they may accept you.'' She again smiled that icy smile. ''They may indeed credit the Guild with restoring their fortunes. Who can tell?''

''I think we may be finished here,'' said Rina. ''How can we bring shopkeepers, bakers, skilled workers, without competing? I am not sure we can fight it. It will be hard for Carla.''

''Fight it? It would be like fighting a pile of feathers or a pool of honey. Sweet, soft, sticky. Would our women become soft if they are trained here? Maybe we don't want to be here.''

They found Marla Hastur sitting in the sun outside Molly's door.

''Marla Hastur?''

''Yes, I am. Are you the Free Amazons the Lady of Dalereuth told me she would send?''

''The Lady said you wanted to return to Thendara.''

''Did she also tell you I should become a Free Amazon because now my virginity is gone I am worthless for any other life?'' Her voice was bitter.

''She did not say it just like that, no, but she did ask us to accept you into the Guild.''

''And what did you tell her?'' Ginevra found it hard to believe the cool manner of this young woman, scarcely more than a girl. She had expected a tumultuous reception from a woman so recently beaten and raped and left for dead.

"We told her the truth. If we took you as a Guild-sister on her request we would be oath-breakers. Our rules do not allow us to recruit, and certainly not to take anyone unwilling into our sisterhood."

Marla smiled a lopsided smile. "Good. I do not know my own mind. I am a fully trained *leronis*, you see, and was only coming here to help Helena as Keeper until such time as she could no longer be Keeper herself. Then I would have become Keeper. I lived and trained at Arilinn Tower since I was ten years old. I know little of the world. Molly and Dikon have taken me in, and their children, especially little Elena, have been good to me."

"Do you want to return to Thendara with us when we go tomorrow?"

"Why would I go to Thendara? My family does not want me. This is a great tragedy for them, you understand. They were proud of me at Arilinn, for I have a great Gift. They were even more proud when I was to become Keeper. Now . . . I don't know where I would go in Thendara. A Free Amazon? To live like a man among the head-blind? Here at least the family has some *laran*, and little Elena is very gifted. I can teach her, train her *laran* so she avoids the threshold sickness. Here they don't think less of me for my misfortune. Molly is teaching me a useful work. And you—you want to live like men, and wield your short swords and swagger about the taverns and bars of Thendara. Why should I want that?"

"I think," said Rina with a glance at Ginevra who was clearly angry, "that you do not have full information about our Guild and our people. But so long as you are content with your life here with Molly and they are willing, I see no reason to encourage you to come back to Thendara."

"We only accept people who want to become Renunciates," snarled Ginevra. "We don't take Comyn ladies who have had a hard knock in life. Tower trained, too. The elite. We have no elite, no aristocracy, we are all equal. We all do useful work, and as many of us wear skirts as pants. We wear these clothes on the trail for comfort and convenience. You think you have had a bad time. You should hear some of the tales our women have to tell. Your one experience pales beside some of these tragedies. Faugh! We wouldn't take you if you begged on your knees.'' Ginevra turned away.

''Forgive my sister, *mestra,* she had a very bad time when we were young and resents those who were more gently reared.''

''Hold your tongue, Rina.''

The three women were silent for a moment. Marla finally spoke. ''I have not asked to become one of you, remember that. I think that one's own experience is one's own. There can be no competition in tragedy. Your experience is your own. It is different from mine, as mine is from yours. Should the time come when I am restored in body, and it will not be long, and should I wish to become a Renunciate and live with you head-blind . . .'' She stopped. ''You are not head-blind, are you? You both have *laran,* and you, Ginevra, are very gifted, but you deny it and do not practice it. That is part of your tragedy. If I should desire to leave this place and be a part of your Guild, I will come to Thendara and apply as any other woman would. In the meantime, I will stay here, and learn what Molly can teach me, and teach the little Elena to be a *leronis* and a scribe.''

Ginevra's anger began to dissipate on the walk back to the inn. For the first time on this journey she had something new to think about. *Competition. Nobody wants it. Marla Hastur says tragedy cannot be compared, there can be no competition, and Carla has said much the same. The women here don't want any competition with their skills. I can understand that. Another midwife would take bread out of Elena's mouth. There's no way to fight our way in, and their soft ways would starve us out in no time.*

Suddenly, Ginevra grinned, and laughed out loud.

Rina looked at her, startled. She was not used to her older sister being cheerful, let alone laughing.

"Rina, how much money do you have after we pay the landlord?" Rina dug into her pouch and produced a fistful of coins. "Good. Go back and arrange for us to leave at first light tomorrow. I am going shopping."

Puzzled, Rina turned in at the inn as Ginevra strode off down the market square. It was a relief to Rina to see the bounce and purpose in her walk. She had found action, but what?

An hour later, Ginevra staggered into their room under a great armload of parcels which she dropped on the bed.

"Whew! I should have taken the pack animal."

"What have you done? We will need another pack chervine to get all that back to Thendara."

"I bought one."

"What! Another pack animal! What will Carla say? You must have wiped out everything she gave us . . . the Guild can't afford this kind of extravagance!"

"Look, said Ginevra."

She began unwrapping parcels: glass, pottery, bolts of fine cloth from the weaver. "This one is dried fish. I won't unwrap it, it stinks, but it's enough for our House."

"Zandru's hells, Ginevra, what have you been up to? Souvenir hunting? And a three-day ride through bandits ahead?"

"No. We, Rina, I mean the Dalereuth Guild House, have a new skill. We have just become Traders."

"Traders?"

"Traders. What is the one thing lacking here. Trade. No competition. Outlet for local products. Caravans coming and going. Bringing what they need from Thendara. Everything. Prosperity." Hands on hips, she surveyed her purchases with smug satisfaction.

Rina began to smile. Then to laugh. "We are a team. Who said we needed diplomacy. We needed information and action. Let's pack up and go home."

DAW

BESTSELLERS BY MARION ZIMMER BRADLEY

THE DARKOVER NOVELS

The Founding

☐ DARKOVER LANDFALL · · · · · · · · · · · · · · UE2234—$3.95

The Ages of Chaos

☐ HAWKMISTRESS! · · · · · · · · · · · · · · · · · UE2239—$3.95
☐ STORMQUEEN! · · · · · · · · · · · · · · · · · · UE2310—$4.50

The Hundred Kingdoms

☐ TWO TO CONQUER · · · · · · · · · · · · · · · · UE2174—$3.50
☐ THE HEIRS OF HAMMERFELL · · · · · · · · · · UE2451—$4.95
☐ THE HEIRS OF HAMMERFELL (hardcover) · · · UE2395—$18.95

The Renunciates (Free Amazons)

☐ THE SHATTERED CHAIN · · · · · · · · · · · · · UE2308—$3.95
☐ THENDARA HOUSE · · · · · · · · · · · · · · · · UE2240—$3.95
☐ CITY OF SORCERY · · · · · · · · · · · · · · · · UE2332—$4.50

Against the Terrans: The First Age

☐ THE SPELL SWORD · · · · · · · · · · · · · · · · UE2237—$3.95
☐ THE FORBIDDEN TOWER · · · · · · · · · · · · · UE2373—$4.95

Against the Terrans: The Second Age

☐ THE HERITAGE OF HASTUR · · · · · · · · · · · UE2413—$4.50
☐ SHARRA'S EXILE · · · · · · · · · · · · · · · · · UE2309—$3.95

THE DARKOVER ANTHOLOGIES with The Friends of Darkover

☐ DOMAINS OF DARKOVER · · · · · · · · · · · · · UE2407—$3.95
☐ FOUR MOONS OF DARKOVER · · · · · · · · · · UE2305—$3.95
☐ FREE AMAZONS OF DARKOVER · · · · · · · · · UE2430—$3.95
☐ THE KEEPER'S PRICE · · · · · · · · · · · · · · · UE2236—$3.95
☐ THE OTHER SIDE OF THE MIRROR · · · · · · · UE2185—$3.50
☐ RED SUN OF DARKOVER · · · · · · · · · · · · · UE2230—$3.95
☐ RENUNCIATES OF DARKOVER · · · · · · · · · · UE2469—$4.50
☐ SWORD OF CHAOS · · · · · · · · · · · · · · · · UE2172—$3.50

PENGUIN USA
P.O. Box 999, Bergenfield, New Jersey 07621
Please send me the DAW BOOKS I have checked above. I am enclosing $_____
(check or money order—no currency or C.O.D.'s). Please include the list price plus
$1.00 per order to cover handling costs. Prices and numbers are subject to change
without notice. (Prices slightly higher in Canada.)

Name _____

Address _____

City _____ State _____ Zip _____

Please allow 4-6 weeks for delivery.

DAW

DAW PRESENTS THESE BESTSELLERS BY
MARION ZIMMER BRADLEY

NON-DARKOVER NOVELS

☐ **HUNTERS OF THE RED MOON**   (UE1968—$2.95)
☐ **WARRIOR WOMAN**   (UE2253—$3.50)

NON-DARKOVER ANTHOLOGIES

☐ **SPELLS OF WONDER**   (UE2367—$3.95)
☐ **SWORD AND SORCERESS I**   (UE2359—$3.95)
☐ **SWORD AND SORCERESS II**   (UE2360—$3.95)
☐ **SWORD AND SORCERESS III**   (UE2302—$3.95)
☐ **SWORD AND SORCERESS IV**   (UE2412—$4.50)
☐ **SWORD AND SORCERESS V**   (UE2288—$3.50)
☐ **SWORD AND SORCERESS VI**   (UE2423—$3.95)
☐ **SWORD AND SORCERESS VII**   (UE2457—$4.50)

COLLECTIONS

☐ **LYTHANDE** (with Vonda N. McIntyre)   (UE2291—$3.95)
☐ **THE BEST OF MARION ZIMMER BRADLEY** (edited
by Martin H. Greenberg)   (UE2268—$3.95)

A note from the publisher concerning:

THE FRIENDS OF DARKOVER

So popular have been the novels of the planet Darkover that an organization of readers and fans has come into being, virtually spontaneously. Several meetings have been held at major science fiction conventions, and more recently specially organized around the various "councils" of the Friends of Darkover, as the organization is now known.

The Friends of Darkover is purely an amateur and voluntary group. It has no paid officers and has not established any formal membership dues. Although the members of the Thendara Council of the Friends no longer publish a newsletter or any other publications themselves, they serve as a central point for information on Darkover-oriented newsletters, fanzines, and councils and maintain a chronological list of Marion Zimmer Bradley's books.

Contact may be made by writing to the Friends of Darkover, Thendara Council, Box 72, Berkeley, CA 94701, and enclosing a SASE (Self-Addressed Stamped Envelope) for information.

(This notice is inserted gratis as a service to readers. DAW Books is in no way connected with this organization professionally or commercially.)